PRAISE FOR
JEREMIAH'S REVENGE

DISCARDS

"An intense read with the classic Brannan
tempo and rebelliousness."

—Daniele Dosch, FBI Victim Specialist

SANDRA
BRANNAN

JEREMIAH's
REVENGE

A LIV BERGEN MYSTERY

RIVER GROVE
BOOKS

Published by River Grove Books
Austin, TX
www.rivergrovebooks.com

Distributed by River Grove Books

For ordering information or special discounts for bulk purchases, please contact River Grove Books at PO Box 91869, Austin, TX 78709, 512.891.6100.

Design, cover design, and composition by Greenleaf Book Group

Publisher's Cataloging-in-Publication Data is available.

ISBN: 978-1-63299-173-7

eBook ISBN: 978-1-63299-174-4

First Edition

The complete list of Sandra Brannan's
Liv Bergen Mystery Thriller Series:

To my real life Ole and Ida.

And to Hobart and Poxy Lone Hill, my Ray and Alice.

Beautiful people.

ACKNOWLEDGMENTS

I AM SO GRATEFUL to my fans—especially to the hundreds of book clubs that keep supporting me and hosting me in your homes, whether in person or via FaceTime. This book is dedicated to two book clubs that chose the striking book cover for *Jeremiah's Revenge*.

The entire team at Greenleaf Book Group is awesome. Sally Garland, Elizabeth Chenette, and Jen Glynn push me to improve my craft, but artist Neil Gonzalez drives me crazy each year by giving me too many excellent book covers to choose from for my next Liv Bergen mystery.

This book was no exception, so I let the book clubs choose the latest cover as my "Thank you" to the fans who continue to read the series.

If you like the *Jeremiah's Revenge* book cover, you have the following people to thank.

Cover to Cover Book Club in Hollywood, Florida
Christina Diaz
Ana Martin
Yvonne Perez
Sandra Salinas
Kathleen Taylor

Ginny's Book Club at the Haakon County Public Library
in Phillip, South Dakota
Suzan Berry
Skye Brucklacher
Kerry Burns
Emily Deveraux
Nancy Ekstrum
Nancy Haigh
Vonda Hamill
Sheryl Hansen
Sally Jankord
Missy Koester
Emily Kroetch and Bob McDaniel
Audrey Neiffer
Laura O'Connor
Norm Payne
Jodi Pease
Lori Quinn
Bobby and Gerry Sloat
Deb Oliver Smith

And of course, the creator of the cover—Neil Gonzalez.

CHAPTER 1

THE BLUE FLASHING LIGHTS in my rearview mirror made me catch my breath, and I felt my heart rev.

Not because I was upset the Wyoming Highway Patrol had pulled me over for speeding. I expected that in Lusk. I'd been stopped at least a half a dozen times here—which would make most people more cautious. But not me.

I needed to get to Denver. It was already closing in on three in the morning, and I had to get to the office before everyone else arrived. I glanced at the dashboard clock again and calculated the remaining time. Three and a half, maybe four hours. I'd never make it by six like I wanted to. Hopefully by seven. Later than I wanted to be. People would start to drift in after seven.

And I wanted to be alone. With Special Agent Streeter Pierce.

If my sister Agatha hadn't insisted that I stop by Rapid City to bid farewell to my parents, I'd have made it by six. But I guess I could see why she had insisted. After all, a sheriff was dead on Mount Moriah in Deadwood. A young man clung to life after surgery at Rapid City Regional Hospital. And the police needed me as a witness to untangle the sordid story that would eventually slip from tongues all over South Dakota for months to come.

It took forever, but Agatha was right. My parents would have inevitably heard about my involvement today in the newspapers and on radio and television—if they hadn't already seen the story on the ten o'clock news last night. But they had: And they weren't pleased to discover I'd found myself yet again in the middle of another mess.

After hugs and kisses, their personal observations that I hadn't been shot, stabbed, or maimed (again), and a quiet reminder that working for my dad might be a much safer bet for me, they set me free. I was on the road by midnight. I'd made my decision: I wasn't going back into the family mining business—I just hadn't told them. Couldn't afford another few hours of them trying to change my mind.

Instead, the dancing blue strobes made me realize I'd made the right choice to stay with law enforcement and how much I absolutely loved working with the FBI. I wanted to get back to work. After my mandated psychological sabbatical, today was the day I was to report for duty. At 8:00 a.m. But I had to get there before everybody else did.

My first order of business was to march into the office of the Acting Special Agent in Charge and tell Streeter Pierce to immediately rip up my letter of resignation. I thought he normally arrived sometime before six, but I had no clue exactly when he got there, since I'd never arrived early enough to verify.

I needed to get moving. After I received my speeding ticket and a well-deserved lecture, of course.

I placed my hands at ten and two on the steering wheel as the trooper eased carefully toward my driver's side open window. In my side mirror, I could see him position one hand on the butt of his service weapon and the other on his flashlight. Then he swept the beam across my hands and face.

"No gun," I said. "Although I do have a concealed weapon. I'm Agent Liv Bergen. FBI. Can I reach for my driver's license?"

The officer hesitated and shined the light into my face. I smiled, still gripping the wheel. I bet I didn't look much like a federal agent. More like a meth-head-bag-lady who'd just stolen a car. I couldn't even remember the last time I had slept. Or brushed my hair.

He nodded. "And your credentials."

I couldn't see his face with the beam blinding me. I fished out my license and credentials from my duffle bag and handed them to him. Then I flashed him another smile, hoping for my best battle-worn-Jessica impersonation from *True Blood*. He swiveled the light onto my identification. My vision adjusted to the dark. From the wash of the patrol car's headlights and from the nearly full moon, I could see the man was young. I'd never met him.

Normally, Carlson was the trooper who'd stopped me on this stretch. And he'd invite me to sit with him in his cruiser while he wrote me a ticket. In the front seat. I thoroughly enjoyed checking out the new equipment and chatting about changes with the friendly hi-po.

This guy was no Carlson. Not so friendly. Not more than twenty or so. I tried to catch the name on his left pocket, but he had his right shoulder toward me.

He handed back my IDs. "What's the rush?"

I tucked away my credentials and license. "Work. I just got off a case in Deadwood. A murder. And I have to be back at our Denver office this morning."

He grinned for the first time. He was much better looking than before, when giving me that stern face. "You've got worse hours than mine. At least when I work weekend nights, they let me off Monday and Tuesday."

"Where's Gerry Carlson?"

His grin faded. "Retired. Maybe I should reconsider."

"Reconsider what?" I asked.

"If you're on a first name basis with the guy I replaced, that means you're not much of a learner when it comes to speed limits and the law. Maybe I should reconsider and write you a ticket."

I worked up a plausible protest. "You weren't *going* to write me a ticket? That's a first."

Then I realized that that might not have been the smartest thing I could have said.

He patted the door, grin gone. "Slow down, Agent Bergen. And have a good night."

"You, too. Stay safe," I called after him, sounding trite and pathetically maternal.

I turned on my blinker and slowly merged into nonexistent traffic on the desolate highway. At Lusk, I'd have to fuel up with my credit card and move on to Cheyenne before I could find any food. But the gas station was open. I purchased two large coffees to ward off drowsiness, some Hot Tamales, and ate a box of chicken fingers that were probably cooked at least ten hours earlier, but I hadn't eaten since yesterday morning, and I was starving.

—————

Reenergized, I cranked the air conditioner to high and turned west onto Highway 18 toward I-25. It would be faster on the interstate and a straight shot into Denver.

I hadn't figured out what I was going to say to Streeter. Or how I was going to thank him for everything he'd done for my family and me since my boyfriend's death. He'd called every day to check on me, even though I wouldn't talk to him about Jack.

The bureau's psychologist was right. I had definitely needed a leave of absence after Agent Jack Linwood's death to get my head back in order. Witnessing a colleague being gunned down right before my eyes was bad enough. Holding my boyfriend while he bled out was worse than anyone could ever imagine.

Spending the sabbatical with my family in the Black Hills had proven therapeutic. Exactly what I needed and what the good doctor had ordered for my mental state. I felt better than I had in years. More confident, and sure of myself and my decisions. And I'd learned to embrace the sadness of losing Jack.

He was a dear, dear man. Kind, gentle, and loving. The last words he'd ever spoken to me played over and over in my mind. I found a sad irony in my memories of loss as I drove past Lost Springs. As Jack lay dying on that porch in Colorado, his blood pooling beneath us, he told me that he'd never killed anyone and how sorry he was to leave. I know he didn't want to die.

The worst part of Jack's double life was that I couldn't blame him. And I'd come to terms with the fact that he had finagled his way into the FBI for the wrong motives. I actually envied him. And Agent Jenna Tate.

They'd tracked down and eliminated some very bad people—who had gotten away with crimes against the innocent for years.

Streeter had told me that night—when I was such a mess, when my grip on sanity was slipping—to remember that I had loved a hero. And that he had, too. We'd all loved Jack Linwood. He was a brilliant agent.

Is that what Streeter said? For an instant, I realized that I might have misinterpreted his words. *What were his words?* Something like, "Remember that you loved a hero. And I do, too." Or was it "And I did, too"? I'm pretty sure it was the former, not the latter. But I'd interpreted his words to mean he wasn't ready to speak of Jack in the past tense. But then why did he use the word *loved*, past tense? If he'd intended to use the words he'd spoken, then it would have meant Streeter was in love with a hero, too. Someone alive. Jenna Tate? Was she his hero?

It didn't matter: She was headed for prison. We had both suffered losses—his worse than mine, in my opinion. At least Jack hadn't killed anyone. But Jenna had murdered more than her share. She was no hero.

I thought back to Jack's final words to me. The ones he coughed out with his last breath—the most shocking of all, particularly since he had never said them before.

"Love you."

Jack loved me. And not like everyone loved me, in that generic "I love you, man" sense, or as an agent, or as a human. He meant it as a man loving a woman.

Clarity had become the theme of my leave of absence.

For one thing, I had finally understood the importance of Special Agent Jack Linwood in my life. I realized I had fallen in serious *like* with Jack. I was crystal clear about that. But *love*? I never had a clue he felt that strongly about me, so his final words had made me examine everything.

I know I wasn't in love with Jack.

I could never fall in love with Jack.

Or anyone, for that matter.

As long as I was so unquestionably tethered to Streeter Pierce.

Ever since that kiss at Storybook Island.

I realized I loved working for the FBI *because* of Streeter Pierce. I was choosing to continue to work with Streeter Pierce over working with my family, whom I loved more than anything. Or almost anything.

I knew I had to explore what it was about Streeter that captured my complete attention, no matter how much I tried to ignore him. And even if he was in love with Jenna Tate.

But how could I explain any of this to him?

He had saved my life again through Mully. That was another issue I needed to resolve with Streeter. *Who the hell is Mully and why is that outlaw biker constantly showing up to save me at the exact moment I need him?*

I'd promised Deputy Sheriff Harvey Nolan, Agatha's new beau, that the FBI would open a new case to investigate Mully's involvement in the Mount Moriah shootings. Carl J. Muldando, aka Mully, the leader of Northern Colorado's chapter of the Lucifer's Lot outlaw motorcycle gang, had actually shown up to save my life yesterday. Hiding amid all those headstones. Wiping down the gun before disappearing. Leaving nothing behind but a smile for me to remember.

Heady.

Mully killed Sheriff Leonard Leonard, who had tried to murder young Michael Jacob, an innocent kid who knew too much. And the very same sheriff who would have killed me, if not for Mully. The entire ordeal was completely overwhelming to say the least. It was a mess I was going to need Streeter's help to untangle. And his honesty. And then there were the headstones. *Winzig—Michael Jacob's aunt. PAULA WINZIG JACOB PIERCE—Streeter Pierce's wife.*

CHAPTER 2

FALL IN THE ROCKY Mountains was an exceptional time of year, particularly in the sleepy town of Conifer nestled in the mountains southwest of Denver.

The temperature rarely got above the seventies during the day, but if it did, predictable, late-afternoon thunderstorms quickly cooled everything down. By early evening, a spectacular rainbow—sometimes two—often accompanied the setting sun in the clearing skies.

Tonight, as often happened even during the summer, the temperature dropped so low that Streeter Pierce found it necessary to build a fire in his wood-burning stove. He was enjoying the steam that billowed up from the cup of coffee he raised to his lips. The forty-five-minute commute each way from Conifer to his Denver office could be difficult at times, but his home offered seclusion, privacy, and the mountain living he loved. This particular log cabin was his refuge and the first home he and Paula had ever aspired to buy. They couldn't afford to buy it at the time it was put up for sale—just before her death. But when he learned he couldn't sleep in their apartment without her for the entire year after she was gone, he'd used the payout from her life insurance policy to purchase her dream home. It was the only way he could see himself ever spending that money he'd known nothing about.

He smiled, remembering how they had lain in bed at night talking about the possibilities. Of the remodeling they would do. About the furnishings they would buy. Right here was where he'd spent so many nights since then, sitting on the deck of his cliff-perched home, facing a wild and empty mountain across a wooded crevasse below. The canopy of stars had provided many spectacular views as he listened to the nocturnal animals and birds during many sleepless nights.

Tonight was no exception.

With only the light from the fire within and the stars above, he stretched out in a wooden lounge chair and listened for movement in the dark wilderness above a sea of black. He heard the howling of the coyotes.

Wrapped in a hunter-green comforter he had pulled from his bed and wearing nothing but the scent of a distant slumber, he drew in a breath of crisp, clean air into his tired lungs. But rather than helping him fall back to sleep, listening to nature's nighttime harmony energized him. Particularly his mind.

Tonight, his thoughts were on Liv.

After a joint stakeout with the Denver City Police Department and the bureau, one FBI agent was dead, one was awaiting sentencing, and another was seriously injured—mentally. The dead agent, Jack Linwood, was Streeter's friend. The one awaiting sentencing, Jenna Tate, deserved to go to prison for the rest of her life. The injured one, Liv Bergen, deserved nothing but happiness and peace.

He was saddened by the loss of Linwood to be sure, but he realized the emptiness that was consuming him had come after he read Liv's resignation letter. Tate could burn in hell, for all he cared. She shouldn't have used him or the bureau like she had to get her way. It was agents like her who gave the bureau a bad name. The three were his responsibility now that he was acting SAC, and he'd have to find replacements for all of them.

In more than two decades with the bureau, he had never been as scared as he was that night, and there was only one other time he had been more devastated. Since the shootout, he replayed the events during countless sleepless hours. He couldn't stop himself from formulating multiple alternatives in his mind of how he could have spared Jack's life.

And Liv's pain.

During his career with the FBI, Pierce had mentored many of the bureau's finest agents on how to conduct criminal investigations, particularly those involving violent crimes. As a new agent nearly a year earlier, Liv had been one of the agents he'd mentored. She was by far his favorite, both professionally and personally.

He'd long crafted the reputation of being a very private man, a loner, who divulged very little if anything about his personal life outside of the bureau to anyone. Liv was one of few people who made him feel comfortable enough to keep it real. To be himself. She asked him many questions—most of them unabashedly direct—which he found impossible not to answer. She had that effect on him.

Since she took leave, he had called her every day, but she'd refused to take his calls. He hadn't understood why, but he decided not to visit. Instinct told him it might worsen the situation for her. So not talking with her didn't bother him. Her letter did.

She had resigned. No mistaking her intent. That's why she'd refused to talk to him. She didn't want him to try to convince her to stay. She was quitting to work with her family's mining business. She wasn't going to report back to work today as she had previously been scheduled to do.

And at five minutes after eight, he would notify Calvin Lemley in DC that he was declining the SAC position in Denver—instead, he'd ask for a transfer to the Rapid City field office. He'd made up his mind. He didn't care how she felt about him. He needed to be near her.

Even if at a distance.

He refused to leave her alone and had spent every moment with her in the first few days after they experienced Linwood's death together and she decided to go home to South Dakota.

During her leave, he'd called Liv's parents. Garth and Jeanne Bergen were wonderful people. And he'd talked with different siblings from time to time. She had so many of them . . . They reported that she had regained some perspective while working through her grief. Based on her progress and determination, the reports he'd been receiving daily from the psychologist confirmed her mother had been correct. The doctor had agreed to release her for work today as long as she agreed to continue her daily counseling and assessment sessions, at least for some period of time. He knew her well enough to know that not only would she continue with the required therapy, but she would also pursue mental healing on her own time with intense self-determination.

She was strong. She had probably already commenced her routine of running at least five miles a day. He was sure of that.

He wrapped the comforter more tightly around his bare shoulders and gripping the mug, he sipped. He had finally made a decision: When she was fully recovered, he'd ask her out on a date. He had such tender feelings for Liv that he feared his romantic inclinations for her might damage their tenuous relationship if he didn't approach her with much care and caution.

Staring out into the silvery shade of darkness, he listened to a persistent coyote crying mournfully to the full moon above. The coyote's howl sounded desperate, and he somehow felt a connection to and a kinship with the beast.

He sunk deeper into the large comforter and wondered at what precise moment their relationship had changed for him. He pictured her, pacing in his office at the Denver division only weeks ago. She was a vision of perfection in its most pure, yet human, form. With hands firmly planted on her athletic hips, the thirty-something special agent often paced back and forth, thinking about a case.

Whether she wore jeans or an elegant evening dress, she was a spectacular blend of beauty and genuineness. His favorite memories of her were when she was dressed most casually, wearing her worn blue jeans, an oversized T-shirt, and a baseball cap with her auburn hair in a ponytail.

He tried to imagine her beautifully brilliant green eyes staring back at him, rare and alluring like shallow water over a sandy beach. He'd noticed the small diamond earrings she always wore. And that she favored no other jewelry. He wondered about their significance. He wished he could craft a pair of earrings made of glass from an antique green bottle that had washed ashore with someone's love note from centuries past. Only that type of gem should be worn so close to such a beautiful woman.

Her attire—at once casual and proper—complemented her relaxed nature. Her studious, intelligent manner sometimes seemed incongruous with her elegant beauty and dazzling smile. Completing her perfection for him was the fact that she seemingly had no idea how extraordinary her appearance and how intimidating her talents were to those who knew her. She was genuinely a kindhearted and thoughtful person with the intensity, loyalty, and voracity for her work that the federal government only dreamed of finding in an agent . . . and he dreamed of finding in a partner. For life.

There was only one flaw: She was more than a decade his junior.

Was she really mentally healthy? Had she really had such a quick recovery? He began to worry. *She showed no emotion at Linwood's memorial service. Perhaps the grieving process hadn't fully begun for her. Particularly given how quickly she became embroiled in trouble at Deadwood. Had she truly accepted the gritty reality of what actually happened?*

Then again, he wasn't sure how he expected her to react. He wasn't surprised by her insistence in postponing her sabbatical until after Linwood's burial in California. The doctors refused to let her go, at first, but then allowed her to attend the service in Denver and to fly to California for the internment as long as he accompanied her.

She showed no emotion and shed no tears. And neither of them spoke, other than what had to be said to get from here to there and back again. When he brought her back to Denver, she had simply relinquished her bloodhound, Beulah, to his care (as mandated by the doctor who had insisted on complete separation from anything and everything bureau-related) and had driven off to South Dakota without another word.

In the deep quiet of night, the soft squeak of the screen door against the frame startled him, and he bolted with a start from the deck chair to his bare feet.

A red nose emerged from inside the house, and his shoulders relaxed as the adrenaline-rush tension melted away.

"Beulah, you scared me," Streeter said and settled back down in the chair.

Liv's big, red bloodhound with droopy ears and sagging jowls squeezed the rest of the way out the door and lumbered over to him, plopped down next to the chair with a grunt, and rested her nose on Streeter's lap, hoping for a rub. Rewarded with long, slow strokes and intermittent scratches behind the ears, Beulah groaned with satisfaction.

"You'll be going home soon," he comforted the dog. "Let's give Liv a few days on her own to acclimate. Alone. Then I'll take you home so she can care for you."

The bloodhound shivered in the cold night air and retreated to the screen door, waiting for Streeter. He rose and opened the door and watched as the gentle dog's large, ferocious-looking shadow crept around the wrought iron furniture closer to the stone fireplace. Eager to snuggle up to the warmth of the flickering fire, the shadow shrunk to a harmless mound as Beulah slumped into a ball of slumber.

He had forgotten how comforting it was to have a dog around the house. He had enjoyed having Beulah with him while Liv was on leave. She would be happy about his decision to keep Beulah with him for a while longer, rather than kenneling her at the bureau's canine unit. She adored that dog and was going to have the hardest time saying goodbye to her when she left the bureau.

As if she would show up today, he scoffed, chastising himself as a dreamer. There would be no sad goodbyes over the dog because Liv wasn't coming back. He glanced at the clock on the mantle. Three-thirty. He had a few more minutes before he had to get ready for work. He padded back and got under the comforter to ponder Liv's decision to resign from the FBI.

But what if she didn't?

The coyote's lovesick cries sounded hopeful.

A smile played around Streeter's lips as he sank down once more and gazed at the canopy of stars overhead.

CHAPTER 3

SNAKE GLARED AT HIS spotter, who was standing above him by the workout bench, and asked, "Ready?"

Squeeze nodded, shifted from one large foot to the other, as he glanced around the empty weight room looking bored.

Snake heaved the bar away from his chest and out of the brackets. Wiry, but deceptively strong, he arched his back. Liked coiled springs, his muscles stretched, and his biceps bulged and trembled under the strain of the weights. His sweatshirt—made sleeveless by his own careful alterations—revealed tattoos of viperous serpents along his forearms, which rippled with every strained movement.

He loved this time of day.

No one was awake at this hour at the Englewood Federal Correctional Institution south of Denver in Littleton. Not even his spotter, Squeeze.

But he could get anyone to do anything.

He'd convinced the guards to let him work out before dawn, arguing that the rest of the prison population would appreciate his absence during regular weight-training hours.

He'd convinced Squeeze that he should join him; that waking up early every morning to be his spotter would be better than not waking up at all.

He held the bar, counting in his head, feeling the small, padded bench against his lower back and planting his feet firmly on the ground. The smell of iron, plastic, testosterone-soaked rubber, and old sweat permeated his nostrils as he breathed through the lift. His freshly powdered hands gripped harder around the bar above his shoulders as a wave of fatigue flooded his muscles. With a grimace, he lowered the bar into its support brackets with little help from Squeeze, who continued being distracted.

Snake sprang to his feet. Angry, and with sweat dripping off his forehead, he charged the large man who'd been absorbed by something near the door. Snake put his nose into Squeeze's massive chest and was not the least bit intimidated by the size disadvantage. "What the *hell*? I almost lost it! I asked if you were ready!"

The spotter blinked stupidly. Only then did Snake really notice the two men who had entered the weight room. One, a guard. One, a prisoner. The prisoner was Jeremiah Coyote Cries, aka The Reverend. The only prisoner tougher than him. The only prisoner more connected.

Not good. Not good at all.

Why was *he* here?

Wishing he'd grabbed the shank he kept hidden under the lip of his sink back in his cell, Snake felt his fingers twitch. Never had he seen anyone in the weight room at five in the morning except when the guard came to take him and Squeeze back to their cells. It was well before wake-up for the rest of the population.

Squeeze, who got his nickname within days of his arrival at the prison because of how he killed his victim in a bar fight, said calmly, "I *was* ready. But then The Reverend came in with the bull. I was checking him out. Seemed more important than you, Snake."

The Reverend stood next to the prison guard, glowering. They were both too far away for Snake to hear what they were saying to each other. He wondered what the guard was telling The Reverend. Whatever it was, it probably wasn't good.

Snake's anger with Squeeze instantly vanished. A renewed rage welled from within him toward the guard. *Traitor.* He would pay for his disloyalty.

The spotter added, "Besides, you didn't need me anyway."

Snake grinned at his weight-lifting buddy and revealed his gold front tooth—the only straight one—before lifting his fists in the air. He flexed the muscles in both arms and kissed the muscle that bulged in his bare right upper arm. "You're right. I didn't need you. But now I do. If either of them comes near me, kick his ass."

"Right. *A guard? The Reverend?* Dream on, little man."

"Oh, come on . . . ignore them. Probably here just like me. To work out before the population wakes up." Snake motioned for Squeeze to follow him, sounding far more confident than he felt. "I need to work some more on my pecs."

They walked over to the universal weight-lifting equipment. Snake laid his sweaty torso down for horizontal pull-downs and instructed his big friend where to put the pin for his initial set of repetitions. With the palms of his hands turned toward his face as he lay supine, Snake reached up and grabbed the bar. The cables attached to the weights behind his head strained along with his muscles. He pulled the handle toward his chest and the heavy weights slid up the metal tracks.

After the initial rep, Snake instructed Squeeze to move the pin down. That added more weight to his load. A lot more weight. He struggled to pull the bar to his chest.

Snake counted the last seconds of his second rep. He felt the burn. The fatigue. When he was about to release the handle, allowing the weights to slowly lower down the cable supports behind him, Snake felt somebody yank his hair.

He let out a low yelp. His slick-with-sweat body slid along the vinyl until his head stuck off beyond the bench. He felt his ears scrape against the cables. The heavy bricks of weight hovered above his wide eyes. He held fast to the bar. His arms were aching.

A quiet, guttural voice cautioned, "Better hold on tight to that, Snake. Or those weights are going to come crashing down on that ugly face of yours."

Snake glanced up.

It wasn't Squeeze. It was The Reverend.

The Lakotan's black, lifeless eyes stared back at him like a shark stalking its prey. His features were sharp and angular. His face, hard. The Indian's thin nose was underscored by the slash of a tight smile. Long grey hair hung over each shoulder, framing his inverted face.

Snake had never been more terrified in his life. He knew The Reverend's reputation.

Staring into his hostile face, Snake wriggled slightly to test the man's grip. The Reverend tightened his fingers and yanked harder on Snake's hair, pinning his head in place.

Snake was staring at his throat from beneath the hovering stack of weights, and The Reverend hadn't even broken a sweat. This was child's play for him. This bastard was stronger than he'd heard. No exaggeration.

"Keep slithering, Snake. You're wasting what's left of your energy—and time—by trying to wriggle free. Your strength is dwindling. Fast."

Snake's eyes desperately darted around the room.

"Guard's gone. Took your spotter back to his cell. That's keeping the bull occupied. And me without any training on how to be a spotter. Guess all you have going for you is your ability to hold on to that handle."

Snake swallowed hard. "What do you want?"

The Reverend snarled. "I hear someone's been ratting me out to the bulls."

When The Reverend tightened his grip, Snake let out another moan of pain.

The Reverend's voice returned to a monotone that was unsettling. "I've been working real hard for Jesus for two decades. Hard time. Some may call that oppression. But me? I see it as redemption. I'm only days away from getting out on parole."

The fingers of one of The Reverend's hands twisted a clump of Snake's hair. The large Indian placed his other hand on the weights and pushed down. The load was heavy enough, but with the added pressure, Snake felt his muscles strain even more as if the tissue in his arms would snap like overworked rubber bands. The stack was nestled against his delicate windpipe. If he lost his grip, the weights would break his neck in an instant.

"I have them convinced that I've found religion. I don't need some rat ruining my chances. If it's necessary, I'll waste whoever's talking about me." The Reverend's wide chest was rising and falling with every breath he took.

Snake pleaded, "Reverend, listen. It ain't me. I swear. I ain't no rat. Please. Believe me."

"Have you read the book of Jeremiah?" The man's grin left Snake cold. "Or do you use the pages of your Bible to wipe your ass?"

Snake shook his head. His sweaty hands slipped on the bar, the cold metal smashing his windpipe by nearly a half inch. He croaked, "I can't . . . hold this . . . much longer. Please."

His arms quivered with the strain from the weight. He held tight with only his fingertips, which were slipping. Knowing his life hung in the balance, he struggled with every ounce of concentration and determination to grip the bar, keeping the weights away from his throat.

"Jeremiah 20:4 unless you answer me honestly." The calm of the Lakotan frightened Snake. He had no clue what was said in 20:4, but he suspected it wouldn't be good news for him. "Who's been talking about my stash with the bulls?"

"I don't know," said Snake, with sweat dripping from his face.

The Reverend lifted the weights easily with his free hand, relieving the pressure from Snake's arms. Then he shoved Snake's body a couple of inches away from him and let the weights drop. Snake seized the bar for dear life. He caught the load just before his face was crushed beneath the stack of weights, which now hovered precariously above the tip of his nose.

The Reverend said, "20:4 says *'Behold, I will make thee a terror to thyself, and to all thy friends.'* Is that what you want?"

Snake screamed, "I swear, I don't know. The Fish, maybe. He's always chumming with the bulls. Maybe it's him, the new guy. Nobody trusts him. He don't even have a joint handle yet, and he's been here three weeks already."

Snake thought he saw the slightest softening around The Reverend's eyes. Although soft for Coyote Cries was harder than granite.

"I'll find out. I can learn things. Please."

The Reverend's eyes narrowed as he stared down at Snake, who felt a shiver skip down his strained neck and spine. Without a word, Coyote Cries released his grip on Snake's hair and walked slowly and quietly away. Snake used every ounce of strength to slide from beneath the weights, and the bar slipped from his grip. The stack of weights came crashing down inches from the top of his head. He rolled onto the floor and gasped for air. He was grateful to be alive.

He was terrified, shaken, and exhausted.

He pulled himself back onto the weight bench and rubbed his throat and his nose. He massaged the ache in his arms and chest. Only now did he realize he was totally alone. The Reverend was gone. If Coyote Cries had wanted to kill him, no one would have been around to contest his story about him not being trained as a spotter. A cold sweat broke out on his forehead, and his body trembled with fear.

He would live to see another day—after having a one-on-one with The Reverend. No one did that.

CHAPTER 4

WHEN I PULLED INTO the parking structure off 36th Avenue, I glanced at my watch.

As badly as I wanted to talk to Streeter alone, I needed a few minutes to make a quick stop at the canine kennel to see Beulah, where Streeter would have brought her this morning after the long weekend with him. It was 6:45. Coworkers would be arriving soon. I hesitated and then decided I had to see my dog first. One quick hug wouldn't hurt. I missed her so much. Streeter would have to wait.

Claudia, the groomer and caretaker for what she called the fed's "day-care for doggies," hugged me before letting me in. Before the kennel door was barely open, Beulah launched into my arms, licking my face. The other bomb-sniffing, cadaver-recovery, and tracking dogs—mostly German Shepherds—howled with envy.

The reason Streeter asked me to join the FBI was because this dog, this bureau asset, had lost her handler, my friend, who was murdered by De Milo, a demented killer, in my house. It was Beulah who motivated me to avenge my friend's death. But I hadn't realized how attached I'd become to the dog as a companion. I had missed her so much these past few weeks.

I settled Beulah into the environmentally controlled kennel and told her I'd be back as soon as I could to take her home.

I ran through security, sharing greetings with all the guards, and sprinted to the elevators, anxious to find Streeter. Speed walking toward his corner office, I was happy to see that no one else had arrived yet.

My heart raced when I smelled his cologne.

Drawing a deep, anxious breath, I stepped through the open glass door. He was sitting at his desk, studying papers in a casebook splayed out in front of him. Before I could say anything, he glanced up, and our eyes met. I could see the expression on his face was one of concern.

The single word that escaped his lips fell heavy and rushed. "Liv."

I smiled. "Do you still have my letter?"

He paused before reaching into his top drawer. He withdrew a single sheet of paper and extended it to me. My resignation.

I tore it in half. Then in quarters. Then in shreds.

He rose to his feet, slowly. He appeared unsteady, keeping the fingertips of one hand resting on his desk, as if letting go would cause him to topple. "You came back."

I nodded. "To stay."

He opened his mouth as if he wanted to say more. As did I. But neither of us said another word.

I rounded the corner of his desk and wrapped my arms around his waist. He hesitated and then returned the hug around my shoulders. With the palm of his hand on the back of my head, he pressed my cheek closer against his chest.

He felt warm. Familiar. His heart pounded against my ear.

A lump was threatening to block my throat and make me cry. I had no idea I'd have this reaction to a simple hug. Clearly, I had needed one. I had craved his company for days now. I had missed him. I felt so isolated without him.

I didn't want him to let go.

But I wanted to tell him exactly how much I had missed him. How badly I needed him in my life.

Then I heard Manny's voice out in the hall. The others were starting to arrive. I let go of him, but he held on a moment longer. I couldn't look at him. I felt stupid. All the things I'd thought to say and now I couldn't find the words.

I stepped back, straightened the jacket of my pantsuit, smoothed my hair, and wiped a tear from my cheek.

"Good talk." I exited without looking back.

What an idiot.

I had practiced for hours during the drive so many ways of telling him how I felt. How much he meant to me. How to thank him for being there for my family and me. How much I valued his friendship. But all I managed to do was rip up my resignation letter and cling to him like a barnacle to a docked boat.

At least I managed that.

He smelled good. He felt familiar. He hugged me back.

Manny immediately hugged me and ushered me to the break room.

Disregarding office policy, Bessie padded her way out of the bullet-proof reception area when she saw us walking down the hall. She disappeared around the corner and reappeared through the heavy metal doors to the agents' offices. Arms outstretched toward me, she folded me into her heavy bosom. "Come here and give me a hug."

So many hugs. And it was barely seven o'clock.

I grinned and bent down to hug her. Finding myself lost in Bessie's bearlike embrace, the familiar aroma of a sweet mixture of vanilla and mint encircled my nose.

"How are you, Bessie?"

"What are you thinking, child?" she scolded as she held me by the forearms. "The question is, how are you? What are you doing back so soon? You need time. To heal."

"I'd go crazy if I had to spend another minute cooped up at home," I answered honestly.

She wasn't finished. "And what did I hear about you trying to save Jack's life by flinging yourself on top of him during that shoot-out? You could have been shot. What were you thinking?"

"I wasn't."

The memory of my decision to protect Jack slammed into my head. The explosion of gunfire. The smell of gun powder and blood. PTSD, I guess.

I was pulled from the flashback instantly when she clucked her tongue. "I'm sure of one thing. You are certainly not as smart as I once thought you were."

I chuckled. "That's fair."

More arms hugging. Lifting me off my feet. Welcoming me back to work. Manny Juarez, Steve Knapp, Kyle Mills, Jon Tuygen, Tim Gregory, Pauly Horwitz, George Nichols, Laurie Frumpley, Raymond Martinez. For an hour, we never left the break room.

We drank coffee, ate donuts, and caught up on office gossip. The entire gang was there, except Phil Kelleher, who wouldn't arrive until precisely 8:00 a.m.

And Jack, of course.

I had missed them all.

"It's so good to see you again." I hugged Steve's massive arm. "You're all a sight for sore eyes."

"Except for Knapp, right?" Mills shifted his glance from me to Steve. "He's so ugly that when he was born, the doctor slapped his mother."

Everyone laughed.

Steve pouted. "Knock it off, Mills, or I'll have to slap you."

As always, in an attempt to smooth the rough waters stirred by the cynical Kyle Mills, Manny Juarez changed the subject. "Grab another donut. Meeting's about to start."

We followed Manny and his box of donuts to the conference room. "Is it hot in here? Are you guys as hot as I am?"

Steve answered, "It's always hot in here. And you ask that every time we have a meeting. And did you just take the one donut with sprinkles again? I think the only day you come to work early is when you know you can get the best donut."

"Some things never change." I said it more to myself than anyone else.

Pauly Horwitz squeezed my shoulders. A sideways hug. "This place was very dull without you."

Considering he rarely said anything without whining or complaining, I was surprised by his compliment. "Thanks, Pauly. Maybe some things do change."

I hadn't meant for the comment to draw so much laughter.

Phil Kelleher, one of the senior agents, walked swiftly into the conference room with a natural air of sophistication. He stopped short at the sight of me, caught off guard by my presence. It was uncharacteristic of the man who was always prepared. "Liv. You're back. Already. How did you manage to . . . recover so quickly?"

I simply smiled at him and shrugged my shoulders.

He sat beside me and patted my forearm. Closest thing to a hug I would ever get from Phil. And he liked me.

Raymond Martinez, the quietest of all the squad members, squeezed my shoulder and sat on the other side of me. "I was worried about you. I heard you went to Jack's memorial, but I wasn't able to go that day. I was on a case. And I didn't come see you at the hospital because I'm scared to death of those places. I had a bad experience once."

Unable to restrain himself, Mills mocked, "Whoa, Martinez. That's more than I've ever heard you say in the seven years you've been here. My God, Liv, look what you did to him? He's a regular chatterbox."

Embarrassed, Raymond lowered his head.

Ignoring Mills, I gently placed my hand on Martinez's forearm. "Thank you for worrying about me, Ray. And don't feel bad about not coming up to the hospital to see me. I wasn't there long. I don't like those places either."

Raymond smiled shyly and whispered, "I'm so sorry about Jack."

The sentiment was touching. And unexpected. I almost lost it.

The thought of losing Jack hit me hard. Again. My happiness instantly disappeared, and my mind drifted to private moments with him. In my reverie, I hadn't noticed the room had become quiet.

I had been blessed with both Jack's and Jenna's friendships over the past year, but I had somehow become more distant with Streeter. Now that my doctor had begun sharing the truth about Jenna's real motivations, her duplicity, I realized she had been using me just like she'd been using the bureau. But Jack hadn't. He had just wanted vindication for his child's death.

I completely understood that.

What I worried about now was how Streeter was coping with the news about Jenna Tate.

She'd had her meat hooks in him from the instant she arrived and likely used him more than anyone else to get what she wanted.

Poor Streeter.

I felt protective of him now more than ever. Not because I had intentionally asked to be assigned to the Denver division just to learn from the legendary agent. And not because he had chosen to work with me after I helped him solve a couple of cases last year as a civilian. It was simply because I cared about him.

I understood why Streeter had turned down promotions in the past. He clearly preferred to be a field agent rather than be stuck behind a desk. But the doctor told me Streeter had accepted the acting SAC role when Cal Lemley accepted a sudden promotion in DC. Must have been important. And urgent. Because he was able only to leave me a message with his goodbye rather than to offer me one in person.

What had surprised me was how easily Streeter seemed to take on the reins. Something I hadn't expected he'd want to do. Streeter's skill and keen intuition in the field were unmatched. And I had no doubt he'd make a great SAC. I just wouldn't have predicted him leaving the field. For any reason.

But I didn't pretend to know everything. Like what had happened to his wife.

Almost immediately upon my arrival at the Denver division from the academy, I had heard the rumors of her death.

Paula Jacobs Pierce. Or *Winzig*, as everyone in Lead, South Dakota, had called the tiny woman.

Instantly, I became very protective of Streeter and intensely jealous of other women in the bureau who seemed to set their sights on him. Like Jill Brannock, SAC Calvin Lemley's personal assistant. Now Streeter's. Ugh. And Jenna Tate in particular.

He was the most intriguing, eligible bachelor in the federal building. I had no right to feel so possessive of him. Especially considering he had been no more to me than a boss. And possibly a somewhat distant friend.

But I felt very differently about him. I always had.

I tried hard not to think of Streeter or to entertain any thoughts of a relationship other than as subordinate and boss. But it had become more difficult now, knowing how much time he had willingly spent with me while I was at the hospital being checked out and how diligently he had called my mom and sisters to find out how I was doing.

I couldn't deny that he did care for me. Yet I wouldn't allow myself to hope for anything more. But that hug. If it meant anything, I wouldn't really care if I got OCRed for an interoffice relationship. Screw it. I'd quit.

While my thoughts were on him, Streeter entered the small, stuffy conference room, with the entire squad in attendance for the first time in weeks. Probably since I had taken my leave of absence.

In his deep, gravelly voice that seemed to resonate in the room like a teenager's stereo adjusted for maximum bass, Streeter began his weekly meeting. "Liv, welcome back. As you all know, we've been three agents down for a few weeks. Four, counting me. Now I'm working the desk. Calvin's job. Temporarily." Streeter stared directly at me. "So we're all particularly pleased you're ready for work."

I said, "Thank you."

"Don't take on anything you're not comfortable handling. That's an order." Then a gentle, boyish grin played around his lips and his steely blue eyes danced with life.

Smiling in return, I answered, "I won't. I'm just glad to be back. Ready to work."

Streeter explained the process of replacing Jack Linwood and Jenna Tate, the commendation Linwood had received from the president of the United Stated posthumously, and the scheduling for Jenna Tate's trial. He reminded everyone about how to handle questions from the public and the press, speculating that a renewed effort by the press to dig up dirt was inevitable with my return.

No pressure there.

Thankfully, he moved on to discussing the trial.

"Tate is not representative of the quality of federal employees who work hard to protect individuals every day as special agents. And Linwood is a hero for revealing her. As is Liv. So protect her from the press. She'll need your help more than any of us."

I wasn't sure what he was saying until he slid a newspaper my way. On the front page was a photo of Jack Linwood and Jenna Tate. The first line mentioned me.

"Damn."

Everyone chuckled.

Streeter said, "They don't have a photo of you yet. So let's not make their job easy, people. Protect Liv. Along with fame as a hero comes the strain of recognition."

I blushed. I never thought of this ever happening. And hoped it never would.

Laurie Frumpley raised her hand like a kid in grade school. Odd, but not for Laurie.

"Mr. Pierce, they've already called. Bessie held them off and eventually transferred the calls to me—*Denver Post, The Gazette, Daily Camera, Chieftain, Sentinel,* and the *Times.* They all wanted a photo of Special Agent Liv Bergen. And to know where she was from."

Streeter asked, "You didn't tell them, did you?"

Her lips tightened with disdain, and she shook her head.

"Good. And please don't call me Mr. Pierce. How long have we been working together now? Eighteen years? Nineteen?"

Laurie pushed her glasses up her sharp, shiny nose, and her doughy face stiffened slightly. "Eighteen years, four months, and sixteen days. You were the first to greet me."

He sighed, thanked her for her service, and asked each of the field agents to debrief the group on the cases they were assigned. Then, he asked us to brief about our expected activities for the coming week.

He looked at me. "We need to get you out of here."

That stunned me. Everyone else laughed.

"Because of the nosey press." Then he leaned back slightly in his chair and held his folded hands against his rugged chin. "We had a call two weeks ago from a man named Matt Juzlig. He operates a small concrete operation in Glenwood Springs. Has for many years."

My ears pricked up. My family was in the ready-mix business, too.

"He called to report extortion by a federal employee. We get so many calls that just don't amount to anything so, initially, I didn't put much stock in the call. The guy hasn't been in business long and even though he sounded sincere, I was leaning toward believing that he had misunderstood the federal inspector in some way."

"And now?" I asked. My curiosity was certainly piqued. This was an industry with which I was familiar. And federal employees, I understood.

Streeter turned and faced me. "Then, late Friday, we received another call from a man named Bert Ridgewood. He runs a little asphalt company in Buena Vista."

"We have a limestone operation nearby."

"The Bergen family? Do you have air permits?"

I nodded.

"Ridgewood said Juzlig had warned him about this guy, and the same EPA inspector called his secretary on Friday. The inspector said he'd be up on Tuesday to see Ridgewood. Before he could get there, Juzlig had encouraged Ridgewood to call us."

"Interesting," I said, feeling my left eyebrow arching. I already wanted this case.

"Ridgewood has been making 'insurance payments' to this guy for months." Streeter actually motioned the air quotes. "Thought it was just common business practice in the Rocky Mountains. Apparently, this inspector threatens to issue a notice of violation, or worse, a cease and desist of operations if the owner doesn't pay."

"Extortion," I whispered.

"Has it happened to you, your family?"

I shook my head. "Not that I know of. But I'll call my brother."

"Juzlig wanted to not only file a complaint against the federal agent but also to offer proof through his friend Ridgewood. If we can get someone up to Buena Vista tomorrow morning, they think we can hear for ourselves what this guy is up to. Are you up to it?"

"Absolutely." I was sitting so far on the edge of my chair that I almost tipped over.

He slid the file my way.

"What's supposed to happen tomorrow morning?" I asked.

"Ridgewood said his secretary told the EPA guy that her boss was out of the office and would be returning Tuesday morning. Which is tomorrow. So the EPA inspector will likely be back to collect his quarterly cash payment. Although only the secretary and no one else in his company knows about the 'protection.'" Again, Streeter made air quotes.

I wondered if my brother Ole or any of our employees had heard of this EPA inspector.

"You want me to arrange for an arrest? Theft of government property or bribery and conflict of interest?" I remembered the charges under the bureau's jurisdiction from my Quantico training.

"Neither," Streeter said simply, surprising me.

"What I'd rather have you do is find out how deep this guy's hand is in all the operators' pockets. If we have two who called us, there are probably several more who didn't. You're from that industry. See if you can find out how much he's extorting. Our case will only get stronger."

"So what do you recommend?"

"Be there for tomorrow's exchange. Wired and recording."

"I'll be there."

Streeter added, "Laurie, help Liv. I want you to dig up all you can on this guy and make a list of possible operators he might be extorting."

"Where do I start?" she asked.

I responded, "Colorado Department of Health. Pull air permits. That's where this guy seems to have found these two victims. At least it's a start. An EPA inspector can argue air, land, or water issues with operators. Sky's not the limit."

Streeter suppressed a grin at my pun. The others chuckled. Someone said, "She's back."

Indeed.

With the meeting over, I couldn't wait to research all the sites around Buena Vista so I could head in that direction right away. I wanted to meet with Ridgewood and figure out our approach to witness the extortion firsthand. I'd grab Beulah and have her spend the night in the hotel with me getting reacquainted. And call my brother on the drive into the mountains.

As I was gathering up a duffle bag of listening and recording devices, I received a call from an old friend at the Criminal Investigative Division at Quantico. Christian Doonsberg had been one of my closest coworkers when I started with the bureau. Although I was ten years his junior, I had always felt a special connection with him—like a daughter to a father or a sister to a brother.

Familial, somehow.

We'd been able to communicate easily and freely with one another.

He had taught my behavioral science course during Academy training and was primarily responsible for all the job offers I'd received as a new Academy graduate and was most certainly responsible for the two promotions offered to me since.

He hadn't stopped there.

He'd been trying for several months to recruit me to come to work for him in the FBI's Criminal Investigative Division as an intel agent.

"How are you feeling?" I asked, knowing he'd been through a serious bout with cancer. "Are the tests still showing clean?"

"I'm telling you," Christian said in his ever-optimistic tone, "I wasn't about to let a little cancer get me down. Everything's still good. It's not coming back. I won't let it."

"I miss being around that kind of optimism."

"That's why I'm calling," Christian added. "I know you said that you wanted to stay in field investigations the last time we talked, but I could really use your talents right now. Especially since this Solomon debacle. And considering your condition . . . "

The pause that followed was extremely uncomfortable.

"I'm sorry," Christian eventually said. "I didn't mean to say 'your condition.' That sounded so insensitive. How are you?"

"Grieving. Stunned. Hurt. Sad. Mad. Everything I'm supposed to be feeling at a time like this, I suppose."

"I wondered if you would reconsider my offer of coming to Washington, DC, and of being part of the Criminal Investigative Division. It may be safer."

"Safer," I repeated solemnly.

"You're not still avoiding safe, are you?" Christian asked.

"Yes."

"Even after nearly getting yourself killed?"

I didn't reply.

"Once again, I may have just ruined my chance to have the most brilliant mind on my team." Christian sighed with exasperation. "So let me try again. Think about this from a different perspective. If there was ever a time for a transition from field investigation to intel analyst for CID, this would be an excellent moment for you."

"I know." It was my turn to sigh. "You're right."

All I could think of was Streeter. If he were moving to DC, I'd jump at the chance to work for Christian. Because I'd be near *him*. But I had fumbled my opportunity to ask Streeter about his plans.

"Think about it, won't you?"

I would. But I needed time with Streeter. To know for sure.

"How much time do I have before you need to move on to someone else?"

CHAPTER 5

SNAKE HAD TO FIND out who was selling out Coyote Cries.

His life depended on it. He had no idea how much time he had left. But the way the big Lakotan was glaring at him across the yard, he knew it wasn't long. The yard was packed. It was a popular place for free time today for some reason.

Maybe they were out here to see a fight. Rumors circulated about trouble. Maybe Snake was at its epicenter.

He wiped the beads of sweat from his brow.

He reminded himself to quit being so damned paranoid. He could take any one of them. Except Coyote Cries. But then suspicion got the best of him. All eyes seemed to cut his way. Or had they? Paranoia would cause him to make mistakes if he weren't careful.

He was indeed stronger and scrappier than any one of them. But he couldn't take them on all at once. His fingers twitched.

Let them stare.

The Reverend might have a congregation of followers both inside and outside the prison. But *he* had guns. He lifted his right arm, made a muscle, and kissed the bulge.

He was focused.

Every one of Coyote Cries's flock seemed to be gathered today to hear his sermon.

Damn it. Why would anyone listen to that bastard? Such a liar. A fraud.

He promoted himself as being a political prisoner because of his devotion and dedication to his Native American customs, culture, and religious practices, including his open support of opium use in the peace pipe ritual. It was an excuse he used in an attempt to peddle inside to the prison population.

But it didn't work. They denied him use of opium, which was good.

The Native American's plight with discrimination, oppression, and destitution was real. Unfortunately, for the Lakotan people, Coyote Cries capitalized on their suffering claiming to be a political prisoner, when in reality he was nothing but a vicious murderer. Inside and outside of these walls. The lowlife used his heritage to gain sympathy for a concocted campaign as the poster boy for the oppressed.

He was evil. Snake knew it. The population inside knew it. The guards should have known it. The fools.

Coyote Cries was no reverend. He was the devil. And his sentence of life by Denver's federal courts was more than justified as far as the prison population was concerned. He'd spent decades crafting a plan designed to fool everyone and manipulated a sympathetic journalist who embraced his story, helped spread his concocted message to the outer reaches, and created a fan base of those who came to believe he'd been wronged.

Idiots.

But Snake had to admire Coyote Cries for his intelligence, for his power cloaked in subtlety, and his ability to effect change. He was frightening as hell. The Reverend had become a legend, an international cultural icon for the downtrodden. Over the decades, his accusations of conspiracy by the judicial system and his claims that he was a political prisoner of the oppressive white government had become more convincing.

Memories had long since faded about what really happened two decades earlier. But Snake knew better. Coyote Cries was no anti-removal revolutionary. Removal of the original people was horrible, as was apartheid for his people. But Coyote Cries wasn't to Lakotans what Nelson Mandela had been to Snake's people.

Mandela never peddled drugs, polluted young minds, profited from the downtrodden, or murdered people who stood in his way. Mandela fought for the oppressed against the white minority through peaceful protests as a tribal leader. Well, mostly peaceful. Anyway, Mandela was a hero. Someone Snake admired. Although he'd admittedly be ashamed if the legend were still alive and could see what Snake had done with his life.

The Reverend unapologetically bragged about the prosperity of his organization and about who sourced and delivered drugs—primarily to the tribal youth—in South Dakota. On the Pine Ridge reservation, specifically. That was, until his arrest. Since then, he'd grown even richer, manipulating those on the outside even more successfully than he had when he was free.

His organization not only survived his conviction. It thrived. His sermons were all about how to create new and expand existing markets, including those for marijuana, heroin, Quaaludes, cocaine, and methamphetamine, particularly on the isolated reservations—and especially with the youth.

Millions of dollars exchanged hands each year with his source in Denver to supply dealers in Whiteclay, which was a small town in Nebraska two miles south of Pine Ridge Village and off the reservation. They'd all heard the story of his multimillion-dollar success. Everyone had heard, except the authorities, apparently.

Which was why Snake was amazed and confused that he'd even be considered for parole. Most of those working for him on the outside, his gang, had been recruited in prison. He'd even tempted Snake. At first, Snake figured he could learn a thing or two from the street-smart drug dealer. About never using the product sold. About recruiting others as mules. About never conducting business anywhere on the reservations— but just outside their boundaries.

He was clever. And tempting. But not enough for Snake to overcome his enormous fear of the man.

He'd end up dead. Like so many others who didn't carry out orders to The Reverend's exacting standards. Other drug dealers sought The Reverend for advice on how to evade the law, how to recruit, how to grow business, and how to better evade detection after being released. Even inside, The Reverend was notorious. A professor in crime. Revered by many, feared by all. His students were eager to reward him with favors once they were released. They were not reformed or rehabilitated by crime. They were renewed and reestablished as smarter criminals.

He'd boast to the "better people"—a term used for the more intelligent inmates—that his system had not only grown stronger while he was incarcerated but also much more sophisticated. And it had. He had found ways to circumvent tribal laws that were so restrictive on the reservation that even the sale or possession of alcohol was prohibited.

Released prisoners repaid The Reverend by providing information and supplies or assuring his business remained vigorous in exchange for his lessons. And for a cut, of course.

Wanting in on the profit, Snake wished Coyote Cries hadn't scared the living shit out of him so much. But he had. Snake rubbed his throat and walked gingerly toward the window to study his reflection in the sunlight. The bruising around his smashed throat from the weights was darkening from pink to purple. He was alive. At least for now. He had to find out who was trying to bury The Reverend. If he didn't, he'd be dead.

Coyote Cries had the power. Live or die.

Asshole.

He shot a glance across the courtyard, afraid he'd conjured up the devil; worried someone might have overheard his thoughts; worried that even Squeeze might turn on him. The Reverend could be persuasive. But Coyote Cries wasn't even looking his way. He was talking to some of his followers, who were laughing.

Blockheads.

He wanted to shove that book of Jeremiah right back in his face. Chapter 22, verse 19. *He shall be buried with the burial of an ass.* Yeah, he knew how to read a Bible. And he wanted to tell Coyote Cries his mama named him after the crybaby prophet. Always bellyaching. He turned back to his reflection in the window and inspected the darkening band on his own throat—unmistakably there to remind him of The Reverend's power.

From the feds' perspective, his sentence was a defeat for The Reverend.

He wondered what they'd think if they learned how prosperous and powerful Coyote Cries had become while he'd been inside. Maybe that was his ticket out of here: to turn on The Reverend. He shuddered at the thought of what would happen to him if he failed.

He'd heard Coyote Cries claim his sentencing *was* a defeat. He had expected to be acquitted. But only twenty-one years old at the time, he admitted he'd been naïve. He should have expected the white government would want him incarcerated. He'd boasted that he was too smart, too talented to be allowed freedom. The white government feared him too much. He'd bragged that he'd made more money in the eight years dealing drugs before being arrested than anyone else had made on the reservation in a lifetime. He thought he was a threat to the feds. He claimed to be somewhat of a local hero, an inspiration on the reservation.

But Snake had heard differently from an inmate who was also Lakotan.

The guy said Coyote Cries was a disappointment to his people. He'd represented a setback for those who struggled to fight true oppression and keep their culture alive through hard work and persistence. Without drugs. Resisting the temptations of an easier life through crime.

That Lakotan had bled out in his cell. No doubt at Coyote Cries's hand. But no one could prove it. The guards found The Reverend praying over the dead prisoner, spouting that the heart is deceitful above all things and desperately wicked. It was a veiled warning to others in the population not to contradict his stories, but the guards interpreted the action as Coyote Cries simply praying for his brother.

That day, The Reverend had scrawled *Jeremiah 22:17* on his wall.

It was not a confession. It was a caution.

Jeremiah 22:17 became the credo by which The Reverend lived. Snake remembered borrowing someone's Bible to look up the passage, barely remembering from his childhood how to look up chapter and verse.

> *Your eyes and your heart are intent only on your own dishonest gain, on shedding innocent blood, and on practicing oppression and extortion.*

The guy was a frickin' loon.

If he'd kill a fellow tribesman, what would he plan on doing to Snake?

Ever since, The Reverend had used that passage to justify his actions as righteous.

Some prisoners complained, but most remained quiet. His incantations appeared to be praises to God. He was simply expressing his religious free-doms. But most knew better. The smarter population had learned early that if The Reverend's cautions weren't heeded, injury or death coincidentally followed.

To increase his chances for early parole, Coyote Cries learned quickly to put his time in seclusion toward crafting his façade, acting as if he were in prayerful reflection. Occasionally the guards would see his solace inter-rupted by another prisoner, which they falsely interpreted as The Reverend counseling his fellow inmates. In actuality, he was peddling—paraphernalia, information, whatever—inside the block.

Fools.

They had no clue. And remained sympathetic to The Reverend. He had been so convincing that two of the guards had even agreed to give personal testimony on Coyote Cries's behalf at his parole hearing on Thursday. Snake had almost puked when he'd heard that.

Another prisoner suddenly stepped in behind Snake, startling him, and began studying his reflection in the mirror.

Snake growled, "*And?* What'd you find out?"

The man said only one word. A name. Dillinger.

Not good. Should he tell him? Or not.

Either way, Snake knew he was a dead man.

CHAPTER 6

AS FAMILIAR WITH QUARRIES as most people are with coffee shops, I knew where to set up for the best advantage to listen in on Bert Ridgewood's conversation with the EPA inspector.

At least until the plant ran into trouble or experienced an upset.

I took off for the feed hopper with aggregate that charged the asphalt plant. I crept down the gravel ramp and hunkered down behind the leg of the cold feeder feeding the hot drum. The steel I-beam was large enough to hide all of me.

I was close enough to catch the wireless feed from Bert's mic in my earbud, yet far enough from the rest of the screening and hot plant that I could hear over the noise of the operation. The EPA inspector had just driven up to the office.

I'd been hiding since long before sunrise and before any of the employees arrived. They hadn't noticed me even though they'd started up the equipment an hour earlier, and it had been running ever since.

The yardman climbed into the loader to charge or fill the cold bins with rock every half hour or so and the first time he did, I feared being spotted. But I wasn't.

So far so good.

I was glad I'd grabbed my hearing protection muffs. With them covering my earbuds, I'd be able to better hear the mic. Everything was in place.

I'd run home yesterday for an hour to pack an overnight bag and to grab what I'd need for Beulah. I could have left her at home, but I missed her too much. She was nestled in her kennel in the back of my Jeep. Probably dreaming about the pizza we had shared the night before in the comfort of our hotel room.

To while away the dark hours while waiting, I had been recalling the great conversation I had last night with my oldest brother, Ole. He was sorry he didn't get to see me to say goodbye. He heard the next day that I'd left—from Dad—and offered his condolences again about losing Jack. Then, as always with my brother, we got right to business.

He'd told me he'd had several strange calls from an EPA inspector named Dick Roth out of Region VIII's office in Denver. Ole's interpretation? Mostly, the inspector seemed anxious and wanted to meet on site. First at our Rifle Quarry; then at our Buena Vista Quarry. Finally he had suggested they meet at our Livermore Quarry. Ole said he had ultimately agreed to meet with the guy at Livermore, the only continuously active quarry of the three.

When I asked him if Roth had made any hint of "protection" money to keep the air permits, Ole said he hadn't. Roth had performed a quick inspection, asked about the other two sites, and left.

Uneventful.

I pressed my brother for more details, and he explained that he had brought a young manager along with him for training purposes after asking Roth if the Livermore site manager could join them for the inspection. He confirmed to me that he was never alone with Roth but that Roth had insisted they talk again. Alone. Sometime in the near future. Ole thought that was strange.

He said he'd thought the conversation was so odd that he'd told Dad about it, and the two of them had planned to meet with this guy if he ever insisted again on seeing Ole.

They wouldn't be alone with him. Smart men.

And here I was watching Dick Roth through my tiny binoculars. The man Ole had described in detail to a gnat's ass—complete with the diagonal scrape in the EPA sticker on his barely used hard hat.

Recording device: ON.

The sun was at the inspector's back. He'd introduced himself to Bert Ridgewood a few moments earlier and ushered him away from the other employees like a cow dog cutting a yearling out of the herd for slaughter. Then he studied the cloud of dust being emitted from the asphalt stack. I could see him shake his head slowly from side to side. I could hear through my mic the cluck of his tongue. Scolding Bert Ridgewood? *Seriously?*

Then I heard the EPA inspector say, "I am not at all pleased with what I see."

I snapped photos and took video of their conversation and then of the plume coming from the plant. Ridgewood, a tall man wearing a soiled, white hard hat and neatly pressed blue jeans, slowly removed his safety sunglasses.

He turned toward the inspector and asked, "What are you talking about?"

Ridgewood was cool and understood exactly how to play the situation. He was thrilled about me showing up yesterday when I'd called from a local restaurant, suggesting we have a coffee at quitting time. Or a beer. His preference. Wisely, he chose water. And we made our plan.

He was following the plan precisely.

I wanted to know how Roth would play this thing, too. I told Ridgewood to throw questions his way; to make him talk; to make him say what it was he didn't like seeing and what Ridgewood had to do to make him happy; to leave nothing unspoken or assumed.

And from where I hid, the opacity from the stack looked great. For an asphalt plant.

"Your stack emissions," Roth replied. "The readings I'm getting far exceed your permitted opacity. I'm reading at least fifty-five percent. And your permit is only for thirty-five."

I was trained to read opacity. From where I crouched, the sun was at my back, too—a requirement for reading opacity. And I would have guessed Ridgewood was running at twenty, not more than twenty-five percent. I made sure I spoke into the speaker of my video camera when I recorded my reading.

Apparently, Bert was as confused as I was.

He alternated slow, careful glances between the Environmental Protection Agency representative and his asphalt plant's stack. "That opacity isn't any more than twenty-five percent."

Bingo, I thought. The two of us could testify as expert witnesses. Bert was obviously a certified Method 9 opacity reader, too. I'd forgotten to ask him yesterday.

"Really," Roth said flatly as he narrowed his eyes. "And are *you* certified, Mr. Ridgewood?"

"Method 9."

Roth arched an eyebrow and tilted his head. *"Really?"*

Ridgewood had told me that he'd never met Dick Roth—until last week when he showed up at the site unannounced. Roth had told Ridgewood then that he'd be back today for a formal reading. He said Roth never explained how or why he'd chosen to visit his small asphalt operation in Buena Vista. But Ridgewood had explained to me over coffee that he had called the FBI after receiving a warning call from his friend in Glenwood Springs to expect a shakedown.

But he admitted he had immediately disliked Roth the instant he'd met him. Even before he'd heard from his friend about the dirty EPA inspector.

Roth had announced himself a half hour earlier to the receptionist of Ridgewood's Asphalt and Aggregates, Inc. As a representative from Denver's Region VIII Environmental Protection Agency, Roth had demanded to see the manager or owner of the operation. Having formed the small asphalt company only three years earlier, Bert Ridgewood qualified as both. Roth claimed he was making the required visit in response to a complaint filed with the agency about Ridgewood's operation. I'd recorded all of this on the device I'd left in the secretary's top desk drawer.

A savvy businessman in his early forties, Ridgewood was no stranger to the construction material industry. He'd told me that for the first twenty years of his career, he had worked all over the Denver area and along the Front Range of the Rocky Mountains in the sand and gravel, ready-mix, and asphalt industries. He'd heard of Bergen. Knew my brother.

Ole said he'd heard that Ridgewood had worked at various levels of supervision for an international construction materials supply company and that he was renowned as one of the experts in the Rocky Mountain region on how to successfully operate plants and quarries. Ole had even offered Ridgewood a job. But he declined, telling Ole that he wanted to strike out on his own.

Who could blame him with all that talent?

Ridgewood told me yesterday that based on his years of experience in the area, he predicted strong economic growth to continue along the Front Range that would eventually arrive at Buena Vista, a small town located southwest of Denver in the Rocky Mountains. I suggested we reopen the Bergen limestone mine north of town or sell it to him. Then I asked him whether he had suggested an expansion idea to his previous employer. What I really wanted to know was if he was ethical or not. Needed to know, actually. And the way he answered told me.

He said that after he tried unsuccessfully to convince the regional manager to expand the company into Buena Vista and profit from the inevitable growth, Ridgewood turned in his resignation to risk everything he owned to start up his own fledgling asphalt operation. He'd even offered to rescind his resignation if they changed their minds about the growth opportunity.

But they hadn't.

So he had ventured out on his own. It had taken him nearly three years to make the small company profitable and all his hard work and persistence was beginning to pay off. After spending sixteen arduous and dedicated months obtaining all the necessary permits and learning everything he could about reaching regulatory compliance with his operation, Ridgewood had been nothing short of astounded by Dick Roth's crooked tactics.

And from where I was watching, he was getting more and more pissed at Roth's assessment.

Ridgewood was explaining to the inspector how he had attended "smoke school" and passed the opacity certification course offered by Colorado's health department two years ago—specifically to understand how to stay within compliance of the air emissions permit. He explained unequivocally that he had become certified because he wanted to know that his employees were operating within the limits of the permit issued to Asphalt and Aggregates, Inc.

He wasn't brownnosing. He truly cared.

As he stood next to the EPA representative, Ridgewood's cheeks flushed. Roth insisted the opacity of the plume from his plant was exceeding his permit limit. Ridgewood repeated that he read nothing more than a twenty-five percent blockage of light from the plume of dust emitting from the stack. He was sure of that and could arguably suggest it was no more than twenty.

I could confirm that assessment on the witness stand. That was my reading as well.

What Ridgewood couldn't read or predict was the motivation behind Dick Roth's unannounced visit and his subsequent accusation of an alleged permit violation. He simply had to wait until Roth unintentionally or intentionally expressed his intent. He grew silent and watched Roth.

Roth stood confidently with his hairy arms folded across his chest. As he rocked back on the heels of his steel-toed boots, a smile spread slowly across his craggy face beneath the shiny white hard hat with the scarred EPA decal. He was not an attractive man, and his arrogant demeanor suggested that he was determined to make those who were attractive—like Bert Ridgewood—pay for Roth being shortchanged in the looks department.

Roth's smug smile widened. "How long ago were you certified, Mr. Ridgewood?"

Ridgewood furrowed his brow with his pale-blue eyes fixed on Roth. "Two years ago. I passed on my first attempt. What I see out there in my operation is a twenty to twenty-five percent opacity, Mr. Roth."

"Well, that *is* a problem, isn't it?"

CHAPTER 7

ROTH FEIGNED A SMILE, removed his hard hat, and scratched his greasy hair with his neatly trimmed fingernails.

I wanted to puke. Without looking back at the asphalt plant, he added, "What I see and what I will report in response to the complaints we've received about your operation is that you are emitting dust at a fifty-five percent opacity, which is far in excess of your permit. You understand what that means, don't you Mr. Ridgewood?"

Even from where I was, I could see Ridgewood clench his teeth with frustration, with his muscles twitching along his strong jaw. He did not like Roth, and I was witnessing an erosion of Ridgewood's initial opinion of Dick Roth from dislike to hatred.

After hearing all of this, witnessing it firsthand, I had no doubt of Roth's intentions to allege complaints about operations, falsify reports of field inspections, and threaten to garner "protection." Now all I needed was "the ask."

On record.

Ridgewood said nothing. *Good job*, I thought.

"That means the department of health will need to issue you a notice of violation based on my report," Roth continued. "As the operator, you could be found grossly negligent or even wanton and willfully in disregard of the law. I can make it a violation. Depending on what I report, you will not only be fined, but you may be issued a cease and desist order, which will close you down."

Ridgewood glared down at the threatening, unattractive man.

Roth smiled back at him with satisfaction, placed his hard hat back on his head, and folded his arms. Rocking back on his heels, his pompous expression seemed to be getting to Bert Ridgewood. It would me.

Unfolding his hairy arms and stuffing his hands deep into his pockets, Roth added, "As for your reading of only twenty or twenty-five percent, Mr. Ridgewood, let me clue you in on a little secret so you won't embarrass yourself in the future. You are not considered a current certified opacity reader in this state unless you recertify every six months."

He was correct. He could disqualify Ridgewood's readings but not mine. I'd kept up on my certification, even though I changed careers.

"That means you are grossly overdue on your recertification classes, considering you haven't been back to smoke school in two years. Your readings today are totally disputable. Whereas mine are not."

The clucking noise of his scolding tongue caused Bert to wince.

Defensively, Ridgewood argued, "Lila Sorenson from the health department was just here less than a month ago. She came unannounced for her annual inspection and is the official inspector for compliance with our air permits. She read no more than a thirty percent opacity, and she took readings every five minutes for nearly an hour."

Ridgewood was doing well, laying out a contradictory opinion. With me present, his official report would be on file. I just prayed his temper wouldn't tip his hand about me. I needed more. I wanted to nail this bastard for what he was doing to hard working, compliant operators.

And my video footage was running on the plant's plume.

"The plant operator didn't even know Lila was here until after she finished her readings. That was the official inspection, and we did fine. In fact, we typically ran at twenty percent opacity. It's in her report. The health department has the official responsibility to inspect us for EPA Clean Air Act compliance and all associated air permits."

I started to think that maybe Roth might not offer the bribe; that with Ridgewood's righteous indignation becoming overwhelming, Roth wouldn't risk getting caught.

"I want to see a copy of the complaint. Otherwise, you can leave. Or tell me under what authority are you here, Mr. Roth?"

I could see Roth's chest inflate. He was defiant.

"My own authority," Roth answered. I noticed a change in his face. His lips moved with a weird exaggerated elasticity. I snapped a photo. Although his smile reappeared wide across his craggy face, his small, brown eyes never left Ridgewood's. "You see, we occasionally do audits of our field offices to make sure they are doing their jobs properly."

Ridgewood appeared stunned by Roth's persistence. My curiosity was growing, and I had no clue where Roth was heading.

"Maybe Ms. Sorenson is having trouble reading your stack for some reason. But I doubt it. I'd more likely believe that you are operating intentionally without your control devices. Because you didn't think anyone would be back to inspect you until next year. Is that possible?"

"Absolutely not," Ridgewood argued.

"That may just be my official conclusion, Mr. Ridgewood." Roth lit up the cigarette he had just pulled from his pocket. "It would certainly explain the discrepancy between the reports to anyone at the health department."

"We don't allow smoking on the property."

I grinned. I knew how Ridgewood must feel. And he was trying to exert what little authority he had left over this asshole.

"You do for me." Roth shook out the match and discarded it on the ground. "You see, if I report that you're intentionally operating without your baghouse, allowing emissions to far exceed your permitted amount, then your responsibility as owner will elevate from negligent to wanton and willful misconduct. Do you understand me now, Mr. Ridgewood?"

I checked the recording device. Light still indicated the capture. Roth was about to incriminate himself. I clicked on the video and zoomed the lens on the pair. Ridgewood turned his back on Roth and studied his asphalt plant, like an artist would examine his painting. I felt sorry for him. He wasn't as prepared as he had thought.

He was probably replaying all the hours he'd spent getting the plant into operation and into compliance and the sacrifices he'd made to get where he was today. He likely couldn't bear the thought of being issued a cease and desist order, thinking of the irreparable damages something like that would cause to his relationships with his customers. It would be a blemish on his otherwise spotless regulatory record and to his reputation in the Buena Vista community.

I understood exactly how he felt. I would have felt the same if Roth had treated me this way when I managed the Livermore Quarry before I came to the FBI.

Roth had him by the nuts.

With a wanton, willful, and scathing misconduct report by Roth, along with the alleged excessive emissions, possibly a Notice of Violation, the penalties would be severe. And the health department might decide to permanently revoke his air permit. Ridgewood's fledgling new business could be shut down—all because of the lies from one corrupt, power-hungry, bully federal inspector.

I held my breath. I was waiting to see how Ridgewood might handle this.

He spun around, narrowed his eyes at the bureaucrat, and asked, "What is it that you want from me?"

I could've cheered out loud. He kept his poise. Even after all that.

"Nothing more than your cooperation." Roth drew hard on his unfiltered cigarette. He flicked the butt down next to Ridgewood's steel-toed boot, shot him a glance, and added, "And of course, your trust in me as a partner in your new venture."

There it was. I had him. Dead to rights. Hopefully.

Ridgewood stood perfectly still and stared at Roth. His jaw moved slowly in and out. It looked like he was grinding his teeth.

"Like I said, what is it that you want?"

"A thousand dollars," Roth said coolly.

I checked the equipment again. It appeared to be recording. I had him—in-person, witnessed, and on the record with video and sound.

"Cash. I want it when I return from lunch." Roth studied Ridgewood's expressionless eyes. "And I'll be back every three months, and you'll give me an additional five hundred in cash when I do."

There it was: the ask. Protection money. Extortion. I wanted to pump my fists in the air and high five Ridgewood.

The muscles of Ridgewood's jaws flexed in bulging knots, and for a moment, I thought he might hit the guy. But he didn't.

Then Roth smiled slyly and attempted to make nice with Ridgewood. "Oh, don't worry, Mr. Ridgewood. You'll get something for your investment in me. After all, this is a partnership in your new venture. In return, I won't file the report for today, and you will receive no notice of violation or any related penalties for the way you are operating so willfully and wantonly out of compliance."

The squat man turned to go. Ridgewood balled his fists.

Roth lifted his index finger as if he'd forgotten something. "The fee you pay me every quarter will ensure that I will do everything I can in the future to allow you the lightest of penalties if you are found to be out of compliance to any degree and will ensure that you receive no future visits by me." His wide grin revealed his tobacco-stained teeth. "That is, no official visits."

"And if I refuse or report you?"

"Report me?" Roth lifted his hands in surrender. "You're a smarter businessman than that. Who would believe you over me? I'm a very powerful man at Region VIII, with an impeccable reputation. Do you honestly think anyone would believe you over me?"

Ridgewood added, "Wouldn't hurt to try."

Roth leaned into Ridgewood and poked a finger in his chest. "You're a new player in the market who knows virtually nothing about the regulations. You're an operator who would do anything to get his business profitable, including ignoring the restrictive permit. And if you file a complaint against me, I'll bury you with my expertise and experience."

When Ridgewood's shoulders and face fell, Roth revealed another thin smile. He shrugged. "Look at it this way. You can spend money fighting me and arguing about the validity of my report to the health department with no assurance that you will prevent me from shutting you down indefinitely—or even permanently—or you can make me your partner. You're a businessman. You're trained to assess risk. Do you really want to risk your business over a couple thousand dollars a year?"

"What you're doing is wrong. How long do you think you will get away with this?"

Roth raised his eyebrow and laughed.

I imagined from Ridgewood's puckered nose that he could smell the blended stench of excess saliva and stale cigarettes that emanated beyond the loathsome man's stubby teeth.

I shivered. Poor Ridgewood.

He'd been threatened with his livelihood and extorted for a relatively inconsequential amount of money by a man purporting to uphold and regulate one of the country's most expansive environmental legislative acts ever passed by Congress.

Regulations that were intended to help, not hurt.

Made by good people, not assholes like Roth.

"For as long as I choose." Roth's sneer faded, and his face hardened. "Don't get smart with me, Mr. Ridgewood. Your principles and cleverness are no match for my spotless reputation."

"I may be outmatched, but I'd rather have principles than be crooked."

Roth warned, "A few have tried to take me on, and they silently watched with hopefulness and horror as I squashed them like the bugs that they were. Keep in mind, this isn't personal. It's just a business transaction. You keep your quarterly payments coming, and I will watch out for your best interests at Region VIII. If you do that, we will get along just fine."

Ridgewood watched the craggy-faced, stumpy man make his way back to his government-issued SUV. Roth waved casually. "Think about it. See you after lunch." Then he drove off.

I'd had time to climb out of my position and check the recordings. They were solid. I had him.

Ridgewood stared at the empty parking lot, looking lost for many long moments before turning back toward his asphalt plant.

I studied him as I made my way through the yard. He shook his head and closed his eyes. He removed his well-worn hard hat whose smudges of grease and patches of dirt were like medals of honor awarded to an experienced commander. He ran his fingers through his thick, black hair and wiped his forehead with the back of his hand.

I imagined he was seriously weighing his options. I approached him and clapped him on the back. "You did it. I have him. Recorded and witnessed."

He let out a deep breath. "What next?"

"Pay him. Cash. I'll record it. Don't worry."

He turned and walked back toward his office.

"Where are you going?"

"To get my checkbook and go to the bank."

He looked so sad. I had to do something to cheer him up. "Bert?"

He stopped and looked back over his shoulder at me.

"Twenty. Not more than twenty-five. Roth was lying about the opacity."

He spun on his heels, gawking at me.

"Two months ago. Recertified. I keep up as a Method 9 opacity reader. And you were right. Your lawyer should call me as the expert witness to your testimony."

The grin that split his handsome face was all I needed as thanks.

CHAPTER 8

COYOTE CRIES STUDIED THE nicks on his bedframe.

He'd been counting the days until his parole hearing. He'd never done that before. There was no point counting days. He had plenty of time to waste. But he'd been waiting for this day, this moment, for two decades. And now it was fast approaching. He had to be prepared.

Ready for anything.

He had flawlessly set a plan in motion to assure his release. A plan to ensure no one would be at the parole hearing to testify against him.

No one.

He'd be freed.

He could almost taste the sweet revenge he'd take against the man who'd stolen his freedom.

After that, he'd move on to the list of all those people who had double-crossed him or refused to help him. More than anything, Coyote Cries hated disloyalty. And there were plenty in his organization who'd been disloyal to him, who had taken more than their agreed share, who had cut product without his permission, or forgotten their place, or made decisions for him. Or *as* him. He intended to make good on that list after he paid a long over-due visit to the man who had arrested him, just to claim Top Tenner status.

When he was arrested, he'd posted bail. He'd had plenty of money socked away for that, even though the prosecuting attorney smirked when the judge announced the excessive amount. They never dreamed a Lakotan like him, one of the original people, had that kind of cash. But he did. Much more, in fact. Business on the rez was good back then. Still is now, after all this time. Not just good, but growing.

When he was out on bail, he'd used the precious days to wrap up his plan for continuing his work while he'd be doing time. And of course he'd attempted to pay a visit to the asshole lawman who'd arrested him. But he'd been unable to complete the job. Instead, he'd had to settle for less.

Coyote Cries loathed settling.

He'd grown accustomed to getting what he wanted when he wanted it. Especially when it came time for grudges and revenge. He needed to settle this old score before he could truly see himself as able to move on with his new life as The Reverend.

He rubbed his thumb across the grooves in the black paint of his bedframe. The day was coming. He would reach the moment of redemption soon, despite someone's efforts to keep him here. He frowned, pressing his thumb against the frame until his skin turned ghostly. The sharp nicks pierced his skin.

He was imaging strangling the neck of whoever'd been sabotaging his release. Someone had been trying to convince the prison guards that he was a fake; that he was not really as spiritual as he claimed to be. Someone had told the prison guards about his stash and the illicit materials he'd been selling to the other prisoners.

But he'd managed to convince most of the guards that the stash had been planted for revenge—against his belief in God and his people—and as a warning to other prisoners to turn their back on reformation and redemption.

He'd successfully explained that rumors about his feigned belief in God were easily and naturally disputed, as evidenced by his decades of unfaltering commitment and dedication to his religion that were witnessed by seasoned guards. Only two guards, who were newly hired, seemed skeptical about the forty-six-year-old Native American's story. The other guards believed every word Coyote Cries spoke because he'd demonstrated for years that he was who he said he was.

Even though he wasn't.

Jeremiah Coyote Cries was disciplined. And he was patient. He could be anyone he needed to be as long as he got what he wanted.

And he wanted out.

But the seasoned guards couldn't persuade the two new guards that Coyote Cries was an honest, forthright man who'd made some bad choices as a young man. Neither could he. In all his years, he'd been able to convince anyone of almost anything. But not these two.

Why not? he wondered.

Not even when he shared a quote with them—a very successful quote he was famous for using that was getting more hits on social media than the cat that did backflips. He told them, "No one can believe in one thing and do another. Maybe for a moment, but not for a lifetime. What I believe and what I do are the same thing."

But they weren't convinced. Someone inside had been brainwashing these two.

He lifted his thumb, sucked off the blood, and grabbed his well-worn Bible. He flipped through the pages and landed on his favorite passage.

Jeremiah 22:17.

His mantra.

> *Your eyes and your heart are intent only on your own dishonest gain, on shedding innocent blood, and on practicing oppression and extortion.*

What dishonest gain might those two be after? Maybe they'd discovered his wealth, his power that he so carefully kept secret. Maybe they wanted a cut? That didn't seem likely with these two Dudley Do-Rights. No, not that. More likely, they'd heard something about him. They were cautious. They distrusted everyone in the population.

They were scared. That could work to his advantage. But first he had to find out exactly who was trying to destroy him. Then, he would make the prisoner who ratted him out to the new guards pay for his indiscretion.

This parole hearing was everything to him.

Although he knew that Snake was no snitch, Coyote Cries suspected he might know or could find out who was talking. And if Snake did know, their "talk" yesterday morning would've convinced him to confess. But he hadn't. So Coyote Cries would be patient. Snake would figure out who was squealing.

He'd been keeping close tabs on the fish, the newest prisoner, who had only been in the joint for three weeks, and Snake had alluded that he was likely the leak, too. But Coyote Cries needed time to confirm it. Until then, he had assigned his most trusted and loyal soldier to shadow the fish.

The gossip at the mainline, the prison cafeteria, was that some prisoners had suspected the new guy was a correctional officer in disguise—a plant or a spy placed in the system to find out information about other inmates. The rumor was that he was no more a wife-beater than the Pope and was too clean-cut to be anything but an undercover agent.

A Dudley Do-Right—like the two new guards.

Maybe all three of them were in it together. A shakedown. He'd keep a closer eye on their interactions and ask his only confidant if the fish had spent any time with the new guards alone.

The underground prison network of communication was a haven of information. No one other than the convicts themselves could participate in the elaborate data link. Even though the administrators were always trying to infiltrate it, they hadn't yet succeeded in any of their attempts.

The thought that this newest prisoner had been introduced into the population as the lawman's latest attempt to break the prison code was completely plausible. And the guards might be his protection. Yes. There was something to that supposition.

He smiled.

He rose from his bed and walked to the door, knowing the quiet time lockdown before dinner was almost over. Just then the locks popped, and the doors opened throughout the cellblock. He padded out of the cell and merged into the flow of prisoners headed to the mainline to eat.

Coyote Cries sensed he was onto something. The two new guards . . . the fish . . . Although he wondered if the feds would allow one of their boys to be "done" by the booty bandit . . . Maybe that story was fabricated, but Dillinger, his number two guy, said it had been confirmed. He was a legitimate source. He would never lie.

On second thought, maybe the correctional plant himself started the rumor about being messed with by one of the booty bandits, wanting the news to spread as quickly as it did so he'd appear to be one of the blues. It made sense. Coyote Cries would find out. He'd either confirm directly with the booty bandits, or he'd corner the newest prisoner and invite him into the confessional.

With The Reverend.

CHAPTER 9

A DOZEN LONG-STEMMED YELLOW roses in a magnificent bouquet that was probably delivered yesterday brightened my doorstep.

My mother said she would be sending me a day brightener to remind me how proud my family was of me for going back to work. She was always thinking of others and had yet to ever let me down. I scooped up the plump vase and fumbled with the keys to my apartment. Beulah nudged my leg with her nose. She had wanted to come home, and we were finally there. To stay.

I glanced over at the family photo on my counter. There are eleven of us.

My parents named all nine of us kids alphabetically for saints. That was Mom's choice. She's Irish Catholic. Our Norwegian middle names were Dad's choice.

I was named Genevieve Liv Bergen. My brother, Dismas Ole Bergen. All the girls but me go by their first name: Agatha, Barbara, Catherine, Elizabeth, Frances, and Ida. My two brothers, Dismas and Hubert, go by their middle names, Ole and Jens.

I'd like to say that a name means nothing; that it predestines a child in no way. But I've found as my siblings age, they were named exactly as they should have been.

Agatha Ardnis, my oldest sister, channels both the patron saint for volcanoes and is an eagle spirit, as her Norwegian name indicates. She's an artist who tends to favor cutting torches over paint brushes, is strikingly beautiful, and can get any of us to do just about anything anytime. She claims to be "the oldest and the meanest." Not true—she's one of the kindest.

Barbara Bera was an officer in the Army. She's afraid of nothing and as tiny as Elizabeth. But never underestimate their strength. Barbara, the patron saint of mining, and Bera, the Norwegian word for spirited, suit my second oldest sister to a tee.

Catherine Carlsdatter is a Catholic nun who loves to eat and dotes on everyone. Catherine is the patron saint of learning, and Carlsdatter refers to my grandmother's maiden name. Everyone loves Sister Catherine. And Sister Catherine loves everything chocolate. Especially Chubby Chipmunk and Mostly Chocolates—locally made Black Hills delicacies. Both are absolutely to die for.

Dismas Ole runs the family business with my dad. Dismas was the good thief who was crucified to the right of Jesus Christ. And my oldest brother is indeed my father's right-hand man. And who the hell knows what Ole means in Norwegian? Just Ole.

Elizabeth Eldrid is the wild-card elfin sister who changes jobs as often as she changes hair color. She amuses me more than anyone on the planet. Saint Elizabeth was the patron saint of widows and young brides, and Eldrid means fiery spirit in Norwegian. She's never been married, which is ironic considering her saint's name. Elizabeth and I tend to get into a lot of trouble together. Fiery spirit, indeed.

Frances Frida is a telemarketer who works from home. She is most certainly her Norwegian name, which means beautiful, and Frances was the patron saint of migrants. Far from being a wanderer, Frances is the omnipresent buoy for all of us during any of life's storms. I tend to think that's why God chose her to raise Noah, my nephew with severe cerebral palsy. Frances is simply the saint of the family.

Hubert Jens is an integral part of the family business and beloved by the employees. Hubert is the patron saint of hunters, and our Hubert loves to hunt or fish in every spare minute of his time. And Jens? I've forgotten what that means in Norwegian. Just simply Jens, I suppose. But he is far from being a simple man and is, in fact, quite complicated and interesting.

Ida Ingrid, the youngest—singer, model, and actress. Not just a singer, an opera singer. No wonder her name means prosperous beauty. She is every bit of it, with the operatic voice of an angel. And quite wise on top of it all.

I was seventh born. Between Frances and Jens. Genevieve Liv Bergen. St. Genevieve is the patron saint of disasters and fever. Go figure. If asked about my name, I stick to Liv Bergen, which means life as a mountain dweller.

My parents, David Garth and Jeanne Kiara Bergen, are incredible gifts.

My dad, Garth, is of Norwegian heritage, owns and runs a mining company, and is a popular local icon. Oh, and a US Congressman.

My mom, Jeanne, is of Irish descent. She's the glue in an incredibly tight family and a saint who owns a Mary Poppins purse. The only thing I hope to inherit from my parents is the magic purse.

I collect rocks that represent each of my family members, and the one that represents my mother is the most beautiful of them all. It's a crystal and my favorite. When a madman serial killer swiped the crystal from my room in Fort Collins over a year ago, the depths of hatred and instant panic I suffered in that moment of recognition that I had failed to protect her drove me insane. The wound was deep and visceral.

No one will ever harm my mother without going through me. And a lot of other fiercely protective siblings, too. Red Rover, Red Rover. Send the assholes over. We'll take care of them.

I set the roses on my kitchen counter where they were visible from everywhere in my tiny apartment, tossed my overnight bag on a chair, and filled Beulah's bowl with water, which she lapped greedily. Now to some food—for the dog, not me.

I poured myself a glass of merlot and glanced through my stack of bills, sorted by priority. While I opened each envelop, I called my brother.

"Genevieve," he said before I could get out a hello.

"Dismas."

I glanced over at the yellow roses and imagined her whipping that huge bouquet out of that tiny purse, putting them in the back of my Jeep without me knowing it, and arranging for someone at this end to place them on my doorstep before I got out of the car. That would be my mom. She can do anything.

"What's up?" my brother asked. "You left a rather cryptic message."

I'd been waiting for Bert Ridgewood to wrap things up in his office after Roth had left. So I made use of idle time and called Ole.

"Wondering if you can help me."

"Of course. Name it."

"Remember that guy I told you about?"

"Dick Roth? The EPA inspector?"

"I wouldn't normally ask, but you mentioned that you and Dad were going to attack this situation together if Roth ever came back. Think I can use you as bait in a sting operation?"

"Happy to do it. When do you need me?"

And that was that. Clearly, they weren't afraid of the risk. No regard for inconvenience or even danger. My brother was there for me, and we'd have a good time taking that lowlife down.

We set the plans and said our goodbyes.

I swallowed more wine and foraged for anything I could find in my fridge. I was hauling out some crackers, an unopened brick of cheese that hadn't yet expired, and some buffalo sausage, thinking at least I had some protein, when someone knocked at my door.

I set my bounty down on the counter and peeked through the fisheye and gasped. It was Streeter Pierce. He'd never come to my apartment. I didn't even know he knew where I lived.

I swung the door open.

I had so many things I wanted to say to this man, but I just stood there staring with my mouth hanging open like a shored guppy. My mind just couldn't wrap itself around what I was seeing.

I must have stood there for far too long, because he finally asked, "May I come in?"

"Oh, of course. Sorry," I said, stepping aside and motioning for him to come in.

I closed the door behind him and nearly bumped into him as he stopped just inside the doorway. He handed me Beulah's lead, rolled into a nice bundle. "I forgot to give this to you yesterday and thought you might need it."

I took the harness and set it on the counter by my Jeep keys. "Thank you. I've been . . . well, I just got back from Buena Vista."

"I know."

He just stood there. And so did I.

What was wrong with me?

It was like I was having an out of body experience watching the most humiliating moment of my life.

Could I be a bigger doof?

"I was just having a glass of wine and some cheese. Want to join me?"

He glanced at his watch.

"You probably have to go, have a date or something." No clue why I said that.

He grinned. "I'd love some wine."

I darted around the kitchen counter and motioned for him to have a seat at the bar. I fumbled with a glass and poured him some wine. Topped off my own. "Merlot okay?"

"Perfect," he said, tipping his glass my way before taking a sip.

I unwrapped the buffalo sausage and cheese, quickly sliced both, shoveled the production onto a plate, and dumped out a sleeve of crackers beside the creation. I slid the plate toward him.

"It's not much, but I just got home."

"Your mom sent you flowers? How sweet."

I stared at him. "How did you know they were from my mom?"

"Jeanne sent me some too. Yellow roses. About a week ago. To thank me."

"Jeanne?" I said, walking slowly around the counter to my stool beside him.

I was most certainly out of body.

When did my mom and Streeter become so chummy?

"You call my mom Jeanne?"

"That is her name." His right eyebrow arched as he took a sip of wine. He plucked a slice of sausage from the plate and took a bite. "The buffalo Jens shot?"

My chin dropped again. "You know my brother shot a buffalo?"

I wondered just how long I'd ignored Streeter's calls and if maybe it wasn't such a great idea. Especially now, in retrospect, that I was finding out he'd been chatting with my family and, apparently, quite a lot.

How much did they tell him? And where was I that entire time?

Clearly, head in a fog. I had no clue.

He said, "Garth invited me up to this year's family pheasant hunt."

"This can't be happening," I said. But I hadn't meant to say it aloud.

"Should I go?" He swiveled his barstool toward the door.

"Oh, heavens, no," I said, grabbing his forearm.

I slapped both hands over my face, embarrassed. I heard him chuckling. I let my hands drop into my lap and averted my eyes. "I'm sorry. This is just so surreal. You being here. In my apartment. When I have so much to say. To tell you."

"So tell me," he said with a shrug.

I looked down at my hands, which I'd begun to wring nervously. I wasn't sure where to begin or how to tell Streeter how much I appreciated him. "You were there for me. That night. All night. And the next day. You took me to the memorial service and then to California. And then you called. Every day for ten days. Twice a day."

"More," he said. He fished a cracker from the heap, placed a slice of sausage on top, and then cheese, and handed the morsel to me. "Eat. You need the protein."

That single gesture alone was my undoing. For the first time in days, I cried—only with a smile on my face. His gesture was loving and caring and genuine. Authentically Streeter.

"Thank you."

Then I ate. I tried to hide the feelings that had overwhelmed me and attempted to regain my poise. I sipped on my wine. I watched as he made himself a similar sandwich stack.

He popped the entire stack into his mouth. Then he lifted his glass. "Good buffalo sausage. Not too spicy." He took a sip. "I see Beulah's happy to be home."

I glanced over my shoulder. She was sacked out on my couch, snoring.

"She did the same at my cabin."

"You live in a cabin?" I asked, feeling my thoughts return. "Where?"

"Conifer. Want to see it?"

My glance cut to his, and I felt my eyes widen. "I do."

I did.

His cool blue eyes were amazingly bright. The setting sun through my deck window painted him beautifully.

Surreal.

I reached out and touched his arm again, just to make sure this was happening.

Streeter grinned.

"I want to thank you for everything you've done for me. Did I already say that?"

"You did." His smile was crooked.

"Taking care of Beulah, covering everything for me at work. You even managed to find me a case that's right up my alley. I'm jazzed."

"I see that."

The emotional rollercoaster I was experiencing—the excitement, confusion, elation, disbelief, timidity, joy—was unexplainable. All because Streeter appeared at my door. The floodgates opened to jumbled thoughts. "My shrink would have never allowed any of this had you not agreed to keep your eye on me."

Streeter leaned forward, close enough that I thought he was going to kiss my cheek. But he didn't. He simply moved a strand of hair from my forehead.

I thought my heart was going to leap out of my chest.

"Are you sure you're okay? With Jack?"

A steep dive down the rails of a rickety coaster, from the highest of highs to a gut wrenching low with the mention of his name.

"You didn't shed a single tear at his funeral."

That was true.

"You concern me."

Sorrow filled me. "I'm okay. Confused. Sad. Stunned. Mad. Pissed, really."

Streeter nodded and fixed another cracker. It felt good to talk to a friend. To be brutally honest with him. Something I'd never had the courage to do with Jack.

"Jack was a dear man. Pained, but dear. I can't excuse what he did—using us, the FBI, the way he did."

"He died a hero." Streeter held my gaze.

"You said that. And I'm sure he did. But I struggle with that. No matter how it came to be and what he had to suffer through, it wasn't right what he did. He shouldn't have died like that. It was like he had a death wish."

"He wanted us to catch the real murderer."

"Jenna Tate wasn't worth that. Wasn't worth his life." I sighed. Then I remembered how Jenna had used Streeter. "How are you dealing with all of this? With Jenna, I mean?"

"She'll be arraigned later this week, and trial dates will be set."

I reached out and grabbed his forearm again, only this time I didn't let go. He met my glance. "I mean personally. I know you two were . . . had a thing."

"A thing?" His expression seemed amused.

"You didn't? You two weren't . . . ?"

He shook his head. "That was Jenna. A tease. But we never had a thing."

I let go of my hold on him. The tension drained out of every muscle in my body. "I thought . . . I worried you were . . . "

"And it bothered you all this time? That we had a thing?"

I realized he was getting the wrong impression.

Well, not wrong exactly.

Damn it. I had to clean up my mess. "I should have felt a bigger loss than I did when Jack died. He said he loved me. But choosing death over life with someone you say you love isn't love. Is it?"

He just stared at me. "I'm not sure I followed what you just said."

"I loved Jack as a dear friend. But I wasn't in love with him. And when he died, I was crushed. Losing him like that—as a friend, as a coworker. I cried a lot for that loss. But in California, at the funeral, I . . . I felt like you, the others, expected me to be his family. I wasn't that. I just couldn't. Does that make any sense?"

Streeter said nothing and shook his head slowly. He was forcing me to explain.

I grabbed my glass of wine, drained and refilled it. "All I felt was a big, empty pity for him. That seems strange, doesn't it? When someone close to you dies?"

I hadn't thought about the implication of what I'd just said. Of course, he'd known what it felt like to lose someone close. He had loved his wife.

"I'm sorry. I didn't mean . . ." I watched as he drained his glass and went to get a refill. "I saw it. Her headstone. On Sunday."

He emptied his second glass and poured a third, staring straight ahead.

"Paula Winzig Jacobs Pierce," I said. "Michael's aunt. Your wife, right? Why didn't you tell me?"

He fiddled with the stem of his wine glass. "I couldn't."

He didn't want to talk about that. So I didn't. "Thanks for sending Mully. He saved my life. I promised the Deputy Sheriff in Deadwood we'd open a case."

"I'll run with it," he said, his tone dull.

"You sent him to help me, didn't you?"

"You don't need to ask. And you don't need to know."

I slid my glass away and rose to my feet. He did the same, thinking I was signaling for him to leave.

But that wasn't it.

I'd waited long enough.

I walked over to him and reached up to touch his face with both hands.

I kissed him like I'd kissed no one before. I melted into him, loved him in that moment like every human being should be loved. I had never felt so strongly about anyone in my life.

I was the first to stop kissing, but I did not stop touching his face. I dragged my fingertips down his cheek, his neck, and rested the palm of my hand on his chest. "I didn't love Jack. I couldn't. There was always you between us."

He leaned down and kissed me back. "And there was never Jenna. Or anyone besides you. Since Paula."

I grabbed him by the hand and led him back to my bedroom.

Beulah slept.

CHAPTER 10

ONLY ONE MORE DAY remained until Jeremiah Coyote Cries could go home, walk in the fields, lie down on a grassy bank, and feel the sun against his skin.

The hum of quiet conversations in the well-guarded visiting room sounded like a distant swarm of killer bees. Every Wednesday morning, the same people arrived to visit their incarcerated loved ones. Most of the visitors were wives and children bearing gifts of family news and food.

Some of the prisoners had no family or families who were non-supportive. They never came to the visiting room. Instead, those prisoners chose to spend their Wednesday mornings playing a pick-up game of basketball in the yard or watching television.

Coyote Cries normally dedicated his Wednesday mornings to the weight room and excessive bench presses and squats. He seldom had reason to participate in visiting unless he was conducting business—unlawful, undetected business—with the outside world.

Today was one of those days.

He shoved through the entrance of the prison corridor thirty minutes into visiting hours. When the doors swung open with a bang, the hum of the room instantly ceased. Heads swiveled in his direction. He walked confidently toward a man sitting alone at the corner table. The tall, strong Indian sat down across from the lone visitor.

The hum returned, and its level rose louder than normal as the prisoners undoubtedly squawked to their families and friends about him. About The Reverend. About the legend.

He felt the gossip even more than heard it. So he sat with his shoulders high, his torso rigid. He rested his muscular arms, disproportionately longer than his short legs, on the table. He looked imposing as he swept his long, shiny grey hair off his high cheekbones and tucked his braid neatly behind his ear.

Glares from angry spouses bored into him from all directions, undoubtedly because of stories of how he had transgressed against their loved ones in some evil way. Mostly true, he was sure. But he ignored them anyway.

Instead, he'd gladly allow them to study his flat profile and his sharp angular features. He wanted them to remember him. Every detail. To never forget The Reverend.

The man across from Coyote Cries said, "What's so funny?"

"I'm not laughing," he said as he glanced at his own reflection in the window and saw that there was a perpetual hint of a tight, arrogant smile on his lips. Like the male version of Mona Lisa. As if he knew a secret he would never share.

No wonder he'd asked.

It was the closest expression to amusement this guy had ever seen on Coyote Cries's face.

He narrowed his black eyes, cold and piercing, to bore into the visitor. And he let his passive tone belie his hostile expression. "The whispered rumors. About me, The Reverend. I find them amusing." His long, strong fingers wrapped tightly around the ratty Bible that he carried everywhere he went in the prison.

"I heard one of them call you a chameleon." The man's glances flitted everywhere. Except on him, the client. He was nervous. Coyote Cries wondered if this idiot had done what he had told him to do. He better have. If he knew what was good for him. Time was running out.

"And what do you think?" His question was intended to mute his visitor and to send a cold chill through his veins. It was his get-back-to-business question.

The man didn't answer. But he got the hint. He informed Coyote Cries about the project's progress.

Coyote Cries listened to his nervous whispers about his activities over the past two weeks. The man was small, good-looking, in his late forties with a full head of reddish-brown brittle hair, cut short. Four of his fingers hosted gold rings. His custom-tailored suit was lined in silk. His blue eyes darted about nervously behind his gold wire-rimmed glasses as he leaned forward to continue his progress report.

Not unlike Coyote Cries, this guy's appearance belied his ability to get things done. He appeared pampered, nervous, and rich. But his results suggested he hadn't been unwilling to get his hands dirty to get the work done.

Good for him, because if he hadn't been, he'd be no better than dead.

" . . . and I wasn't sure if I would ever get it from her. But I finally did. It cost me, though," the man explained.

Coyote Cries leaned back, glancing around to see if anyone was listening.

The guards and prison staff paid little if any attention on visitors' day—especially with his visitors. He had convinced nearly every staffer that he was a devoutly spiritual man who had made one mistake in his youthful years.

The guards adored him and believed The Reverend had been made an example—given a stiff sentence for trumped up charges of drug possession and trafficking just because he was Native American. He was seen as the victim.

Nobody was listening. No worries.

But the other prisoners and their visitors did present a problem. Disdain and defiance were etched deeply on their faces. He imagined the room was buzzing with stories of past penances and explanations of the transgressions that triggered The Reverend's wrath. Most fellow prisoners justifiably feared him, which was why they were desperately trying to hush their loved ones.

With his back against the wall, Coyote Cries laid his worn Bible on the table in front of him and placed his large hands casually in his lap. "How much, Vic?"

"Four G's. I had enough left in the account you set up for me to cover it. You still have about a hundred twenty left. The market's great these days. I'm making more in the free market than I am from the organization."

"Is that before or after I pay your annual fee for keeping up on my investments?"

"After," Vic answered. "I'm telling you, you're making money at this. You won't even have to get back into the business once you get out of here if you don't want to."

Coyote Cries actually smiled. It was brief, and it was barely detectable, but he was sure Vic noticed. He wanted that. "That's good. Because I won't be able to pony express to the reservation after I get out. At least not for a while. They'll be watching me too closely at first."

"Look, Jeremiah." Vic couldn't maintain eye contact: That wasn't a good sign. "I can't promise you anything at tomorrow's parole hearing. Chances are—"

He cut his lawyer off. "Chances are, I'll be free. Because of you."

He could see the Adam's apple in his lawyer's throat bobbing up and down. "Where can I find you? After you get out?"

"I'll find you," Coyote Cries said, still sitting rigid in his chair, casually studying the others in the room. "I have a job to do right when I get out. But after a few weeks, I'll be able to let Dan know if I can pony for him or not. If not, I'm going to need a ticket to get lost."

"When . . ." Vic licked his lips nervously. "The ticket, I mean."

His mouthpiece clearly wanted Coyote Cries gone; out of Denver. As soon and as far away as possible.

"My parole hearing is tomorrow," Coyote Cries said flatly. "That's where you should focus."

Vic nervously fidgeted with his glasses. "So . . . what's your plan?"

"What's yours? Shouldn't you have a strategy by now? For tomorrow?"

He watched as the man's tongue circled his dry lips. "About that."

Coyote Cries raised an eyebrow and held Vic's stare.

"There's always next time. I don't want you to get your hopes up."

Like the dawning of a new day, Coyote Cries suddenly realized his attorney wasn't working to get him out. Quite the opposite. He had no hope or intention of freeing him tomorrow.

Coyote Cries cut his glance to the nearest guard who was not within earshot of the two. "I need your help one more time."

Vic nodded.

"I need you to get me some things. Leave them at Dan's mountain home. I'll pick them up." Seeing Vic's nervousness intensify, Coyote Cries added, "Don't worry. I won't be staying there."

Vic let out a sigh of relief. "Good, because Alcott would kill me if anyone messed with anything up there."

Coyote Cries enjoyed hearing this. He might be able to use that tidbit of information to his advantage if Vic or Dan ever crossed him.

Becoming increasingly uncomfortable, Vic's hands started to tremble. Coyote Cries calmly enumerated the items on his list. He resisted the urge to grin, watching his lawyer scribble the descriptions down in detail.

"Tell Dan I'll call him." He picked the day and exact time to expect the call. "I'll have my answer by then on whether or not I want back in the business."

Vic glanced over his shoulder to see if anyone had moved into earshot. He leaned forward and removed his glasses, catching his gaze. "Alcott's going to be pissed if you drag this out too long."

Coyote Cries squinted. He resented being lectured.

Nervously, Vic explained, "I'm just saying—"

"I know what you're saying." Coyote Cries leaned across the table and lowered his voice. "Just get everything on that list. Have it at Dan's by noon tomorrow. Tell Dan I'll call him. Got it?"

Vic nodded, averting his gaze.

No one was paying attention to them.

Vic sighed and stuffed the scrap of paper into his shirt pocket.

Coyote Cries casually pushed the ratty Bible he had laid on the table toward Vic. His attorney sat perfectly still, staring at the book. This idiot would eventually figure out that he was trying to give him something.

Vic's eyes grew wide. Clearly from his body language, he didn't want anything from his client. He never did.

Coyote Cries knew exactly what he was thinking. That something from the Lakotan always meant trouble. That he hadn't even wanted to visit this client today. Or ever.

But Vic knew if he hadn't come, it would be worse. Jeremiah Coyote Cries was probably the most ruthless man Vic had ever known. And he'd known his share of merciless people. Coyote Cries hoped these types of thoughts raced through this idiot's mind every time they met. He wanted that amount of control over Vic. All he needed was to manipulate this asshole for one more day until he successfully argued for his freedom tomorrow.

Vic stroked his cropped hair with his thick, gold-studded fingers, and it sprang back into place like a thick shag carpet.

He was the epitome of ridiculousness in Coyote Cries's mind. He was weak and greedy. He probably lost sleep wondering how he ever got himself into this mess in the first place. He was a wealthy, successful lawyer who boasted about his mansion in Cherry Creek and his profitable law practice. His third wife, a gorgeous blond, was nearly half his age and wanting nothing more from life than to shop for expensive clothing and to be sexually pleasing to him, with the former being a prerequisite to the latter.

Yet look at him. He was pathetic—a prisoner to his fortune.

"*Galeshka*," he said aloud, not intending to have voiced his thoughts.

"What?"

"Nothing," Coyote Cries said. But he'd said "spotted" in the Lakota language, thinking of 13:23 and knowing the answer. This leopard certainly couldn't change his spots. He was disloyal twenty years ago, and he was the same today. Still spotted.

Between Dan Alcott, his primary client, and Coyote Cries, his most feared client, Vic Webber had built his practice on defending the most prominent and profitable drug traffickers in North America and winning. Most of the time.

No doubt, he hoped Coyote Cries was going to lose tomorrow.

Coyote Cries saw the sweat dripping down Vic's temples. He no longer needed proof that he had double-crossed him, purposely worked toward him losing the parole hearing tomorrow. He knew in his gut the man was spotted, and he was going to make sure Vic Webber's obituary ended up in *The Denver Post* within the week.

Vic had accomplished everything exactly as asked over the years. Not the least of which was in his Bible. Vic had obtained the forged letterhead for him and gave it to Coyote Cries during the last visit. Now Coyote Cries was giving it back to Vic. Only this time, the letterhead was no longer blank. Coyote Cries had never told Vic why he'd requested it. Instead, Coyote Cries personally typed and sealed the letter that would be hand-delivered today.

It was a forged letter from the parole board office in correctional services at the Englewood Federal Correctional Institution in Littleton. Board of Prison terms were stenciled across the forged blue and black emblem embossed on the crisp, white paper. Beautiful. He'd been pleased with Vic's ability to get him what he wanted. And it was better for Vic that he'd asked no questions and knew as little as possible. He'd be safer.

He was nearing the finish line.

But Vic stared at the Bible as if it were a coiled rattlesnake ready to strike. Eventually, in response to Coyote Cries's stillness and silence, he sighed, wiped the sweat from his groomed brows, and reached for the worn, tattered book.

Coyote Cries curled his thin lip. "Try Jeremiah chapter four, verse thirteen."

Vic rifled through the pages slowly with trembling hands. He was flipping the pages, clearly unfamiliar with the references to books such as Jeremiah. Not a spiritual man.

Just as he retrieved the small sealed envelope marking the page, Coyote Cries chanted, "Look, the enemy is coming like clouds. His war chariots are like a whirlwind and his horses are faster than eagles. We are lost. We are doomed."

Vic grimaced and slipped the envelope into the inside pocket of his suit coat. "So dark. Morbid. Ever try reading *Penthouse*?"

Coyote Cries simply stared and remained silent.

"What's your fascination with the Bible, anyway? With the book of Jeremiah, specifically?"

Coyote Cries's voice was low and quiet. "Besides being my namesake? It's the longest book in the Bible. His people ignored him. He warned them. They disregarded the increasing danger that resulted in their disobedience." What he chose not to reveal was that Jeremiah was accused of being a false prophet since his prophecies never came true.

"God's wrath and all, right? Disobedience of His laws?" His lawyer wasn't at all good at casualness or interpretation.

Jeremiah blamed all for disobedience, warning of God's impending wrath that never came. So instead, he blamed God and took matters into his own hands. He grinned. "Sure."

Vic shuddered and looked away.

He would eventually figure out that the passage was intended as a distinct message for the leopard whose spots had never changed—a warning for him. But by the time he did, it would probably be too late for the greedy lawyer.

Coyote Cries knew more than he was letting on. But he didn't know everything yet. Vic would find out soon enough that Coyote Cries had discovered that Vic and Dan Alcott had intended for him to be imprisoned two and a half decades ago; that they'd screwed him; that Coyote Cries now knew that Dan had felt threatened and wanted a part of his action—which is exactly what he'd gotten.

But Coyote Cries would exact his revenge. It was all part of his plan.

Pretending to ignore the ominous message, Vic steadied his trembling hand and casually slid the Bible back toward Coyote Cries.

He stared at Vic. "Put the envelope in locker twenty-two across from gate twelve in concourse C at Denver International Airport by noon. Today."

"What's your plan?"

Coyote Cries didn't answer.

"Do you really think you have a chance to get out of this place?"

He sat rigid. Staring.

"Because, I'm good, but I'm not that good."

Coyote Cries didn't respond.

Finally, Vic added, "He has a girlfriend."

This got Coyote Cries's attention. "After twenty years?"

"A new fling. But they're spending a lot of time together. It's not a one-night stand. We've got some photos, and we're trying to get a name and anything else we can get." Vic recited a license plate number and address that Coyote Cries committed to memory. "My guy did what you told him to do last night. Now what?"

For a moment, Coyote Cries didn't respond. Then, he said, "As humans, we cannot avoid blood from being shed, since we are predestined for guilt despite being born innocent."

Vic said nothing.

Coyote Cries slowly wrapped his fingers around his Bible and left Vic sitting at the corner table.

To ponder.

CHAPTER 11

THE WAKE-UP ALARM startled Snake.

He nearly dropped his soap as he glanced around the shower room. He hurried to finish up before everyone arrived but froze when he noticed Dillinger walking toward him. He tossed the bar aside and reached quickly for the shank he stored in the soap tray. He stepped out of the streaming shower, naked, and squared off with the fully dressed man. He, too, had a blade in his hand.

Dillinger stopped two feet from him. "Asshole."

He darted as the man stabbed at him and sliced his right forearm. His breath quickened.

He lunged again, narrowly missing Snake's ribs. The blade glanced off his side. Blood spilled on the tiles.

"What did I do?" But Snake knew. He'd ratted him out to Coyote Cries. And Coyote Cries had ratted on Snake to Dillinger.

So why was Dillinger still alive?

Snake jabbed back at the big man, missed his chest, and struck his left arm as he turned away. More blood flowed onto the floor.

People started to congregate in the shower room and huddled around the battling pair. Snake barely noticed, knowing none of them would come to his rescue. That was an unwritten rule in the population. The best he could hope for was to stay alive until the guards caught wind of the fight. Then maybe he'd survive.

Dillinger rushed him again, only this time Snake's wet foot landed on the bar of soap, and he slipped directly into Dillinger's blade. In that instant, he tried to catch himself by grasping at Dillinger's shoulders, but the only thing that was still gripped firmly in his hand was the shank.

He felt a pain in his gut just as his own shank buried deep into Dillinger's neck.

Both men collapsed on the slippery floor.

Snake could hear the mumbles of the other prisoners. Someone instructed them to get out, clear the room.

He felt the pain overwhelming his belly, and he could hardly keep his grip on consciousness. But he didn't want to die. He had to make sure Dillinger wasn't going to kill him. He squeezed his eyes shut to chase away the grey that clouded his vision.

Then he opened his eyes and found himself staring directly at Dillinger's face. His eyes were wide and lifeless. Blood spurted out of the hole in his neck. Without aiming, Snake had sunk his shank into a jugular. He had won. He would live.

Then he saw movement. Two legs were behind Dillinger. It wasn't the uniform of a guard—it was a prisoner. He blinked hard and tried to call for help. Then he saw the prisoner squat behind Dillinger's body.

He heard the man ask, "Snake? Are you okay?"

He blinked. The man's face came into focus. The man who'd come to help was The Reverend.

He hadn't ratted him out to Dillinger after all. He'd come to help him. To save him.

Snake tried to smile, to nod, to thank him. But the pain was too intense. And he felt his consciousness come and go in waves. He felt the blood ooze from between his fingers as it poured around the shank Dillinger had stuck in his belly.

He thought he'd seen The Reverend retrieve a towel from a nearby hook. His towel. He was coming back to help him, to cover him while he went with him to the infirmary. Snake held Coyote Cries's gaze as he squatted beside him.

The Reverend laid the towel over Snake's shivering body. He was grateful for the man's gesture, his kindness. Then he felt Coyote Cries's hand through the towel cover his own, over the shank. He felt the blade twist in his gut and probe deeper. Then he heard him say, "Forty," before passages from the Bible, from the book of Jeremiah, escorted him out of this world and into hell.

CHAPTER 12

COYOTE CRIES SCANNED the visiting room through the thick glass as he followed the guard down the hall.

He spotted the man immediately. The guy had never been to a prison. Ever. He could tell immediately from the skinny man's body language. His spine was too erect. His shoulders were bunched up around his ears. His eyes were wide, and his hands were folded and stretched on the tabletop—to stop himself from fidgeting.

A newbie.

He shook his head and tried not to show his disappointment.

The new mouthpiece appeared weak. Fragile, even. And he, only hours away from a hearing that meant more to him than any other, had hired this string bean . . . He should have listened to Dillinger. He'd suggested a local defense attorney. A guy from Denver who had a winning track record at parole hearings. He would have been a familiar face to the board deciding his fate.

Not this yahoo from the boonies that Todd Long Soldiers had recommended.

But something told him to trust Long Soldiers over Dillinger. He couldn't put his finger on what had changed in the past few days.

But everything had.

Maybe the rumors were true. Maybe the prison guards had really abandoned their belief in him. Maybe they'd indeed yank their support of him for release today rather than testify to his demonstrated change and good behavior.

Maybe it was the way Vic Webber had backpedaled over the past week. A bit too eager to remind Coyote Cries he just might not get out of prison today.

Maybe the prison yard gossip about how the feds had planted a fish to uncover a conspiracy had made him doubt the secrecy of his plan and caused him to be paranoid.

Which only Dillinger had known.

No matter what the answer, his sense was that traitors had penetrated his inner circle. Somewhere. Somehow.

And Snake had confirmed his suspicions late last night about Dillinger's betrayal, setting this morning's brutal event into motion. Both men had to die.

But no matter.

He was on his way home.

Or he'd better be.

All heads turned as he and the guard weaved through the occupied tables to where his visitor sat. He glowered at his new attorney, chose a chair directly across from the man, and slumped hard into the seat. The guard offered a nod and retreated toward the door, standing post between the visitor's corridor and the hall leading to the cells.

The man flashed a nervous smile, followed by an even more awkward greeting. "Jeremiah Coyote Cries?"

Coyote Cries stared at the small man.

"I'm Duke Raven." He stuck out his spindly fingers.

Coyote Cries grabbed them and shook, tempted to break every little bone in the man's limp-fished hand.

He also wanted to tell the asshole what a stupid name Duke Raven was—too big a name for a skeleton of a man.

Instead, Coyote Cries said nothing.

The big-eared man's smile faded. His serious expression matched his tone. "You called me. You don't want to talk? Fine. I am perfectly content letting someone else help you."

He gathered his papers and stuffed them into his briefcase.

He rose from his chair, startling Coyote Cries—which pleased him. The man might be worth something after all.

Coyote Cries grabbed his wrist as the attorney spun to leave. "I did call you. I'd heard you were good."

"Then no games. We've got work to do," the attorney said, settling back into his chair. "My job is to make sure you receive a fair chance to be heard by the parole board." He cleared his throat. "Without any surprises."

Coyote Cries snapped to attention. "Such as?"

The dork retrieved a file from his case and slid it across the table.

At first, Coyotes Cries's stomach lurched, thinking the file would reveal he'd sent a fraudulent letter to Special Agent Streeter Pierce or that his parole hearing would be canceled or at best postponed pending investigation for interference of due course.

The weasel attorney asked, "Know her?"

Coyote Cries noticed the name on the file with today's date: his. He flipped it open.

Then he gasped, thinking he'd seen a ghost.

The photo was of an attractive white woman. Number Thirteen. He'd remember her anywhere.

Striking sea-green eyes.

But instead of hair the color of wheat, the woman in this photo had chestnut brown locks. Were they dyed?

He glanced up at Duke Raven. "Is this a joke or something?"

The new attorney shook his head and demanded, "Look again. It's not Paula."

Coyote Cries slid his gaze down to the photo and studied the woman's face.

No, this wasn't Thirteen. It wasn't Streeter Pierce's wife, after all.

Her eyes were the same color but far more intense and purposeful. This woman had a mission. And she seemed to be taller, more athletic than the woman he'd dominated and annihilated twenty years earlier.

"Their daughter?" Thirteen had told him she was pregnant. Maybe the fetus lived. He thought his research was thorough and accurate. Could he have missed such an important piece of information? Was there a Pierce offspring?

The woman in the photo could be Thirteen's twin.

Raven shook his head. "No relation. She's thirty. Works with Pierce."

"A special agent?"

He nodded. "Her name's Liv Bergen. I found this photo in Vic Webber's case files."

Coyote Cries's heart raced. The name didn't ring a bell. Webber hadn't mentioned her. He held his breath, waiting for his attorney to deliver bad news.

"You think she's going to show up today to testify?"

Coyote Cries shrugged. "Perhaps. But I don't know the woman."

"If she does, I'll argue that her testimony has no bearing on your case. That she has neither firsthand knowledge of you during your incarceration, nor of your crime. All I need to know is if she knows you in any way."

Relief flooded Coyote Cries and his brain freed itself from the fog. "I've never seen this woman before in my life." And he hadn't. "Where in Webber's files did you find this particular folder?"

The attorney shrugged. "In the case file box. It was with another file called Julius Chavez. Know him?"

He furrowed his brow and shrugged.

But he *had* heard of him. He was the guy Webber had hired to shadow Pierce's girlfriend. Lady friend. Whatever they're called these days. So that's the woman who belongs to the license plate and address Vic had given him.

The woman he'd been following must be Liv Bergen. Streeter's girlfriend.

Why else would those files be together? he thought.

He held the photo closer to his face and studied every inch. So this is the young lady who'd been spending the weekend at Streeter Pierce's place? Helpful. Interesting.

No wonder Pierce had been attracted to this Bergen woman. She was the spitting image of his late wife Paula Pierce. Thirteen.

His thirteenth victim.

It was a lucky number, and it was also the number of one of his favorite verses in Jeremiah. He felt a grin sneak onto the corner of his lips, but he resisted the urge and quickly composed himself.

It was best if Raven knew nothing about his plan. He'd already had to order one attorney silenced. That was number Thirty-Eight.

Most of the count since his imprisonment had happened at his direction. Not by his hand. But he was very much looking forward to getting back to practice.

And of course, as of this morning, he had left Thirty-Nine and Forty together in the prison shower room, bleeding out on the tile floor near the drains after an apparent shank fight to the death.

The shower room had been carefully selected. There was no point in making the guards who would be testifying on his behalf later today waste their time cleaning up after that mess. He needed them rested and focused—on him.

Of course, he had demonstrated just the right amount of remorse, shock, and pity that they'd come to expect from The Reverend when they found him kneeling over to the two bodies, praying. And he'd gladly obliged, along with boldly and unapologetically reciting Jeremiah 9:4.

> *Beware of your friends. Do not trust anyone in your clan. For every one of them is a deceiver. And every friend a slanderer.*

The guards hadn't even seemed to notice the meaning behind the passage he'd used. They probably assumed The Reverend was warning others to beware of fellow prisoners—when he was all but admitting he had killed the two men himself.

"If she has no connection to you," the attorney said, "then I am confident I'll be able to minimize the impact of anything she says if she shows up today, objecting to any reference made to what Pierce might say or think as hearsay."

Coyote Cries gave his new attorney a nod.

"I just loathe surprises. So we must prepare for the unexpected. The guards' testimonies should overwhelmingly convince the board to release you."

"Today?" he asked.

Raven nodded. "Today. I'm requesting you be released immediately to a halfway house. On work release, at least—for a time. But soon you'll be out of the program completely."

This time, Coyote Cries allowed himself a smile. "*Pilayama*."

"You're welcome," Duke Raven replied.

"You know Lakota? *Tuktél yatí hwo?*"

"Some. And not where you think," he replied to Coyote Cries's question of where he lived. "I actually live in Boulder."

"Curious," Coyote Cries replied. He'd misjudged this man. He knew better than to judge a book by its cover. Yet he'd done it again. And he'd been wrong.

As he gathered up his files, Raven offered him final instructions for the hearing, which was less than an hour away.

Coyote Cries could barely focus. He was reveling in the choices he'd been forced to make in the past twenty-four hours. All of them wise. Especially siding with Long Soldiers's choice of attorney.

With everything going on inside the yard, he'd had to make a choice.

Dillinger, his longtime confidant on the inside, or Long Soldiers, the man he'd left to run the operation for him at the rez. Only Long Soldiers had been strongly influenced by Alcott and Webber over the past twenty years, whereas Dillinger had never been very far from his side during that time.

He owed Dillinger his life after everything the man had done to protect his back while imprisoned. Yet he'd known Long Soldiers his entire life. His choice had been difficult, and it had resulted in Thirty-Nine and Forty.

Both Dillinger and Snake had to die.

They had known far too much.

CHAPTER 13

I SAW THE TELEPHOTO LENS before Streeter did.

"Hey," he called to the photographer. Then Streeter bolted toward the car parked along the curb. The lens retracted into the window, which was followed by the squealing of tires.

"Streeter, let it go," I called.

But he was too far from me now and likely too angry to listen to me anyway. I watched as he chased the car down the street, straining to make out the license plate number. I glanced over my shoulder to see if anyone in the federal building was watching. I'd assumed that the security guards at the entrance would have at least taken note of an agent in pursuit of a car.

But they hadn't. *Not very reassuring*, I thought.

I moseyed closer to the parking garage entrance and waited for Streeter. I leaned against the nearest column and folded my arms.

He was marching across the grass toward me.

I imagined my arms wrapped around his neck, my legs wrapped around his waist, and I smiled. I nearly purred thinking of him beneath me. Not a thought I'd ever entertained near the hallowed halls of work before, but this man was delicious.

His blue eyes pierced my soul, came alive and mischievous when we embraced. Beneath his thick shock of white hair, his rugged, cleanly shaven face was a magnet for my palms and fingertips. I absolutely couldn't stop touching him.

I wanted to reach out right this moment and touch his cheek, make his brilliant smile come to life.

But we were at work.

And with my luck, now would be the time the security guards would take notice of what was happening out here.

I straightened when Streeter arrived. "Did you get the plate?"

He shook his head. "Partial."

He walked in silence toward his car.

I headed off toward my Jeep. "Why does it bother you so much?"

He spun on his heels, barely noticing we'd separated. "Oh, sorry. I was thinking."

"I know," I said. "That's why I'm asking. Why does that bother you so much? The paparazzi?"

He hesitated and then took a couple of steps toward me, scooping his arms around my lower back, ignoring the consequences of being discovered. He clearly didn't care what people at work thought about our relationship. He held my gaze and said, "Because I don't think it's the paparazzi."

He kissed me. Lightly. Like a butterfly lighting on my lower lip and then taking flight the instant it landed.

"I thought you told everyone on Monday to watch out for the paparazzi; that they were trying to get photos of me to keep the story alive about Jack's death."

He kissed me again. Twice. "I did."

I was losing it, and I wanted to go home. Now. Or take him in the back seat of his car.

He clearly felt the same, because he kissed me and pulled me closer. I could feel him against my hip, his heart beating, his breath quickening. Our desire for one another was insatiable, and we both found it nearly impossible to separate long enough to come to work.

"It's Friday. We have all weekend. Come with me."

"To your cabin?"

He hummed an affirmation, kissed my ear, my throat, my chest.

"What about Beulah?" I managed.

"She's coming with. Or leave her here. I really don't give a damn." His words were rushed, hungry.

I heard footsteps on the sidewalk and pulled free of Streeter's grip. We didn't recognize the federal employee approaching, but we both kept our emotions in check just long enough, until he disappeared up the ramp of the parking garage.

"Follow me?" he said, heading to his car.

I nodded and sprinted toward the caretaker's quarters to collect my bloodhound, ran to my car, and put her in the back seat's kennel. I pulled into the lane behind Streeter, who smiled at me in his rearview mirror.

Then I had a thought and called him.

"You are even more beautiful when your cheeks are flushed," he said into the phone.

I grinned. "How fast can you drive?"

I saw him smile back at me.

"Why don't you think it's the paparazzi?" I asked.

I could see his expression change instantly. "Think about it. This is the third time this week that someone's taken a photo of you—long distance."

"And? So what?"

"Have you seen your picture show up on the news or in the papers or on the Internet?"

I had to think about that. "Not like I've been really looking. I've been kinda busy."

I tried to catch his eye in the rearview mirror, but we were both too focused on traffic.

"But we would have heard from someone."

He was right. I would have heard. From someone at work or a neighbor. "Maybe they're holding out for the highest bidder?"

"Three days? They're not that patient," he said.

"Another good point. Then who?" I asked.

I heard him sigh. "I don't know. But I don't have a good feeling about it. So I'm thinking I better keep you close. Just until I'm sure."

"Promise?"

CHAPTER 14

COYOTE CRIES SAT ERECT, his hands folded in his lap.

He'd been called up to "the big boss's office" by his shop floor supervisor. He'd only been on the job one day, a few hours, and he'd been beckoned by the owner. Couldn't they just leave him alone to make cardboard boxes in peace?

Instead, he was probably going to get a lecture about how crime doesn't pay.

He didn't need this shit—not from a rich asshole like this guy who hired parolees from a work release program to keep his costs down. He had plans. And this prick was interfering with them.

He read the placard on the man's desk.

Bernie Dewitt, President.

His glance cut toward the big man standing by the picture window. To Coyote Cries, he looked like a former football player. He had big, wide shoulders—unlike his shop foreman who was slight, this guy couldn't be snapped like a twig.

His foreman fidgeted in the chair next to him.

Dewitt stared out the window down onto the shop floor that was filled with machines in motion, scurrying employees, and cardboard—lots and lots of cardboard in various stages of production. He was staring at an empty machine that Coyote Cries should have been manning, doing a job he'd just learned how to do hours ago.

The building had no windows, but the ceiling was covered with lighting fixtures that mimicked natural daylight. Dewitt's employees seemed to be appreciative of their shift work conditions, from what he'd heard so far. The operations for pressing, folding, and packaging the cardboard sheets into various sizes of cartons ran around the clock.

His supervisor had told him that Dewitt struggled with keeping enough people employed on all shifts. The economy in the Denver area had remained strong, which meant low levels of unemployment. Coyote Cries had experienced the same thing in his business. People just weren't as eager to turn a quick, easy buck as they used to be.

"As president and owner of Colorado Cardboard Company, welcome," Dewitt said, finally turning from the window and extending his hand to Coyote Cries. "It's important to me as manager of this manufacturing facility to greet all my newest employees in person."

The cardboard packaging building, which covered nearly half a city block southeast of Denver, was bigger than any building in South Dakota, Coyote Cries imagined. And the guy had designed the place so he could see every square inch right here from his office perch. Windows encircled the large room, and TV monitors were like guards lined up in their ceiling brackets. That meant cameras—everywhere.

Coyote Cries would use that to his advantage.

"The economy is booming. So good, in fact, that I've been forced to seek creative employment tactics to replace turnover."

His foreman added, "Which is constant around here."

Dewitt shot the twitchy man standing next to Coyote Cries a withering glance. "I've found the steady source of new employees through the work release program at the federal correctional facility in Littleton useful to me. And as my newest employee, I have to tell you how impressed I've been with your skills and work ethic."

Coyote Cries noticed a familiar file lying on Dewitt's desk. The file with his name typed on it. The file that his parole officer, Gilmore, had asked him to give his new employer a few hours ago at two o'clock when he'd arrived.

"I've already decided to offer you a job. A permanent one—on Carl Wilson's shift," he announced, his face beaming.

In his mind, Coyote Cries answered, *And I've decided to offer you a reprieve and not slice your slimy throat, on behalf of all the little people who would have to mop up the mess.*

Instead, he said nothing.

Dewitt nodded to the foreman. "You'll like Carl. His shift is the Sunday through Wednesday swing shift from two o'clock to midnight."

Dewitt sat on the corner of his desk, his leg nearly touching Coyote Cries's knee. "I'm not intimidated by you, Jeremiah Coyote Cries, or the fact that you have committed involuntary manslaughter or that you dealt bad drugs to a junkie twenty years ago. I don't care."

He leaned forward, smiled, and patted his shoulder.

Is this asshole serious? Does he really think he is endearing himself to Coyote Cries?

He stood and rounded his desk. "I've hired much tougher characters than you over the years. And I've found many of them to be exemplary employees who tend to put forth their best effort and do as they're told. I suppose that's because it is work release."

"Plus, you guys are usually strong and used to hard work," his foreman added.

Here come the generalizations and stereotypes. He knew plenty on the inside who were weak, not at all used to hard work. But Coyote Cries was used to being typed.

"I've never regretted seeking employees through the program. An uncooperative WRP employee's rights are suspended if they don't perform to my standards. Did they tell you that?"

Coyote Cries said nothing.

"Not much of a talker," Dewitt said to the supervisor. "I never have to deal with them again if they don't do what I ask. They're much easier to manage than normal employees."

He picked up the file that Gilmore had sent in with him to give to Dewitt. "You are particularly intriguing. I've never had a Lakotan working for me before. Actually, I've never even met one. Are they all as big as you?"

Coyote Cries could feel his anger simmering.

"And are they chatterboxes like you?" His laugh was as pleasant to Coyote Cries's ears as if he had dragged his knuckles across a cheese grater. "Not sure why I'm so intrigued. I've employed many people from various backgrounds and ethnicities, which is probably why I'm such a popular employer."

He swept his arms in the direction of a small wall where a dozen plaques hung.

In response to Coyote Cries's nonplussed expression, Dewitt leaned closer. "Do you speak English?"

Coyote Cries resisted the urge to snatch the guy by the throat and strangle him.

"He does. I've heard him," the shop foreman said.

Coyote Cries rose from his chair, towering over Dewitt. At nearly fifty years old, he was far from aged. He was massive compared to the pudgy football star, several inches taller than Dewitt, and at least thirty pounds heavier with rock solid, well-toned muscles.

"I speak English, Mr. Dewitt. And I'd prefer to work tomorrow. On his shift," he said, jamming a thumb toward his shift foreman. "Before you assign me to Carl Wilson's shift on Sunday."

Dewitt nodded. His eyes were too wide and his mouth partially open.

"Can I get back to work now?"

Dewitt tried to hold his gaze but averted his eyes and said, "Sure."

Coyote Cries flipped his long grey braids over his shoulders and smoothed his freshly pressed work clothes before stepping around the chair to leave. To further put the asshole in his place, he said, "Pleasure to meet you."

Dewitt called after him, "Do you go by Jeremiah or Jerry?"

Coyote Cries didn't answer.

By six o'clock, he was loading cellophane-wrapped cartons from the conveyor belt onto pallets alone. His foreman had finally gone about his business. Dewitt left for the night—probably for the weekend. The office hovered above like an alien spacecraft—dark.

He spent the next six hours steadily stacking pallets and working through his breaks despite his supervisor's insistence to the contrary. By midnight, Coyote Cries had punched his card at the time clock. He met his escort from the halfway house on the corner where he was instructed to return after his shift. There was no sight of Gilmore, his parole officer. He was probably home in bed.

He noted that the escort arrived promptly at ten minutes after midnight, just as he said he would.

The next morning, Dewitt would read nothing but good things about Coyote Cries in his shop foreman's shift report. He was a stellar new employee. He smiled, thinking how there was no doubt Dewitt would place the promised call to the coordinator of the work release program, glowing about Jeremiah Coyote Cries.

One more day, and this would be all over.

Dewitt had no clue that during his calculated bathroom break at 4:45, Coyote Cries was standing outside his door, listening to the call he'd had on speakerphone.

"Gilmore, this is Dewitt."

"Right on time. Four forty-five."

"It's Friday, and you and I both have better places to be. Want some good news to end your week?"

"Sure," came the grunting response.

"That Coyote Cries is getting great reviews from his shift supervisor. And believe me, that doesn't happen around here. He said Coyote Cries works like a horse. First day and he's refusing to take breaks and is getting more done than the regular guy for sure. At least when it comes to stacking pallets. You got more like him?" Dewitt asked.

"He's a one of a kind, all right," Gilmore responded.

"What's the deal on this guy?"

Coyote Cries glanced down the stairs and leaned closer against the door, so he could hear.

"Did he get railroaded just because he was Native American or something?" Dewitt asked bluntly. "He seems like such a nice guy. Not much of a talker."

Gilmore laughed. "He is a nice guy. They call him The Reverend over in the pen. Some like him. Some hate him. But most stay out of his way. He was in for life with possibility of parole. Been in for twenty years. He was granted parole yesterday morning. First time in front of the board, and they let him go."

Dewitt whistled. "That almost never happens, does it?"

"Not often," Gilmore went on. "But what he had going for him was some of the prison guards spoke on his behalf. And no one spoke against him—not even the guys from the FBI who put him in prison originally."

Dewitt whistled again. "I thought bureau guys never missed a chance to keep their perps behind bars."

"Apparently the parole board sent a notice to the arresting FBI agent about the hearing. Everyone expected him to show up to testify against Coyote Cries. There's some sort of personal problem with Coyote Cries."

"What kind of problem?"

Gilmore said, "I can't say that I blame the guy. The agent's wife was murdered during the trial, and he thought Coyote Cries had something to do with it. But they could never prove it."

Coyote Cries grinned. He remembered Thirteen. He fantasized about that white meat often.

"That's rough."

"The agent had a nervous breakdown or something."

Good to know, Coyote Cries thought. He hadn't heard that.

"Anyway, the guy is located at the Denver division, but he didn't show up. The parole board just assumed that by his absence, it meant the bureau had no objection to granting Coyote Cries parole. So there you are."

Dewitt grunted, "Well, I sure like him. He's one hell of a worker. I'll take anyone you got over there like Coyote Cries. Has he called in as you instructed?"

"Yep," Gilmore answered. "Talked with him an hour ago. He said he enjoyed the work so far. Said the guys were really good to him."

"Look forward to seeing him again tomorrow at two o'clock."

"Unless something comes up between now and then," Gilmore quipped.

Without a sound and knowing his plan was working, Coyote Cries tiptoed back down the stairs.

What Bernie Dewitt couldn't know is how his weekend was destined for nothing but a shit storm. First, one of the primary 250-horsepower motors on the press machine would fail shortly after Coyote Cries left at midnight, and his three maintenance men would spend much of their weekend on the phone trying to locate a replacement motor.

The floor would be chaotic as employees scrambled to keep the other machines busy by running stockpiled and scrapped pieces through the process. His production team would stumble with their quotas since the motor wouldn't arrive at the plant until the next morning.

He would have a rough day, indeed.

And in all that chaos, no one would notice—until twenty minutes after midnight, early Sunday morning—that Jeremiah Coyote Cries had not reported to work on Saturday.

Dewitt's world would further erode to shit when he received the call about this from one of his supervisors.

The federal escort would pitch a fit, wanting to know what had happened to his prisoner, Jeremiah Coyote Cries. But Dewitt would have no answers—even if the cameras did confirm the escort's story that he'd dropped Coyote Cries off for his shift. But the new employee had never clocked in.

No one ever noticed that Jeremiah Coyote Cries had never shown up for his shift.

He'd be long gone. Nowhere to be found.

Missing.

CHAPTER 15

MATT JUZLIG WORKED THROUGH various mix designs for a customer's special project.

"Look who's here," the woman behind the desk called to her boss.

He didn't have time for her games. "Who is it, Judy?"

"That snake, Dick Roth."

Juzlig glanced over his monitor toward the front door. *On a Saturday?* "Weekends are becoming a pattern for him."

Judy's disgust was obvious. "Because he wants to catch you doing something wrong. And he figures you won't be expecting him on the weekend. Am I right?"

He didn't answer. Of course she was right. The last thing he needed today was a visit from Roth—not because he was doing anything wrong, but because he was busy.

It was the busiest time of year for construction. His biggest customer had a pour starting on Monday, and he still needed to find a mix design that would meet specs and be profitable for his company. He had a lot to do, and he didn't need an unannounced inspection on top of everything else.

He'd been working since five o'clock that morning trying to deliver mud to customers. This time of year, there never seemed to be enough daylight hours or enough ready-mix trucks, and the demands on his small company seemed to be growing exponentially each day.

He'd already visited three job sites this morning. Customers were grateful but wanting more and wanting it faster.

The last customer Juzlig visited had actually thrown his hard hat against the newly poured basement wall because Matt refused to double the agreed-upon number of trucks delivering. The subcontractor on the new jail being built in Glenwood Springs had expected a different reaction from what he got: Juzlig had simply waved and left the job site.

Demands by the ever-growing number of people in the small mountain town were increasing faster than Matt could supply. He was having trouble hiring drivers and purchasing new trucks. Almost every job was delayed in the area because no one could find the people to complete them. Unemployment in the booming economy of Colorado was at an all-time low, and although his profits were soaring along with the growth, Juzlig couldn't capitalize on the natural expansion of his small business as much as he wanted.

He knew the game: The subcontractors were using him to tighten their construction timeline, so they could either minimize penalties for completing the jail late or earn bonuses for finishing early. Either way, he wasn't going to jeopardize his business to profit that subcontractor.

There was too much at stake. And other projects needed his mud.

He'd only been back in the office for fifteen minutes, enjoying the first peace and quiet he'd had all day, when Roth showed up. For Matt, that surely meant another drain of cash from his growing business. And if he knew the slimy inspector, it probably meant the greedy bastard would want even more than last quarter.

It wasn't that he couldn't afford the protection money. What bothered him the most—disgusted him, really—was how much power such a small-minded man as Roth wielded. It made his skin crawl.

The federal government, and the EPA in particular, were designed to protect people from those in the industry who were unethical enough to put profit ahead of health and the surrounding environment. Although the majority of businesses in the industry were ethical and practiced corporate responsibility, they were all considered suspect under the regulations.

Yet here was this guy, working for the powerful regulatory agency, who was more unethical than those in the industry who were ignoring their responsibility or snubbing the laws. Matt just wanted to do his job and do it right—without interference or a shakedown.

He had been paying this slime for over two years, and each time it seemed to become more difficult for him. It was getting painful. He just couldn't keep his mouth shut any longer. He'd called the FBI because he was sick and tired of Roth's demands and the people like him who got away with bad behavior—while people like him worked their asses off to earn an honest living.

He'd told the special agent that he was fairly sure it was not Congress's intent when they passed the Clean Air Act to allow someone like Dick Roth to extort money from operators like him using his air permit.

Yet, that's what had happened.

He not only called the FBI but also contacted all his friends in the industry, warning them.

Two years earlier, Roth had threatened to issue a notice of violation with a stiff monetary penalty and possible jail time. Matt couldn't believe what that short, pot-bellied man had told him on that cool day in September. It had been so unbelievable that he'd asked Roth to leave the property or he would call the police. Roth responded with a stubby-toothed sneer that sent a shiver up Matt's spine. From that moment on, he understood that the man was not playing any other game but hardball.

He reluctantly paid Roth and had regretted it ever since.

What I wouldn't give to see Roth rot behind the same bars he threatened to put me behind two years ago.

With exasperation, he reminded himself that he was in trouble as deeply as Roth. Matt had continued to make the extortion payments— payments the federal government would simply consider bribes—that were just as illegal as Roth's demands. Somehow it would be his fault, despite the special agent's reassurance to the contrary.

The dilemma between doing the right thing—reporting Roth to the authorities, risking his own reputation, his business, and his freedom— and doing nothing, jeopardizing his own self-respect and morals, had been intensely perplexing and burdensome. A day hadn't gone by that Matt didn't struggle with the dilemma. Every time Roth slithered out from under his rock to pay Matt a visit, he was only reminded of how in peril his principles had become.

Today was no different.

He hadn't heard anything from the FBI, so he'd assumed they had ignored his call, filed the report, and forgot all about him as small potatoes.

What can I do now?

"Tell him I'm not here," Matt shouted to Judy.

"Then where are you?"

"On a job site. Anywhere. Just get rid of him for now. Tell him I won't be in until next week."

He rubbed his eyes with both hands. He got up and shut the door to his office and turned out the lights. Just as he shut the door, he heard the front door to the small office building open with a jangle of bells and then slam shut. Roth's irritating voice greeted Judy. With each word, he pictured Roth's tongue flicking between his almost nonexistent lips like a snake's.

Matt quietly slumped back into his chair as he listened to Judy's feeble lies. In the dark office, as his gaze scanned his cluttered desk, something in the daily newspaper caught his attention. The headline of a small article in the bottom corner of the front page gave him an idea. Without another thought, he lifted the receiver and pushed a button. He could hear Judy respond to his call both on the phone and through the door.

Matt whispered, "Tell him to come back next Tuesday morning. Tell him you're sure that's when he can catch me in the office since that's when accounts payable checks are due, and I'll be in signing the checks. Just pretend this is Junior."

He quietly hung up the phone. He heard Judy's muffled voice saying goodbye to Junior, one of their loader operators who hadn't shown up for work today. He heard her repeat to Dick Roth what he had just told her.

He lifted the newspaper and read the small article regarding the FBI's involvement in an embezzlement case by a federal employee at the Immigration and Naturalization Service. The immigrant had taped a wire under his shirt and captured the INS employee's racist comments. Matt Juzlig's migraine and stomachache instantly disappeared with his decision to offer proof to the FBI. He would be wired the next time he spoke to Roth.

Tuesday.

Maybe then Special Agent Pierce would listen to him and pay attention to his calls.

And do something about Dick Roth.

CHAPTER 16

COYOTE CRIES WAS a free man.

His parole officer wouldn't know for hours that he hadn't shown up to work this afternoon. By the time he knew, The Reverend would have settled several scores and regained a firm hand as the sole proprietor of his business now that Dan Alcott had ceased being his partner. Number Forty-One.

So much to do. So little time.

He'd put business first and pleasure later.

It wasn't even ten o'clock, and he'd learned more about his employees on the rez than he'd ever learned while behind bars: who had remained loyal, who had not, who had skimmed, and who had been honest.

Dan Alcott had been willing to tell him more than he wanted once he realized his life depended on it—which it had. After arriving at Pine Ridge a half hour ago, he'd been busy assessing the business firsthand. Nothing in the world could take the place of boots on the ground. If he'd learned nothing else, at least he had learned that in prison. He'd been cheated for so long not knowing what was really going on out here.

He stood quietly behind a tree, listening.

"Come on, baby. At least try it." Todd Long Soldiers could be convincing, even charming. The young girl he had pressed himself against next to the bonfire stared at the flickering flames in the late night and bit her lip. Todd slid his arm around her thick waist and slipped his hand underneath her shirt. At first, she tensed and pulled away from his grip. Then, as he continued to coo in her ear, she began to relax and allowed him to touch her. An older teen was watching the two from twenty yards beyond the bonfire's light and was the only one separate from the crowd gathered around it. The boy was small and wispy, a twig, sitting on the picnic table in the dark, seemingly bored. Coyote Cries would need to keep an eye on him, although he didn't see him as much of a threat yet.

His attention returned to Todd Long Soldiers. He'd nearly convinced the teen to do something she didn't want to do. She wouldn't be able to resist—not Long Soldiers. He was the best pusher he had.

Noticing movement on his left, the twig drained the last of his pop and threw the empty bottle to the ground as he slid off the picnic table. Apparently, he thought Todd Long Soldiers had gone too far. Perhaps the girl was related or a best friend's baby sister. Drugs were one thing. But pedophilia was entirely different.

"She's only fifteen," the twig called to Long Soldiers.

"Who?"

"Edith Walking Crow," the boy said, bunching his fists.

"Old enough."

"I'm fine, Larry," the girl said as she straightened her shirt.

Larry, the twig, closed the distance.

"Bug off, Standing Bull," Long Soldiers said.

So the older teen's name was Larry Standing Bull. He was clearly not a fan of Long Soldiers—or his business.

"Just leave her alone."

Edith stared at the two men. She wasn't a very pleasant looking girl. But to Coyote Cries, she appeared thrilled by the attention.

"You and Jimmy do your thing and take off," Larry said. "It's our party."

Jimmy Blue Owl was another employee of Coyote Cries. Both were responsible for Pine Ridge High School and Middle School. Both charged with increasing demand, and he wanted to observe their skill level and commitment. He needed to decide if they had grown too old to get away with their tricks. He'd seen Jimmy sneak off behind the cluster of bushes near the creek with another teen just as he'd arrived. Clearly Jimmy wasn't too old.

Larry reached down at his feet, groping in the dark for the pop bottle. His fingers wrapped tightly around the neck, lifted his hand high above his head, and slammed the bottom of the bottle against the picnic table. The glass shattered.

Coyote Cries grinned. *The twig has balls*, he thought.

Larry quickly glanced over his shoulder at Todd Long Soldiers and Edith Walking Crow. They hadn't noticed him. The roar of the other high school kids partying near the bonfire had drowned out the sound of his bottle's crash. Larry walked slowly toward them, breathing heavily.

Coyote Cries wasn't the least bit tempted to warn his employee. Instead, he wanted to see how he handled Larry.

"Leave her alone."

Todd Long Soldiers ignored Larry. "Just try one of these Quaaludes," he said to Edith Walking Crow. "They're the best. They'll make all your problems go away. I can get you more next week if you like them. Try this one on me."

Larry's nostrils flared. His wispy arms trembled beneath his oversized, mesh-material football jersey. He gripped the broken bottle.

Coyote Cries chuckled.

"I said leave her alone, Long Soldiers."

This time, Long Soldiers noticed but only because the girl had taken an interest in the twig. "Larry, what's the matter with you?"

Long Soldiers clutched Edith's thick elbow, pulled her away from the angry twig, and resumed his conversation with her. Larry reached up and gave Long Soldiers a shove.

"Hey, buddy. Watch it, will you? Are you drunk or something?"

"I don't drink."

"Then leave us alone here, you freak." Long Soldiers straightened his silk muscle shirt.

Larry squinted in the firelight. "You don't even recognize me, do you?"

Long Soldiers squinted back at the small man. He stepped aside so the glow could shine on the twig's face. "Yeah, I know you. You're the wimp who stopped buying from me last year because you found Jesus. What a pussy."

"Keep your hands off Edith, and leave her alone."

Long Soldiers laughed. "Or you're going to do what?"

Larry held up the jagged bottle. "Or I'll cut one of your nuts off."

Long Soldiers took a step back and nearly stumbled backward into the fire. "Whoa, little man. What the hell has gotten into you? Put that thing down. I was just seeing if Edith wanted to party with me. That's all."

"I said, leave her alone." Larry Standing Bull jabbed the broken bottle at Long Soldiers, who had distanced himself.

"I heard you, man," Long Soldiers replied, his hands defensively in the air in front of his chest. "No problem. I'll leave her alone."

Coyote Cries was impressed. Long Soldiers opted to dissipate the situation, rather than escalate the tension. Mature. Smart. They didn't need the Bureau of Indian Affairs intervening.

Then, to Coyote Cries's further amazement, Long Soldiers capitalized on the opportunity when the small crowd had gathered around. "Look, I thought she might want to try some of the best shit out there. I've got some free samples. Considering her brother loves this shit, and he's such a good friend of mine and all, I just thought maybe she'd want some, too."

The other kids listened intently. They were curious. It was a perfect opportunity to make new friends, to offer some bait for those who had always wanted to get their hands on something new. He had managed to name drop by mentioning what Coyote Cries imagined to be the most popular guy at Pine Ridge High School as one of his customers. Smart move.

Infuriated, Larry jabbed the jagged bottle in the air in front of Long Soldiers. "That's not true. Logan doesn't use your shit anymore. He's clean, just like everybody else here."

No one moved or disputed the twig.

He spun on his heels to face the others. "Don't forget what Mr. Two Bears said. We matter. We can beat this, if we stand together."

Who the hell is Mr. Two Bears? One of the old brothers? The Jesus freaks who imposed themselves on me when I was a kid? Pretending to be father figures to those of us without one? Pretending to care? What the hell do they have to do with these kids?

Coyote Cries had to find out, because at the mention of his name, the other kids turned their attention to the twig.

Facing Long Soldiers, the twig said, "We're not going to buy anymore, Long Soldiers. Find a new place to peddle. Get out of here."

Long Soldiers chuckled and scanned the faces in the small crowd to measure their acceptance of Standing Bull's ideas. The crowd remained passive. Coyote Cries frowned.

"Take it easy, little man. People are buying my shit here tonight. I've sold at least two cases of beer and a few odds and ends on top of that. People need me here, Larry. Maybe you don't. And maybe even little Edith doesn't. But others do. And I'm not going anywhere."

Long Soldiers wrapped his long, spindly arm around Edith Walking Crow's neck. "I'm happy to leave Edith alone when she tells me to. Understand, pussy boy?"

Edith stared at Larry with bewilderment and sheer terror. Larry asked, "Edith? What do you want?"

Coyote Cries raised an eyebrow, curious to see who would win this little battle.

The girl finally opened her mouth—just barely. "I want to go with you." She scrambled free of Long Soldiers's embrace.

He shrugged. "No problem. Just means more for me to enjoy, unless anyone wants to join me? World's greatest highs?"

The murmurs of the crowd rose as the high school teens encircled Todd Long Soldiers. Larry grabbed Edith's pudgy hand and led her back into the dark recesses of the night. Coyote Cries gave his employee a passing grade, even though he had lost two potential users.

Within the hour, Long Soldiers responded to Coyote Cries's text and met him behind the abandoned warehouse in Whiteclay. Long Soldiers's sweat was pouring off his forehead in the cool night. He was nervous.

"*Toníktuha he?*" His fingers trembled as he shoved a thick wad of money toward Coyote Cries.

Coyote Cries said nothing. He just nodded.

They stood in the shadows of the abandoned building. Long Soldiers fidgeted and occasionally kicked an empty bottle or pop can with the toe of his boot.

"I didn't know you were out. Alcott never told us."

Coyote Cries stared at him. "How's business?"

"I haven't been able to convince anyone to use either the heroin or the sample Quaaludes. They want meth. I told Alcott that. We all have. The older ones are still interested in this shit—the ones who graduated from high school a few years before Jeff Two Bears came to the reservation to teach."

"Jeff Two Bears?" Not the old codgers, Ray and Fred.

"He's a problem."

Coyote Cries's eyes narrowed.

"I'd convinced a few of the students at the Catholic high school to buy some heroin. And one of the Holy Rosary students even tried a Quaalude. They're Two Bears's students. But I've had to offer more freebies." He nodded at the wad of cash Coyote Cries was holding. "That's why it's so light."

Coyote Cries said nothing and thought about the situation.

Long Soldiers glanced at the wall of the brick building and paced.

Coyote Cries leveled his stare at him and scanned the wall with his peripheral vision.

The bricks had been spattered with spray paint in a multitude of colorful messages adorning the backside of the abandoned warehouse. One message that caught Coyote Cries's eye read *Jesus Lives* painted in bright blue beneath the crude sketch of a sorrowful Jesus Christ. The crude drawing depicted Jesus with his arms outstretched to the viewer, his comforting hands open for an embrace.

"You look so old," Long Soldiers said.

Coyote Cries resisted a smile and stuffed the money into his pocket. "It's been twenty years." He pulled a bag from the other pocket and handed it to Long Soldiers. "Kiddies will love these."

Long Soldiers studied the bag, held it close to his face, and kissed the bag. "Meth. Thank God. I couldn't get him to listen to me. But you did. How'd you convince him?"

"Convince him?" He raised an eyebrow.

"Alcott, the boss," Long Soldiers said, stuffing the bag in his jacket pocket.

Coyote Cries's fingers snatched his collar with lightning speed, like a cat pouncing on its prey. Long Soldiers clawed at Coyote Cries's hand and Coyote Cries demanded, "What's happening? At Pine Ridge High?"

Long Soldiers gasped, "They won't touch any of this shit. They tell me where to go. They say they don't need it. They've got plans for themselves. I don't know what's gotten into them. I tried, Jeremiah. Really, I did."

Coyote Cries asked, "Skimming?"

"I would never do that. Alcott would kill me."

He tightened his grip and lifted the large man off the ground with one hand. "Alcott's not the boss anymore. I am. And you're already dead."

Long Soldiers's eyes widened. Panic overtook him, and he wet his pants. "No, please. Let go. I'm telling you the truth. Two Bears has brainwashed the little shits into thinking they're hot shit. They're really messed up. I practically gave this shit away, and I'm dog meat to them. They wouldn't touch it."

Coyote Cries grumbled. "You know the rules. Whatever it takes to get those kids hooked. You should have been willing to pay them to take it, you idiot."

"But Jeremiah, I tried. I did everything I could. Alcott didn't want me giving out cash to—"

Coyote Cries lifted one finger on his free hand to his tight lips and mocked a hushing motion like a father to a child in church. Todd Long Soldiers stopped struggling. A slash of a smile appeared on Coyote Cries's hard face, and he snatched the blue bandana off Long Soldiers's forehead. He dropped him to the ground, gagged him with the bandana, and felt his wiry body quake.

Long Soldiers's face appeared as sorrowful as the crude Jesus painted on the warehouse wall. Coyote Cries leaned down, smelled the fear pouring off his clammy skin, and said, "Alcott is dead. And he was never the boss."

Coyote Cries slipped the belt from Long Soldiers's jeans and beat him until he stopped screaming.

And moving.

CHAPTER 17

COYOTE CRIES NOTICED the man entering the front doors of the Indian Health Services.

The bald man in a brown suit was definitely not BIA. He was likely FBI. But not Streeter Pierce, as he'd expected. Maybe Pierce didn't know about his escape yet and still hadn't figured out the letter about the parole hearing delay was a fake.

If he had, he'd be here. This meant Coyote Cries had more time for his plan. He wouldn't be so rushed, and that was good. He set his coffee cup down, unfolded himself from the lobby armchair, and followed the suit.

He made sure to stay far enough behind the guy, so he wouldn't notice he was being followed. He went right, down the hall, then left, and into the second door on the right. He was definitely a fibbie, a coworker of Pierce's.

Coyote Cries walked past the ICU room and tucked himself into the next alcove to listen.

Thick layers bandaged Long Soldiers's head. Drainage, feeding, and oxygen tubes emerged from various orifices covered by the multiple sheets of gauze. Both hands and wrists were in casts, and dressings covered several areas on the patient's upper torso and arms. He couldn't see Long

Soldiers from the alcove, but he'd already checked. He had been in the room earlier when the nurses weren't paying attention.

The methodical wheezing and pumping of the machines and the steady beep of the monitors were the only sounds in the quiet hospital room. He hoped they wouldn't drown out the conversation.

He ducked behind the wall when a tall nurse shuffled toward the door to document vitals and make a periodic check on the patient. The two would talk even if Long Soldiers couldn't. He'd find out what they knew.

The nurse had the body of a football player yet was graceful in her movements. Her skin was dark and leathery, but he imagined her touch was gentle, which aroused him. He heard her introduce herself as Norma Chasing Dog. He was FBI Special Agent Roger Landers. He could hear just fine from his hiding place.

"His name is Todd Long Soldiers. He's forty-six. A resident. Unmarried."

Her voice had no inflection, but it sounded familiar.

The agent asked, "Who brought him in?"

"Someone dropped him off at the emergency entrance but didn't even stay to check him in. That was early this morning, just after two. It wasn't my shift."

"What do you know, Norma?"

"I think he was brought in by some kids who were out drinking last night. My boy told me he had heard some other boys talking about their trip to the strip joints in Chadron. When they returned, one of them had to pee. They had stopped at Whiteclay behind one of the buildings and found Long Soldiers."

Coyote Cries heard the young nurse walking down the hall before he saw her. When he did, she was studying a clipboard and hadn't noticed him.

He listened and wondered what he'd missed.

The nurse said, "It took awhile to figure out who this guy was. He didn't have any identification. Luckily, one of our custodians recognized his boots and the blue bandana gagging his mouth. CCG. Long Soldiers was notorious for his dingo boots."

Coyote Cries didn't understand CCG.

"Blood alcohol?"

"Nothing. He was completely clean. He's not a user; he's a supplier."

A long pause followed before the agent said, "Found at Whiteclay—so I suspect he was bootlegging or peddling. Do you think he was beat up by someone who didn't like what he sold them? Or by someone who didn't like his profession?"

"Hell, yes. Any or all of the above. But that sure as hell won't be the story he tells if this guy ever comes out of it. Whoever beat the snot out of him used a metal pipe or brass knuckles or something. He had some serious damage to his head and face. It looks like Long Soldiers tried to protect himself and broke lots of bones in his hands and both forearms in the process."

The agent asked, "Will he live?"

Coyote Cries didn't hear the nurse's answer. She either nodded or shook her head.

"Head injuries?"

The nurse answered, "Not so bad that he's a vegetable. But he's messed up. He's been unconscious the entire time. He's stable, and the swelling is going down. He'll come out of it."

"What's the doctor saying?"

"They don't know anything. Doctors stationed here lately have been a bunch of white kids who couldn't afford to put themselves through medical school. So they promise to 'do their time' on the reservation in exchange for financial help from the government. Chalk it up to another failed program implemented to assuage centuries of white guilt."

Coyote Cries suppressed a grin. He was more attracted to Norma than ever.

"Who do you think did this to Long Soldiers?"

"I heard Long Soldiers was trolling at the Pine Ridge High party last night. One of his marks was the young Walking Crow girl. Her older brother, Logan, is one tough little shit. Maybe he was teaching Long Soldiers a lesson."

Coyote Cries was pleased to hear Norma throw out a reasonable suspect to cover for him.

"The truth. You don't believe it was Logan Walking Crow. Do you?"

Coyote Cries strained to hear her answer. He wanted an excuse to pay her a visit.

"Who do you think did this, Norma?"

"I could be killed for telling you." He heard Norma's heavy sigh. "What the hell. I'm going to die someday anyway. Todd Long Soldiers is rumored to not only be one of the bootleggers for alcohol on the reservation. He's also one of the drug dealers. So is Floyd Tice."

"The guy that got the crap beat out of him a few weeks ago?"

"These guys are with CCG."

"Coyote Cries gang?" the suit asked.

Coyote Cries hadn't heard that his team had been labeled CCG. It was a great tribute to him. He was a legend. That was another reason Long Soldiers deserved the beating—for not telling him.

Norma explained, "A bunch of lowlifes work for the scum from Colorado—the asshole who took his place when Jeremiah went to prison. He pretends to know our people, but really all he's doing is draping himself in Jeremiah's reputation. He's like a fancy dancer under a coyote pelt. One greedy bastard and unoriginal too."

Coyote Cries vowed to find out who this woman was. Somehow, she thought like he did. She felt his pain and knew his very core.

"A name? Have you heard?"

"Guy named Alcott. Dan or Dave. A white guy."

"We're on him," the suit said.

And so was Coyote Cries.

He'd been "on him" within an hour of his escape. He had called him from Alcott's Denver mansion after he'd retrieved everything he'd instructed Webber to leave there for him and after he'd confirmed that his men had indeed taken care of that traitor, Vic. They had—although in the most unoriginal fashion.

And a good thing they had. Because the hit was so unoriginal, Alcott never suspected Coyote Cries was behind the murder—which was why he had parked his car in the garage and stomped inside to meet the released felon instead of speeding off in his Lamborghini like he should have done.

Coyote Cries enjoyed every minute of his time with Alcott—listening to him bargain for his life and promise him the world if he let him live; seeing his expression when he quoted Jeremiah 12:6: "For even thy brethren has dealt treacherously with thee. Believe them not, though they speak fair words unto thee"—and watching him die as he choked on the wad of money he had stolen from him.

Coyote Cries grinned.

Glancing down the hall in both directions, he retreated quickly to the exit. He'd heard enough. There was plenty of time to exact his revenge on everyone who'd betrayed him.

And a little left over to visit Nurse Norma.

───────────

Jeremiah Coyote Cries stood between some parked cars outside the construction area waiting for Jeff Two Bears to take his late afternoon break. He'd learned through his sources that Two Bears had been moonlighting as a flooring hand on weekends with the new construction at the high school.

He was leaning against an old pickup truck with Pennington County plates. He knew that Jeff Two Bears was from Rapid City and probably hadn't had time yet to change out his plates. But he had no idea what Two Bears looked like. He'd known the man's dad years ago, but he doubted that would help.

Someone had given him a general description and told him that the Two Bears were a *wacipi* family—a family that not only celebrated but taught others their culture by traveling to powwows around the country and advocating clean living. They believed in no violence, no alcohol, and no drugs—which meant no tolerance for him.

Old man Two Bears had tried to convince the Catholic grade school to accept Coyote Cries when he was ten. He had pleaded his own case, since there was no one else around to do it for him. He had begged them to have mercy on him, considering he'd been beat to near death by his stepfather the year before. But they wouldn't take him. Then in eighth grade, three years later, another old man Two Bears had caught him with a knife in his hand after slashing a teacher's tires.

But he hadn't ratted him out. He had just told him to get his life turned around before it was too late and that he'd be watching him.

He didn't know which old man had fathered Jeff. But none of the Two Bears he knew would have any appreciation for his altruistic desire to exact revenge on the very people who had destroyed their culture in the first place. They were naïve. They equated forgiveness without consequence to weakness.

He glanced over at the sun and waited.

By twenty minutes to one, most of the cars in the construction yard and parking lot had been retrieved by the workers. Coyote Cries watched as two men approached the lot. Both men were Lakotans, both in their early to mid-twenties. That fit the general description.

He studied their faces, but neither claimed the pickup. A third man emerged from the Pine Ridge High School. He was tall, slender, and had a confident gait and looked to be just over six feet tall with a face that gave him the look of a young boy. But the sureness in his steps was unmistakably that of a mature man.

The man was running his long, slender fingers through his stylishly groomed hair, which sprang obediently back into place. Although he was alone, a wide, perfect smile sat upon his handsome face.

Coyote Cries mumbled to himself. "A pretty boy. This will be easier than I thought."

He watched as Jeff Two Bears waved a friendly goodbye to the last of his fellow coworkers and approached the truck. He pulled up short when he saw Coyote Cries standing near the bed.

Coyote Cries stepped away from the vehicle as Two Bears opened the door and crawled into his truck. Coyote Cries hurried to the driver's side window when he saw the other two workers drive out of the lot.

They were alone.

Two Bears showed no fear. "What's the problem, friend?"

"Are you Jeff Two Bears?"

He nodded.

Coyote Cries swiftly covered Two Bears's mouth with his left hand, pinning him to the seat and jabbed a hypodermic needle into his upper arm straight through his denim shirt. Two Bears struggled for a brief moment before going limp behind the wheel.

"You're the problem."

Wanting the death to appear to be an overdose to shake up the core beliefs of that pitiful powwow family, he worked quickly. He rolled up the sleeve of Two Bears's shirt and strapped a rubber tie around his exposed arm. He placed the emptied needle in Two Bears's limp, left hand and scattered a few more pieces of drug paraphernalia on the seat and floorboard.

Then he stepped away from the vehicle. He smiled when he imagined the rumors that would spread like wildfire once the news of the man's death hit the street. Two Bears, dead—from the same vice he preached as evil and destructive. Students would consider him a traitor, a hypocrite, a liar.

Within no time, his customer base would blossom with the distractions like Two Bears's "better way of life."

Making sure one last time that Two Bears's slumped body was no longer moving, Coyote Cries turned to leave. Out of the corner of his eye, he spotted a young woman turning off the road into the parking lot of the high school several yards away.

For a split second, their gazes locked.

The expression in the woman's eyes was one of apprehension—maybe even fear.

He quickly disappeared behind the nearest building, hoping the woman hadn't gotten a good look at him. As he wove his way through other random buildings and through the tall grass of the fields beyond, he heard the young woman's distant scream.

She'd found Two Bears.

Coyote Cries recognized the woman. He knew her face. He'd seen her working with ICU nurses on Long Soldiers's tribal and allotment status down at the hospital earlier that morning before the suit arrived. She would be easy to identify.

As he reached his Camaro, cleverly parked and hidden in the bushes beyond the high school, Coyote Cries smiled. He wondered if she'd be back at the hospital later today.

Perhaps when sweet Nurse Norma's shift ended, and he pulled her into an empty, secluded room, she wouldn't be able to resist whispering in his ear what he needed to know about the woman.

And where she lived.

CHAPTER 18

I HAD SPENT FIVE glorious days and nights with Streeter.

Three of those days were at work—trying to stay focused on my job and rushing home in the evenings to make him dinner so we could maintain our stamina—and two of them at his cabin in Conifer. It was sheer bliss—the best weekend of my life.

By Sunday night, I was elated and fulfilled—at once energized and exhausted. I drove east on I-70 toward downtown Denver, then south on I-25 to my apartment. Beulah nestled in her kennel in the back.

At the Mousetrap, which wasn't all that crowded compared to rush hour during the week, a grey, distressed pickup sped up and cut in between my Jeep and the car behind me. The guy looked pissed and full of road rage with his mouth set in a slash. His eyes were hidden behind mirrored shades. *Kind of late to be wearing sunglasses, but who am I to judge?*

The driver might have been Hispanic, although it was hard to tell. He was shouting something. Maybe to someone on a phone call? Hands-free? Or perhaps he was singing. But it appeared he was shaking a fist at the driver behind me—yelling at him as he passed.

I cornered the off-ramp from I-70, careful not to hit anyone as I merged onto I-25 South. I eased into traffic, which was backed up at 20th Street.

Must be a Rockies game about to start.

I stayed in the lane as far to the right as possible without getting entangled in the baseball traffic, hoping the road-rage driver would scoot left and pass me.

But he didn't.

He hugged my bumper in thick traffic and dropped back when we settled into a more consistent speed. Something niggled in the back of my brain: *This is not right.*

I reached into my console looking for something to write on but only found a pen. I glanced into the rearview several times to retrieve the license plate numbers. I pulled up my shirttail and tucked it between my teeth and scribbled the numbers directly on my stomach—right side up for me, but upside down to someone looking at me.

I was trying to see the last number on the plate when a car squeezed in between the truck and my Jeep. I swore out loud, wishing the lady in the Lexus had waited just an instant so I could complete the plate. But it was too late. I'd get it in a minute. Besides, I'd narrowed the license down to ten plates in Colorado.

I floored the gas and lurched forward away from the Lexus that had begun to slow and ease into the right lane. I sped up enough to duck in front of three cars to my left then moved over two more lanes before reaching the high occupancy lane. I hit the gas again. Not so much that it would seem I was trying to lose the driver in the pickup, but I did want to see if he tried to keep up with me.

He tried.

I saw his grey beater weaving in and out of lanes to reach the inside high occupancy lane I was driving in, so I flicked on my blinker and merged right and then eased into another lane right. I slowed down as if I was targeting an off-ramp.

The pickup sped past me but not before I saw his head swiveling to find me in the crowded lanes to the right. It was growing dark and easy for him to lose sight of me as I dropped over and back.

I saw him shaking his fist at other drivers and heard horns honking. He'd removed his sunglasses and his hat. I didn't recognize him, but it was definitely me he was following.

It was too late for him to follow, and I merged onto the off-ramp, one exit short of my apartment complex.

Dick Roth popped into my head, and I wondered if this guy was somehow related to his "protection" organization. But I doubted it. Roth was likely a lone ranger—more money for him and less chance of being discovered.

My brother had everything set up for me at Livermore on Wednesday, and I would be meeting him for dinner Tuesday night in Fort Collins. Everything was moving smoothly toward nailing the pig.

My cell phone rang. Streeter Pierce's name popped up on my display.

"Missing me already?" I asked.

"Where are you?"

"Almost home. I'm on Evans."

"Why'd you turn off so soon?"

"Had a guy following me. Just didn't want him to know where I lived." There was silence. "I'll be there in thirty minutes."

I chuckled. "No, Streeter. I'm fine. We're both exhausted and need a good night's sleep."

"Who was he?"

"I don't know. Driving a grey F150, probably a 90s model. Old, beat up. License plate . . . hold on." I saw a gas station parking lot and parked under a lamppost. I lifted my shirt and read off the numbers. "Colorado license plate. I got cut off before I got the last digit."

"Good girl. I'll have someone do some digging."

"It's probably nothing. Just someone with road rage."

Silence again. "How long had he been following you?"

I lowered my shirt and glanced around to make sure no one saw me using my belly as a tablet. "I don't know. Figured it out on I-70 as I was coming onto I-25."

"From my house?"

My turn to be silent for a moment. "I don't know. What are you thinking?"

I wondered if he was worried about someone at work finding out about us. I didn't care. I loved the man. But he was my boss, so the implications would be far more dangerous for him than for me.

"I'm just being careful. I'm worried about you. I'll be right there."

"No. I'm serious. I'm fine." For some reason, his hypervigilance pissed me off. It wasn't endearing. I'd been alone most of my life, and I didn't need a man's protection. Then I felt bad for barking at him. "Sorry, Streeter. I just need a good night's sleep. It's been fun, but I need rest. You're killing me."

He chuckled. I told him goodnight and said I'd see him tomorrow at work.

I pulled out of the lot and merged back onto I-25, headed for my apartment off Yale. When I pulled into the parking lot of my building complex a few minutes later, I spotted the grey truck in the back row, nose out in the space. Maybe he wasn't following me. Maybe he lived here. I had never noticed the truck here before. But maybe he was a neighbor.

The hair on the back of my neck rose, and a shiver skipped down my spine. I didn't trust this guy one bit. I parked under a lamppost on the far side of the lot and sat in my quiet Jeep for so long the hot engine stopped pinging. I studied the grey pickup across the lot and saw no movement. No one was inside.

I gathered up Beulah, strapped on her harness, attached the lead, and headed for a neighboring apartment building. Not mine. Just to be sure. I ducked inside, ran down the hallway as quietly as I could, and exited the back. Rounding the corner, I waited to see if anyone followed. Nothing. I tiptoed near the back fence past two buildings and froze when Beulah started baying.

"Shhh." I pulled her lead, closed the distance, and crouched to calm her. "Beulah, hush."

But she was having none of it. Something in the distance caught her nose—a smell she didn't like. I saw a figure standing near the back door of my building. I thought about my next move and decided to approach, using Beulah as my guide.

I instructed her: "Find."

She did and bolted for the man near the back door. When she closed the distance, the man moved quickly around the corner of the building, tossing his cigarette in the grass. I pulled my dog away and headed for the back door. I fumbled with my key, trying to distract my bloodhound from howling. Once through the door, I took the stairs two at a time to get to my floor.

I poked my head around the corner. There was no one in the hall. Then I sprinted for my door, key ready, Beulah in tow. I stabbed the key in the lock and flung myself through the door, flipping the deadbolt as I did. Beulah immediately calmed down and lumbered to the couch. I pressed my back against the door and slid down to the floor.

How did that guy know where I lived? He was waiting out back at *my* building. Not the one I'd parked near. Beulah lifted her head off the couch, started a low growl, and lumbered to her feet again, moving quickly toward me and the door.

Then there was a knock.

Streeter, I thought. He decided to come after all. I had to admit, I was relieved.

I tried to hush Beulah, but she wasn't to be comforted. I kenneled her and threw a blanket over the cage. Lights out.

Another knock.

It had to be Streeter.

I grabbed my SIG Sauer and stuffed the pistol in the waistband of my jeans at the small of my back. I peeked out my peephole. No one was there.

The peal of my cell phone startled me. The display indicated it was Streeter. He must have called when he couldn't get me to open the door. He was worried.

I answered, turning the deadbolt to let him in.

"Streeter, I thought I told you not to—"

A man's hand snaked around my mouth, and another wrapped around my waist.

I heard Streeter shouting my name through the cell phone I'd dropped.

I kicked and scratched and tried to get to my gun. I tried to scream.

He had me from behind, his body up against mine. I bit his hand and stomped his instep. He let go for an instant. I whipped around and reached for my gun. It was gone.

I glanced quickly at his face. *The guy from the pickup—definitely Hispanic. Long, black hair. Forties. Average height and weight. A scar just under—*

I saw something flash in the hand he lifted. It was my gun. Then I felt something heavy against my skull.

My world went pitch-black.

CHAPTER 19

COYOTE CRIES FOLLOWED Nurse Norma under the light of the nearly full moon with his headlights off.

She hadn't noticed him in the parking lot, nor had she noticed him pull in behind her. Within minutes, she'd parked her Kia under the carport and used her keys to enter her small, dark house.

No one was home but her. There was no movement up or down the street, except for the images from a television near the front window of a house two doors down. He glanced along the neat row of houses in her neighborhood. Every yard had been tended. Houses painted and maintained. He marveled at how much had changed since he'd been gone. When he was a child, only one house in the neighborhood would have reflected care and attention to the home and yard. Now, that attitude was the rule, not the exception. He beamed with pride for his people. Except for the neighbor's property across the street. Movement to his left caught his eye. He spun on his heels. A collared goat tied to the base of a satellite dish stretched its tethered neck toward a rusty engine that dangled from the center of a tripod three feet off the bare, dusty ground. The driveway was strewn with parts from a stripped and aged Impala. The heart of the beastly automobile was hanging from a makeshift engine rack erected from three downed tree limbs and some old rope.

The pet could reach just far enough and, oblivious to the visitor, the goat was licking the gooey mess that had coagulated on the underside of the engine.

He saw a horse's tail swishing as it stood near the house to the right of Norma's. Its head was jammed into the hole where a windowpane should have been. Probably the owner had busted out the window and was using the sink as a feeding trough, so the man or woman inside wouldn't have to brave the winter weather to keep the horse fed.

He suddenly missed his mother. He'd check to see if she was still alive before he left town.

He opened the car door, having carefully removed the dome light and dimmed the dashboard. He snuck across Norma's perfectly manicured lawn and darted quickly into the backyard. He could see her preparing a meal in the kitchen, which gave him plenty of time to enter the house through her bedroom window.

He stood motionless behind her door and waited.

Within minutes, she came into the bedroom, flicked on the light, and unbuttoned her nurse's uniform. She stopped suddenly when she noticed the open window.

Before she had time to react, he slid up behind her and covered her mouth, pulling her against him. She tried to bite his hand and wriggle from beneath his arm banded around her ribs, but he reached back and turned off the light, leaving them awash in the glow from moonlight through the open window and the kitchen light around the corner. The breeze against them felt cool and the bare skin of her waist soft beneath his hand.

He hushed her and whispered in her ear to be still.

Which she didn't.

She fought him like a bearcat.

Which only made him want her more.

He chuckled. "Norma. Sweet Norma."

His lips brushed the top of her ear. Her muffled cries and ferocious battle beneath his arms pleased him—until he felt a tear against the fingers that clamped her mouth.

He quoted Jeremiah 29:11.

> *For I know the plans I have for you. Plans to prosper and not to harm you. Plans to give you hope and a future.*

His words seemed to calm her. The energy behind her fight drained with each word he whispered. He pulled her closer to him, so she could feel his strength, his erection. But her back arched away from him, and her fight renewed.

"Be still. And you'll have that future. I promise."

She grew still.

He wanted to push her onto her bed and take her right there, because he could.

But he didn't. He was enjoying her too much, and he wanted her to want him back. He had decided to spare her. She was too much like him.

"Now, Norma. I like you. Very much." He tilted his hips toward her, his member hard against her back. She whimpered. "I'm going to let go—of just your mouth—long enough for you to answer my questions."

He was also going to unsheathe his knife at the same time in case she screamed.

"Two questions. And if you answer me honestly, I will slip out that window and never bother you again. If you scream, I will have to kill you."

He felt her tense beneath his grip.

"Do you understand me? Nod, if you do."

She hesitated, and then she nodded.

"Good girl."

He relaxed his fingers and calculated his next moves if she tried to scream. He would clasp his hand over her mouth quickly and use his right hand around her ribs to retrieve the knife. He'd kill her quickly. He didn't want to strangle this one. He had too much appreciation for her spirit. She deserved to die fast.

But she didn't scream. She said only one word. "Ask."

"The woman today giving you information about Long Soldiers—her name and address."

She stiffened beneath him. He pulled her closer to him with his right arm, dragged his fingertips down her cheek, and wrapped them around her delicate throat as a warning.

She swallowed hard. "Why?"

"I need to know."

"Who are you?"

"Someone very much like you."

"We are nothing alike. I would never frighten someone like this."

He relaxed his fingers from around her throat. He slid his hand around her neck down her chest, stopping as his fingertips touched her cleavage. "I am not trying to frighten you. This is called foreplay."

She whimpered again. She was a smart woman. The message of consequence was not lost on her. "I don't know where she lives."

He believed her. "Her name."

She remained still. Then she ripped free of his grip and bolted for the window, actually diving headfirst out the opening. She tried to scramble away, her hands and knees clawing at the ground for purchase.

But she didn't get very far. He was on her in no time and pinned her to the ground in the backyard with his face inches from hers. He pressed his knife against her throat. Her eyes were wide.

"Norma. Why? I liked you."

She shook her head quickly. "Don't kill me. Please."

He leaned down. She jerked her head to the side. He kissed her cheek gently. She tried to head butt him, so he pressed his lips hard against her cheek, her chin, her neck, and then he ground his hips into her. She pleaded for him to let her go.

"You've betrayed me, dear Norma." Then he bit her neck.

She stifled a scream. Tears streamed down her temples. "I didn't. I haven't. I'll tell you whatever you want to know. Just don't kill me."

He eased his weight off her so as not to hurt her but kept her pinned. She started to sob. He kissed her face gently. Her forehead. Her nose. Everything but her lips.

"You have one chance. Her name."

Her sobs were for the woman she was about to betray—not for herself. He knew her strength well enough to know she would have died keeping the other woman safe, if she could have. But the will to live was stronger than her desire to save another.

They were all the same when it came down to this moment. The pleading and the power he held over them once they realized they were about to die at his hands. She stared into his eyes and held his gaze for many moments. She wasn't going to tell him. She needed a bit more convincing.

Because he didn't have that much time, he pressed the blade against her beautiful throat. Enough to cut but not kill. The familiar odor of blood rose between them, and he held her gaze and let her study his face. He didn't care if they told her who he really was when she described him; when they pieced this altogether in the weeks to come. He'd already be long gone. And she'd realize how lucky she was that he let her go.

She would owe him. Tears poured from the corners of her black eyes, down her temples, and into her hair.

"Your last name?"

"Chasing Dog."

He grinned. "And hers?"

In a tiny voice she said, "Good Run. Julie Good Run."

"Norma Chasing Dog." He kissed her forehead and disappeared in the dark, leaving her to her thoughts of him.

CHAPTER 20

I WOKE UP IN the emergency room, woozy, and with the worst head-ache of my life.

I was alone, behind a curtain. I tried to get up, but my head pounded, and I regurgitated into a nearby bedpan.

Damn it.

I glanced at the clock. 11:15. How did I get to the hospital so quickly? Last I remember, I was skulking around behind my apartment complex at 10:30. I remembered being clobbered . . . which I wished I didn't remem-ber . . . but I did. Everyone else I'd ever known had a bit of amnesia around a violent event. I seemed to remember every gory and brutal detail.

Unfair.

I recalled everything about the guy who'd been following me, even the crazy scar along the right side of his nose. It looked like he'd been punched by a right-hander. Probably a boxer's punch—not a jab or an uppercut but a hook—well executed and strong. He had likely broken the bones of his nose in a bout. The scar was exactly like those after tiny nose bones slice through the ridge of the cheek. He was definitely a fighter.

I lay back down and groaned. I reached for my forehead to ease the pounding, only to find my arm tethered with an intravenous needle.

How did I get here?

A nurse pushed the curtain aside, stepped closer to the foot of my gurney, and slid the privacy drape closed. "You're awake."

"You mean conscious?"

"I mean, awake. You were conscious when the paramedics arrived. You fell asleep almost immediately and have been out since."

She bustled around my bed, scowled when she saw the bedpan, and clicked her pen several times on, then off, after each documented reading. Each click was like a .45 being fired next to my ear. I wasn't so out of it not to wonder why the hell she didn't leave the damn pen alone until she was all done with her exam.

"Name and date of birth?"

I answered. Accurately. She checked my reply against my hospital bracelet.

"Wait, how did you know?"

"Driver's license," she said, not glancing my way. She was too busy affixing another blood pressure cuff. "Don't talk."

I didn't, knowing if I did, the blood pressure reading wouldn't register accurately. After a long minute or two, the air hissed in release. My head throbbed. She ripped the Velcro strap off, and the grating noise amplified in my brain. She quickly wound the rubber hose around the band and shoved the contraption hurriedly into a cabinet. The wooden door closed with a bang.

I cleared my throat. "Would you mind telling me what's happening? Apparently, I've been asleep for a few minutes and missed all the excitement."

She smirked. "You're at St. Joe's ER. We're busy. Which is why you still don't have a room. And since you were so sound asleep, we just let you stay here last night. Not a few minutes. Try twelve hours."

I glanced at the clock again. *11:30? In the morning?* Yikes. "So what happened? When can I leave?"

She finished her tasks with speed and efficiency, never landing a glance my way other than fleetingly. "The doctor will be in shortly. After the phlebotomist. We'll need your labs."

"But—"

"Your friend will fill you in." She snatched the sullied bedpan, ripped the curtain aside, and disappeared.

"Friend?" I asked.

Streeter stepped through the opening, grinned, and quietly slid the curtain closed behind him. He looked awful—and wonderful. I was so glad to see him.

"You didn't listen," I said, grinning back. "You came anyway, didn't you? You never got a wink of sleep."

He shrugged, sat down on the edge of my bed, and leaned down to kiss the right side of my forehead, opposite of where I'd been clocked. "How are you feeling?"

"Like Sleeping Beauty, only not so much the latter."

He tucked a strand of my hair behind my ear.

"What happened?"

The pained look in his eyes scored deep.

"I called."

"I answered." I remembered. I had thought it was Streeter who'd knocked on my door. "Someone had knocked on my door. Twice. I thought it was you."

"You didn't check?"

I nodded. "Of course. No one was there. I grabbed my gun and went to answer the door . . . and was about to turn the knob when you called."

"You thought it was me," he said, sadness flooding his face. "I found you in the entrance of your apartment. The door was open. Do you remember anything?"

"Yeah, unfortunately. I remember everything." I tried to sit up but got woozy again. I didn't want to puke in front of Streeter, and I probably smelled and looked like hell.

"Careful," he said, helping me settle back onto my pillow.

"I'd give anything to brush my teeth."

His grin was lopsided. He fished something from the pocket of his jacket and held up a packet with two mini-toothbrushes "with a freshening bead of paste built into the brush."

"It was either this or M&M's. And you think I wasn't paying attention all weekend?"

"I am a bit of a nut about my oral hygiene," I said, offering him a crooked smile. "And about my chocolate. Would you mind helping me?"

He opened the plastic wrapper and gave me the first tiny brush. I used them both, spitting into the plastic cup he'd handed me. Heaven. My mouth felt fabulous. My breath had to smell better, too. I tossed the two used brushes into the cup. "My mouth thanks you. The nurses thank you. My doctor thanks you." I glanced over his shoulder. "My phlebotomist thanks you."

"I need your labs. Do you mind?" The young woman didn't appear old enough to be out of high school. But she was quick and efficient like the other nurse and was in and out.

"What are they looking for? When can I go home?"

"Everything's normal. They're worried about concussions or any other damage—like eyesight problems or seizures."

"And if everything comes out okay, can I go home? I'm late for work."

He held my hand. "You're not coming to work. Liv, this is serious."

I withdrew my hand from his. "I have plans. I promised Bert Ridgewood and my brother."

"I know, I know. But your health is far more important."

He grabbed for my hand again and patted it. His tone was condescending—like I was a child. That pissed me off. "My health is fine. I just got a bump on my head. That's all."

"We don't know who did this."

"I do. It's the guy with the grey truck." I pushed back the blanket, lifted my hospital gown, and pointed at the fading numbers written in pen on my stomach. "This guy."

"You saw him? And you remember?"

"Every detail—including the scar running down the right side of his nose. Five eight. Hundred and seventy pounds. Straight black hair below his ears, tucked. Scruffy, but like he'd shaved, and it quickly grew back. Black eyes. No glasses or tattoos visible. Early forties. Hispanic."

I stopped, breathing heavily. My anger subsided. Streeter appeared stunned. Then he arched an eyebrow in amusement. "Every detail. Of course."

I knew I wasn't normal. He knew that, too. "And he didn't want to hit me."

"How do you know that?"

"A feeling. He clocked me with the butt of my own gun."

"I thought you said this guy was a road rager?"

"At first, that's what I thought. But then I realized he was just a tail. He was smoking a cigarette at the back door of my apartment complex. He got there before I did."

"He knew where you lived." Streeter's eyes widened.

"Exactly. So I snuck up on him and pretended I was sending Beulah to attack him. He ran and dropped his cigarette." I thought back to exactly where I saw him drop that smoke. I would retrieve it as soon as I got out of here. I'd bag it, in case we needed his DNA for something. "Then I ran up the back stairs to my apartment."

"But if he was a tail and knew where you lived, why did he follow you to your apartment? And why would he knock on your door?"

I shrugged. "Don't know. But what I do know is that I surprised him. I opened my door. I had a gun, and I attacked him when he jumped me from behind. I'd stepped out looking for you."

"Maybe he was surprised you were on the phone."

"I just don't think he was intending to do anything with me. Other than follow me." But then I wondered if I'd been wrong. What if he'd intended to rape me?

Streeter plowed his fingers through his short, white hair. "What is this about?"

"Dick Roth?"

"I don't think so."

"Mully?" I asked, knowing that couldn't be.

"No way." Streeter covered his face with his hands and rubbed his eyes. "Think, think. Why would someone have a shadow on you? You've been out on sabbatical, not involved in any open cases for weeks."

"The press?"

He glanced up at me.

I shrugged. "You said yourself that they were trying to find me. Maybe it's just a paparazzi thing—this guy was hired to find out where I lived. Maybe the knock on the door was a photographer he'd called in to take my picture."

"And instead, he assaulted a federal agent and stole her gun?" Streeter asked.

"He stole my SIG?"

Streeter was about to answer when the curtain slid back again.

It was the doctor.

Before she could say a word, I asked, "When can I get out of here?"

CHAPTER 21

"SO WHAT DO WE have on this guy?" I shifted the cell phone gingerly to my left ear.

The entire right side of my head felt like an exposed nerve. The doctor said that if everything remained normal, she'd release me when she returned for her afternoon rounds. Until then, I was bedbound. It might take me time before I could get rid of the goose egg on my forehead, but thinking didn't hurt a bit. And she never said I couldn't work.

Laurie Frumpley said, "Dick has been a very bad boy. Since last Tuesday, when you recorded the shakedown of Ridgewood, he's leaned on four different operators. That's just under a week and all of them on Saturday."

I scooted to the edge of my bed as I listened, then bent at the waist, and stretched down to my toes with a groan. The throbbing worsened. I pulled myself erect, straightened my hospital gown, and scooted back against my pillows. "How'd you find that out?"

"That tracking device you managed to slip into his wallet? The one that looks like a credit card? It showed me exactly where he's been. How long will that device last?"

I'd managed to plant the tracking device without him knowing. He had told Ridgewood he'd be back after lunch for the money. Dick Roth clearly valued food, so after shaking Ridgewood down, I suspected he'd go eat somewhere besides fast food.

One thing I loved about having a big family was that I was surrounded by experts in various fields. My sister Elizabeth treasured cutting-edge technology, particularly surveillance equipment. I wasn't sure if she really hired out as a PI from time to time or if she used that as a cover to amass her stash of equipment and weapons—or if she secretly worked for the CIA.

The futuristic credit card had been a gift from her—in case I ever needed it.

I had thought about planting a tracking device in his car, but it was government issued, and he probably used his personal car on weekends for most of his heavy work, assuming he was smart.

I spotted his car at a local saloon. He was eating at the bar, his eyes transfixed on a television mounted near the ceiling. His cell phone and wallet were lying on the counter to his right beside his plate.

So I tipped the bartender to fumble his Coke, spill it on his belly and crotch, which she did. He rushed off to the bathroom to mop up. And when he did, I slipped the card into his wallet, tipped her a fifty, and swore her to secrecy.

"As long as he has his wallet within three feet of his cell phone, the device will recharge itself."

"His government car was checked in on Friday afternoon. But other than Ridgewood, he had only official visits on his log throughout the week. So he must have driven his personal car on Saturday."

"And took Sunday off?"

"Appears so," Laurie said. "Personal car remained parked at his house since Saturday night until this morning when he went to work. I called all three operators and told them you'd be calling and confirmed that EPA Inspector Dick Roth had paid them an unofficial visit."

"Three? I thought you said he visited four?" I studied my notes. With Ridgewood, Juzlig, and Ole along with these four, I thought the bureau had a good chance to nail this guy.

The doctor told me I had a linear skull fracture, a slight fracture, visible on my X-ray. I'd be fine and back to my normal routine in days. Never mind the warnings that I might not be thinking straight for a few days. I had my coworkers like Laurie to keep me in line until the muddle cleared. The pain was from swelling and contusions, and the concussion meant I'd lost alertness and some awareness. Probably not good in the field, but as long as I kept my movements to a minimum and eventually iced my wound once I got home, I'd be back to my usual routine in a matter of days.

"I did say four. I just got a call from Matt Juzlig. Roth visited him Saturday again. He thinks we're not doing anything to help, so he's taking matters into his own hands. He plans on being wired up Tuesday when Roth returns."

"That could be dangerous." I pulled my hair into a loose ponytail and secured the thick bunch with an elastic band.

"I told him I'd have you call him back today. Are you up for it?"

I looked at the clock. It was 4:30. "I'm on it. I'll call all four of them and Ridgewood. I'll keep them posted." I jotted down the names and phone numbers she recited. "What else do you know?"

"I know you're in the hospital and not supposed to be working."

"Yet here I am . . ." I wasn't going to get any more out of her. I was busted.

"Just don't tell Streeter. Otherwise, we'll both be fired. You okay?"

Laurie Frumpley was cooler than I thought. She had moxie.

"Perfectly fine. Anything else?"

"Our boy's been busy. I found his other bank accounts."

Impressed, I said, "You *have* been busy. Good job."

"He has four total, all at separate banks. One of the accounts he uses publicly and openly for everyday business like deposits, writing checks, and withdrawing cash."

"Amazing. How did you learn about this so fast?" She was a remarkable data jockey, and IT geeks were golden to us field agents. I had never worked with Laurie but was learning why Streeter kept her to himself.

"The other three accounts have very little activity, cash deposits on occasion but no withdrawals to speak of. He didn't even bother to come up with a false name or a different social security number."

"Bold," I commented.

"Or stupid," she added. "The odd thing is that he uses Richard M. Roth on his daily account, and he uses R. M. Roth on the other three, with social security numbers matching exactly. So it's not like he didn't think about changing the name."

"How much does he have squirreled away for rainy days?" I arched my back, beginning to feel the soreness of being bedridden. I needed to get out of here.

"He has over five thousand in his daily checking account." I heard tapping on Laurie's end of the phone. Her fingers were on a keyboard. "And he has some other assets with one of the local investment companies totaling nearly fifty thousand labeled "Retirement." In his other bank accounts, he has a hundred thousand in two of them and ninety-seven thousand in another."

I whistled. "That means our boy is about to open his fourth bribery account soon. He's spreading his money around so that he doesn't have more than $100,000 in any one account."

The guard standing watch at my hospital room poked his head around the door and mouthed that someone was coming.

"Laurie, I have to go. Anything else?"

I hoped it wasn't Streeter. He'd have my ass.

"No wife. No kids. Modest home. He's living within his means from his government job for sure."

"Not drawing attention to himself," I said. "Smart."

Streeter Pierce came into the room, talking with my doctor.

Laurie continued, "He doesn't do much. He does his job during the week and watches television at night. He works like a dog on Saturdays leaning on people and is a major couch potato on Sundays. I'll bet you he does the same thing this weekend. A pretty predictable and routine sort of guy, if you ask me."

"You're probably right," I agreed.

The doctor stood by my bed and folded her arms across her chest. She was annoyed at me. I mouthed "one second" and held up a finger. Streeter scowled.

"If he's truly retiring in four years, and he's building a secret nest egg that he doesn't want anyone to find out about, do you think he'd risk picking up new customers in his operation so late in the game?"

"No, ma'am. I think he has all he wants for right now." I tried to keep my words to a minimum.

"So what about Ridgewood? And your brother?"

The doctor glared at the clock. Maybe she'd be so pissed she wouldn't let me go home.

"I'll let you know when I see him on Tuesday. I'll give him a hug for you, Mom."

"*Mom?*" Laurie asked. "Is Streeter there?"

"Absolutely. Gotta go. Call you back." I ended the call and glanced up at Streeter and shrugged. "My mother. She wants me to call her after I have dinner with Ole tomorrow night."

"You're not going to Fort Collins tomorrow." His voice sounded like a lawnmower had discovered a horseshoe.

"The hell I'm not."

The doctor cleared her throat.

"Doc, can I go home now? Please?"

She finally smiled. "Everything does appear safe for you to go home. But we'd like you to stay at least until tomorrow morning."

"Tomorrow? Why?"

"We'd prefer to watch you another night, particularly since you haven't hit the twenty-four-hour mark yet. Concussions can have delayed consequences. We want to make sure you are all right. Plus you indicated on the admission paperwork that you live alone."

I exchanged a glance with Streeter, who flashed me a crooked grin. I noticed his eyes were steely and focused. All work. No pleasure. Damn it.

"So the discharge order will come tomorrow morning during my early rounds."

I was not happy. "What about Beulah?"

The doctor cocked her head, curious.

"Her bloodhound." Streeter touched the doctor's elbow. I envied the woman. "Which I'll handle. Thank you, doctor."

She left, calling back over her shoulder, "You two have a good night."

I gathered the blanket around me and slid down under the covers.

Streeter walked slowly to my bedside, sat on the edge of my bed, and pried my fingers off the blanket. At first, I resisted. Then I figured, what the hell. I let him tug the covers off me, revealing that I was fully dressed, ready to go—shoes and all.

"Seriously?" he asked. "You thought you could fool us by slipping a hospital gown over your shirt?"

"Streeter, I—"

"Don't 'Streeter' me. Now strip. Get back into that gown. And be a good patient. Please."

I could hear the guard outside my room laughing, and I pointed to the doorway. "Is that really necessary?"

"Absolutely. Until we figure out what this is all about. Even when you go home."

I leaned into him and whispered, "But can't you be my protection? Sleep with me?"

He closed his eyes, bussed my right cheek, and moaned softly. "You know there's nothing I'd rather do."

I sighed, leaned back in my bed, and crossed my arms. "When the doctor releases me, do you mind if the bodyguard escorts me home to gather my things for Fort Collins? Because I'm headed there tomorrow afternoon. I have work to do Wednesday morning."

He hesitated. Then he said, "I'll make it happen."

I was surprised by his answer. I thought he'd fight me. But he didn't.

Before he left, he dropped a small tube of toothpaste and a real toothbrush on my bed, along with a pack of M&M's. My hero.

I stared at my bounty for longer than I realized, when I noticed it was 5:30 and panicked. I punched numbers into my cell.

"Laurie? Oh good. I thought you'd left."

"You said you'd call back. I was waiting." She was an eight-to-five woman. So her staying this late and being willing to adjust her schedule meant the world to me.

"Listen, you're probably right, and you're the field agent and all. But I was thinking. Maybe Roth's about to retire, has been really careful up until now, and won't be adding new accounts. But what if greed gets the best of him?"

"Could be, Laurie. It would explain Ridgewood. When did the activity in his other three accounts start?"

I heard more tapping on the keyboard.

"One account was opened nearly five years ago." I heard her pause again.

The guard peeked around the corner again and smiled at me. I covered the phone. "My mother."

"Right," he said, flashing me a thumbs-up.

"The other two were both opened over the past two years. The activity seems to have leveled off over the last year with consistent monthly deposits of about twelve to thirteen thousand dollars."

I whistled again. "Nearly $150,000 a year? We're in the wrong business." Laurie chuckled. "True."

Then something struck me. "That means our boy is going to be a millionaire by the time he retires in four years."

Laurie said, "Correction. He would have been a millionaire if he hadn't been caught. By the way, what did Bert Ridgewood have to pay last Tuesday?"

"A thousand." I kicked off my shoes, peeled off my jeans, and removed my shirt. I was leaving my underwear and socks on. Bare feet on floors grossed me out. I folded my clothes and crawled back into bed. My head ached less and less as the day wore on. "And he said Roth comes around every quarter."

She let out a thoughtful hum. "So he's leaning on a dozen or so every quarter? Did I do the math right?"

I calculated. "A hundred and fifty divided by four is thirty-five to forty-thousand divided by say two thousand a year per operator. Yeah, I'd say he's squeezing at least twenty to thirty operators."

"At least. Can you imagine how those operators must feel?"

"Outraged, helpless, dirty, used, embarrassed, and ashamed. Out of control and pissed. Yeah, I can imagine. I got an earful. Ridgewood was livid."

"So was Matt Juzlig."

I looked at the clock. "I'll call them tonight if I can. How many gave you cell phones?"

"All of them. Those are the numbers I gave you."

"Got it."

By 7:30, I had talked to all four of the operators on Laurie's list. Matt Juzlig felt as violated as any rape victim I'd ever interviewed. The others were equally upset. Roth had threatened to shut all of them down if they didn't cooperate. On top of that, he'd convinced them he had a lily-white record with the EPA, an impenetrable reputation, and no court in the land would believe low-life polluters over him.

They believed him.

He'd wedged those operators' asses in a sling, and they couldn't do anything about it. They had to just grin and bear it. And it pissed me off. Not only for the operators as victims, but also that it gave regulators and the EPA a bad name. And I knew how that felt, considering all of us special agents were under scrutiny after what Jenna and Jack had done.

I understood that there were people who chose to do bad things in every business and that no line of work was above reproach from infestation by cockroaches. But for some reason, this guy had a particular knack for getting under my skin. Maybe because he targeted people in an industry I happened to love.

I thought of Ole. There was nothing that could keep me from driving up to Fort Collins tomorrow. Not even Streeter.

I wondered what was wrong with me to be so laser-focused on taking down Dick Roth that I hadn't even thought about the guy who'd attacked me. Maybe it's because I knew Streeter would be working on that, and there was no way he'd let the perpetrator get away with what he'd done to me.

So I left the grey pickup guy to him while I worked on a strategy to make a solid case against Roth. I placed one more call to a detective friend of mine in the Glenwood Springs PD, so that Juzlig had professional help getting evidence on Dick Roth.

Then I fell asleep dreaming of cuffing the bastard.

CHAPTER 22

STREETER COULD NOT REMEMBER a time when he was as happy as he'd been over the past few days with Liv.

She was everything he'd imagined.

His feelings for her inspired him to work even harder while he looked for the thug who had attacked her. He would find him and make him pay for what he'd done to her. He had all night. She was safe at St. Joe's with a posted guard.

He studied the reports from the DMV that had been sent over earlier: the names and addresses of ten individuals. He narrowed the list down to four possible suspects and, addresses in hand, he drove the streets of the greater Denver area, finding the locations and checking them out personally.

The first house had no car in the driveway. Maybe it was in the garage. He could see an elderly white couple through the front picture window of the house, so he drove toward the next—while he thought of Liv.

She was warm, caring, witty, and wonderfully genuine. She'd renewed his youth, faith, and love after decades of solitude and loneliness. The past weekend was absolutely perfect. Whether it was their time together at his cabin in Conifer, or several weeknights at Liv's apartment in Denver, it didn't matter where they were—they never had enough time to talk. And touch. And learn.

The fall nights were cool and still, cloudless and full of stars. During the week, they'd enjoyed each other's company as they prepared meals together, cleaned the dishes, and took Beulah on strolls along city sidewalks.

Over the weekend, they took easy hikes in the Rocky Mountains. He worried about this time of year, being on the heels of serious rattlesnake season. And he worried about her changing her mind about him—running away after realizing it was far too soon after Jack's death.

But she hadn't, and she appeared to be as happy as he was. He couldn't help but notice how her happiness painted her in an even more beautiful light than she already was—which he didn't think possible.

Liv meant everything to him in a different way than Paula had. It was hard not to compare them, and Paula had meant the world to him, too. Their life together had been brief and preoccupied with achieving goals. Now he'd allowed himself to dream of how his and Liv's lives could be someday.

Paula and Liv were very different from each another. But so was he— he'd changed with age. He appreciated precious moments of togetherness and intimacy much more than he had in his younger years—whether they were walking hand in hand or he was gazing into her sea-green eyes that danced with life and understood his thoughts.

Streeter absolutely, and without hesitation or condition, loved Liv Bergen and had loved her for quite some time. He vowed to never take his time with her for granted.

He pulled into the second neighborhood and found an old car in the driveway of the house. It was the right license, but the wrong car—not a grey beater, as Liv had called it.

He drove on through the night.

Work had not been the same since Liv had kissed him last Monday night. He frequently found his thoughts preoccupied with tender memories of her during their late nights together out on his deck drinking coffee and listening to the orchestra of nocturnal wildlife. He had shared thoughts with her that he'd never uttered to another human being—not even Paula. They hadn't been apart for a moment since—until she decided to go home last night. He didn't know why he felt so uncharacteristically comfortable with her. He felt she was safe somehow, and his trust in her was unconditional. He knew she would never repeat his words, and his faith in her allowed him—for the first time in his life—to let down his guard completely.

He thought about the emotional freedom he felt with her. She hadn't pried, yet she had an insatiable hunger to know everything about him. He chuckled at the thought of how she managed to pry out of him that he'd never worn a costume as a kid trick-or-treating and how much that idea seemed to bother her—like he'd been cheated somehow out of childhood.

He, too, hungered to know everything about her. The more she shared with him, the more he needed to hear. Meaningless tidbits, like how her mother sewed all nine of the Bergen kids' costumes each year and that Liv's favorite time was when they were all dressed as clowns. Maybe he *had* missed out on something in his childhood.

In the short time they'd spent together, he'd realized how perfect they were for one another and how foolish he'd been for not pursuing her sooner. He couldn't even remember what it was that had made him resist her. It didn't matter now. They were together.

He turned right on the street of the third address, and his gaze instantly landed on the F150 grey pickup truck. It was a beater. He cruised past, verified the license, and called in for backup.

Within fifteen minutes, he and Phil Kelleher were on the front porch knocking on the door.

The man who opened the door was exactly as Liv described.

"Julius Chavez?"

"Who wants to know?"

Streeter flashed his credentials. "Special Agent Pierce. Mind if we come in?"

"Shit." He turned his back to them and walked slowly to his recliner. The door was open. His hands were visible.

Streeter exchanged a glance with Kelleher, and they both followed.

He scanned the room. There were no pictures on the wall just a single crucifix—Catholic; one recliner, occupied by Chavez; one dirty couch; a TV tray; and a television. It was an old-fashioned one with an antennae with aluminum foil balled up on the rabbit-ear ends. It felt like they'd been dropped back in time.

"This your parents' house?" Streeter guessed. "Are they home?"

"Dead," he said.

Streeter sat on the couch. Kelleher chose to stand. He probably didn't want to get anywhere near that filthy couch, and Streeter couldn't blame him. He was particular about his suits and germophobic.

Streeter grabbed the remote from the TV tray and muted the set. "Where were you last night?"

Chavez bunched his shoulders to his ears. "Nowhere. Turn it back on, man. I'm missing my game."

It was preseason Monday night football. He was watching the Broncos pummel the Patriots.

"Look, it's getting late." Streeter hoped his compromising tone didn't belie his true desire to beat the mess out of this guy. "How about telling us who hired you, and we'll leave you to your game."

Chavez cut a glance toward Streeter. "Hired me to do what?"

"Follow that woman last night to her apartment."

Streeter noticed a tremor in Chavez's right foot. He was nervous. "Need a smoke to help you remember?"

The walls had a dingy yellow tint and the odor of permeated smoke seeping from the drywall, indicating several chain smokers had lived here.

"Maybe. Yeah." Chavez reached for his pocket. Both agents reached for their guns. Chavez held out his hands in surrender. "Hey man, you offered. I'm just getting a cig from my pocket, okay?"

Streeter nodded as the guy fished a stick from the box in his breast pocket. He popped it between his lips.

"Now my lighter." Hands up in surrender, he pointed to his pants.

Neither agent removed his hand from the butt of his service weapon. But this time, both nodded.

Chavez reached into his right front jeans pocket and retrieved a lighter with a white skull etched on the metal frame. He flicked three times before the flame stayed lit and slipped the lighter back in his pocket.

Both agents slowly released their ready positions. Chavez relaxed with each inhale.

The tremor in his leg slowed.

Streeter waited.

Chavez drained his beer. "Want one?"

Both agents refused to respond.

He drew a few more pulls on his cigarette before tapping off ashes. "Your loss. Who is she to you?"

"A coworker," Streeter said.

"He never told me she was a cop."

"Not a cop. An agent. FBI."

He mumbled a string of curses that were meant for someone else.

Streeter held his gaze. "Want to tell us who 'he' is? Who hired you—so you can get back to your game?"

"I am so screwed." He leaned back in his chair, sucked on his cigarette, and lay still for a long time staring at the ceiling. "I'm dead either way."

Streeter agreed. No matter what, he wanted to see this guy dead, even if he had to kill Chavez himself. Instead, he asked, "How's that?"

"My job was to shadow her. Follow her. Confirm her patterns. Her address." He sat up and stubbed out his cigarette. "I didn't know she was with the FBI, so I'm a dead man walking with you two."

"And if your boss finds out you killed her?" Streeter noticed Kelleher cut a glance his way, hoped Chavez hadn't noticed.

All the color in his face drained. "She's dead? Not again. Ah, man. I am truly screwed."

He slapped his hand over his eyes.

"Again?"

The guy lowered his hand, straightened in his chair, and hung his head. "In the ring. I killed a man, but I didn't mean to. It's why I hung up my boxing gloves. For good."

Streeter glanced over at Kelleher, warning him to stay quiet. "Your boss. How much did he pay you?"

The man leaned back and appeared defeated. "Five hundred up front and another five when I confirmed."

"Last night? Or this morning?" Streeter narrowed the scope of the investigation quickly through his interrogation.

"Last night. But he never showed." He shook his head, visibly upset.

"Tell me about his plan."

"I was supposed to have the information to him Friday, but I only got a few shots of her coming and going from work. So I didn't get the rest of the information he was looking for. And I didn't put eyes on her until last night. She was at some guy's house all weekend."

Streeter shot another glance at Kelleher. No reaction.

"He told me where to look for her car and gave me several addresses to check out. I finally found her in the mountains at an address that he'd told me would be the least likely place to find her but an option. She was there."

This was *his* house. This guy was hired by someone who knew his address. Streeter's gut twisted. He knew exactly what this was about. It was about him, not Liv. "So you followed her."

He nodded. "She's dead? Seriously? I killed an agent?"

His foot trembled—then his knee, then his entire leg. Instinctively, he reached for another cigarette. And the agents instantly reached for their guns.

"Give us another minute before you light up again." Streeter acted like he was wrapping up. "One more thing. Who hired you?"

Chavez shrugged. "I never met him before. I answered a personal ad on Craig's list."

"But you did meet him. You saw him. What'd he look like?"

"Yeah, last Wednesday. He looked rich. A suit. How the hell do I know?" He threw up his hands in exasperation.

Streeter laced the fingers of his hands, scooted toward the edge of the couch, and shifted his weight to the balls of his feet. He wanted so badly to punch this guy in the mouth. "Try harder. Race. Height. Build. Hair color."

"I told you, I don't know. I need a cigarette."

Streeter sprang to his feet and snatched Chavez from his chair. He pinned the man like a moth to the bare wall. His fist wrapped tightly around Chavez's collar and bunched it tight. He pushed against his chest while his other hand whipped out his handgun. Then he pressed the barrel against Chavez's temple.

"Try harder."

Chavez's eyes went wild. He panicked. He couldn't breathe. He wriggled beneath Streeter's grip.

Kelleher stepped up beside Streeter. "Easy."

Streeter let loose of the man's shirt. Chavez coughed and grabbed at his throat.

"Let him talk," Kelleher urged.

Chavez's stare bounced between him and Kelleher. "The guy was white. My height—maybe taller . . . soft . . . all shiny. Gold rings on every finger. A ginger."

"A name," Streeter growled.

"I. Don't. Know." His eyes grew hard as he glared back at Streeter.

"He doesn't know," Kelleher repeated.

Streeter cocked his revolver. "Then I don't need him anymore."

"Vic. The guy's name is Vic." Spittle flew from Chavez's nervous lips. "That's all I know."

Streeter released the hammer and lowered the gun. "The SIG."

"What?"

He threw his hands up in surrender when Streeter again pressed the barrel against his forehead. "Where is it? The gun you stole last night."

Chavez's eyes slid over to the recliner. Streeter slammed him up against the wall and let him crumple to the floor. When Streeter darted for the chair, Kelleher stepped in and stood over Chavez, his service weapon trained on his chest. Streeter slid his hand between the cushion and the armrest on the right side of the chair and pulled out Liv's gun, stuffed it in the waistband of his khakis, and tightened plasticuffs onto Chavez's wrists.

Kelleher helped him lift the thug off the floor. "Julius Chavez, you're under arrest for assault and battery of a federal agent. Read him his rights before I kill the bastard."

Streeter left Kelleher with Chavez as he rushed out the front door to cool off. The night air was brisk and fresh. He drew in a breath and told himself not to go back into that house; not to punch him liked he'd hit Liv. Instead, he focused on recounting everything he'd just learned from this creep.

Within a half hour, they were back at the bureau, with Chavez in federal custody.

It had been one of the longest Mondays on record. Or at least it felt that way. Streeter needed some sleep. Instead, he settled for stale coffee and a quick retreat to his office while Kelleher processed the criminal.

Case files, mail, phone messages, and piles of work loomed on his cluttered desk. For the first time in his career, he'd blown off work over the past week and had done virtually nothing—besides Liv—since last Monday. He didn't regret a single consequence from his choice. She was worth it.

He wasn't sure if he wanted to address any of this work or tackle the piles of neglected mail, intercompany memos, or caseloads. Then he sighed. If he knocked out some of the tasks, he'd have more time for Liv when she was released.

The first thing he did was check his cell phone to see if he had any messages from her, but there was nothing, which hopefully meant she was fast asleep. He sent a text to the police guard on duty, inquiring about Liv's condition. The officer quickly responded that she was indeed sound asleep in her hospital bed.

Good news. She was healing.

His spirits elevated at the thought of going to Fort Collins with her tomorrow as her personal escort and guard. He just hadn't told her yet. He'd share the news in the morning when he picked her up to take her home and then they could spend the night together in the hotel. He smiled at the thought as he flipped through his stack of phone messages and mail.

One particular envelope caught his eye, and dread filled him as he tore open the ominous envelope. The letter dated last week was simply notifying Streeter that the upcoming parole hearing for Jeremiah Coyote Cries had been delayed.

What parole hearing, he thought? *What have I missed?*

His heart sank. This was a serious consequence of his neglect of his work this week.

He rifled through the rest of the mail and scattered envelopes across the desktop and onto the floor, until he found a similar envelope. He tore it open and read the parole board's letter. It was an invitation for him to join the proceedings scheduled for last Thursday at nine. He looked at the calendar and swore.

Then he looked at the newer letter. The delay was until Tuesday next week at nine.

"Oh my God." Streeter groaned gutturally. He didn't even recognize his own voice. It was animalistic, fearful, and unexpected.

Jeremiah Coyote Cries.

He had almost missed it. If not for the delay, he wouldn't have been there to testify to make sure that monster remained behind bars until he rotted. He thought of Liv and was sickened at the thought of what might have happened to her because of his carelessness.

Next Tuesday. Nine o'clock. He would be there. Nothing would stop him.

Then he remembered an earlier thought he'd had about Liv—that he'd opened up to her about topics he'd never discussed with another human being. He'd shared all his innermost thoughts—except this. There were still secrets left to share and demons to exorcise. He would tell her tomorrow night. He would share everything.

Then a name on the letters caught his eyes.

A name following the cc: at the bottom of the page. It was the name of an attorney—for Coyote Cries.

Victor Webber.

Streeter spun toward his computer, searched for the attorney's name, and saw the image of a soft, rich lawyer with red hair, a suit, and gold rings on every finger.

Vic.

Streeter slammed his fist on the desk.

Liv's attack *was* all about him.

About Coyote Cries.

Feeling the hot flash of nausea flood his cheeks, he slapped the letters onto his desk and ran for the bathroom. He made it just in time as he upchucked the coffee he'd just drunk. He splashed cool water on his face and looked at himself in the mirror. His eyes were wild and distant. His hands were trembling.

He gripped the sides of the cool porcelain sink and locked his elbows, allowing his head to sag between his tense shoulder blades. Unaware of how long he'd been standing there, he was startled when a hand reached out and touched his shoulder.

He spun around, nearly jumping out of his skin.

"What's the matter?" Phil Kelleher asked. "You look like you've seen a ghost."

Streeter caught his breath and forced a smile on his lips. "Long day."

He released his grip on the sink and walked past Kelleher.

"You're a bit shaky," he offered quietly. "What's happened?"

Streeter saw the concern in Kelleher's stare, but instinct told him to keep quiet until he could understand more about what was happening. He needed to find control and balance before endangering others.

"Is there something I can do?"

It was then that Streeter's plan began to formulate. "Would you mind escorting Liv to Fort Collins tomorrow if you can spare tomorrow and Wednesday?"

Kelleher nodded. "Like old times."

CHAPTER 23

STREETER'S SLEEP WAS FITFUL.

Thoughts of Paula, his life as a young adult, and his days on his first assignment in Rapid City, South Dakota, came flooding back to him like a long-lost home movie. A horror movie.

As the painful and distant memories resurrected themselves, his insecurities and indecision about how to explain to Liv what was happening also sprang to life. His reaction to the letter and being sickened at the mention of Jeremiah Coyote Cries's name revived his grief for Paula.

It was an instant recollection of suppressed memories of finding the mutilated remains of his once beautiful wife.

He had thrown up so many times that evening twenty years ago when he saw her in their Denver apartment that he eventually went from regurgitation to dry heaves to throwing up blood. The shock and horror of it all had nearly killed him. Only the anger and the need for revenge had motivated him to stay alive.

The blood coursed through his veins so intensely after finding her body that his heart pounded with hatred and his face reddened with fury every time he thought of it. His thick, brown hair had turned stark white—overnight. His sole focus had become finding the demon who had murdered his wife.

Coyote Cries changed Streeter's life forever and brought a darkness to his world that was colder and more blinding than anything he could have ever imagined. Even his combat experience in the Special Forces as a US Marine paled in comparison to what he had witnessed and suffered with his wife's brutal murder.

He had finally earned a peaceful sleep this past week, but now he was being plunged into his haunted past with the permanent reminders of the evil that existed through those damned letters. The monster was eligible for parole. He couldn't let that happen, and he had to decide where Liv fit into all this blackness. It was smothering him and permeating his nostrils and heart.

On one hand, Streeter could not imagine how the correctional system could possibly consider parole for such an evil human being or what possible reason they could use to justify even the most remote possibility for his release. On the other hand, he realized that times had changed, and criminals who had been convicted for drug trafficking were granted much lighter sentences than Coyote Cries had already served.

If the parole board freed Coyote Cries, Streeter had no trouble imagining the thrill the lowlife would get out of further torturing him through Liv if he discovered her importance to him—which he probably already had through Julius Chavez and his attorney, Victor Webber.

How could this be happening?

The man was pure evil, and he blamed Streeter for his incarceration. Even though Coyote Cries totally devastated Streeter by murdering his beloved wife, he would not be above continuing the excruciatingly painful war that he had waged against Streeter decades ago. Death by a thousand cuts. It wasn't over.

Streeter was rightfully concerned about Liv's safety, especially considering the barbaric way Coyote Cries had taken his revenge before he was imprisoned. He had to decide if the chances of Coyote Cries being released were worth risking the love, trust, and happiness he had finally found with Liv. He couldn't bear the thought of Coyote Cries touching her. He would rather die first.

His only option was to end the relationship with Liv for her own protection. He had to be convincing, and he had to do it swiftly before anyone learned of his feelings for her. He would have to figure out a way to stop Coyote Cries from finding her. He'd pay a visit to Victor Webber first thing in the morning before the lawyer passed on anything to his client that Chavez had learned about Liv.

He seethed and shuddered. Squeezing his eyes closed, he laid his hand on Beulah's head. She lay beside him on the big feather tick comforter. She breathed heavily as he scratched behind her ear.

How could he possibly say goodbye to Liv? Convincingly?

He didn't want to let go.

Why did he allow Coyote Cries to have such a visceral effect on him? Why hadn't he killed the man when he'd had the opportunity?

If he had, Paula would still be alive. And Liv would be safe.

He had let them both down.

He covered his eyes and rubbed. He answered his own question and reminded himself that life was only ten percent of what happened to him and ninety percent of how he reacted to it. That was how he had always survived challenges.

The upcoming parole hearing would be held in the administrative offices in Littleton next to the Englewood Federal Correctional Institution next week on Tuesday at nine o'clock.

He rehearsed the testimony that he'd be giving at that hearing. He would vehemently request the board deny Coyote Cries's parole. He would list not only his numerous criminal activities as a teenager and young adult but also the laundry list of inhumane treatment he had inflicted on many of the people at the Pine Ridge Indian Reservation, on the federal agents, and on his own dear wife—the innocent.

Certainly, the parole board could not possibly recommend this criminal for conditional release once they saw the cold, black evil that lurked in his eyes. Certainly, they wouldn't. He glanced at the clock. It was four in the morning.

He would go to the hospital.

And end this.

Streeter arrived at Liv's hospital room shortly after six.

She was awake, staring out her window. She hadn't heard him come in.

"Hey," she said, smiling when he stepped into view.

"Morning." His heart was heavy. Kissing her tentatively on the cheek, he said, "Sorry it's so early."

Liv stared at him with concern. "I was awake. Good timing. It's shift change."

The thought suddenly occurred to him that Liv was from South Dakota and so was Coyote Cries. He shuddered at the thought of them ever having crossed paths when she was just a young girl and shifted uncomfortably to shake off the sudden chill that danced down his spine.

"Is something wrong?"

"We arrested the guy who attacked you. His name is Julius Chavez. He said he was paid to verify where you lived. So I've assigned full-time police protection for you at home and at work."

She grinned and grabbed his hand. "Are you going to be my bodyguard? Round the clock?"

He slid his hand free and turned his back to her. He couldn't lie directly to her face. "Liv, about that. It was fun, but we really shouldn't have. I'd like to put all that in the past and forget it ever happened."

She said nothing. He could feel her stare boring into the back of his head trying to read him.

He continued with his lies. "It's just not for me. I took advantage of you after Jack's death. I was just feeling sorry for myself losing Jenna." That was total lie. There was nothing between him and Jenna Tate.

"I've turned over your case to Phil Kelleher. He'll be coordinating your protection. He'll be here to escort you home today and then to Fort Collins. He'll accompany you on your case tomorrow, and he'll also be responsible for the police protection until we can get this case sorted out."

"Now I'm a case?" Pain dripped from each word.

"Liv, the last week has been fun, and you're a wonderful girl . . ." He didn't turn to see her reaction. "But all good things must come to an end."

She said nothing.

"I just don't want anyone to get hurt here. You're such a nice young woman. And I'm just a stubborn, old man. I'm set in my ways. And I love my life as a bachelor. I just don't want you to get any ideas about us."

He had rehearsed a line where he depicted himself as a salty old playboy, but he knew no one would buy that story. Especially Liv. So, he had settled on the "I want to be alone" routine and hoped she'd believe it.

"What are you saying?" Liv finally asked quietly.

"I'm saying it would really be best for both of us if you would take that job that Doonsberg offered you," he said as evenly as he could manage. "Kelleher has your ticket to DC for your official interview and transfer to CID. It's all arranged this week."

They had shared with one another all the offers that had been made and their thoughts through the decision-making process, both admitting their choices had depended on one another. To tell her to take the offer in DC truly signaled it was over and that he wasn't going anywhere. He hadn't expected her reply.

"But I love you."

Streeter's heart broke into a million pieces. He resisted the urge to spin around and embrace her, abandon all this malarkey, and tell her he loved her, too. He struggled to control his breathlessness and the lump that rose in his throat. Knowing it would be one of the most hurtful things he could ever say to her, he managed to feign a chuckle. "Don't be silly. You don't even know me."

He'd said it—cruelly and deliberately. He hoped the words would make her hate him and that they were words that might save her from Coyote Cries's wrath. If someday the threat of his demon's release from prison no longer existed, then he trusted Liv would find it in her heart to forgive him and take him back. But he didn't hold out much hope. He knew he'd wounded her deeply with his deliberate message filled with coolness and disrespect.

Her words sounded squeezed from her throat. "No, I guess I don't. I didn't mean to offend you. I apologize."

Streeter turned around and took her hand in his and patted it clumsily. "Apology accepted, but really it's not necessary. I just want you to realize that I have had a most enjoyable time with you. Maybe we can see each other again sometime—maybe the next time I'm in DC. You'll make one hell of an agent for CID. They'll be lucky to have you."

Streeter knew Liv was one of the most open and honest people he had ever met, but he hadn't anticipated the question that followed. He had expected anger, tears, apathy, something other than how she responded.

Almost childlike, she asked sincerely, "What did you mean when you said you never wanted to let me go?"

He swallowed hard. He turned away from her and started for the door. "Just a term of endearment. A line. What can I say?"

"Oh," she choked.

Seeing her from the corner of his eye, he knew his plan had worked. He had devastated her, and he'd hated doing it.

He reminded himself that it was for her own safety. But he couldn't take one more minute of this. "Look, I have to run. Everything's okay here, isn't it? We can still be friends?"

He saw her nodding slowly, her arms limp at her sides.

It took everything he had to keep walking away, not to turn back, to tell her it was all a lie. To protect her.

He made two quick phone calls on her behalf: one to Phil Kelleher and a second to the man he knew would die protecting her.

He made it out to his car, climbed in, and laid his head on the steering wheel.

CHAPTER 24

I WEPT.

I tried to cry as quietly as I could into my hospital pillow. I didn't want a nurse or the officer by my door rushing in to comfort me.

I was hurting. But I didn't need medical care or protection.

Just all the king's horses and men to put my heart back together again. It had suffered greatly.

It felt like an old wound that had barely healed had been ripped back open. One of Cupid's jagged arrows was poking around inside again. Only this time it was deeper. Not closer to, but in my heart.

What is happening to me? When did I become so vulnerable?

For most of my life, I'd had complete control over my emotions and had never once been accused of flightiness or superficiality. And it wasn't like I'd ever allowed myself the luxury of grasping for attention, school-girl crushes, or human contact through one-night stands.

It just wasn't me.

So what was I thinking this past week? Have I lost my frigging mind? Who have I become, wallowing around in this ocean of pain and sorrow?

I had convinced myself that what Streeter and I had for the past several days was powerful and meaningful—much more for me than for him, clearly. I was normally such a great judge of character. I never once considered Streeter to be an opportunist or casual about anything relating to the human heart.

Was I blind with grief? How did I let this happen?

Then I realized I wasn't thinking clearly enough to properly assess this new information. Streeter's blow had left me too wounded not to be blinded by my pain.

Deal with all this later, I told myself. Much later.

I closed my eyes. I focused on the timing of monitored beats to slow the tempo of inhales and exhales. I controlled my breathing. I lay still and replayed his words over and over—stunned, for what seemed like hours. Until Phil Kelleher arrived.

His voice scattered my thoughts. Deep, even, monotone. "I was instructed to give you a ride to your apartment after the doctor releases you. Then, I'm to escort you to Fort Collins for the evening."

I swiped at my face with the back of my free hand as if I'd been sleeping, making it appear that my tear-stained cheeks blossomed red from slumber rather than sorrow.

"Thanks. I must have dozed off. I'm still waiting for my doctor to come by during her early rounds."

I scooted up in my bed and grimaced from the pain.

He must have noticed. "You okay? Need help?"

I tenderly touched my forehead. "I'm okay. Actually, there's something you can do. Would you mind stepping out for a minute while I get dressed?"

His left eyebrow arched.

He nodded once and left my room, closing the door behind him.

I scooted to the edge of the bed, careful not to tangle the IV tubes. I lifted the nearly empty saline solution bag off the hook and squeezed it like a sausage through the sleeve of my blouse and hung it back on the rack. I slid on my pants, socks, and shoes, straightened the covers of my bed, and sat in the recliner next to the window.

Within seconds of finishing, the door swung open without a knock. The doctor's expression seemed even less amused than yesterday afternoon. Apparently, she wasn't happy with whatever Phil had told her, because she burst into the room with an expression so sour it was as if someone had squeezed a lemon on her chapped ass.

"Most impatient patient I've ever had," the doctor scolded. "I said I'd consider your release today. I didn't promise."

"I have to get back to work, Doc," I said.

"You don't have to do anything except rest and heal. You're not taking this seriously." She lifted the stethoscope to my heart and listened. I remained quiet until she pulled away.

"I am taking this seriously. I take everything seriously." I couldn't help cutting a glance Phil's way, soliciting some support for my claims.

He didn't offer anything.

She went about her assessment without another word. She checked my vitals, my eyes, my reflexes, and read the charts and notes from overnight. She removed the bandage and examined my stitches and then instructed the nurse to replace the dressing.

Before she was done, I explained, "I'll do whatever you ask. You can trust me." She caught my glance. "I just can't take one more minute in here. Please. Too much time to think."

She hesitated and seemed to consider my request. She clearly knew about Jack and about the sabbatical the bureau had forced me to take.

She finished bandaging, wrote some notes on my chart, and handed the clipboard to the assisting nurse. She sighed. "Alright, Agent Bergen. You win. I'll release you but only to the care of Agent Kelleher for the next twenty-four hours."

I smiled, and he drew in a deep breath, as if the responsibility for me was the weightiest he'd ever carried. I rolled my eyes.

"But that means every minute during the next twenty-four hours. You understand?"

I nodded.

"No exceptions. No excuses. No cajoling, convincing, or arguing." She turned from me to Phil. "Don't listen to any of her BS. She is not well enough, and her body doesn't know better than I do as her doctor. Keep her movements to a minimum. She needs lots of rest and quiet activities."

"You do know she's—"

I cut Phil off. "That I'm going straight home from here. That's where Phil is taking me."

"Good." The doctor eyed me suspiciously and exchanged looks with me and Phil. "Then you are officially free to go home. The nurse will complete your discharge papers, and she'll have you on your way."

My grin widened.

"Not so fast. The nurse will go through your 'At Home Care' information that you will *both* need to sign." The doctor stared at me and then at Phil.

He sighed again, audibly pained. "A moonbeam in my hand."

That earned a slight smile from the doc. "Agreed. But you're up to the challenge."

We were headed toward the bank of elevators in no time. No way would I admit how dizzy I was. And how much my head pounded with every step I took.

Phil took me straight home from St. Joe's Hospital and refused to wait for me in the car. I had not only wanted to shower in privacy but also to call my sister to cry on her shoulder for a minute and get her advice about how to fix the mess I'd obviously created with Streeter. But Phil remained close on my heels like my shadow, waiting for me in the living room while I showered and packed in the rooms nearby.

Beulah was nowhere to be seen. And neither were her lead or harness. Streeter had told me he'd take care of her, and he had.

Within minutes I was packed, and we were on the road headed to Fort Collins.

On the long drive north, I tried to remain focused on the case—on Dick Roth and the plan for tomorrow; not on Streeter. Only once did I press Phil for some answers.

"What happened? To Streeter's wife twenty years ago?"

I noticed his lips purse and his fingers tighten on the wheel.

After he said nothing for many moments, I asked, "Why is it such a secret?"

"It's not a secret. It's a mystery. Only Streeter knows the real story. He's never talked about it, Liv. And we all must respect that." He was right, of course. But I didn't want to hear it.

"What *can* you tell me?"

"His wife was killed. Murdered in their apartment."

I waited for a long moment. I thought that I could outlast him. But I couldn't. "Come on, Phil. A little help here."

He said nothing.

We drove the rest of the way in silence.

Just as we arrived at the hotel, he added, "And he was devastated."

That part, I knew.

Upon Phil's insistence, Ole and I were going to eat at the hotel restaurant, which was sad. Fort Collins had so many great places to eat. And I was stuck here. I waited for Ole in the lobby. When he approached the doors, I rushed him, shouting, "Dismas!"

I hugged my brother for a long time—maybe to avoid his judgment once he had a good look at my face, and maybe because I just needed a hug from home. Maybe because my short jaunt over to him caused some serious warbling of my mind. I really wasn't well enough to do this. But I had to. For my own sanity.

Ole was my limestone, the single rock representing our family business. He was just like Dad—a literal chip off the old block. I had found a piece of limestone with a corner still barely attached. I let it fall on its own over time, metaphorically representing that my brother was born of my dad and had eventually separated from him to become his own rock-solid self.

He pulled away from me. "Genevieve? Are you okay?"

I glanced back to find Phil. "Ole, I want you to meet Special Agent Phil Kelleher."

"I've heard a lot about you," my brother said.

Phil raised an eyebrow. "I'm not Streeter Pierce."

"Aren't you the agent who stayed with my sister when our employee was murdered in Fort Collins last year? Before she became an agent?"

My brother was correct. And he had a fabulous memory.

I noticed Phil smile.

"Thank you, by the way, for keeping her alive and out of trouble." Ole shook Phil's hand. "That's a huge accomplishment."

Phil waved his hands in surrender. "You're welcome. But I cannot promise you miracles. There isn't a soul on the planet who could keep this young lady out of trouble."

"True," my brother said. "Want to join us for dinner?"

Phil declined. "But I will eat at the same time you two dine to keep an eye on her."

My brother chuckled.

"He means keep an eye out for me. Not on me." I was not liking where this was going.

Phil said, "Have it your way, Agent Bergen."

He swept his arm to allow us to be seated first. Then he selected a table for one out of earshot but close enough to protect me, if needed. I thought it was rather ridiculous. I was safe with Ole. Safe in Fort Collins.

"Is he here because of that?" Ole asked, pointing to the bandage on my head.

"Everything's been blown out of proportion."

"Sure. And does Mom know?"

I shook my head, which only brought stars fluttering into my vision. "But she did send me roses. As a welcome home."

"Yellow."

I nodded.

"You're having a streak of bad luck. Sure you don't want to come back and work with me?" His eyes shone like cobalt.

I knew he was deeply concerned about me and offered him a smile.

We ordered dinner and drinks. I drained a Coors Light and ordered a second. We caught up on work, what was happening at the Livermore Quarry, and the plan for tomorrow morning when Dick Roth arrived. I explained everything we'd need to do and the care we'd take in capturing evidence.

I thanked him for his help.

My brother reached across the table and grabbed my hand. He'd never done that before. "Genevieve, listen to me just this once. I am truly sorry about what happened to Jack. And I'm worried about you. Can't you reconsider? Working for the bureau has proven to be dangerous—even deadly."

He'd never talked so seriously to me about anything besides business. His honesty brought out mine. "The truth is I don't care. About the danger,

I mean. Or even the deadly. I love my job. I'm happier than I've ever been. And I'm pretty good at what I do."

I thought about the ticket to DC.

I noticed him glance up at my bandage.

"Most of the time," I added.

I almost told him that Streeter had transferred me to CID to be safer. But I didn't. I hadn't even begun to wrap my mind around what had happened earlier this morning yet. What Streeter had said to me; what he'd done to me. He bought me a fricking one-way ticket, without even asking my opinion about working for Doonsberg as an intel agent.

"Be honest. What happened?"

"A guy was paid to follow me, to confirm my address. But I startled him. He panicked and clocked me on the noggin. That simple."

He arched an eyebrow.

I jerked my chin in Phil's direction. "And I've had round-the-clock police protection ever since. Until we can figure this all out."

"I'm just worried that— "

Suddenly, a flash temporarily blinded me. Ole stopped mid-sentence, stunned by the man who'd rapidly approached our table—a photographer or a journalist.

Phil was right behind him by only milliseconds. And then he was escorting him away, probably interrogating him, and forcing him to delete the photo.

My brother across from me appeared stunned.

"This is about the case where Jack was killed. Apparently, the story has gone a little crazy, viral, since I've been gone."

"I've heard. That's all the employees could talk about today, last week, the week before that. You've become quite the celebrity. Some people have been approached to sell photos of you for lots of money."

My mouth hung open.

"Don't worry. Not one has sold you out."

My heart swelled with pride. Great people. The best coworkers ever. I knew they'd have my back.

He finished his beer and pushed his plate aside. "I don't know how you handle all this stress. I couldn't do it."

When we got up to leave, I hugged him again.

He sighed when he let me go and said, "As hard as it is for the rest of us to stand by and watch, just be you."

That was the nicest thing he'd ever said to me.

CHAPTER 25

NOTHING ANYONE COULD SAY or do would stand in the way of Streeter protecting Liv.

Not his boss, not his badge, and not his conscience. Not this time.

He wouldn't let Coyote Cries get away with this.

His first order of business was to find out why Vic Webber had hired Julius Chavez to follow Liv and what he had told the beast behind bars. Streeter crouched behind the wheel of his car and stared at the locked office doors of *Victor C. Webber, Attorney at Law*. The sun was rising and had begun to climb.

He glanced at his dashboard clock. It was just before nine.

How late did attorney's sleep, anyway? Forget banker's hours.

If Webber didn't show in the next few minutes, he'd head for his home in Washington Park. He should have gone there in the first place and surprised him. But he was closer to his office than his house and had hoped to catch him early at work. Apparently, that was not Webber's style.

He drained the last of his cold coffee and reached for the key. Movement in the corner of his eye made him stop. He cut his glance to his right.

A small black Audi R8 revved into the lot—an expensive vehicle four times pricier than anything Streeter had ever owned.

Must be Webber, he thought.

The driver whipped into a space near the door and a long leg, shapely and bare, extended from the sports vehicle. She was wearing gold high heels.

The buxom redhead adeptly unfolded herself from the car, hands full, bumped the door closed with her hip, and toddled toward the door. She yanked the handle and nearly toppled backward, apparently expecting it to swing open. It didn't. It seemed to be locked tight.

Nearly dropping her purse, she slung the strap back over her shoulder and swung her gaze across the virtually empty parking lot, barely noticing Streeter's car. She frowned, shifted the coffee cup to her other hand, and tried the door again. It was still locked.

She glanced around, removing her oversized sunglasses for a better look, in case she had missed something. Streeter didn't budge. Her gaze skipped over his car, quick and dismissive. Apparently she hadn't noticed it was occupied—by him.

If Webber could pay his employee enough to buy an Audi R8, Streeter could only imagine what vehicle he drove.

She hitched a hip and looked pissed. She wasn't used to being greeted by a locked door. She appeared to be wondering how to handle the situation—one she hadn't dealt with before—judging by her confused expression.

The woman was striking, if a bit heavily painted and fluffed. Coffee in one hand, the large purse—one of those expensive brands—in the other, she gawked a third time around the parking lot, looking for her boss. She stared at her coffee, toddled back to her car, and set the cup on the hood. She hefted the purse to her hip, digging in the bag with her free hand. Then she stopped searching, slung the purse over her shoulder, and scratched the side of her head with her long, painted nails.

Then she rushed to the passenger's side of the Audi and opened the door. Leaning in, nothing but a well-shaped rump extending from the inside, she surfaced with a set of shiny keys—apparently a set she rarely used but kept in her glove compartment. Leaving the car door open, she hurried toward the office, stabbed the lock with her key, and pulled the door open. Her bosom heaved as if she'd exerted more energy than she was accustomed to.

She walked back to her car, replaced the keys, and closed the passenger door. She retrieved her purse, then her coffee, and she disappeared inside. No one else had arrived, and it was nearly 9:15—unless the stripmall-style building had parking in the back.

Perhaps his first instincts about Webber had been right—that he was an early riser. This woman was clearly used to him—or someone—arriving at work long before she did. But he wasn't here this morning. Something was different.

He imagined that Webber worked alone with only this woman as an employee, an assistant to answer phones, type letters, and perhaps perform light legal research for him.

Whatever legal assistants do, he thought.

He watched as the dark space came alive with lights. He grabbed his binoculars and studied the signs on the other doors to either side of *Victor Webber, Attorney at Law*. One was a dentist—Monday through Friday, ten to six; Saturday, ten to noon. The other had no sign. The windows were covered.

Then he focused in on Webber's office.

The redhead stood at the reception desk with her hands on her hips, her head swiveling around the space. She picked up the handset and pushed buttons on the phone. She kept pushing buttons and then hung up. She began to drum her long fingernails against the desk. The placard on the edge of the desk had a brass plate with engraved black letters that read "Tiffany Holden."

Formulating a plan, he stuffed the binoculars back in the case, turned the key in the ignition, and whipped his car through the lot up to the space by her Audi. He noticed her glance up just as he whipped into the parking space.

He hurried out of the car, slammed the door, and rushed into the office.

"Vic, is he here?"

She glanced up. "Who are—"

"Come on, Tiffany. I don't have time for this. Vic said he needed my information right away, and I haven't been able to get a hold of him."

"When did he call you?" She looked pissed.

Streeter had to play this exactly right. "Not since Wednesday. I have some information about the woman he hired me to tail."

Recognition registered on her face. "You're the guy who answered his ad on Craig's list. Chavez?"

I nodded.

"You don't look like a Chavez," she said, the corners of her mouth dipping.

"That's racist of you. I don't have time for this crap. I want my money," Streeter said. "So where is the asshole?"

"I wish I knew," she shrugged. "The asshole stood me up, too. We were supposed to . . . we had a business meeting planned in Vegas on Thursday. And he didn't show."

"At your place? The red-eye flight Thursday night?" Streeter guessed.

She tilted her head. "He told you?"

"He said if we didn't meet up Wednesday night that I was supposed to pick up my package from the front seat of his car last night, after I called to confirm I was coming. He gave me the address. But no return call. And no car."

"That's what I told you. He never showed up Thursday night." She slammed her balled fists against her hips. "Never saw him all weekend."

"Yet no missing person report?"

"Well . . . it's Vic."

"What about yesterday? Was he at work?"

She shrugged. "I don't work on Mondays. It's my day off."

"Wife? Another girlfriend?" Streeter decided to flame her ire.

"It better not be another girlfriend. And the wife's a total bitch. Spends most of her time in Miami." She glanced past his shoulder to the parking lot, looking for Webber.

More cars started to arrive, likely for the dentist office.

"Maybe she flew in unexpectedly."

"Nah, she only flies in on her broom when he needs her for something. She's perfectly content staying far, far away from the asshole." She glanced back to his large office behind her desk. It was clearly empty.

"Did you try him at home? On Franklin?" Streeter hoped he hadn't pushed too far.

"You know about that, too? You're a goddamn unknown from Craig's List. When will he ever learn to shut his trap?" She shook her head and then answered, "Her rule. He can do whatever he wants except not at their house. She's worried about what neighbors will say. So no. I didn't check his house."

Streeter pressed. "Just give me my money."

She slumped into her chair. "I don't have it. Besides, I don't know what he agreed to pay you. Did you confirm where the bitch lives? What she does?"

He bit the inside of his cheek so as not to react to her calling Liv a bitch. "I'll tell Vic everything I know. I'm not leaving here until I have my money. Or Vic."

She seemed unimpressed by his demand—like she'd heard it before. Nor did she find his imposing presence threatening, despite his efforts to appear larger and to sound menacing. Instead, in a calm tone, she said, "I gave him the photos you dropped in the slot Tuesday night and Friday night. But the photos from Friday are still on his desk."

Her eyes jerked to the mail slot in the door. His heart sank. So Vic did receive photos from Chavez—probably of Liv. He waited a beat and leaned across her desk. "This happen a lot? Him skipping out on a deal?"

He realized she'd be far prettier without the mask.

She shook her head and offered a coy smile. "He's a master of delaying payments. But he never skips. Reputation is everything in this business."

He appreciated her honesty and relaxed. "Did you look at the photos?"

She shook her head. "Of course not." Then she winked and leaned forward, whispering. "Very pretty."

So she had opened the envelopes.

He was about to ask more, when she offered, "Good close-ups, too. Vic was happy with your work. And he'll pay. I promise. But you'll have to be patient. This is all too confusing. He never, never misses work. Not one day. Too many people depend on him."

He believed her. She appeared concerned. "Any ideas where I could find him?"

She flipped to his appointment calendar.

Even upside down, it was hard to miss that the calendar was still on last week. And Vic had been scheduled to meet Coyote Cries both on Wednesday and on Thursday. She flipped the page to this week. The first appointment today was a phone call scheduled for nine o'clock with a man whose name he also recognized.

A call Vic had clearly missed—Dan Alcott, a slippery drug felon.

"No clue." Her fingernail slid down the page.

He committed the unfamiliar names to memory. He'd have Laurie look them up and confirm that they were likely all associated with felony convictions or charges that probably needed a defense attorney.

Streeter growled, "Tell Vic I was here and that Julius Chavez is pissed as hell. And that I want my money." He walked toward the door but not before noticing that she barely acknowledged his departure—or his threat. She didn't seem to care. Like she had more important issues to consider.

So did Streeter.

Fifteen minutes later, he was driving north on Franklin Street along the east side of the greenway toward Smith Lake. Just past the elegant boathouse on his left, at the south end of the lake, he scanned to his right for the numbers on the row of expensive houses.

The one with all the trees along the curb was the home he wanted. There was no car in the driveway, and the garage door was closed. Streeter glanced around the neighborhood before getting out of his car and approaching the front door. He rang the doorbell three times—no movement or sound. He glanced in the front windows—nothing out of place.

He stepped back and stared up at the second floor terrace, a deck for the occupants to overlook the lake across the street. He could see nothing up there.

He tried the door. It was locked.

Six newspapers lay scattered on the front porch. He bent down to review one. It had today's date: Tuesday. Which meant the last time Vic was home to retrieve a paper would have been last Wednesday.

He had a bad feeling about this guy. He had either skipped, or he was dead.

He stepped to his right, checking for unlocked windows and doors. Nothing. No sign of a break-in, foul play, or a hasty departure under the cover of darkness. And one of the two cars registered in his name was in the garage.

Vic Webber wasn't here. Where'd he go?

He hadn't spent the weekend away with his girlfriend in Vegas or at her apartment, unless she was lying, covering for him. But the way she had responded this morning when she didn't know he was watching would suggest she didn't know anything either.

He wasn't in the office. And he clearly hadn't been home.

Chavez had told him that Webber had wanted to know Sunday night what he'd found; that he'd called to make the exchange to confirm Liv's address and her routine. He was going to tell Vic more—about how he had panicked and clobbered the woman—after he got his money. But Vic had never shown.

Vic had told Chavez to meet him at a bar west of I-25 on I-70 between Wheat Ridge and Golden. He'd waited at the dive for several hours, tried calling several times, and headed home when the bar closed at midnight.

He'd waited the entire day yesterday, Monday, and had heard nothing from Vic.

Vic was missing. Or running.

He remembered the calendar and placed a call to Laurie Frumpley. "Anything yet?"

She cleared her throat. "All of them are either convicted felons or charged with a felony, awaiting trial."

"Let me guess. Drugs?"

"Or crimes normally associated with dealing drugs, like the illegal use of the telephone, just like you suspected."

Streeter paused. "Have you heard from Liv?" He panicked when Frumpley didn't immediately respond. "Or Kelleher?"

His heart raced. Maybe the news wasn't good about Liv's release. Maybe he was too hard on her.

"She hasn't called. Phil called Bessie about an hour ago to say that he had dismissed police protection and that Liv was in his care."

He let out the breath he was holding and felt thrilled to know she was released and in the competent care of his best agent. He refocused his attention on removing the threat.

"Did you find addresses? Phone numbers?"

"Most of them had something on file." He heard the clacking of keystrokes.

"Any addresses around Golden or Wheat Ridge?" It was a long shot, but worth taking. It was all Streeter had to go on before paying a visit to Coyote Cries in prison—to find out if Vic had visited and provided him with photos. If he had, Streeter would kill them both with his bare hands.

He did not want to have to visit Coyote Cries unless he absolutely had to. He'd rather the element of surprise be on his side. Until then, he'd keep his distance from the scumbag.

"There's one off Lookout Mountain near the park. Must be one of his richer clients. Know where that is? West of Golden?"

He did. "Whose?"

"Daniel Alcott."

"I should have guessed."

After she gave him the address and directions, Streeter was on his way. West on I-70 to Highway 40; north on Paradise Road to Lookout Mountain. He found the fortress at the end of Golden Point Drive, nestled in the woods on the mountaintop. Secluded. Rich. Gated.

They probably had cameras mounted all over the driveway, along each expensively angled roofline of Alcott's home—alarms and sensors everywhere. Streeter didn't care. Because, as he rounded the last corner to the parking area near the massive underground garage, he spotted Webber's missing vehicle: The fully loaded black Mercedes S-Class Coupe, with a shattered bullet hole through the driver's side window.

Vic Webber was behind the wheel, sitting very still.

And very dead.

CHAPTER 26

ALONE FOR THE FIRST TIME in days, I closed the shades of my hotel room and the adjoining door to Phil's room, grabbed my cell, and flopped down on my bed.

I sent a text thanking Ole for dinner and that I'd see him in the morning.

Then I called my sister Ida.

"What's wrong?" Her voice was genuinely alarmed, and I could barely hear her over the din of the crowd, wherever she was.

I almost started crying the instant she asked. She clearly knew me well enough to know I was reaching out, needing a shoulder for a good cry.

"Am I interrupting?" I knew how busy she was all the time. She was super popular with everyone she met. She was rarely alone because of her magnetic personality. So I wasn't surprised at hearing numerous people calling for her to get off the phone.

"Give me a sec," she said.

I imagined her—not unlike Rosalind Russell in that late 1950s movie *Mame*—trying to appease her adoring dinner-party suitors to let her go for just a moment to step into another room of her elegant apartment and take my call. I could almost hear her saying a modern version of Auntie Mame's famous line, "Life is a banquet and most poor suckers are starving to death" to hold them over until she returned.

The line was quiet. "Okay, I'm back. What's up, Boots?"

"Nothing. Everything. And don't call me Boots. I retired them. For good." I was referring to my steel-toed boots that I wore in the quarry, a nickname my siblings had dubbed me because I was so infatuated with the life of hard-rock miners—even from an early age.

"Whatever. Is it Jack?" my baby sister asked.

I sighed. "Actually, not Jack and everything Jack. I don't know."

"You just need someone to talk to. You're surrounded by all those stuffy suits you work with every day. My word, Liv. How do you do it? They're all as cuddly as porcupines, if I may be honest."

She always had a way to get to the point and make me smile. "You can always be honest with me, Ida. Are you at a bar?"

"Dinner party."

I groaned. "Let me guess. In New York. At your apartment. I've got to go."

"Don't you dare," Ida said. "Talk to me."

"You have guests."

"And two of them include Lee Child and Bob Stine. They will keep everyone entertained while I talk with you. Don't worry."

Stunned, I realized she was talking about the authors. Jack Reacher's daddy. And the mastermind behind Goosebumps, R.L. Stine. My sister, a total rock star. It sounded better than if I said she was a total supermodel or opera star—neither of those had quite the same meaning.

"Talk. And be truthful. I know when you lie to me."

She was right about that. And I was humbled that she genuinely wanted to spend time listening. "I need some advice. And you know everything there is to know about relationships."

"Because I've had so many?" she asked, an edge of defensiveness in her tone.

"Because you're worldly. And wise."

"You have me eating out of your hand. So what's the problem?"

I told Ida the entire story about Jack and Streeter. I told her all my private thoughts about the two of them and the struggle I'd had since the first day I met them both and about the dream weekend with Streeter Pierce.

I told her what happened on Sunday night—how I'd been followed, struck, stitched, and dumped. How I now had to be under police protection and how annoyed I was with the entire ordeal.

She didn't interrupt me. Not once.

I ended the saga by adding, "And all this has to stay between me and you."

"Of course," Ida said. "So what's your problem?"

For a second time, I was stunned. *"Weren't you listening?"*

"Of course. You're madly in love with Streeter Pierce, and you're both resisting the opportunity to capitalize on your shared feelings." She paused and repeated. "So what's your problem?"

"My problem is Streeter."

"No, your problem is that you're being a big coward." She stopped talking to me and told someone to give her a minute. The first voice sounded all yummy and English. The second voice, a lot like Tom Cruise.

"I'm back."

"Was that Tom Cruise?"

"He's here with Lee Child. They're stumping their third Jack Reacher movie. Now where was I?" *What a life Ida lives.* "Oh yeah. Streeter is not a problem. He's your opportunity. You're in love. He's in love. You're both terrified. Now get over it. No problem."

I pulled the phone from my ear and stared at the display as if I could see the seriousness of her words by doing that.

She read my mind. "I'm serious. He just wanted you to hate him for some reason. If I were you, I'd figure out why."

"But he dumped me."

"He didn't dump you. He's pushing you away from him. He's scared—of losing you. That's my read. He's scared to death." She waited a beat before adding, "Do you love him?"

"Deeply."

"Then, fight for him. Find out why he's so afraid."

"But the ticket to DC." I knew my argument was weak before I ever said it out loud.

"Rip it up. Running isn't the answer. You know that. So does he. But he's scared."

I ruminated on her words. She was right. "How did you get to be so wise?" She said nothing.

I asked, "What do I do?"

"Call Monsignor Shannon. He knows."

Of course he knew. He was the one who led me to Paula's grave. And mom told me he was out of the hospital, back at Lead. "Ida, you're a genius. How can I thank you?"

"Let me sing at your wedding."

My cheeks flushed. I said my goodbyes and called Father Shannon.

He answered the phone on the second ring. "Trouble maker."

"Caller ID? And yet you took my call," I said. I got up and unwrapped my bandage, looking in the mirror at my angry stitches. "How are you?"

"Better. Glad to be home."

He had to spend some time in the Rapid City hospital after falling and hitting his head. So I knew how he felt.

"Is that all you wanted? To know how I was doing?" He had a brilliant way of cutting to the chase with me.

"I wanted to ask you about Paula Pierce . . . Winzig Jacobs . . . and to thank you for leading me to her grave Sunday—Sunday before last. I'm hoping for some answers."

"More questions?" His voice was steady and comforting.

"What happened to her?"

"She was murdered."

I knew that. I needed more. I didn't know how to ask if the rumors I'd heard were true and if she'd been decapitated. "Did you see her? I mean, did you bless her? Before she was buried?"

There was an interminably long pause before he answered. "Liv, sometimes answers just lead to more questions. Mine are multiplying as we speak."

I knew the eighty-four-year-old priest as well as anyone did. I knew he had to know where I was going before he helped me get there. So I opened up to him. "I'm in love—with Streeter Pierce. He's pushing me away and always has. But I know he loves me."

I heard him shift the phone, take a drink of something, and set the mug down with a slight thud. I could envision him sitting at his kitchen table wearing a flannel shirt in the Parish house at Lead. I forced myself to remain quiet.

"The two were very much in love. Streeter suffered such a deep loss—one from which he will never fully recover. He's damaged severely, Liv. You can't help him fight his demons. It's a battle he has to fight alone—without you."

"That's redundant."

"And sometimes you need to hear things twice."

He knew me pretty well, too. "I understand this is a solitary journey for him. And I understand the guilt. But how *can* I help him?"

"Listen. Let him talk. He has no one to talk to. He sees himself on an island. And only he can swim to shore. You can't save him." After a long pause, maybe a few more sips of coffee, he added, "And I know how tempted you must be to commandeer a boat, pick him up, and drop him to safety on the other shore, but you can't. Alone means alone."

I knew he was right, but I wanted more.

"Okay, I'll listen. I'll do everything I can to zip my lip and open my ears."

"More than your ears, Liv. Open your heart. Then you can really hear him."

I sighed. "You know me, Father. If I'm surprised or ill prepared, I'll ask questions, and I'll blow it. If I'm supposed to listen, I need to know what happened—ahead of time. So I'm not shocked when he tells me." I prayed he'd believe me. After a very long pause, he asked me what I knew. And confirmed what was true and what wasn't.

The door between Phil's and my room suddenly swung open. His expression was stern. I covered the mouthpiece and told him I was almost finished talking with my priest. He rolled his eyes and stepped back into the privacy of his room.

Once he was gone, Father Shannon told me what little more he knew beyond what I'd heard.

Which was enough to get me started in my quest to figure out Streeter Pierce.

CHAPTER 27

STREETER WALKED DOWN the narrow aisle, hunched at the waist to avoid hitting his head on the low ceiling of the small turboprop plane.

He could see the ten passengers ahead of him through the postcard-sized windows descending the flimsy stairs of the lowered airplane door one at a time. His heart raced like it had the first time he'd arrived in Rapid City when he had accepted his first office assignment from Quantico in this small resident agency more than two decades ago.

He had never even heard of this South Dakota town back then. Although, he had heard of the two federal agents who had been killed on an Indian reservation two hours south, near Oglala, in the 1970s. And he knew about the demonstration at Wounded Knee.

Agents from all over the country had gathered to assist the small FBI resident agency the day after their comrades were found murdered. The racial tension in the Black Hills of Western South Dakota became a common topic of discussion within the bureau, as well as in the private sector, for decades to come.

Back then, young Streeter had been thrilled by the prospect of learning and understanding more about what was happening on the reservations and who the Native American people really were, and he had seen his assignment as the opportunity of a lifetime. But, he had been apprehensive about what he might discover in this isolated, sparsely populated plains state. He'd been ready for an adventure as an agent and couldn't possibly imagine what might be exciting in such a place. There were fewer people in the entire state than there were in the Chicago area where he was born and raised. This place had more cows than people.

The only other time he'd even heard about the small state was from an obscure Beatles song that mentioned the Black Hills and some raccoon named Rocky. He hadn't even remembered whether it was South or North Dakota that had the four presidents' faces carved on Mount Rushmore. But the most memorable moment was the first breath of the clean, fresh air he'd caught from the open door of the plane.

Roger Landers, the resident agency's Supervisory Senior Resident Agent, or SSRA, had greeted him. He'd explained the difference between bureaus and resident agencies since South Dakota had none of the first and four of the second. He explained how they not only had jurisdiction over cases such as kidnappings and bank robberies just like bureaus, but that they primarily worked with tribal police and BIA as an ICRA—an Indian Country Resident Agency—working violent crimes such as homicides, child sexual abuse, human trafficking, arson, rape, domestic violence, and assaults with weapons. It was Streeter's first introduction, up close and personal, to reservation work.

Landers taught him so many important realities and dispelled an equal number of myths about life for the Native Americans, starting with the fact that most of them referred to themselves as Indians and a few called themselves first people or original people—to separate themselves from other groups who were native to America.

He'd had so much to learn back then and even more now.

Even after all these years, the fresh air seeping beyond the opening of the door as he headed toward the stairwell struck him as overwhelmingly clean and special, even precious.

He disembarked the plane and found Landers waiting for him in the airport.

He shook his extended hand and patted him on the shoulder. "Friend. How are you?"

"Old," Landers said, rubbing his head. "And bald."

Streeter chuckled. "Thanks for picking me up so late."

"Like old times."

"What's new since we talked?"

"Too much. The funeral is tomorrow for Two Bears."

"Ceremony?" Streeter asked.

"That was four days ago. It went well. After Mass, they'll have the burial and meal. It's tomorrow at eleven."

"Did you get me a car?"

"No, I'll drive you, Miss Daisy. And when you need to take off on your own, you can just drop me off at work." Landers led Streeter down an escalator. "But listen. Another woman was found dead today. It's related."

"To Two Bears's death? How?" Streeter felt a chill skip down his spine. Something about all of this was off. Webber. Alcott. Two Bears.

"Her name was Julie Good Run. No relation to Two Bears. Just a nice, clean, buttoned-down woman by all accounts."

"What'd she do?" Streeter asked. "For a living, I mean?"

"She worked for BIA. She issued allotment checks. When she didn't show up to work Monday morning, they didn't think much of it at first. It's the rez and all. So they didn't even go over and check on her at home or call in a missing person's report."

The two agents walked slowly through the airport, Streeter clutching his overnight bag. He'd noticed his friend was struggling to keep pace and figured he must be nearing sixty-five and may have had some kind of surgery on his right knee or hip from the way he favored that side.

"No family?" Streeter asked, intentionally slowing his gait, even though he was anxious to reach the outdoors.

The instant they stepped outside the airport, he drew in a long breath of fresh air and glanced out toward the Black Hills. It was too dark to see, but he knew they were there beyond the glow of the city lights of Rapid City. He longed to see them again. The hills made him feel more peaceful than the Rocky Mountains for some reason.

Landers shook his head. "She lived alone, but this morning when she didn't show up for a second day, a coworker became concerned."

His friend led him to the cruiser parked on the curb with a police officer standing nearby. Streeter tossed his bag in the back seat and climbed in the front passenger seat. Once inside and pulling away from the curb, Landers said, "The coworker peeked in through the windows of Good Run's house and found her dead on her bed with blood everywhere. Her throat was slit."

Streeter grimaced. "Two Bears was a drug overdose. Why do you say they're related?"

"Timeline. I think Good Run saw something on Sunday. That was the last time anyone saw Jeff alive. They were working on the high school remodel project."

"I thought Two Bears was a teacher?"

"He was. But he was laying tile on the side to earn some extra money. Same as Good Run. Only she was not working directly with Two Bears. She was doing all the receiving and accounting for the subcontractor on the job. She was a goods receipt clerk or something."

Streeter's mind was working overtime. "And they were both working Sunday?"

"Two Bears was found in the parking lot. He was one of the last to leave that day. Good Run clocked out after Two Bears. Only three others out of thirty-two left after that—the rest had already left. But none of them saw anything. You hungry?" Landers was driving into town and signaled to turn right. "McDonald's okay?"

Streeter said, "Sure. Any of the three see anything? With Two Bears or Good Run?"

"Nothing. But Good Run was the one who called in Two Bears's death."

"I don't believe in coincidences."

"Me neither." Landers glanced around the seedy neighborhood of East North Street, looking for the bank of fast food establishments until he spotted the golden arches. "She found him in the truck. She gave a police report saying she saw a big man walk away, but she couldn't describe that much about him except that he was tall, with wide shoulders and long grey braids."

"What did she say he was wearing?"

"A baseball cap, jeans, and a button-down, long-sleeved white shirt with a wide plaid pattern—maybe maroon lines. It was a new shirt. Classy. That's how she described it."

"Did she remember anything else? Anything at all?"

Landers pulled into the drive-through and ordered two meals; then he turned to Streeter. "What do *you* want?"

Streeter grinned. "I thought one of those meals might be for me."

"Nope."

"I'll take a hamburger. And a water."

"That's it?"

Streeter nodded.

As they approached the window to pay, Landers added, "Not much else." After they pulled away, he added, "She gave the tribal police a rough description. But it was his eyes she most remembered. She said the instant he looked at her, she knew he had killed Two Bears."

"Just by his look?"

Landers had stuffed a burger in his mouth, chomping off half, so all he could do was nod until he finished chewing. "She wanted police protection because she said she feared him coming after her. They said they'd drive by her house and keep an eye on her."

"And did they?"

Landers shook his head and took another bite.

"It's not really their fault. It's not like you can put protection on someone over a look."

Streeter's senses were tingling. Something was *very* wrong. He plowed his fingers through his hair and worried about what he was missing.

"The cap. Any particular color?"

"Purple. With a silver logo, but she couldn't place why it looked familiar." Before Streeter could comment, Landers added, "And we have another witness."

"Who? Where? What did he see?" Streeter owed the Two Bears family. He had to prove their son didn't overdose. He had to confirm what the dead witness suspected was murder.

"A woman. Norma Chasing Dog. She came forward the instant she heard the rumors that Julie Good Run was dead."

"What did she witness?"

"The man she believes killed Good Run broke into her home Sunday night and sliced her throat."

When they arrived downtown at the federal building, they both reeked of Landers's two biggie French fry servings. The guards nodded at them as they passed through security and made their way to the second floor, where another agent kept Norma Chasing Dog company in a small interrogation room.

Streeter glanced at the clock. It was 9:40 p.m.

When Landers and Streeter entered the room, the female agent greeted them, introduced Norma to them, and excused herself, telling the woman she'd be back.

Norma said, "I have to get up early and work."

The agent nodded before leaving but said, "Might not be such a good idea."

Streeter studied the woman. She appeared to be older than he was but not by much. She was maybe forty-five at the most. She had long black hair pulled up in a loose bun at the base of her skull, just above the bandages wrapped around her neck. She was a beautiful, large woman with probing eyes—wide-set above her plump cheeks. A serious woman.

Then he recognized her. *"Norma?* You wouldn't happen to be the granddaughter of Eva Yellow Beard?"

She eyed him, squinting. "The hair. I didn't recognize you."

The tension seemed to drain from her body. Streeter grinned. "You're even more beautiful. So much like Eva."

"Thank you," she said, lowering her eyes to the floor out of respect.

"What happened?"

She told the story of the man waiting in her bedroom—explained every detail. What he said, what he did, and how he'd left. The only time she shed a tear was when she explained how she had given up Julie's name. "I am so ashamed."

"You didn't cause this. He did." Streeter wanted to ask to see her throat to examine if the perp had intended to kill her.

Before he did, she noticed him staring at the bandages. "It was no mistake. He was good with the knife. He cut only to make me talk but very intentionally to let me live."

"How many stitches?"

"None. They used adhesives. That's what I mean. It was enough to make my throat sear with pain but not enough to cause me serious harm.

He . . . spared me." Her eyes cast to the floor, she reached up and softly touched her neck.

"Norma's been helping me work another case. A man was beaten and left for dead at Whiteclay."

"Drugs or alcohol?" Streeter asked, remembering the sorry town in Nebraska just south of Pine Ridge. With Pine Ridge's tribal leaders banning alcohol sales on the reservation, residents headed south across state lines toward Whiteclay, Nebraska, to buy their beer—and illegal drugs. The highway, littered with empties, trash, dirty diapers, food containers, and cigarette packs, had earned notoriety as being the filthiest stretch of highway in the country.

Landers answered, "One or the other. Some teens found the vic and dropped him off at the ER."

"A CCG," Norma said.

Streeter cocked his head.

Landers explained, "CCG is what they call the notorious gang around the rez known as Coyote Cries Gang."

Streeter felt his stomach twist. His evil presence was still here. He had his hooks in the youth even after being incarcerated. He should have known. "Who is he? The vic. Is he conscious?"

"Todd Long Soldiers. A longtime notorious dealer." Norma raised an eyebrow and stared at Streeter.

He looked at Landers for an explanation. "Small time, smart, and slippery. Tribal police have incarcerated him several times over the years, but he always gets released as soon as the tribal leadership changes—which is every two years."

"Nothing we can do?" Streeter asked, referring to the bureau.

"Like I said: smart and slippery. They do all their business off-rez. Probably in Whiteclay. We can't get them."

Streeter seethed at the thought of Coyote Cries having such a long reach from behind bars. "Do you think the asshole who did this to you was from CCG?"

She nodded. "I have no doubt they're all connected. Me, Julie Good Run, Jeff Two Bears, Todd Long Soldiers, and Floyd Tice."

"Floyd Tice?" Streeter asked.

"Beat to a pulp two weeks ago," Landers answered. "He's not talking. I personally have no doubt it was Long Soldiers, but I just can't prove it."

Streeter asked, "Is this an internal gang war—a power struggle or something? And do you believe Tice was the one responsible for Long Soldiers's beating?"

Landers shrugged. "Could be. But something tells me no. With the escalation, the rez has become a dangerous place for anyone with CCG."

"Maybe a territorial grab? Another drug ring like the one from California that came in a few years ago dealing meth?"

Landers shook his head. "Alcott took care of all of them. He chased them off before we could. There's a pretty strong army under Alcott."

"Alcott's dead," Streeter said, trusting Norma Chasing Dog with the information. "Murdered. So the real question is how CCG is reorganizing and who is in charge now."

Norma averted her eyes.

"Norma? Do you know the man who attacked you?"

She said nothing. "Ask Logan Walking Crow. He'll know. But I think Jimmy Blue Owl is leading CCG for the moment."

"Did Jimmy do this to you?"

She shook her head.

"We'll find Logan and Jimmy. Can you describe the man who attacked you?" Streeter asked the question a different way.

She dragged her stare back to him. "Big. Smart. Strong. Unafraid. Skilled. Scary." Tears squeezed out of the corners of her eyes and down the sides of her plump cheeks.

He reached across the table and held her hand. "I'm sorry. I know you're scared."

"Terrified."

"Give me some descriptions of his physical appearance. Please."

She closed her eyes. "Lakotan . . . grey braids . . . six foot . . . two hundred twenty pounds . . . all muscle . . . arms the size of that WWE wrestler—The Prototype."

"John Cena?" Landers asked.

She nodded.

Streeter had no clue who they were talking about but got the idea. "Was he familiar to you?"

She nodded and then shook her head. "No idea. It was dark. He turned the lights off. All I had was the moonlight, and it was casting light behind him, not on him. But something was familiar about him."

Streeter knew she was holding back. "What was familiar? Can you describe how he might have seemed familiar to you?"

She sighed and opened her eyes. "I can't say. It's more like I *should* know him. He's not someone I would have missed or forgotten. He has a . . . a presence." Then she shuddered and mumbled, "Poor Julie. It was my fault."

"It was not your fault. You're alive to help us. Both of you would be dead if you hadn't told him." He patted her hand and let go. "Anything else?"

She shook her head. The two men rose when the female agent came back into the room. They thanked Norma and headed for the door.

She called to them, "He cited something. A quote. Poetic."

Streeter paused, turned slowly, and saw her staring at him.

"I don't know, but that was also familiar somehow. He said something about plans for me. But the way he said it was like quoting from Shakespeare or Mary Oliver—or someone."

Streeter found that odd. *A killer quoting Shakespeare?*

Landers asked, "Can you recall exactly what he said?"

She shook her head. "I was terrified. Let me think." She closed her eyes. "He said something like, 'For I know my plan is not to harm you, but to give you hope.' Something weird like that. It was the cadence, the order of the words he used that made it sound stiff, like a quote."

Streeter handed her his business card. "If you think of anything else, call me on my cell. Please."

CHAPTER 28

AS THEY LEFT the Sacred Heart Catholic Church, Streeter pulled Alice Two Bears closer to him.

Her tears were flowing freely as she buried her face against his chest. Ray Two Bears was stoic and stunned. They had made it through the ceremony, the three-day wake, and now the Mass—without a tear.

Brushing the strands of her straight, shoulder-length hair away from her face, Alice had never appeared more fragile to Streeter than she did at this moment. He asked tenderly, "Are you going to be okay?"

She drew in a deep breath and wiped the tears from her cheeks. "That was a beautiful Mass. It's just that my son was such a wonderful man and so young."

Streeter patted her shoulder as they walked slowly to their cars.

"Streeter, Fred and Pearl are struggling," Alice said.

They had looked terrible—but not nearly as haggard as Ray and Alice. "They look like they haven't slept in days."

Jeff Two Bears was Fred and Pearl's nephew, Ray and Alice's son. Streeter found it touching that Alice appeared more concerned for others than for herself. That was just her way. And Ray's.

Streeter answered, "They probably haven't."

They walked the rest of the way in silence. When they arrived at the car, Streeter embraced Ray. Neither let go. Ray sobbed silently into his shoulder. Friends from decades ago; sharing battles that could never be forgotten.

The only way Streeter knew how to repay the Two Bears family was to find whoever had killed their son, Jeff.

"Are you sure you don't want me to wait around until after the internment and the meal to give you a ride home?"

"No, thank you," Ray answered quietly.

He glanced over at Alice who was preparing the colorful squares for the giveaway at the meal after the burial. Women embraced her repeatedly as she busied herself with the traditional work.

Ray added, "I appreciate you being there for us today at church. But later, Alice doesn't want you to stop her from . . ."

His words trailed off.

Streeter had no idea what Ray was going to say about what Alice would do later, but he knew Ray well enough not to press the issue. And he was far from being an expert on the Lakotan traditions. His instincts told him it had something to do with the razor-sharp cigar cutter Alice kept in her smock pocket and fiddled with all through the service.

Was she planning on cutting her hair at Jeff's gravesite? He hoped not.

Ray added, "I know funerals aren't your favorite."

"Doesn't matter. Being here for you is important to me."

"I really needed you to be there with us through the Mass. Let us say our goodbyes, and we'll meet you at home for supper."

Dumbfounded at being dismissed, Streeter stopped arguing with Ray. He glanced around, realizing he was the only white person remaining. The others had left after the Mass.

They both turned as they heard the drums begin to beat and the wailing cries of song rise into the air. The masses flocked back inside the hallway to help prepare the meal for after the burial.

Streeter shook Ray's hand and headed for the car. He removed his dark jacket and threw it in the back seat. He called over to Ray and Alice, "It's at least a hundred degrees today. Don't forget to drink some water."

Alice offered a sad smile and a nod. Worry encircled her wide, deep-set eyes. Her hand tightened around the cigar cutter in her pocket.

Streeter couldn't imagine how Ray and Alice must feel losing a child. It must be unbearable—even worse than when he'd lost Paula.

And they'd been there for him.

So many of the Lakota people had been there for him. He owed them so much.

Pulling away from the curb, Streeter avoided the memorial procession headed toward their cars from the church for the burial. He had arranged to meet Landers in ten minutes in front of Logan Walking Crow's house.

Streeter parked in front of the house next to Walking Crow's. In no time, Landers arrived on foot, spotting Streeter behind the wheel of his cruiser.

Streeter stepped out as he approached. Out of breath, Landers huffed, "The Walking Crows may not be here. The car's gone."

"They're probably at the meal. Seemed like the entire community was planning to attend after the burial."

They walked to the door, and Landers knocked.

A young teen opened the screen and scowled when he saw them.

"Are you Logan?"

He nodded.

Landers flipped open his credentials. "Agent Roger Landers. We're here to talk to you about your sister Edith."

"She's not here. She's with my parents. At a meal."

Streeter offered the teen a smile. "Jeff Two Bears—I was there. Can we come in?"

The young man hesitated and then opened the door wide for them.

He sat down in a recliner, wound up the cords to a gamer control handset, and turned off the television. "I didn't feel like going."

They hadn't asked, but he must have felt a need to explain.

"Been tough lately?" Streeter asked. The boy looked away. "We heard about what Long Soldiers did to your sister last Saturday night. Brave of Larry, standing up to him like that."

He glanced up at the two men and half smiled. "He's a good friend."

"We heard he was just doing the same thing you did a few weeks ago. Said you were the first. Started a revolution. Encouraged others to do the same."

"I don't know about that. I was stupid. Didn't do it right. Larry did. And it was Mr. Two Bears who started the revolution. I just did what I thought he'd do."

No way could this young man be responsible for the beating of Long Soldiers or Floyd Tice. Someone a lot angrier and less timid than this young man had done that damage—unless he had a split personality or something.

"I heard Mr. Two Bears was an amazing teacher," Streeter said.

The boy leaned forward and sat on the edge of his recliner. He folded his hands with his elbows on his knees and stared at the floor. Streeter couldn't see his face but noticed the drops of tears hit the hardwood beneath him.

"I knew Mr. Two Bears when he was a boy—younger than you. You remind me of him."

The boy looked up, anger on his face. "I am nothing like him. Mr. Two Bears was brave. And wise. He was a hero."

Streeter nodded. "Yes, just like him. Humble. And brave enough to stand up to Long Soldiers."

He shook his head. "I wasn't even brave enough to go to Mr. Two Bears's meal."

"I understand. One of the most difficult things a man has to do in life is say goodbye."

The teen swiped at his tears with the back of his hand and then balled up his fist and rubbed his eyes. He drew in a breath and asked, "Why are you here?"

"To ask you what you know." Streeter didn't sugarcoat anything. "Long Soldiers was in charge of CCG. Who's in charge now that he's in ICU?"

He shrugged. "Jimmy, I suppose. But the whole world is upside down, now that Mr. Two Bears is gone. How could he do that? Why?"

His face screwed into a knot of confusion and anger.

"He didn't," Streeter said. "At least, I for one believe he didn't do drugs. Someone killed him. But that's between you and me, Logan."

His features softened. His mind was clearly working overtime. Slowly, he nodded.

"And you're going to help us find out who did this."

He sat up straight. "How?"

"Jimmy Blue Owl. Do you think he had a reason to do all this? To take over?"

He shook his head. "He likes being a big shot. But he's too weak."

"What do you mean?"

He shrugged. "He wouldn't want to be boss. He doesn't like accountability. He just likes the benefits—screwing around with all the girls."

The kid made sense. Streeter had to agree.

"So what's your guess?"

"No guesses."

"For your sister Edith's sake, do you know who beat Long Soldiers?"

"Not me."

"I didn't say you did."

"I'm not sad about it, if that's what you're asking. And I don't know who did it." The teen wrung his hands. Streeter waited, knowing he was contemplating whether to share what he knew. "Rumor is that the CCG man from Denver sent someone up to clean house—to shut things down and start over. I heard Jimmy's laying low. Scared to death. No one's seen or heard from him since Sunday."

Streeter exchanged a glance with Landers, who nodded.

Landers asked, "Did you hear a name? Of the guy they sent from Denver?"

Logan flicked a glance toward Landers and then at the clock and the door. It wasn't locked.

Streeter added, "It's okay, Logan. No one will know what you've told us."

"I heard it's a preacher man, a guy quoting out of the Bible. But he's a freak. A big, scary-looking guy."

Streeter thought how similar his explanation was to Norma Chasing Dog's.

"That's why I didn't want to go to Mr. Two Bears's Mass." Tears streamed down the teen's face. "My sister called me a coward, and my parents told me I was being disrespectful."

Streeter rose and approached the young man. He held out his arms. The boy rose and gave him a hug. "You are so much like your teacher, son. In life, we're faced with difficult choices every day. And sometimes we don't choose what others think we should. Mr. Two Bears had to make difficult choices that his parents didn't agree with, too. Like teaching you at the high school."

The boy sobbed. "He was such a good teacher. He was a rock for all of us."

"And he would be honored for you to take his place. You need to be strong. Be that rock for the other kids through these difficult and dangerous times. Can you do that?"

The boy held tight to Streeter and nodded, his cheek against Streeter's chest.

Streeter rubbed his back. "Good. Mr. Two Bears would be proud of you—for what you did a few weeks ago. And of Larry Standing Bull, for Saturday night. And for what you're going to do from now on: Be strong."

Logan let go, drew in a big breath, and wiped his face with the sleeve of his T-shirt. Streeter handed him a card. "Call me if you hear anything else."

Once back in the car, Landers said, "A preacher? From Denver? What's that about?"

Streeter remembered what Norma Chasing Dog had said about quoting poetry. "Landers, can you get someone in the office to search biblical passages for what Norma said her attacker told her? About plans and her future, rather than being harmed or hurt . . . whatever she'd said?"

"Good idea." Landers placed the call.

<hr/>

Within a few minutes, they were knocking on Jimmy Blue Owl's door. An old woman approached, a fried chicken leg in her hand. She said nothing.

Landers asked, "Is Jimmy home?"

"Nope. He hasn't been home since Sunday."

"Are you his grandmother?"

"Great-grandmother."

"Do you know where we can find him?"

"Try Long Soldiers's place."

No way was he staying at Long Soldiers's home. That place was crawling with BIA and FBI.

"If not there, any other ideas where he might be?"

She shrugged.

They left a card in case he returned, bid her farewell, and headed back to Rapid City.

Landers made a call to post a BOLO for Jimmy Blue Owl as a person of interest. Then he asked Streeter to drop him off at the office so Streeter could use his cruiser for the evening. He insisted he'd get a ride from his wife and that he'd call him if anyone found Blue Owl or if they discovered anything about the preacher.

Streeter made his way to the Two Bears's small home in North Rapid City.

Staring out the window, he thought through everything he'd learned since arriving for the funeral. Jeff was left for dead in the parking lot of the new high school on Sunday with a band on his arm and a needle sticking from his vein.

Jeff didn't do drugs. Streeter would never believe that he had—no matter what the BIA and FBI found. He told them there was no way Jeff was a user. Although they argued that Streeter had been away from reservation work for decades and never knew Jeff Two Bears as an adult, Streeter argued back that he knew Jeff's family.

That was enough for Streeter. But he knew it wouldn't be enough for the investigators. Paula had spent many hours caring for little Jeff when he was just a toddler. Jeff was the reason she wanted children. He was bright, curious, loving, and full of joy.

Streeter prided himself on never sharing the details of his work with his wife at home. He wanted his home to be his own, not dominated by thoughts of work. What he did share with Paula was basic information that could have been learned from a local newspaper or from normal street gossip.

He had always refrained from sharing the intimate details or the theory behind any of the cases he was working—not only to avoid thinking about work every waking hour, but also because he wanted to protect his wife from any harm that might come to her for ever knowing too much.

But the Two Bears was an exceptional family, and that's where he crossed the line. Ray Two Bears had become his best friend; Ray and Alice, his most trusted resources on cases he'd worked to keep the reservations safe. After Paula was murdered, Ray moved his family from Pine Ridge to Rapid City to be able to raise Jeff with their culture, but safely. He'd had enough of being *ate,* or father, to so many. It was time for him to be the father to one.

Streeter had no problem finding their house. The small, three-bedroom home on the north side of Rapid City had been easy to find.

It was the white house with green trim two doors down from the infamous purple house on Maple Street.

Many of the residents in North Rapid City used the purple house as a reference point to guide new visitors in the area. Ray had told him that the elderly woman in the purple house had once read somewhere that burglars avoided gaudily painted houses. She guessed burglars assumed the owners had bad taste, no money, or both.

The house was still there, and he hoped the neighbor woman was, too, after all these years. That purple had truly been her best protection.

Streeter retrieved the key from beneath the broken step, where it'd always been, and let himself into the quaint living room. It was decorated in warm, earthy colors with a long tan couch beneath the big bay window with white, lace-trimmed doilies on both armrests. The two rocking armchairs in brown floral print had the same covers on the armrests and were separated by an oak table with a lamp resting on yet another white lace doily.

It hadn't changed a bit since the last time he had been here—which was for Jeff's graduation. Each end table, the mantle above the fireplace, the top of the television set, and even the windowsills were covered with religious relics and American Indian artwork, statuettes, and trinkets. On one wall hung a beautifully framed, crocheted United Sioux Tribes star. They'd likely receive a star blanket during the meal in memory of Jeff, and surely Alice and Ray would find a prominent place to display that.

On another wall were photos taken at various powwows throughout the country: the entire Two Bears family dressed in traditional outfits from their Lakota heritage; Fred and Ray together in traditional breast plates; Alice and Pearl captured during a traditional dance, the hems of their deer skin dresses swinging to the beat; and Little Jeff Two Bears holding a ribbon after a fancy-dance competition in one photo and grinning during a grass dance in another.

A third wall held several family photos in a collage arrangement: Ray and Alice Two Bears with their three adult children, a boy and two girls, and three grandchildren. On a third wall hung a simple, yet beautiful Catholic crucifix. Above the mantle was a large painting of the Madonna and child.

Studying the photos, Streeter chuckled at how much Ray looked like his brother Fred. They were identical but such different people. Fred wore well worn, less fashionable clothes. Both men had just turned sixty. Streeter knew this because when Roger picked him up at the airport, he said that he hadn't seen Ray in a while, but that he'd stopped by Fred's house to wish him a happy birthday last month.

Both brothers were nearly six feet tall, with skinny legs, wide chests, and large bellies. Both had crew cuts, although Ray wore his hair just a little longer than Fred. They both had warm smiles and contagious laughs. Fred wore thick, black glasses, and Ray wore silver wire-rim frames. When they were together, it was hard to distinguish between their voices. And the twins frequently talked at the same time, exchanging barbs and funny stories. Occasionally, Ray would slip in words from the Lakota language; Fred frequently did, too.

Alice was a short, thin woman in her late fifties. Her impish grin made her look at least two decades younger than her age, and her gem-studded glasses framed her bright, laughing eyes. She had worn a light-green smock dress with a wide, ivory-colored collar and matching pumps to the funeral. A small silver cross hung around her neck. And of course, she had the colorful scarves—to share with the other women in celebration of life.

Fred's wife, Pearl, was also short, but very stout. Her deep-set eyes nearly disappeared when she flashed her wide grin, and she could certainly be described as jolly. She wore a floral-print, summer dress with well-worn moccasins on her otherwise bare feet. The major difference between the two women was that Pearl's cheerful face was etched from hard work and difficulties, making her appear much older than Alice even though she was the same age. Alice appeared to have had an easier life, which she probably had, in many respects—up until this week.

He noticed a photo of an old woman, possibly from the turn of the century, surrounded by children of all ages and holding a swaddled baby. Underneath the photo, someone had written in ink, "Alice's great-grandmother, Iayanke." He studied her hands and noticed a missing digit. He remembered hearing about the old Lakota tradition that was rarely, if ever, practiced in modern times.

Instantly, he knew the reason they didn't want him to attend the burial and meal. She was indeed planning to use the cigar cutter in keeping with an old Lakota tradition for a mother grieving over the loss of a child, which was to cut off the tip of one of her fingers in honor of Jeff.

CHAPTER 29

I KNEW THE OWL Canyon Quarry like the back of my hand.

I used to manage this operation and loved every employee as if they were part of my large family. But I didn't recognize some of the new employees hired over the past year, and a pang of regret filled my belly for the first time since I had committed to law enforcement. I missed being a part of this extended family unit—and being a miner.

I was thrilled when I introduced Special Agent Phil Kelleher to my father and brother, reminding Dad that Agent Kelleher was the man the FBI had assigned to live with me during the serial killer case over a year ago.

My dad shook Phil's hand and then hugged him. I nearly chuckled at Phil's response: rigid and awkward because of another man's physical touch. That was just my dad. And me. We were both high-fiving, fist-bumping huggers. Phil was not.

We made a quick plan, wired up the office of the site manager, who was away on personal leave for the day, and strapped mics on both my brother and father, instructing them to play it cool with the inspector. Neither appeared nervous or uncomfortable with his assignment.

I looked at the clock. There was plenty of time.

My cell phone buzzed, and I stepped away from the three men to take the call.

Laurie Frumpley greeted me. "I just got a call from Matt Juzlig."

"From Grand Junction?"

She hesitated before saying, "Glenwood Springs."

Clearly my head was still muddled. "Now I remember him. He's the guy who warned Ben Ridgewood about Dick Roth."

And I didn't say the guy on whose behalf I had called my friend at the Glenwood Police Department to assist him. If I had, Laurie would know my thinking wasn't all that clear and that I shouldn't be working.

"Juzlig sent me some audio files. He said you'd want them. He had some help from law enforcement up there. Was that your doing?"

I said nothing. I'd worried about his safety.

"Anyway, they got some excellent sound bites. The prosecuting attorney reviewed the audio clips and said we're close. Hopefully, with what you get today, they'll be able to arrest the bastard."

"*Ms. Frumpley!*" I said, never having heard her curse before.

She giggled. "You bring out the shero in me."

"Shero?"

"The female hero. I love helping you, Liv. You empower me. You don't treat me like a desk jockey like so many others do."

I felt my cheeks flush. "Laurie, you're damned good at what you do. Don't ever forget that."

"Ms. Bergen. Did you just swear?"

"Way too often. Gotta go. Thanks!"

I wandered back to my old office, the new site manager's office. "Twenty minutes. Places everyone!"

Phil and I took off in the SUV and drove to a hogback ridge where we could park out of sight but still be high enough so that the antenna could reach the recording devices from anywhere in the three-mile complex. Then we waited.

Although he wouldn't let me take the risk of walking up to the ridge, I took one of the biggest risks of my life as we sat waiting. "Phil, I'd like to ask you something. And I'd ask if you could please keep what I say confidential."

He said nothing and stared straight ahead at the gravel entrance road off Highway 287, watching for Dick Roth.

"Will you? Keep this between you and me?"

He nodded once.

I let out a breath. "Do you think Streeter is irreparably damaged?"

I detected a slight buckling of Phil's eyebrows followed by an interminably long silence.

I realized I had to offer more to get him to talk. "I am madly in love with Streeter Pierce. Probably always have been."

The corner of his mouth twitched and possibly curled.

"Jack Linwood was dear, but I could never get over my feelings about Streeter."

I got nothing from the stiff man sitting next to me, although the hint of a smile still played on his otherwise stern lips.

"And I think he loves me back. Not to kiss and tell, but we've spent the entire week together."

He cleared his throat before growing rigidly still once again, possibly resisting a smile for only a brief instant.

"And this morning, before you arrived at the hospital, he broke up with me. He told me he was basically just having a fling with me."

His eyebrow arched.

"I don't believe him, either. That's just not Streeter."

He said nothing.

"I think he's scared. I think he's afraid to love me, to be in love with me—to love anyone after Paula . . ."

His eyebrow collapsed, but he didn't say a word.

" . . . which makes me wonder if he truly is as irreparably damaged as Father Shannon claims."

We both sat in silence for a long moment staring at the deserted entrance road that was occasionally traversed by a truck retrieving or delivering rock somewhere.

"He said you have tickets for me to DC. But I had no say in the transfer."

Phil reached into his pocket, eyes still on the road, and handed me the itinerary.

It was for tomorrow morning—one-way.

I sighed. "I'm not giving up on him. I'm not running. I love him. So between you and me, don't waste your time trying to take me to the airport tomorrow."

The corner of his lip curled once again as he pointed at something.

I recognized the car that pulled in off the highway. I keyed my mic and said, "Dick Roth is here. Recording: ON."

My brother and Dad both acknowledged that it was show time with a quick affirmation.

Within minutes, Dick was escorted back to the site manager's office. We heard Roth say, "Oh, I thought you were alone."

"This is my dad, Garth Bergen. He stopped by unexpectedly on his way to Rawlins."

"Nice to meet you." I could picture my dad's wide smile, his firm handshake, and his magnetic personality drawing Roth in like a moth to a lit firecracker.

They talked for a few moments, my dad expressing his appreciation for the EPA—genuinely and with direct knowledge and details about numerous regulations many owners or presidents may not know firsthand. But my dad did. And so did Ole.

The conversation steered toward time being of the essence. My dad, taking the hint, chipped in a great leeway, "I'll let you two be on your way. I've kept you long enough. I've got to get going."

I spoke in a whisper. "Dad, what are you doing?"

"Good luck, son. Make sure we do whatever this fine man tells us to do. You have the authority to make any necessary improvements to the plants and operation, as long as Mr. Roth suggests best practices. On my way."

"Dad!" I whispered. *"Dad?"*

I watched in horror as he stepped out of the office toward his pickup truck and drove away.

I turned off my mic and turned to Phil. "What in the hell is he doing?"

Kelleher grinned. "Disobeying our instructions. He's just like you."

"Ole's on his own now. Damn it."

I listened intently to Ole and Dick Roth's conversation. Ole played up to everything Roth said, placating him in any way possible, stating often how he needed to please his dad, never receive a citation, or Garth would be sorely disappointed in him.

Within minutes, Roth was delivering the same load of shit as usual—reading the opacity at the crushing plant as twice the permitted limit. How disappointed Garth would be in Ole at the notice of violation he'd have to write up, and how sorry he was that he'd have to do it because he liked the two so much.

And Ole had him eating right out of his hand, asking how he could make this go away, what he could do to convince him that his crushing operation was in compliance.

The "ask," the deadline for coming up with hush money, the handshake agreement—all recorded. All within two hours. Dick Roth drove out onto the highway headed south to Fort Collins for a long lunch, Ole having asked for at least two hours to drive back into town to retrieve the cash.

The instant Roth's taillights disappeared, I saw my dad coming from the north and turning into the entrance. He had never left. He had been there all along.

"Sneaky."

Phil actually laughed out loud. "The apple doesn't fall far from the tree. He sized up the situation perfectly, made himself scarce, and set up his son for a home run."

"But that wasn't the plan," I protested.

"Since when did a Bergen ever follow a plan?"

I shot a glance his way and headed toward the site manager's office to congratulate them for a situation well-played, even though it was off-script.

Phil said, "He's scared to death."

"Who? Dick Roth? Or my dad?" I had no clue where he was getting that idea. I didn't see any of the three frightened at all.

Then he surprised me more than I ever thought possible, tying up my earlier monologue with a bow.

With four simple words.

"Streeter. Of losing you."

CHAPTER 30

LATER THAT EVENING, after dinner and over a plate of Alice's famous plum cake, Streeter asked what had been happening with the Two Bears family.

Alice still worked for one of the public schools as part of the clerical staff. Ray planned to retire from his quarry job as a dozer operator after forty years with the company. And Fred continued to ranch on the reservation, which was leased and operated by one of the few Caucasians who lived on the reservation. *Wasicu*, as Fred called them, were not permitted to live on reservation land unless they were married to an Indian, which Fred's boss was.

Pearl worked several part-time jobs at the hospital in the cafeteria and as the village seamstress to make ends meet. Even between Fred and Pearl, they had barely made enough money to keep their four children fed as they were growing up, but now they enjoyed a few luxuries since all four had moved out on their own. Fred and Pearl's total income, including the allotments for living on the reservation, paled in comparison to Ray and Alice's, who could no longer receive an allotment since they had moved off the reservation.

Streeter commented, "So you two stayed?"

Pearl flashed a grin. "My family's there. I've lived there all my life. I need to stay and help some of the young people who don't choose to provide a life for themselves."

Streeter said nothing, shoveling more cake into his mouth.

"Some of our youth fall into the trap of believing that more government funding is the answer," Pearl explained evenly. "They stick their hands out expecting a big, fat check just like little, helpless birds in a nest waiting for the next worm. As their hunger grows, so do their demands for more worms."

"Not birds. *Khukuhse*." Fred stuffed another forkful into his mouth.

Pearl's eyes disappeared when she laughed, which Streeter enjoyed. He laughed, too. He knew enough Lakotan to know that Fred had called them pigs.

Pearl continued, "Instead of flying out and finding the worms for themselves, they sit and wait for the next, grumbling about their hunger. Pretty soon, their wings become feeble and useless. Then all they can do is sit in the nest and squawk."

Fred added, "They need to work to earn self-worth."

Pearl summarized her thoughts less directly, more in keeping with the Lakota style. "That's no way for a bird to live. They should fly on their own."

Streeter held out his plate for another piece of cake offered by Alice. "When I tell people I've worked in South Dakota, they jump to a reply either about Mount Rushmore or why the government hasn't provided more funding programs for the reservations to make life easier."

"Easier?" Pearl asked as she helped herself to a second piece of cake, too. "As far as money goes, yes. But life is not about how easy it can be. It's not about how much you're worth in dollars. It's about whether life is worth living. So few people understand that concept."

Alice added, "Handouts are like a bully. They take, rather than give."

Talking over one another and finishing each other's sentences, first Ray chimed in. "When you live your life dependent on someone or something other than yourself, it is difficult to realize your own self-worth."

Then Fred said, "The only way to find self-worth is to know self-reliance."

Then Ray again, with, "Self-reliance means caring for yourself, doing for yourself, earning for yourself."

Fred responded, "It is very difficult to rationalize that you have earned for yourself by simply being a descendent of the original people. There are centuries of descendants who were promised money in exchange for original ancestors being ostracized from the rest of the country."

"And even more difficult to rationalize that you've earned something just because of the color of your skin," Ray wrapped up.

Streeter asked, "So what about Jeff? Why did he go back to the reservation? You raised him here in Rapid City so he'd be safer."

Pearl dabbed at her eyes but was the first to answer. "Jeff considered himself very fortunate. He'd say he was blessed with wonderful parents and a wonderful family."

The elder Two Bears blushed in unison and cast their glances downward—humbled.

"He told me at his graduation party that you taught him to be proud of his heritage and to work hard for what he wanted." Streeter remembered the young man's beaming smile when he talked about his parents.

Pearl added, "Most kids on the rez are not so fortunate. When Jeff graduated from college with his teaching degree, he wanted to return to the rez to make a difference. He would say, 'Even if I could touch one child, help him reach for a dream and then teach him how to work hard to achieve it, I would feel like I made a difference.'"

Streeter knew Jeff would be proud of Logan Walking Crow. Jeff had definitely made a difference in that young man's life.

Fred added, "Half of the two million Indians in this country live on or near reservations. What the *Wasicu* call Sioux represent about five percent of that total population. I guess Ray was the half that left, and I was the half that stayed."

Ray said, "About a third of our people are listed under the poverty line. The average number of violent crimes committed against Indians as a percentage of the population is nearly two and a half times higher than all the races combined."

Alice rose to remove the plates and retrieve the coffee pot. "My boy had a way of putting things in perspective. He'd say, 'Imagine one hundred of my students in this room. I could separate thirty-three of them and say, 'You are going to live in poverty.' I could take another thirty-three of them and say, 'You have to live with some disability,' and fourteen of those thirty-three will have to live with a severe disability.'"

"Many from car accidents," Fred added.

"Drunk driving," Ray said.

Streeter knew the Two Bears would eventually get around to talking about Sunday's tragic event, but this was their way of weaving the story, leading up to what had happened with Jeff and to their firm belief that he had never touched drugs.

Alice poured coffee in each of the cups. "My boy would say, 'I could take another seventeen of them and say, 'You seven are going to be assaulted. You four are going to suffer aggravated assault. This one is going to be raped. This one robbed. Three of you will be neglected or abused as a child. One of you may be murdered.'"

Pearl said, "Sounds harsh. But Jeff was right."

Streeter did the math and sipped his coffee. "That leaves seventeen students."

Alice set the pot down and joined them. The odds are not good for them. Of the seventeen remaining from the original hundred, thirteen will commit suicide."

Pearl argued, "That's not as high as eighteen to twenty-four-year-olds who are white, but it's but second highest by race."

Alice said, "The point is, unfortunately, that the number is growing each year."

"Tragic," Streeter said, shaking his head.

Alice lowered her head and lifted the napkin from her lap, delicately dabbing her mouth. "Our son did such a great job bringing awareness to our people. These statistics may sound startling. But they don't even cover the violent crimes that go unreported."

"I never understood why folks didn't report crime. I ran into that so often when I worked the reservation," Streeter said.

"Repercussions," Fred said.

Pearl nodded. "Many of our people will report the crimes against them, which are perpetrated by strangers or people of another race. And many more will never report those crimes committed by their own family members or loved ones. So many people on the rez are afraid of the repercussions—like Floyd Tice, Todd Long Soldiers, Julie Good Run."

"Do you ever just want to throw your hands up? Surrender?" Streeter asked, as he acknowledged his own feelings on the situation and how they had changed as he had aged. He felt profound weariness, like he wasn't effecting change as he should.

"It's hard to say," Ray answered with a sigh. "Our people must realize that it does not help to cover for those who are evil, just because we have the same blood or the same color skin. We will be unable to rise above the atrocities until we do."

Pearl said, "A woman where I work part-time, at the Red Cloud Indian School, did not show up for work for a few days last spring. Some of us became concerned and went looking for her. Her husband said he did not know where she was."

Streeter remembered just such stories from when he was an agent in Rapid City. And he knew her story wasn't going to have a happy ending.

"We found her not far from her house. She was naked in a field bleeding from numerous lacerations. But she was still alive. She had been lying there for four days and three nights."

Streeter realized accepting the SSRA job in Rapid City would be tortuous for him. And he offered up a silent prayer that Liv wouldn't quit her job at the bureau over the transfer to DC and wouldn't move back to Rapid City—because he would most certainly follow if she did. He realized he'd made a big mistake by forcing her to go.

Pearl continued the story of her coworker. "Her husband and she had gotten into an argument over the last donut in the box. He slashed her with a carpet knife, over and over again, and left her in the field to die. We took her to the hospital, and she is fine now, but she refused to press charges against him. She said it was nothing, just a few small cuts she got at home."

Fred finished for Pearl, "Before she had even been released from the hospital, she called the school to say her husband would be by to pick up her paycheck and asked if they could please release it to him."

Pearl nodded. "The school could do nothing to stop it from happening.

The tribal police did everything they could, but the woman was unwilling to press charges against him. He's in prison, thank God, even though she tried to stop them. The US and tribal attorneys did their jobs and convicted him on an evidence-based prosecution with her egregious injuries and doctors' testimony."

Streeter lowered his gaze, knowing what they were saying was all too true.

Ray added solemnly, "It hasn't changed, Streeter, since you left. Some will always believe they are helping by protecting their own."

Fred said, "That only compounds the problem. *Hechitu yedo.*"

Streeter knew that meant "That's the way it is."

Ray jabbed Fred. "Sounds like you're jumping on a pity pod, brother."

"*Maka.* Nothing more degrading."

"Did he just call you a skunk?" Streeter asked Ray. Ray and Fred elbowed one another. "About Jeff. He chose the reservation life for what reason then?"

Alice jumped in to explain. "To help. So many people, including our own, do not know the American Indian life. The reservation is not representative of the Indian culture. Our culture is about work, offering our gifts—our skills and talents—to the community. Celebrating life."

Pearl added, "I've lived there my whole life. But I have never mistaken the reservation as somehow the very essence of who we are."

Ray said, "We were rounded up like cattle and herded onto the reservations in 1894."

"Actually, 1830."

"Ah, you're right, brother. The Indian Removal Act. But President Andrew Jackson only focused on removing those of our brothers in the south and relocated them west to Oklahoma. He hadn't turned his focus on us in the west. That was later."

"There was no gold yet. Then the Indian Nation really started to shrink," Fred added. "From six to ten million of our people to only a quarter million after the turn of the century. The 1800s were riddled with devastating government policies designed to eliminate us."

"Be fair, brother. Not all of that was the US government. Much of our people's loss was from disease and malnutrition," Ray countered.

"Because of the movement west. The settlers brought with them dis-ease and germs, decimating our food sources."

Ray batted a hand at Fred. "We can argue later. We can agree that res-ervations were created in 1830 to separate us from the white man."

"Not separate—remove us from the white man," Fred muttered. "It was called the Removal Act."

Ray continued, "President Jackson designed this new way of living—new homes, new communities."

Fred scoffed. "Jackson's design was seriously flawed from the get-go. Our 'new' lives isolated us from the rest of the country. That was not our way of life."

Ray said, "Some Indians in Rapid City feel guilty for never having experienced the reservation life. As if it is honorable or culturally stimulat-ing. It is neither."

Streeter recalled a quote from a US senator with the Whig Party against Jackson in 1830 that the proposed act's "evil was enormous, the inevitable suffering incalculable." It was one of the only quotes he remem-bered from his time on the reservation twenty years ago, because he had witnessed the suffering firsthand.

Edwards? Everett?

Something like that. He couldn't remember the senator's name. But his prophecy had been correct.

Alice circled back to Streeter's question. "These two get a bit too preachy sometimes. But let me try to answer your question, Streeter. My boy lived here—in Rapid City. But he chose to work on the reservation at the high school because he wanted those kids to think for themselves. To earn for themselves. To become self-reliant. He wanted to teach those kids that the true American Indian heritage lies in the traditions and stories shared by our elders with our young—just like in any culture or in anyone's heritage."

Streeter nodded. "And he must have done well and touched many lives, evidenced by all those who attended the Mass today."

Pearl added, "And many more who attended the meal."

Streeter thought about Logan Two Bears and wondered how many other kids were too frightened to attend. Perhaps when the drums started beating, they finally came.

Ray explained, "I told Jeff when he decided to go back that there is no honor or intrinsic value in living on a reservation, any more so than for those of us who do not. The honor is in becoming the best individuals we can be. In contributing something during our lifetime that otherwise may not be contributed—"

His words were cut short by his own grief that was sudden and violent.

Everyone lowered their eyes and pretended not to see him cry. Streeter reached out and grabbed his hand. He held tight and ignored nothing.

Ray composed himself and laid his hand over his heart. "Jeff knew that the intrinsic value of life is in realizing that this is where the magic of our people—of any people—begins. And ends."

Alice lifted her gaze to her husband, moved closer to him, and held his hand with both of hers. For the first time, she didn't stuff her left hand in her dress pocket or place it in her lap under the table. Her pinky finger was bandaged tightly with thick layers of gauze.

Streeter drew in a deep breath.

When Alice noticed him watching her, she slid her hand back in her lap and offered Streeter a thin smile and an answer to his unasked question: "Tradition—like so many other things we taught our son: how he believed that life was to be celebrated; how adding value to life began with that first job; sharing your skills and talents with others; experiencing the joy and pride of earning that paycheck as teenagers or young adults."

Pearl exchanged a glance with Fred. "He tried to caution everyone on the reservation to become less dependent on the government programs and more willing to share his or her talents with the rest of the community. And I heard he used me as an example. Can you believe it? Me? A nobody."

Alice said, "You are not a nobody. Jeff would say, 'Like Aunt Pearl says, use their own wings and find their own worms before it's too late and their wings become weak and useless.'"

Pearl sobbed, covering her face in her hands.

Streeter had been moved by their stories of the young man's passion and vision. "I can see why he chose the profession of teaching. I have learned so much tonight—from him through you. Those kids at Pine Ridge High School were lucky to have him."

Ray grinned. "Thank you. He believed strongly in our country, in the Lakota people, and particularly in our youth."

Fred replied, "Such *woksape* for a young one."

Pearl and Alice nodded.

Streeter asked, "What's *woksape?*"

Ray, the proud father, beamed and said, "Wisdom."

CHAPTER 31

STREETER TOOK A LONG drink from his tepid coffee and said, "The drugs. What's your theory?"

Ray and Fred started with their tag team talking.

"I think it has something to do with what happened to Floyd Tice last month," Fred said.

Streeter's ears perked, and he tried not to react overtly. Roger had said he'd been working on the case for several weeks. And Norma Chasing Dog believed all the beatings and murders were tied with one another, too.

Then Ray offered, "He was beat up pretty bad."

Fred said, "So he couldn't testify against Marvin Perret on those child abuse charges."

Ray said, "Floyd Tice is Monica's uncle. Marvin is her dad."

Roger had told Streeter that it took him forever to convince Floyd to do the right thing. Then he saw him at Cubby's, and Floyd ignored him and pretended not to see the FBI agent.

Fred said, "His face needed stitches in several places. His eyes were purple and swollen when I saw him last week."

"He refused to testify. Monica's testimony was the only one offered during the trial."

"But they got the conviction against Marvin."

Ray said, "Somebody must have scared Tice off from testifying. They assumed that 'the somebody' was somehow related to or protecting Marvin Perret."

"But many people had reason to beat Floyd."

Streeter asked, "Why is that?"

Pearl continued, "Everyone on the reservation knows that Floyd Tice deals drugs and sells alcohol from his house just off the reservation boundary. No one likes thinking that somehow, sometimes, that stuff gets to our kids at the high school. But I know it does. I see it."

Streeter asked, "Would he have something to do with Jeff's death?"

They all hesitated. Fred shrugged.

"What does that mean? If he deals drugs, wouldn't Jeff have gotten them from Floyd? Or is there someone else?"

None of them said a word. Streeter wondered why not. He wondered if he'd hit a stone wall. He stayed quiet until someone else spoke.

Ray sighed. "Perhaps Jeff simply lost the battle."

"Hey, you know that's not true. Jeff would have never given in to them," Fred said with a shrug. "But Ray's being humble. Most parents want to find someone to blame, because there could be no way their child was involved in something like this—illegal drugs. But so many of our children are. Particularly with meth. So who would believe you?"

Streeter said, "I do. You all know Jeff was not a drug user, and he did not voluntarily shoot that drug into his vein. It makes no sense."

Ray shook his head. "No sense at all."

His brown, doughy face was haggard and sagging. Beneath his thick black glasses, the intense sadness in his eyes was accented by his slanting, thick eyebrows, which were transfixed in a sorrowful peak. He held his mouth slightly agape.

Fred was wringing his large callused hands between his knees and leaning forward as he sat on the edge of the couch. Pearl stood quietly in the corner of their small living room with a rosary clasped tightly between her fidgeting fingers. She had removed her dentures the instant the meal had ended and was gnashing her gums nervously.

Alice busied herself with the dishes because she couldn't bear to watch her husband implode. And Streeter imagined her severed finger hurt like the dickens. He moved beside Ray on the couch and held his hand. "Ray, listen to me: Jeff didn't do this. He was too bright for that. And I'm going to prove it."

Ray looked up hopefully into Streeter's face. Pearl had stopped fidgeting with her beads. The clock on the mantle above the fireplace ticked loudly in the hopeful silence. Streeter glanced over at Fred who had folded his arms across his expansive middle and stood staring at him with one eyebrow raised.

With all of them fixated on him, Streeter explained, "This is at odds with everything I knew of Jeff. He was educated, focused, energetic, and filled with the kind of hope that can only come from being high on life; not high on drugs."

Ray mumbled, "We know that."

Pearl retreated to the kitchen and blew her nose with a loud, unapologetic honk.

Fred leaned back in his chair and laced the fingers of his hands defiantly across his chest.

"The toxicology report from Indian Health Services came back on the drugs in Jeff's system indicating a cocktail," Streeter explained. He refrained from adding that the forensic scientist had added, "Sleep tight, Two Bears" when she'd handed him and Roger the report. "The indication is that the cocktail was a combination of drugs used in doses large enough to basically knock the user out and then send them into a deep sleep almost instantly."

The room fell silent.

Streeter added, "Within minutes the heart stops completely."

"At least, he wasn't in pain," Ray announced. Alice wailed. Ray rose to his feet and embraced her.

Streeter stood, too, and raked his fingers through his thick, stubborn hair as he paced. Browsing through his memory, he reasoned, "I talked to one of his students today—Logan Walking Crow. The rumor is that everything is changing because of a preacher—from Denver. The kids are scared of him. They think he's a freak. Does that ring a bell with any of you?"

All four of the Two Bears simply stared at him.

"Jeff never mentioned anyone quoting from the Bible? Someone violent?"

They all shook their heads.

Alice wiggled her way out from under Ray's embrace and moved closer to Streeter, no longer hiding her bandaged hand. "Like what?"

"Something about plans. Not a plan to hurt you, but to profit," Streeter loosely interpreted Norma Chasing Dog's memory.

Ray asked, "Were those the exact words?"

Streeter shook his head. "More like harm, not hurt. And prosper, not profit. Something about the future."

Alice grabbed her Bible, winced when she balanced the book on her left hand, and flipped through the pages with her right. "Sounds like prophecy. Unfortunately, the words prosper and harm are used a lot in the Bible, so it really doesn't help narrow anything down."

"That's what I was afraid of," Streeter said, holding out little hope that Roger's team could find anything with Norma's lead either. "But I have to try. A woman was killed in her home—probably Sunday night."

"The same day as Jeff?"

Streeter nodded. "But she wasn't discovered dead until Tuesday."

"Oh dear," Alice said, covering her mouth with her fist.

"Who was she?" Ray asked, leaning forward in his chair.

"The woman who found Jeff."

Pearl gasped. "Julie?"

Fred said, "Who?"

"Julie Good Run," Pearl explained. "Leonard's granddaughter."

"No," Fred said, cradling his head in his hands.

Ray said, "A good friend of Fred's. Leonard Good Run."

"I never knew." Fred was mumbling. Pearl was trying to comfort him.

Streeter focused on Ray and Alice, who studied him intently. "She reported to the police that she'd seen a man leaving Jeff's pickup. Then she found Jeff dead."

Ray's face brightened. "He was murdered."

"That's what I've been trying to tell you. He didn't overdose. He was injected. Killed. I can't prove it—yet. But I have every intention of finding out who did this to him."

Alice rushed to Ray's side and hugged him. They both wept.

"The girl. She was injected, too?"

Streeter shook his head and cut a glance toward Pearl and Fred. Quietly he answered, "He cut her throat."

"Barbaric," Ray mumbled.

"Floyd Tice, Todd Long Soldiers, Julie Good Run, and Jeff. We think they're all tied to this man, the preacher."

"Why?" Ray asked, at first hopeful and now disgusted.

"Do you have any theories? Any of you? Based on what you've heard about the changes on the reservation lately? The rumors. The deaths and beatings."

"The organization." Pearl said the words but stared directly at Fred.

Fred mumbled, "*Sungmanitu.*"

"What?" Streeter stammered. "Who's Sung may . . . ?"

"*Sungmanitu,*" Ray answered. "That means coyote."

Streeter's mouth went instantly dry. "You mean CCG? The Coyote Cries Gang?"

"No, *Kola.* Not the gang. The man," Ray said.

Fred added, "*Sungmanitu hothun.*"

Ray levelled his gaze at Streeter and nodded.

Streeter understood. He shook his head. "Not Coyote Cries. He's been behind bars for decades."

Fred said, "Jeremiah Coyote Cries may be behind bars, but his black heart continues to infect our children. Even after all these years."

"Why didn't you tell me?" Streeter asked Ray.

"Because it is not a battle you can win for us. We must fight him as one people. Besides, you didn't need any more worries about the man. You've had enough." He eyed Streeter before addressing Alice. "Did you make a sandwich?"

She nodded. "On a plate near the sink."

Streeter exchanged a glance with the couple.

Fred said, "This has been a heavy burden for all of us."

Streeter offered consolation, saying, "Yes, I know. It's tragic loss for all of you. For everyone. For me."

Fred sighed. "I didn't mean that his death has been a heavy burden. Of course it has. What I was referring to was that Pearl and I believed that Jeff was murdered—he told us."

Pearl said, "And now, to hear that your theory is that Jeff *was* murdered?"

Streeter glanced over at the sandwich again. "*He* told you?"

"In a dream. He came to both of us," Pearl said. "He asked us to be there for his parents."

Fred explained, "When a person dies in the Catholic faith, the soul leaves the body and wanders about in a place called purgatory until it can advance to heaven. In purgatory, the deceased must be purged of all sin, cleansed before entering heaven. The only way that person can be cleansed of sin is for people on earth to pray for that person."

Streeter listened carefully to Fred's inflectionless story.

Ray looked around the small kitchen and pointed to the counter. "Alice leaves food for Jeff every night on that counter in case he gets hungry while he wanders about in purgatory."

Genuinely curious and not comprehending, Streeter asked, "Catholics believe people eat in purgatory?"

"Not Catholics," Ray answered evenly. "Indians. At least this Indian does. I believe that Jeff has been wandering and will be going to heaven soon. Many are praying for his soul. But he has been hungry—hungry for the truth to be known. Last night, he ate half of the hamburger that Alice left for him."

Streeter turned slowly to look where Ray was pointing. The counter was very empty except for the uneaten sandwich. Ray looked at Streeter and smiled softly. "I am not crazy with grief. I know that Jeff is in a better place—a place that we can only hope to be one day. He loves us and awaits us."

Fred added, "We are just family concerned about our own. Jeff was a very good man; a leader among us. He was God's child, and we will miss him."

Ray and Alice simultaneously bowed their heads in a quick prayer.

Streeter stole a glance at the sandwich, praying there hadn't been a bite taken since he'd last looked.

CHAPTER 32

COYOTE CRIES WATCHED Floyd Tice pace.

Floyd's long arms swayed carelessly at his side like branches in a breeze. With effort, his legs moved clumsily beneath him as he strode across the length of his two-bedroom house.

He was pacing. And thinking. He was trying to figure out how to escape his destiny like trapped prey just waiting for the predator to pounce.

Coyote Cries smiled as he watched the two men through the open back window.

"Are you sure it was him?" Floyd mumbled nervously.

The thin man sitting on the edge of the overstuffed chair wrung his hands nervously. His bony elbows propped precariously on the peaks of his uplifted knees. He nodded.

Both men were in their early fifties and aged by worry, from what he could determine. It must be from the news he had made sure they heard a few hours ago. The news Tice had just received must be more frightening than the beating he'd endured several weeks earlier.

And to think, he still isn't walking quite right yet.

Coyote Cries studied him.

Floyd was a much larger man than he'd remembered—over six-feet-two inches and weighing nearly two-hundred-fifty pounds—which he carried almost entirely around his waist. His black hair was thick, peppered with grey, cut short above his ears, and held in place by a ratty, folded, blue bandana. He wore his jeans beneath his expansive waist and an old T-shirt with a worn logo of a cartoon truck driver and the saying 'Ten-four, good buddy' beneath it. There was nothing on his long thin feet.

Johnnie Red Cloud, the young man sitting quietly in the chair, was wearing a sleeveless, blue sweatshirt, tight designer jeans, and brown dingo boots. His long black hair was secured loosely with a black elastic band. A folded blue bandanna was tied across his forehead.

The boots and bandanas were trademarks for members of the CCG.

"Shit," Tice mumbled.

"He told me he'd be here at your house at seven," Red Cloud added, nervously.

Both men instantly looked out the door, at the microwave clock, and sighed in exasperation.

Red Cloud stammered, "Look. I'd love to stay here for you, buddy. But I got two little ones at home, and my old lady will kill me if she finds out I met with Coyote Cries."

Tice couldn't disguise his fear. His jaw went slack, his eyebrows arched, and his expression hollowed. He'd stopped pacing.

Red Cloud rose, diverted his eyes from his friend, and left without a word.

Tice knew what Coyote Cries wanted. He had told him. He wanted to know why Tice had been meeting with the federal agents. He'd heard they'd been at his house twice already this week.

"Damn feds," Tice growled through clenched teeth and began pacing across his living room, wearing a distinct path where his long, heavy feet dragged through the brown shag carpet.

Coyote Cries waited until Red Cloud was gone, rounded the house through the side yard, and knocked once on the door.

He imagined Tice mumbling to himself on the other side, pissing himself.

Tice opened the door wide, a forced smile plastered on his face.

Coyote Cries stood on Tice's porch with his hands tucked deep in the pockets of his black leather jacket. His feet, which were clad in custom-made black leather cowboy boots, were spread shoulder-width apart. His dark blue jeans had been expertly pressed with a precise crease running up the front of each pant leg.

His grey hair was twisted neatly into two long braids. He sported a menacing grin and let the eerie silence underscore his calm demeanor.

In a tight voice, Tice greeted him nervously. "Jeremiah. Come on in, friend."

Tice waved a shaky, long hand in a generous fashion toward his living room. He probably secretly hoped Coyote Cries would refuse the offer. But he didn't.

Coyote Cries sauntered over to the television that was sitting silent in the corner of the living room. He stood in front of the tube looking straight ahead at the wall—at the large, colorful star embroidered on a quilt hanging in front of him.

The familiar star was the symbol of the United Sioux Tribes. A four-pointed red star was in the center encircled by a bright blue band that provided the base for the outer star's points, which were actually red and white teepees signifying the number of tribes comprising the coalition. The recognizable symbol signified the united front of tribes, whose leaders were organized to speak out against issues negatively affecting the Indian people.

Coyote Cries smiled ruefully and thrust his hands deep in his coat pockets as he positioned his feet firmly beneath him: in case Tice got stupid and attacked him from behind.

In the reflection of the television screen, he watched Tice slowly make his way to the couch on bent and wobbly legs. With a defeated expression, he slumped down into the soft cushions.

Tice had probably heard the rumors about Coyote Cries's reaction to anyone who spoke about his business with the FBI, the BIA, or the tribal police. Jeremiah Coyote Cries carefully crafted his intolerant, and often ruthless, reputation.

He wanted everyone in his organization to know that he had no fear—and even less respect for life. He'd spread rumors about himself that he'd slit the throats of anyone who shorted on payments, cut product without his instruction to do so, or for any other infraction of the rules.

But under Alcott, many people had become soft. They'd become careless.

Coyote Cries simply asked, "What have you heard?"

"That you were back; that you escaped from prison; that you killed a bunch of guards; and that you're exacting your revenge on everyone who defied you," Tice said, his voice quivering.

"And?"

"That Alcott's dead and that you put Todd Long Soldiers in the ICU. But I haven't heard why. And that Jimmy split."

Coyote Cries slowly turned toward Tice and glared at him. "And you?"

"I've had two visits from the feds. Two feds—yesterday and today. The same guys."

Coyote Cries remained standing, even though Tice continued to sit on the couch. He noticed Tice had trouble maintaining eye contact. But so far, he had told nothing but the truth. For his sake, he'd better continue.

"What did they want?"

"Information about the main pipeline of all the drugs that came into the reservation and about you."

Tice thought about it for a moment. "I told them that there were lots of rumors and that the drugs were mainly couriered out of Denver by Dan Alcott. Only because I knew by then he was already dead."

So far, Coyote Cries liked what he heard.

Tice added, "I told them a variety of stuff was sold, like marijuana, heroin, Quaaludes, cocaine, and methamphetamines; that other drugs were available when the market demanded but only on special occasions. I told them that the business was booming in meth and that they could pretty much count on finding a meth lab in every other house on the rez. They didn't like hearing that."

Coyote Cries clenched his fist in his pockets. "Is that true? About the meth labs?"

"Nah," Tice said, waving a hand dismissively. "But there are several. The biggest demand is for meth. We told Alcott that, but he wouldn't listen. So demand outstripped supply and well . . . you know the business. Someone's going to make it if we don't supply it."

Coyote Cries formulated a plan. "If I supply, can you sell?"

"Absolutely."

"Are you equipped to step in for Long Soldiers?"

"Of course. I think it was that asshole who had me beaten. Wasn't you, was it?"

Coyote Cries raised an eyebrow. "Beaten?"

"Yeah, six weeks ago. It almost killed me. They busted my legs with a metal pipe. I'm still not right yet."

Coyote Cries hadn't heard about Tice being beaten. Not from Vic, not from Alcott, and not from Long Soldiers. He'd first heard the news from Norma Chasing Dog when she was talking to the suit in Long Soldiers's hospital room.

"Who do you think beat you?"

"I was supposed to testify in a case against a pedophile. This little girl was being touched up by—"

"I don't care." Coyote Cries was losing patience.

"Look, I don't know who beat me. I'd never seen the guys before. It could have been the pedo taking me out as a witness. It could have been Long Soldiers, jealous that my sales numbers were dwarfing his. It could have been Alcott, pissed I was helping the feds on the pedo case. Who knows?"

"How'd you sell so much more than Long Soldiers?"

"With new techniques. Hitting on the high schoolers wasn't working. I moved down to elementary and middle schoolers—with meth."

Coyote Cries noticed the man had no shame in his technique. He liked him. But he had to be sure. "What did you tell the agents about me?"

"That you started dealing in drugs when you were only thirteen; how savvy and street-smart you were at twenty with experience and criminal skills far beyond your years, even then; how you were destined for a life of crime and psychological impairment given your background. But those of us who really knew you would simply explain all that away as evil."

Coyote Cries couldn't believe what he was hearing. Never before had someone been so forthcoming with the facts. And they were facts. Everything the FBI probably already knew from twenty years ago. This guy was either the most brilliant man on his team—or the stupidest.

"That you were the bastard and eldest child born to a young mother of five; that your stepfather was abusive to the children and the mother, who had increasingly found solace in the bottom of a bottle."

That was Number One for Coyote Cries: his stepfather. He had killed him and set him on fire. And no one had missed him—not even his mother.

"That at age nine, young Jeremiah Coyote Cries had been expelled from the tribal schools and was refused by the Catholic school, considering his deviant and dangerous background; that he had started a fire in the art room at one school; slashed the tires of an unpopular teacher's car at another; and threatened to kill a principal at a third."

Tice shifted on the couch and actually lifted his bent leg to relieve the pain, from what Coyote Cries could interpret from his pained expression.

"That your records clearly indicated a pattern of disrespect for the rules, particularly the ones banning weapons on school grounds; that the schools collectively turned their educational backs on you when you brutally beat another fourth grader to near death over an argument on the playground; that you received a nearly fatal beating from your stepfather for being expelled; that the teachers would describe you as being vacant of human emotion, numb to the pain you inflicted on others, and of the view that life is valueless."

For once, Coyote Cries remained speechless.

Tice shrugged. "That's it in a nutshell. Oh, plus I threw in that all of what I told them was true, but that since your incarceration, you'd had nothing to do with the nefarious activities on the reservation and you were a completely changed man who had found religion."

Coyote Cries grinned.

Everything he said was true, except that he had nothing to do with CCG, and he didn't know the gang had the moniker.

"Who came up with CCG?"

Tice grinned. "I told them it was me who made up the CCG to keep them off the trail of the real mastermind behind the drug ring on the rez: Dan Alcott."

"Brilliant," Coyote Cries said.

"I thought so. Long Soldiers and Blue Owl disagreed with me, but hey."

"Blue Owl is a coward. And Long Soldiers is as good as dead."

Coyote Cries moved toward the couch. He thought Tice may have flinched. But he held it together. He extended his hand. Tice grabbed it and shook.

"You're the new man. My lead. I'm headed out. But you tell everyone you're in charge of CCG. That Red Cloud is your right-hand man and Blue Owl is out. Make sure you take care of him. I'll take care of Long Soldiers. Got it?"

Tice rose, clapped Coyote Cries on the back. "Got it. Thanks, boss."

They walked toward the front door.

Coyote Cries stopped suddenly. "Their names?"

"Whose?"

"The agents." He knew one of them would no doubt be the suit, Roger Landers, the bald man he saw at Long Soldier's hospital room. But he wanted to know for sure.

Tice opened his mouth to speak, then snapped it shut. He waited a minute. Then said, "I'm drawing a blank. Roger Landers and . . . the name's on the tip of my tongue."

Coyote Cries waited.

"For the life of me, can't think of it. But I will."

"When you do, let me know."

He started out the door.

He heard Floyd Tice blurt the name as it came to his mind. "Streeter Pierce. That's it. Roger Landers and Streeter Pierce."

Coyote Cries nodded again.

He knew he had to get back to Denver and prepare.

But not before visiting his mother.

He drove to her house—a hovel, really. The place hadn't changed since he'd last been here—to say goodbye. He never imagined he'd see her again. She hadn't been well, even back then, even though she had only been in her mid-thirties.

His heart raced as he plucked his way through a yard full of discarded garbage bags. He wasn't sure how he'd feel if he learned she had died, and he was even less sure what he'd say to her if she was still alive. He kicked a dead bird off the second step leading to her door.

He knocked.

The house hadn't been painted in all these years. The screen was dangling from one bent hinge and nearly fell off in his hands when he swung it open to knock on the door a second time.

But then he heard it. A chain rattled. The knob turned.

An old woman opened the door and asked, "Who is it? Who's there?"

The woman was large, weighed nearly three hundred pounds by his estimation. Her eyes were a milky brown rather than the black he remembered.

"Please. Speak up. I am blind and old and can't stand here all day."

She was ill with diabetes then, but she was far worse now. Heavier. Blind. Not well at all. "Mother?"

Her jaw dropped. Her eyebrows arched. Several strands of hair fell forward across her face as she trembled. "Jeremiah?"

She reached out her hands to him, wailing.

He stepped inside and held her, kept her from collapsing to the ground.

Without a second's thought, she recited the words he'd heard since birth, her cadence a lullaby that would lift his spirits through the darkest hours.

Jeremiah 1:5:

Before I formed you in the womb, I knew you. Before you were born, I set you apart. I chose you . . . a prophet . . . of our Indian Nation.

CHAPTER 33

I LOOKED AT the clock.

My plane to DC would be taking off from DIA right about now.

I smiled.

I sent a quick text to Christian Doonsberg that I wouldn't be on the flight so not to bother sending someone out to pick me up. I told him I appreciated the offer, but I was staying put in Denver.

His reply was quick. It read, "I told Streeter you'd never get on the plane. But I have to admit, I really wish you had. Be safe."

I had so much to do.

I was working from my apartment. I told Kelleher I had the stomach flu and planned to stay in bed all day. But instead, I had a million things to do before Streeter came back from his trip. I'd asked Laurie Frumpley to quiz Jill Brannock about when Streeter planned on returning. She had told Laurie he wouldn't be back until Monday.

But Laurie called me back and said she had taken advantage of the opportunity when Jill took a powder room break and noticed on the calendar that Streeter's flight returned Friday around four o'clock. He had no appointments in the office after that, so he'd probably head home.

I'd grown quite dependent on Laurie's skills.

I heard someone cough outside my door and peeked through the peephole. It was a uniformed officer with his back to my door. Kelleher had posted a guard to protect me. Or to make sure I didn't leave the apartment on my own.

I logged onto the work computers, my fingers flying over the keyboard as I pulled up one archived file after another. I read every word of every file dealing with Jeremiah Coyote Cries. I scanned the national newspaper archives for any article ever written about him. So much had been written, it took me hours to take it all in. I had a huge stack of printouts from my home printer.

I glanced at the clock. It was just past one. I dialed the Englewood Correctional Institution in Littleton. "My name's Liv Bergen, Special Agent for the Denver division. I'm calling to ask someone about Jeremiah Coyote Cries."

"Hold please," the woman said, not asking twice about the prisoner's name. I heard a series of clicks and my call being transferred.

"This is Warren Holden."

I told the man who I was and that I was looking for information about Jeremiah Coyote Cries.

The man hesitated before saying, "I need to transfer you to his case manager."

And I was off surfing the series of clicks again.

"Daryl Blackenship."

"Are you Jeremiah Coyote Cries's case manager?"

"Who is this?"

I told him who I was. And again, I was met with a very long and awkward pause. Finally the man said, "Look, I'm just a unit officer. You really need to talk to his case manager. Let me put you on hold and transfer you."

Before I could protest, I was off on another sea of beeps and clicks.

"Romeo Ortega. How can I help you?"

"By not transferring me again."

The man chuckled. "Who are you looking for?"

"Someone who can talk to me about a prisoner. I've heard I need to talk to his case manager. Are you a case manager?"

"I am. We take a team approach for each prisoner. We call them Unit

Programs. The team includes a unit manager, a case manager, a case management coordinator, an education representative, a correctional counselor, a correctional officer, and a unit secretary."

"And who would I ask for if I were trying to interview someone about a prisoner?"

"Depends on what it's about."

"His overall well-being, behaviors, patterns, fit within the prison population, how he reacts, his disciplinary log, his release plan, any issues you might have with him," I said.

"Let's start with me, and we'll see if I can help. Who's the prisoner?"

"Jeremiah Coyote Cries," I said.

The line went quiet again—for a third time. I quickly said, "Please don't transfer me. Please. I just want to ask you some questions."

Another long pause.

"Can you just tell me in general, what kind of prisoner he is?"

The man sighed. "Exemplary. For twenty years."

That took me off guard.

"Do you know him? I mean, you have eight hundred prisoners in that place. Are you reading this from a computer report or do you actually know Coyote Cries."

Again, a pause. "I know the man well. He's been here a long time. We've had no problems with him in the past."

"Any incidents that stand out? Any threats to other inmates? Any fights he's had?"

"No fights. No incidents. Never sent to solitary confinement. Never disciplined, that I know of. Always attended any educational opportunities, counseling, voluntary work programs. Like I said. Exemplary."

"Any threats? To other inmates, staff, guards, or quirky off-handed comments about people outside the prison?"

"What are you getting at, Agent Bergen?"

I had to fess up. "Look, I'm concerned about his parole hearing. Worried he might come after one of our agents if he's released."

"Ma'am, I need to let you talk to our unit manager. Let me transfer you."

"Romeo, wait. *Romeo?*"

The unit manager wasn't much help. And this was the run-around I received for the next hour, gleaning little, transferred a lot. At one point, one of the folks I talked to called Coyote Cries "The Reverend," which I found odd.

Another called him a 102, but he didn't stay on the line long enough to explain what a 102 at Littleton meant. And I couldn't recall any reference, in bureau terms or police slang that referred to such a number.

I finally gave up trying to talk with anyone at the correctional facility, although I left my name and number with the warden, the assistant warden, a correctional counselor, and the unit manager. Just in case any one of them decided to talk.

I looked at the clock and decided I'd better try calling Streeter to tell him I hadn't gotten on the plane, before Phil told him—or someone else did. I dialed his cell phone number, but it went straight to the message center. I didn't leave a message.

One last attempt at research, and I finally hit pay dirt.

A series of articles by Nolan Buffington written about Jeremiah's life story in *Civil Writes* magazine chronicled a case study that stated that the Lakotan was a political prisoner deserving of the Pulitzer Peace Prize rather than a life sentence as a convicted murderer.

A series of quotes from Coyote Cries peppering his life story made the man come alive for me. Sadly, the author believed Coyote Cries had been convicted of a crime he hadn't committed, he was the poster child for "horrid travesties of the US justice system," and that Coyote Cries's prosecution and conviction were solely driven by his participation and exercise of his First Amendment rights: his freedom of speech. Incarcerated only to silence him, he was the victim of racism, oppression, and bigotry.

In between articles, I studied the photo of Paula Pierce to remind myself what this monster had done, because Buffington was a creative writer—enough so to make even the most hardened heart bleed for Coyote Cries's plight.

But not me. I had experienced firsthand the damage this monster had caused to Streeter.

Buffington suggested letters be sent to the correctional facility to free Coyote Cries on behalf of all Native Americans who had suffered as victims of war, disease, poverty, oppression, and racism. The journalist went so far as to state that Coyote Cries was in poor health, having been beaten several times by fellow inmates and denied medical help by the staff.

I jotted down a note to ask for confirmation or denial of such accusations by the case manager or unit manager, should they ever decide to call me back.

Buffington reported that Coyote Cries wasn't given a fair trial and denied a jury of his peers, citing none of them were members of the Oglala Sioux Tribe, even though four were Indians living in South Dakota. He was convicted on perjured testimony that accused all the agents and tribal officers of lying under oath; then railroaded, after it was revealed that the judge had met with federal agents before the trial.

Beyond the irritatingly naïve presentation of unsubstantiated factoids by Buffington, I was most struck by the tragic story of Jeremiah's childhood—assuming it was true.

I had been fortunate to have such a loving, caring family. To hear that he had no father, that he was oldest of five children born to a mother when she was only fifteen years old, and that he was beat to near death by his stepfather, it was no wonder Jeremiah was expelled from all schools by age nine and was dealing drugs by thirteen to provide for his family.

But for a man to recall his last evaluation in school with a teacher describing him as "vacant of human emotion," "numb to the pain he inflicted on other children," and that he "regarded life as valueless" and agreeing with their assessment of that nine-year-old child, I found the entire situation sad.

The horrors he had committed as an adult—the degradation of young children, spoiling innocence through drug addiction, profiteering from others' pain and suffering, the beatings, the murders—were all unforgivable, all unjustifiable no matter what his childhood had been. Paula Pierce had not deserved to be beheaded.

By all accounts, Jeremiah Coyote Cries may have taken responsibility for nearly a dozen deaths, at least from what I could read between the article lines. Deaths he would never be held accountable for in court because there was not enough evidence.

So incredibly sad.

And like a pebble thrown into the still waters, each one of the deaths had a rippling effect on so many others—including me.

I had to get out of here. I had to slip past the guard at my door and drive to Littleton to talk to someone. I called my neighbor downstairs to see if he was home. He wasn't. I grabbed my grappling gear and simply climbed out my back window and lowered myself to the ground. Unstrapping the rope and harness, I darted around the corner of the building and slammed smack into a man in a leather jacket.

Mully.

He grabbed me before I hit the ground. He was wearing his Lucifer's Lot colors. "Princess, what did you do to your head?"

As head of an MC gang, he was certainly more polite and caring than I'd ever imagined a criminal organization leader to be. And I'd forgotten all about being clocked on Sunday night. I reached up and touched the stitched and tender goose egg. "Oh, just a little accident. Ran into somebody."

He lifted my chin with his fingertips and examined the wound. "Looks more like you ran into someone's fist."

I nodded and scanned the parking lot.

"Were you expecting someone?" he asked.

"No, I . . ." Then I had a thought. "I was looking for a ride to the Englewood Correctional facility in Littleton."

If I could get a ride from Mully, the police officer wouldn't be alerted by my Jeep being missing.

Mully motioned me toward his motorcycle. "Your carriage awaits."

"Are you sure? Am I interrupting anything?"

He didn't answer. He just smiled and mounted his Harley.

CHAPTER 34

STREETER STOOD NEAR THE corpse lying behind the bushes by the front step.

"Poor Florence," Roger said through unmoving lips as they stood in the front door. "I tried to warn her this might happen."

Florence had greeted them before they'd ever reached her door. Her short, massive body, draped in a simple, one-size-fits-all maroon dress, filled the entire doorway. The moccasins on her wide, bare feet were tattered, and her grey-streaked hair was short and ratty. She hadn't bothered to put in her dentures this morning, nor had she bathed—probably since her husband's death two days earlier.

In an even tone, she said, "Garnett isn't here yet."

Roger whispered to Streeter, "Tribal police."

They followed her to the living room and found a place to sit.

Roger replied, "He's right behind us. He said he'd be just a minute."

The thick and pungent odor of stagnant death clung to Streeter's lungs like a heavy, musty blanket. He disciplined himself to take infrequent, shallow breaths. He thought he could smell the aftermath of greasy meals cooked on the open range, stale cigarettes, spilt whiskey, and bad hygiene.

Streeter shot a glance at Roger, who sat on the couch across from

Florence. He wondered why the odor of two-day decay didn't offend Roger as much as it did him. Then he remembered: Roger had swiped some cream or salve on the inside of each nostril just before they arrived. Streeter realized he'd forgotten his jar of medicated rub in Denver.

Roger said, "How long have I known you and Neil?"

"A long time," Florence answered, wringing her hands and staring at her feet.

"Nine years," he replied.

"I should have listened to you. I should have left him. But I told you, I love him. I still do."

Streeter figured that Roger had anticipated the tragedy. He'd probably been called in by the tribal police numerous times to help them with the domestic disputes. He'd probably warned Florence that it might end this tragically if she didn't do something about Neil's abuse.

As Roger leaned forward with his elbows propped casually on his knees, Florence spoke evenly and calmly, "I knew you would be here sooner or later. I'm ready to go now."

Roger replied, "Well, Flo, you know we have to arrest you."

"Yeah," she answered without emotion. She propped her flabby arms across the rolls of her stomach and forced her thick legs together enough to link her ankles. "I know. But thanks for giving me a few days to get my things here at home in order first."

Roger answered, "Sure, no problem."

Streeter knew Roger hadn't given her a few days. He wouldn't have ignored his duties. A man was dead, and if Roger or the tribal police knew about Neil's death, his murder, they'd have come sooner. It was Florence who had called Roger, and Roger had called Garnett.

Light-headed, nauseated, Streeter longed for fresh air. He wondered how Florence had remained in the home this long with her husband's corpse just outside the door.

"Tell me something, Flo. Why now, after all these years of putting up with him? You've been married to him forever. What in the hell made you shoot him?"

Florence shrugged her shoulders like a little girl and curled her lips into a bashful smile.

Roger leaned back on the couch and glanced out the living room window. The two tribal police officers, Wayne Garnett and Vern Chasing Elk, were making their way slowly up the driveway. Roger knew that Florence wouldn't answer any of their questions in front of the tribal police. She and Neil had told Roger on several occasions that they had no use for them and that they didn't trust them—especially Chasing Elk, who was allegedly molesting his own young teenage daughter.

Roger encouraged her. "Come on, Flo. Wayne and Vern are coming. You can tell me before they get here. Please. What did Neil do to you to deserve this?"

Shrugging again, Florence answered, "Wouldn't give me the channel changer. I wanted to watch my soap opera. He wanted to watch something else."

She snapped, Streeter thought. *Couldn't take the man's abuse anymore.*

The knock on the screen door was followed by Garnett's low growl, "Hello. Anybody home?"

Florence puckered her lips with disgust and answered without raising her voice, "Come in, Wayne."

She did not resist the arrest. She'd anticipated it, even prepared for it. She expected to be incarcerated for a long time and hadn't planned on coming back to this house. Florence Short Eagle had arranged for her nephew to move into the house and gave him all of her and Neil's possessions, including the goats, the discarded truck bed in the weeds, and the gutted pickup.

Before she was led off in handcuffs, Streeter asked, "Florence, we weren't here about Neil. We came by to see if you've seen your grandson. Jimmy Blue Owl."

She nodded. "Someone came by yesterday looking for him. I'll tell you what I told him. My guess? He's probably pitched a tent down at Oglala Lake."

Once in the car, Streeter drew a deep breath.

Roger said, "You've lost your edge."

"You've lost your mind."

Roger tried not to smile. "There are two things you've forgotten about being an agent in Indian Country, Streeter."

"What's that?" Streeter asked. "Never trust you? And what else?"

"No. First thing you need is to remember to do your job." Roger held up his index finger, then two. "And secondly, you need to remember to not take it personally."

Streeter shook his head. "Lives on the rez are so hard."

Roger sighed, "I hate to say it, but you get used to it."

Streeter jerked his head in Roger's direction. "What do you mean you get used to it? You're joking, right? Tells me you've worked IC too long."

Roger shrugged one shoulder. "Eventually, you get used to Indian Country. The odd way that life seems to have no—or at least little—meaning on the reservation with some of these folks."

"Most Lakotans embrace life *more* than the rest of us. It's not everyone on the reservation."

Roger jerked his chin skyward as if he agreed, but then he said, "I was on a case right before you came back where an eighteen-year-old knifed his uncle to death for eating the last piece of chicken from the bucket; snapped for the uncle touching him up for years. Same thing happened again at another home when a woman shot her uncle for taking the last beer. She mizzed out after too much meth. I watched an intoxicated man celebrate a victory, arms flailing overhead with fists clenched, because he had beat his buddy in a swimming race. Both men had been drinking excessively, and the reason he beat his buddy was because his buddy had drowned. He was floating facedown in the water."

Streeter stared out the window in disbelief. "Like I said, this is a tough life on the reservation. Many have so little hope because of the few who have little respect for life."

"Some of them don't give a damn about life. Not even their own."

He realized how important Jeff Two Bears's efforts really had been on the reservation and how much he'd be missed.

Streeter noticed Roger headed toward Oglala Lake. "A few months ago, I went to a funeral for a guy who was axed to death. And his buddy who had wielded the ax was the loudest mourner at the wake. It's odd. Didn't you notice Florence? How unfazed she seemed to be about her husband's death?"

Streeter swiped his fingers through his hair. "I think that's what shook me up the most. It's disturbing, and I recognized the signs of shock, even though now she's free from his abuse."

"Like I said. Only two things you need to work the rez: Do your job. Don't take it personally. You've forgotten both."

"Actually, I haven't forgotten. I do my job and take the impacts on victims incredibly seriously after tragedies like this."

"Which is why you burnt out on IC so quickly."

Streeter was tired of arguing. He knew that it was Roger who'd stayed too long, becoming cynical and jaded.

They drove into the center of Pine Ridge Village toward Oglala Lake.

Roger asked, "Want to grab a snack first?"

Streeter glanced at his watch. He hadn't eaten anything since early this morning. "Sure."

Roger pulled the bureau-issued Ram Charger into the empty lot of Cubby's and pulled up to the gas pump. A Plymouth full of teenagers drove by with all the windows rolled down. The car was rumbling from the methodical Native chant blaring from the radio, which was tuned to 90.1 FM KILI radio station.

Roger nodded toward the boys who each nodded once in return.

One boy in the back seat lifted a finger as a wave goodbye to Roger.

As the car turned the corner and slowly crept out of sight, Roger let out the breath he'd been holding. "I can't stand the uneasiness that has settled on this town ever since Long Soldiers was beaten and Two Bears was killed. It used to be more peaceful."

"They're just a bunch of kids," Streeter said and pointed up the empty street.

Roger replaced the fuel hose into its designated slot. "Same bunch of kids who I found spray painting that graffiti all over the Billy Mills Hall after one of the community wakes last year. They were all strung out on something. I wanted them to repaint the hall, but Wayne told them all to go home and get cleaned up or he'd throw them in jail overnight with the drunks."

"They looked clean to me just now, but maybe I'm losing touch."

"Actually, they are clean," Roger said, walking toward Cubby's. "Completely drug-free, thanks to Two Bears."

"He made the difference?" Streeter asked.

"Big difference," Roger said. "He turned a bunch of these kids' lives around. He'll be missed—just like you and me, right?" Roger winked.

They entered the convenience store and perused the shelves for snacks. Roger patted his expansive girth, "I'm getting old. If it wasn't for all the preservatives in the processed foods I eat, I'd probably be falling apart."

Tribal criminal investigator, Howard Walking Crane, darted from the bathroom and nearly toppled Roger.

Roger straightened his crooked glasses. "Whoa, Howard. Where's the fire?"

"Sorry, Roger. Got a call. Got to go."

"What's up? Do you need help?" Streeter asked.

Walking Crane, a man in his early forties with a shaved head and black rimmed glasses similar to Roger's, was a rather slovenly man. His disheveled appearance was by no means indicative of his competency as the tribal criminal investigator, however. During the two short days he'd been working the reservation with Roger, Streeter had found Howard to be very proficient and competent.

Howard tucked in his shirt. "I just got a call. There're two men up at Oglala Lake. The woman who called said that she thought one of them had killed the other with a hammer. We'd better check it out. I radioed Vern and Wayne. They'll meet us down there. Come along."

Roger exchanged a glance with Streeter. "We were just heading that way. We're right behind you."

Within minutes, the three men arrived on the grassy banks of Oglala Lake.

Several small houses and a few trailers scattered the landscape. West of the last house on the dirt road, beyond the abandoned cars and deserted furniture strewn in the grassy fields, an infrequently traveled, barely visible trail wound around the banks of the lake.

The caravan of three cars bumped across the overgrown trail leading to the uninhabited bank, where the two men had last been seen according to reports.

Streeter glanced over his shoulder through the rear window. "Wayne and Vern are behind us. Guess Howard's leading us into uncharted territory."

"God damn it," Roger said quietly. "I thought those two were supposed to have checked this situation out before now."

"Doesn't look like it," Streeter said as he craned his neck to see around Howard Walking Crane's pickup truck in front of them. Streeter jerked his head to the right and pointed out his window. "There's one of them."

"We might be coming into something hot." Roger honked his horn lightly and waved to Howard, who was looking at them in his rearview mirror.

Streeter pointed to the bank of the lake.

Howard bolted from the truck and slowly made his way to the staggering man. Just as they arrived and parked their cars, the tall, staggering Lakotan dropped to his knees in the thick grass. Streeter and Roger exited the Ram Charger to follow Howard, both with their pistols in hand. Wayne and Vern stopped their vehicle, got out, and joined them.

The only thing the five men could see of the man kneeling in the grass by the lake was his head. They approached him cautiously with their weapons drawn but not leveled.

Howard called out to the man, "*Toníktuha he?*"

The man's head turned in their direction. His ruddy face was soiled and drenched with sweat. His eyes were barely open as a result of alcohol consumption and the swelling from being punched in a recent brawl. He stared at the five approaching men as if he were trying to get them in focus and having a difficult time doing so.

Howard quietly spoke over his shoulder to the other four men. "It's okay. I don't think he's quite with us at the moment." Then, he called to the man in the grass, "Could you do me a favor, and show me your hands?"

"Huh?" the large man in the grass grunted in confusion.

"Put both hands in the air, will you?" Howard repeated, slowly inching closer to the man on his knees.

Confused, the man lifted both hands slowly into the air. In one hand, he gripped the handle of a heavy sledgehammer and in the other, the neck of an empty bottle.

Roger slipped his pistol back into his holster.

Streeter whispered, "What are you doing?"

He answered with a shrug.

Howard called, "What happened to your friend?"

The man looked down at the grass in front of him and answered in a slurred voice, "Uh . . . don't know. He hasn't moved much lately. Think he might have . . . had one too many drinks or . . . or something."

"Or something," Howard repeated with disgust.

The five men surrounded and closed in on the kneeling man. After a few minutes, they were all staring down at the bloodied man lying in the grass.

Roger muttered curses under his breath when he recognized his face.

Howard Walking Crane knelt beside the kneeling man. "What's your name, young man?"

"Kyle," the dazed man said as he stared down at his buddy in the grass.

"What's your friend's name?"

"Jimmy."

Jimmy Blue Owl lay in the grass, very still. His nose had been smashed to bits. Beyond his swollen lips and gaping mouth, the bloodied gums where teeth had once been were oozing. The unconscious man's breathing was gurgled and fading. He was still alive, but barely.

Howard carefully tilted the unconscious man's head to the side to allow the drainage from his swollen lips to spill onto the ground, rather than down his throat. "What happened to Jimmy?"

Kyle shrugged. "Fell asleep or something."

Pushing his glasses up the bridge of his nose, Roger gave Streeter a sideways glance and smirked. No one had to hear Kyle explain that he had smashed his friend's face with the sledgehammer. The wounds were obvious. Kyle also didn't have to explain that he and his friend had been drinking.

Checking the unconscious man's pulse, Howard looked at Vern. "Call Benny and have them send over the paramedics." Then, he asked Kyle, "Why'd you hit him?"

Kyle narrowed his eyes and looked at his friend lying on the ground. In an angry huff, he ripped off the blue bandana that encircled his head. "He wouldn't give me my bottle back."

As Vern made his way back to the tribal patrol car to radio for help, the others said nothing as Jimmy's pulse grew reedy and weak.

Vern returned. "I just heard. Todd Long Soldiers died."

Streeter exchanged a glance with Roger, who said, "Damn it."

The sun beat down on the men from the late afternoon sky. The horse flies buzzed around Jimmy's limp, unconscious body. Howard swiped the air around his broken and bleeding nose and mouth to discourage them from landing.

The pungent odor of alcohol, spent body fluids, and blood wafted thickly through the intense heat. Tribal Investigator Wayne Garnett took two steps back from the group and turned his back on the men to clear his lungs. Kyle broke the silence by chuckling and holding his empty bottle high in the air above his head in victory. His slurred words were loud and proud. "He wouldn't give it back, but I got it back. I got it back, all right."

Roger shook his head and mumbled more curse words. Streeter walked toward the lake and watched for the arriving paramedics.

Knowing it was far too late for Jimmy Blue Owl.

CHAPTER 35

HORRIFIED ABOUT WHAT I'd learned so far, I needed more on Coyote Cries.

So on Friday, I decided to return to work to search all the bureau files that hadn't been scanned, looking for everything and anything related to Coyote Cries: the case files, the newspaper articles, the court transcripts.

I even read every word of Jeremiah Coyote Cries's deposition. And Streeter's.

My heart ached for him.

The ringing of my phone nearly sent me sailing out of my chair. I glanced at the clock. It was already 1:30, and I hadn't even stopped for lunch. According to Laurie's reconnaissance, Streeter's plane would be arriving in a few hours. I had to finish all of this, put everything back in its rightful place, and archive the files down in storage. He didn't need to know anything about my snooping.

Or my visit to the correctional facilities yesterday with Mully.

He'd only worry.

"Agent Bergen," I said, answering on the third ring.

The man announced himself as the warden for the Englewood Federal Correctional Institution. "Are you Special Agent Liv Bergen who visited us yesterday?"

My mouth went dry, remembering the stonewalling I had received from several of the staff yesterday. All I wanted were answers. I got a few—confirming that Buffington's story had misrepresented much about prison life for Jeremiah Coyote Cries.

"Yes, that's me."

"And you work with Special Agent Streeter Pierce?"

"I do, but he's away from the office until Monday."

"I know. That's why I'm talking to you. We have a letter personally addressed for him," the man announced.

"For who? Special Agent Streeter Pierce?" I was confused. Admittedly I didn't understand the parole process. "From Coyote Cries?"

The man said, "Yes, for Pierce, but not from Coyote Cries. It's from another inmate who was found murdered in his cell a week ago. And we're just now disposing of his personal effects."

"Was he a friend of Coyote Cries?" I asked.

"They were friends," the man admitted. "And when we cleaned out his cell, we found a sealed envelope addressed to Agent Pierce with a handwritten letter inside."

I thought about what he was telling me. "How do you know it was handwritten?"

"Because we opened it. We always do that," the warden said, unapologetically. "Anyway, are you sending someone down to retrieve it or would you like us to scan and email?"

"Both, please. I'll send a runner into Littleton. But if you could scan and email me the letter as soon as possible, I'd appreciate it."

"On its way," the warden said and hung up.

I called Bessie and relayed the request that we send a runner. I'd leave the letter on Streeter's desk and explain everything on Monday. Until then, why worry him?

He didn't need to know.

Within seconds, I had a handwritten letter on lined legal paper, several pages long, addressed to Streeter Pearce—name misspelled—signed by a man named Mort Dillinger.

The letter was documentation of Jeremiah Coyote Cries's prison confession: a story he entitled "The Beheading—A Near Complete Victory."

My stomach lurched.

I wasn't sure if I could read this—let alone share it with the man I loved about the woman he loved.

The story's preface explained that Dillinger's letter was documentation of what Jeremiah Coyote Cries had told him while they were incarcerated. And that if anyone was reading this letter, it was likely that Dillinger had met his demise, probably because of Coyote Cries.

Jeremiah had explained to Dillinger that a beheading in the Bible signified a complete victory over the enemy and that the Bible was riddled with just such examples of why this style of execution was so important and popular.

Then Dillinger went into great detail about an enemy Jeremiah had called "New Guy" and how New Guy had destroyed his life.

In his early teens, Jeremiah had started a profitable business that made him a millionaire by the time he was twenty-one. The success had afforded him riches, power, and women beyond his dreams. As he grew, he learned. And the respect of his people for his ability and brilliance expanded beyond his wildest dreams.

Until New Guy.

Then the people of his community had turned on him. They believed the fork-tongued New Guy who spread rumors about him. His business dipped. Customers not only stopped buying but demonized him. His employees sought other opportunities—with his competition.

And when New Guy trumped up phony charges against him, he had to choose between losing the business he loved and turning the reins over to a partner while he served time. Times were desperate, and he had to make desperate choices.

Dan Alcott became his partner.

He grew to loathe Alcott even more than he had when they competed. But not more than New Guy, because everything was his fault.

As his empire began to crumble, he decided to destroy everyone who'd become an obstacle in his journey to success before he was incarcerated. So he acted fast and did what he had to do. He admitted to nothing—except complete victory over his enemy, New Guy.

He described to Dillinger how he had stalked his prey for days, waiting to catch New Guy unaware, to slice his throat, hold his severed head high, and holler a battle cry for all his enemies to hear. But on that final hunting day, the day he had planned for so long, he'd been forced to make adjustments.

He watched as New Guy's bride steadied the grocery bag on her knee while she fished for the apartment key in her jeans pocket. She pushed the door open and grabbed the bag from her knee. She was making dinner for them. He would be home soon.

He followed her inside. Silently. Patiently.

The pale blue and silver streaks of dusk painted the empty living room—across the kitchen cabinets and down the dark hallway. New Guy's wife stood just beyond the kitchen, down the hall in the quiet apartment.

He held his breath, listened to the sounds of emptiness, and pressed himself inside the coat closet in the entryway while her back was turned. Then he peeked through the open door.

They were alone.

The woman let out a sigh and made her way quickly across the living room to the kitchen. She dumped the grocery bags on the counter and snapped on all the lights in the kitchen, the living room, and the hallway.

He imagined that she was scared and thought the light would scatter any bogeymen.

She was wrong.

She busied herself by unloading her bounty and storing everything away. She hummed. Perhaps silence screamed constant reminders of her solitude.

She was preparing homemade soup for New Guy—vegetable soup.

He saw the bottle of cheap champagne she'd bought. Were they celebrating New Guy's arrest of a Top Ten fugitive? Probably.

But she had no clue he was already out on bail.

Her excitement grew as several people called to pass on their congratulations to New Guy. She replayed dozens of messages from the day. She chopped vegetables. She smiled, sang, and sipped champagne. And prepared their meal.

Their last supper.

He waited for what seemed like hours. He'd have to report soon or give up his bail money, which he'd worked hard to earn.

He checked the time and watched as she cut celery.

His patience with New Guy was wearing quite thin. The man was ruining his plan. He'd have to go soon.

She chopped the last of the celery and threw the pieces into the boiling water.

Time's up for New Guy. On to Plan B.

The closet door creaked when he opened it. The wife stopped cutting vegetables and glanced up. She'd heard him. She'd held her breath. Listened.

She closed her eyes. He remained still.

Eventually, she let out a long, quiet breath and started to hum again, chopping the carrots more vigorously. As she scraped them into the pot of water, he crept up behind her on the soft carpet.

He'd moved quickly toward her. She gripped the knife, and her body stiffened.

"You're Streeter Pierce's wife?" he'd asked, in a low, emotionless voice.

She'd whirled around to face him, the knife gripped tightly in her right hand.

"What do you want?" she'd asked.

Not a puddle of tears, but rather a pillar of strength. *This is going to be fun*, Coyote Cries remembered thinking. *Nothing worthwhile comes easy.* He remembered she had crouched like a cougar preparing to pounce in a ready stance, gripping the knife tightly in one hand. She was trying not to panic. He was trying not to laugh at her.

With his hands stuffed deep in the pockets of his black leather jacket and his legs spread apart, he had blocked her only exit from the kitchen.

It was that easy.

She couldn't reach the phone or the door without going through him.

She said, "What do you want?"

"Don't you want to know who I am?"

"I know who you are," New Guy's wife had answered. "You're Satan. Pure evil."

Coyote Cries had laughed.

She appeared confused.

He'd pulled his hands out of his pockets.

She'd gripped the knife with both hands, waved it between them. Slice, slice.

His hands were empty, and he'd held them up to her in surrender.

He remembered telling her, "You are as clever as your husband, my enemy."

She'd only *thought* she'd known fear. He'd show her. Teach her. Her hands had trembled. Her glance had darted toward the clock. Then dread had whitewashed her already porcelain features.

"Feels like a nightmare, where you're unable to move or speak," he'd told her. "He won't be home in time."

She'd caught his glance, and fear had enveloped her. "What do you want with me?"

"I want to teach your husband a lesson. He messed with my business, my reputation, my freedom."

Coyote Cries had flicked his head quickly, sending the long, black braid that had fallen forward over his shoulder sailing.

"Please. Don't kill me. I don't want to die."

The boiling pot of soup splashed and hissed on the stove behind her. Startled, the New Guy's wife nearly dropped the knife.

"Vegetable soup?" he had asked.

She'd nodded. "I understand you're angry. But more violence will not help your situation. It will only make everything worse."

Coyote Cries had laughed. "And what do you know about my situation?"

"I know you sell drugs to the kids on the reservation. I know you must have had a difficult childhood. I know you could probably use some help."

Coyote Cries had corrected her. "Everybody who grows up on the reservation has a difficult childhood. I overcame my difficulties. I did something with my life. I ignored my miserable existence on that godforsaken reservation, and I became somebody. I'm rich. I'm important."

"You're a murderer and a drug dealer." She must have said it without thinking.

"People look up to me. They want to be just like me."

Panicked and afraid he was about to make a move on her, she'd lunged in his direction. Jabbed the knife at him. Coyote Cries had clutched her wrist and had given it a quick twist. The knife had clattered to the floor. She'd whimpered in pain.

He'd twisted her wrist until a bone snapped. He'd pushed her into the living room.

Sobbing, she'd pleaded, "Stop. You're hurting me."

He'd made sure she'd felt his hot breaths against her sweat-soaked neck, standing behind her, twisting her arm, and mocking her in a pathetic whine. "*Poor baby.*"

The words must have triggered something in New Guy's wife because he'd felt a change in her: complete submission. "Please stop. I'll lose the baby. I just found out this morning. Streeter doesn't even know. Please don't hurt my baby. I won't say a thing."

Two for one.

He'd pushed her facedown on the carpet. He'd dug his knee into her back, pinning her against the floor. He'd unzipped his jacket.

She must have thought he'd unzipped his jeans, and she'd begged him not to rape her. Tears streaked her face.

His hand had gripped a clump of her hair and yanked. He'd heard a crack somewhere in her neck and felt a clump of hair pull from her scalp by the roots.

"One thing is true. You won't say anything. I'm making sure of that."

He'd pressed the long, sharp knife against the skin on her neck hard. He made one slice. Then he hacked and chopped.

New Guy would find her.

Complete victory.

He had bragged to Dillinger how he'd thrown her head against the wall by the couch.

Dillinger's final paragraph explained that his story had been repeated by Coyote Cries so many times that he'd been able to document his words almost verbatim. And that if something should happen to him, it was probably Jeremiah Coyote Cries who'd killed him.

And now Dillinger was dead.

I set the letter down on my desk.

My hands trembled. Absently, I realized I kept touching my own neck.

I could never, never let Streeter see this letter.

CHAPTER 36

THE INSTANT THEY LANDED, Streeter pulled out his cell phone and dialed.

"Please. It's about Liv. I heard she didn't fly to DC yesterday. I'm going to pick her up from work now and take her to my place."

Mully asked, "Who's after her?"

"Jeremiah Coyote Cries. The man who beheaded my wife twenty years ago."

The long pause at the other end of the phone unnerved him. He may have made a mistake. Mully might decide to kill him and take Liv to safety on his own.

If he was smart.

Streeter added, "But I need your help. I need you to shadow her. Never let her out of your sight."

The man agreed. "When and where?"

"Starting Monday morning." Streeter gave him his home address.

"What about this weekend?"

"She'll be with me. Safe."

Mully's ominous voice sounded, "Believe me, Pierce. If one hair on her beautiful head is harmed in any way, I will kill you myself."

"You won't have to. I'll already be dead." He slipped the phone in his pocket.

Streeter had never been so sure of looming danger in his life. Coyote Cries had already been busy making the dominoes fall in Colorado and at the reservation.

No doubt, Jeremiah was behind all this destruction—even if he was still behind bars.

He couldn't afford for Liv to be swept up in the death toll. But the work of Julius Chavez indicated Coyote Cries had his sights set on Liv.

He had a new plan.

Pretending he didn't love her wouldn't work. No one would buy that—especially Liv. And even if she did, Coyote Cries wouldn't spare her. The murders on Pine Ridge were proof enough that he was taking over the business, even before the parole hearing.

Sending her away hadn't done the trick. She was too damned stubborn for that.

So on to Plan C. He called Denver Chief of Police, Tony Gates.

"Did you find Vic?"

"Exactly where you said he would be."

"Anything?"

"Not yet. We're running everything."

"What about Alcott?"

"Unfortunately. He was inside. What a mess. Who would shove money down someone's throat until they suffocated?"

"A sick bastard like Jeremiah Coyote Cries," Streeter said. "And I plan to prove it."

"Happy to help."

"Mind posting protection? At my cabin?"

There was a long pause. Streeter knew he needed more of an explanation.

"For Liv, not me. I'm picking her up now from work, in case Julius Chavez shared anything with Coyote Cries about her place."

"Smart move," Gates added. "I'll have someone up there 24/7."

"But not obvious. I'm not telling her about your officers. Just post them in the trees near the road to my place. There's only one way in and one way out."

Streeter rang off when Gates made him promise to be careful.

He sped down Penya Boulevard, hoping to be stopped for speeding so he'd have an escort to the office. He needed to retrieve Liv and take her to his cabin. He'd leave Beulah in the care of the bureau dog kennel. They needed to stay alert.

Liv seemed stunned to see him. She glanced at the clock several times. She rose slowly from her chair, rounded her desk until Streeter held up a finger to his lips and motioned her with his hands to stay where she was.

He leaned down to write a note:

> *Grab your things. We need to go. I'll follow you to the cabin. Don't tell anyone. Don't call anyone. Leave Beulah. I'll explain.*

She read his note. Her brows furrowed. He walked out without a word.

The last time he'd seen her was at the hospital Tuesday morning. And he hated himself for saying the things he had. He loved her more than anything. And he hated to see the pain he'd caused.

But now, he prayed she'd listen to him and obey.

Her life depended on it.

<hr />

Stunned, I forced myself not to react.

I read Streeter's note several times. It was so cryptic. He must have been worried about bugs or office gossip or something.

I gathered my work and tidied my desk.

Without another word, I headed toward my Jeep in the parking garage.

With mixed emotions, I anticipated nothing from my arrival at Streeter's home in Conifer. I had no clue what his odd behavior was all about—both earlier in the week and just now.

But I admittedly wanted answers.

I was also dreading the worst; that there might be more than I could handle in all this drama. Unfortunately, the drive to Conifer was a long one. And my fertile mind conjured up several wicked reasons why he'd dumped me earlier. And why he was so cryptic now. None of the reasons were good and all of this was so uncharacteristic of Streeter.

By the time I arrived at his house, I was trembling with worry.

Another surprise—he ushered me into his second garage and closed the door behind me.

When I stepped out of my Jeep, carrying nothing but some files, Streeter pointed me into his cabin through the inside garage door. "Please come in."

I noticed him do a quick scan of the surroundings beyond the garage windows before shutting and bolting the door.

"What are we looking for? What's going on?" I asked.

He ignored me, hurrying me through the house, opening every door and closet, with his gun extended.

He was afraid someone was there.

When he returned, I couldn't think to do anything but hand him a file I'd been working on in his absence. "I dropped this report off with the district attorney today. He said I had plenty of solid evidence and that he's going to arrest Dick Roth tonight. I was going with him, until you showed up."

Streeter took the file, dropped it on his kitchen counter, gathered me in his arms, and held me for what seemed like forever.

Just held me.

It surprised me when I heard myself say, "I love you, Streeter. I know you're in trouble somehow. And that Tuesday morning was all about protecting me. But please don't. I don't need your protection. I need your trust and the truth. That's it. And no matter what game you play with me, it won't stop me from loving and caring about you. I'm worried."

None of those were even one of the options I'd rehearsed or contemplated over the past several days. Not even close. But I'd said it anyway. And it had come from the heart.

Streeter finally let me go. Cupping my hand in his, he looked at me with a sorrowful gaze. "I did not want to hurt you. I never wanted to hurt you. You must believe me."

I bit my lower lip and nodded cautiously. "I know that. But you have to trust someone. Whatever it is that's bothering you, whatever demon you're battling, you don't have to fight it alone. I am here for you. You can trust me."

He closed his eyes and hung his head, with his shoulders slumped.

"I can't help you if I don't know what's happening. *Please*, let me into your life."

He glanced up again. A familiar softness filled his expression. A hint of a smile played around the corner of his lips. "You *are* in my life. That's the problem."

I stood perfectly still, knowing Streeter would explain in time, in his own way. He kissed me hard on the lips. His fingers gently held my head.

We kissed until we were both breathless.

Then he pulled away and gazed into my eyes. And then he surprised me again by asking, "Coffee?"

I nodded. I made us something to eat from his refrigerator while he brewed a pot. Neither of us spoke. We prepared the food as if we'd lived together for a lifetime.

We ate in greedy silence since neither of us ever remembered to eat on a regular basis. The kiwi, cheese, crackers, and grapes tasted amazing. And the coffee was heavenly.

I stole glances at him from time to time, studying his expressions.

He was deep in thought—and worry.

Without looking at me, he pushed himself to his feet with the effort of an old man and walked slowly to the sliding glass doors that led to the deck. I watched him stand at the windows, with his hands deep in the pockets of his khaki pants. I could see the weight on his shoulders beneath the crisp, white shirtsleeves. He was heavy with thought, as if an invisible, beastly monkey had just climbed onto his back.

At first, I was barely aware that he had started talking, his words were so soft and distant.

"A man named Jeremiah Coyote Cries is up for parole. He's been in prison on drug trafficking charges for twenty years. I was the one who put him there."

I tried to make it appear that the name was new to me. I leaned forward on the couch and strained to hear each word, careful not to misinterpret anything he was sharing.

His head hung low. For a moment, he said nothing. Then, he added, "He's scheduled to go before the parole board this Tuesday."

I knew differently. He'd already been before the parole board more than a week ago.

Mully and I learned about that yesterday when we'd visited the correctional facility. The warden finally owned up to what was happening—perhaps because of my pleading, but likely it was Mully's unveiled threats to impose bodily harm on someone "if the princess didn't get what she wanted."

I admitted to myself that having a Lucifer's Lot gang member as a friend had its advantages. On the long bike ride home, I tried to thank him by informing him that I was far from being anything like the Princess of Turandot, and I was not coldhearted. And when I waved goodbye, I was sure he hadn't heard me call him Prince Calaf.

Ever since our first meeting, which was more like a standoff between me and the entire biker gang, he'd referenced the three-act opera by Giacomo Puccini. I can still hear my sister Ida belting out the aria in her lead role. One time during a rehearsal, she replaced the actor who was playing Calaf, singing—just for me—the best version of "Nessun Dorma" I'd ever heard since Luciano.

And she was the only female opera singer I'd ever known to embrace the famous aria.

Her voice played over and over in my head as Streeter's silence grew deafening.

But I didn't want to interrupt. I bit my lip and refrained from asking the hundred questions that swarmed around in my head. Just like I told Father Shannon, because I'd been armed with information, I managed to keep my lips zipped.

I knew he'd explain, in his time.

Streeter drew in a deep breath and lifted his head, staring blankly at the mountain ridge across from his cabin.

My mind drifted again in the quiet to how much I loved the way the log structure blended in with its natural surroundings and perched advantageously on the edge of a cliff. It was like a nest at the entrance and like a perch out the back and was probably the most comfortable home I'd ever been in besides my mom and dad's.

His voice had risen slightly above a whisper, and I wasn't straining as much to hear.

"That's when I came to see you—on Tuesday morning. I had just read the announcement for the parole hearing."

Unable to stay silent any longer, I asked, "Why did the letter upset you so much?"

"Because of Julius Chavez. How he hurt you Sunday night. Targeted you. I didn't want them near you. Because of me."

"You think Coyote Cries hired him?"

"His attorney hired Chavez."

He held my gaze. "And Tony Gates found the attorney this week."

"Found him? Was he lost?"

"He was dead. Shot in the head behind the wheel of his car."

CHAPTER 37

I GULPED.

Audibly. The news stunned me. I hadn't been prepared. I felt like I'd been living under a rock.

Maybe Coyote Cries hired Chavez. Maybe Coyote Cries murdered his attorney.

He'd escaped on Saturday—a 102. I'd learned that from the warden yesterday. A 102—the third most serious offense by a prisoner—escape from escort; escape from any secure or nonsecure institution, including community confinement; escape from unescorted community program or activity; escape from outside a secure institution.

Coyote Cries had escaped during his work release program without a trace—with nothing captured on the business's elaborate security monitoring system. How in God's name could that be? First, he was granted parole. Then, he escaped on his second day of work release.

Clearly, Streeter hadn't heard. And I struggled with how to break the news to him without interrupting his story or sending him into cardiac arrest. Mully had virtually threatened to choke the warden right there in front of me because of the system's failure. It took every ounce of persuasion I had to stop him from carrying out his threat.

I had to think. Fast.

"Streeter, how was it your fault that Chavez hurt me? And how can you be so sure it had anything to do with Coyote Cries?"

I touched the tender goose egg on my forehead. The knot had slowly begun to dissolve, although the bruising had worsened. The stitches would be out soon. At least my ability to think hadn't been permanently compromised.

Streeter pulled his hands from his pockets and folded his arms across his strong chest. With his back still turned to me, I couldn't read his expression. I worried that my questions might have caused him to withdraw.

"We found a file in the attorney's possession with information about you. There were photos."

"The paparazzi. You were right. It wasn't them."

He nodded. "As far as Coyote Cries's role in all this? It's a long story."

"I have time." My words sounded more like a whimper.

He glanced back at me over his shoulder and grinned. "I guess you do. I did kind of kidnap you for the weekend."

He moved slowly toward me, his gaze fixed on mine. He noticed I'd been touching my wound and his expression melted into sorrow.

"*The whole weekend?*" I inflected as much energy as I could muster and pulled my fingers away from my forehead.

He sat down beside me, reached for my hand, and gently touched the side of my head. "I'm so sorry about all of this." He kissed my head. "For what happened to you Sunday night, for what I said to you on Tuesday morning, for trying to send you away. I was just . . . "

I wanted to hear him admit he was scared—for his sake, for his healing. Instead, I let him off the hook and said, "I know."

I sat very still, worried any move might interrupt his train of thought.

He tore his glance from mine and turned, so we sat side by side again on the couch. It was a deliberate deflection. He was working through his demons. And he couldn't seem to talk about them when he looked at me.

I reached over and turned off the lamp. Dusk had settled in, and the living room was cast in shades of grey. *Better for him*, I thought.

And it was.

He spoke, "I first ran into Jeremiah Coyote Cries during my first assignment in Rapid City. Coyote Cries was dealing drugs in South Dakota, primarily on the Pine Ridge Indian Reservation. He was the wholesaler. His business was supplying all nine reservations by selling to the retailers as part of a large, Midwest drug ring that was based here in Denver."

Streeter had calmed. His words were even and cool. And he'd grown less passionate about the subject. Almost weary.

I held my breath, praying he wouldn't stop talking again.

He rose and paced.

After several minutes, he suddenly spun on his heels to face me. His face was hard. The muscles in his jaw, taut.

In a low growl, like a disposal working on a metal spoon, he said, "This man is evil. Truly evil, and he should never be released. If he is, there's no telling what he will do."

I wasn't about to tell him that Coyote Cries was already free. That he had escaped.

"I don't know if he still carries a grudge or if he will come after me in any way. But if there is the slightest chance, your safety is not worth risking, no matter how remote the possibility. This can't be taken lightly. I couldn't bear to live if something happened to you." He trembled with rage.

Startled by his vacillation between passivity and passion, I vowed not to tell him about the parole board's decision last Thursday. He might lose it altogether.

I grabbed his clenched fist in mine and pulled him beside me on the couch and held tight. He sat stiffly on the edge of the cushions with his feet flat on the floor, his spine as rigid as rebar. I gently touched the small of his back. He recoiled, and I quickly withdrew my hand.

He was in a different dimension. In another place, at another time. I allowed him the solitude of deep thought and sat quietly beside him.

"It was the most hideous thing I've ever seen . . ."

His wife . . . Dillinger's letter . . . I could only imagine. Another piece of this puzzle I would never allow Streeter to know that I knew. Only pain could come of that knowledge.

"I thought he would be locked up for the rest of his earthly life."

Me, too. Especially after reading his cellmate's letter and after hearing the fear in the warden's voice when he'd admitted they'd all been wrong about The Reverend.

"I knew he was eligible for parole after twenty years. But I convinced myself that it was a lifetime away. And now that time has come." Streeter's words trailed off to a whisper.

He hung his head with his chin touching his chest.

This time when I patted his knee, he didn't recoil. Instead, he slowly encircled me with his arms and drew me close. Tightly, like bands of indestructible steel. His trembling ceased. Heat radiated off him like a slow, simmering pot.

I felt his labored breathing and imagined his blood had been polluted with oceans of adrenaline. For the first time, I wondered how his father had died and hoped it hadn't been from a heart attack caused by high blood pressure.

His voice tender, he said, "I didn't know what to do, Liv. I couldn't bear the thought of anything happening to you. It was hard enough to watch you lying there in the hospital, not knowing if you would live or die and knowing someone had attacked you."

He was back to Chavez following me to my apartment and clocking my skull.

"My heart ached so badly holding you while you were unconscious— lying there in the hall of your apartment complex. It took forever for those emergency response people to come to help you. I swore to God that if you came through this, I would never let anything happen to you again."

He kissed the top of my head and rocked me in his arms.

I imagined his overly protective response had been born of the guilt he carried over Paula's death. Even after all these years. Such a burden.

"If I actually was the reason you were hurt, if Coyote Cries has found out about you, I would never be able to forgive myself. Or live with myself."

Streeter hadn't eased his grip on me. My shoulders throbbed beneath his hug. I laid my head against his shoulder, feeling his hot skin radiate through the cool white cotton shirt, and I kissed him gently on the neck.

I said, "Don't talk like that."

He continued to cling. "I tried to make you believe you meant nothing to me. I knew what I said would hurt you. And I didn't want to do that."

"Yeah, that was stupid. I didn't believe you," I said honestly.

He loosened his grip. A rumble, almost a chuckle, sounded low in his throat. I was glad I could still make him happy—at least a bit.

"The ticket to DC."

"You knew better," I said.

"I hoped I didn't. Kelleher told me you refused to go."

"Phil is a good man. So are you. But I'm the only one who can make those decisions for me. And I choose you." I kissed him again on his neck, and he finally released his hold on me.

He slumped. "But it was all I had and better than the alternative. Liv, he can't know anything more about you. If he finds out that you're my Achilles heel, he will send one of his henchmen after you. He's already exacting his revenge."

A chill danced down my spine. "How so?"

"His attorney, his business partner, two of his retailers on the rez, an eyewitness to the murder of a teacher—a very good man and son of my best friend—all dead."

"When?" I choked.

Streeter put his head in his hands. "This week."

Finally, the reality of impending danger sunk in—to my bone marrow. I realized sneaking out and waltzing back into my apartment yesterday past my posted guard had been reckless behavior. I could have been killed and not just by one of his henchmen.

By Coyote Cries.

Worse, I could have caused the police officer to be killed. Or Mully.

My throat tightened.

I drew in a ragged breath.

I reminded myself I was safe for the moment. I was glad I was here and thrilled I'd been with Mully yesterday and Kelleher Tuesday and Wednesday.

Oh my word. My brother and father: I'd put them all in danger, too, because I hadn't taken the threat seriously.

This was not the time to tell Streeter Coyote Cries had already been released and had escaped, his whereabouts unknown—that I'd confirmed all of this with the warden yesterday.

My face was flushed with heat.

"I got a letter last Friday, but I hadn't opened my mail in a week with all the changes. Cal Lemley, Linwood, Tate, you. I was behind."

"Doesn't Jill open the mail for you?" I noticed no reaction at the mention of his assistant's name, which was good for me. Because everyone and their dog in the office knew she had the hots for Streeter.

He shook his head. "I open my own mail. Anyway, the correctional facility forewarned me that they'd moved the parole hearing back thirteen days. It wasn't last Thursday. It's this Tuesday instead. I have a few days to prepare my statement."

"A letter? From the Englewood Federal Correctional Institution in Littleton?" I knew that couldn't be true.

There was no delay. The hearing had been held on the original date. A date Streeter would have missed anyway because he hadn't opened the mail until Friday. One more mistake he'd never be able to forgive himself for.

Streeter shot a glance at me. "Did I mention that Coyote Cries was at Littleton?"

He hadn't. I'd slipped. Rather than lie, I asked, "Are you planning on testifying?"

His eyes appeared tired and like they had aged. "Of course. Why wouldn't I? I plan on going down Monday for a dry run; to confirm that I'll be one of the people requesting to be heard at his parole. I'll be the only one. The other agents who were qualified to testify against his parole have all passed away. His crimes happened so long ago."

"What did the letter say?" I pressed. My curiosity was piqued.

"You mean the follow-up letter?"

I nodded, not wanting him to know why I was asking. It had to have been a mistake . . . or a calculated misdirection . . . a forgery. By Coyote Cries.

"They regretted any inconvenience it might cause me, but they had to reschedule the parole hearing for the week after next, a Tuesday . . . scheduling conflicts with some of the members on the parole board." Streeter rubbed both of his hands through his hair.

"And you haven't called to confirm?" Clearly, the second letter was forged, which meant Coyote Cries and his attorney had a sophisticated operation. I'd have to ask Mully how Coyote Cries's organization had managed to forge the federal facility's letterhead. He'd know.

He shook his head. "Like I said, I plan on going down Monday. And, no, you can't come with me."

I placed my hand tenderly on his thigh. "Just a lowly drug dealer. Keep telling yourself that. Don't give him power over you. You've dealt with worse."

Streeter mumbled, "Maybe worse situations—but not worse criminals. I have never come across anyone as ruthless as Coyote Cries."

I watched him struggle with his internal conflict, wrestle with unspoken demons and haunting memories. And I remembered Dillinger's letter and the account of Paula's horrifying final minutes.

For several minutes, I sat sill and listened to him slowly regain control of his breathing. When he finally took a deep breath and folded his hands in his lap, I moved closer to him and laid my hands over his.

He smiled weakly.

He looked at me again with pleading eyes. "Liv, will you do something for me?"

"Anything," I answered without hesitation.

"Take that job in DC. Move back there—before next Tuesday—this weekend. Please."

His request stunned me. I'd never heard him sound so desperate.

"At least until this is all over. Maybe for a year or so. Please, Liv."

"You know I can't do that."

"Then no contact with me, at all. We'll stage an epic break up at work on Monday to make sure everyone knows."

He sounded more desperate by the moment.

"If he finds out about you, he will try to get to me through you. And he will succeed."

"Slow down," I said, frightened by his panic and even more frightened to imagine his reaction if I revealed the secrets I'd been keeping. "He's probably forgotten all about you. It's been twenty years, Streeter."

Knowing the growl through his clenched teeth was not directed at me, I listened carefully to his warning. "You don't know this man. I do. He will not forget me. And I will not forget him. It's not over between us, and one of us will end up dead if he's released."

His breathing quickened once again. The heat radiating from his skin intensified.

"I think you're proving he's already got a head start."

He shot a glance my way.

"Listen, he has you worried. Worry is nothing but a bully. It takes and takes and takes until you have nothing more to give. And then you're as good as dead, don't you think?"

He studied me. I thought he was going to blow. Instead, his features softened.

I added, "Don't let him have any power over you. This is your life. You gain nothing by battling old demons. Especially him."

Streeter said softly, "I'm sorry. I'm terrified of losing you. Will you move to DC for me? Please?"

I held his pleading gaze and realized how much I loved this man. I gently kissed him on his lips, which were warm and full and unresponsive to me. I gently dragged my fingertips across the stubble on his warm cheek as he continued to hold his question in his steely blue eyes.

How could I refuse him anything? Yet, how could I possibly leave him at a time like this? I didn't have an answer for him.

"I will do anything you ask," I said in a low, steady voice. "Anything. But you will need to do something for me, first."

Streeter stared at me. Waiting for my request.

"Let me get you a glass of water," I requested tenderly. "Then, what I want you to do is tell me the whole story from the beginning. Everything you can remember. Because this is like an octopus you've had trapped in your gut for a long time and it needs to come out. The tentacles have to give up their grip. Then, if you choose to shove this all back inside, that's for you to live with. And I'll honor your choice. If you see that it wasn't so scary to examine the beast, then maybe we can formulate a plan together."

He blinked.

"Streeter, I love you. I want to help, in any way I can. We have to start somewhere."

He walked out onto the deck and gripped the wooden rail. He stared out over the shapeless trees in the rugged cavern blanketed in black. There was no wind, no movement of any kind.

I sidled up behind him, wrapped my arms around his waist, and laid my right cheek against his back.

"I was once comforted by the nocturnal cries of the coyotes. Now I'm thankful only for the brightness of the sun with rays that mute their love songs like a lit basement silences crickets."

His symmetry was lost on me.

I imagined the canine scavengers uncomfortable in the daylight, revealing their nocturnal secrets, as I laid out my proposal about his very private past.

I felt him suck in a deep breath, and he was probably gathering his thoughts on how to tell me a story he hadn't discussed in two decades.

I encouraged him. "Everything is less frightening under bright lights. Even slimy old octopuses."

CHAPTER 38

AS HE DRANK an iced tea laced with tequila, Dick Roth stretched out lazily in his recliner and sucked down the excrement that had gathered in his nose and throat with a loud snort.

His overweight, grey poodle jerked her head in his direction. She snuffed and drifted off to sleep once she was certain that the loud noise was not her master getting up to forage for more food.

Dick lifted his ratty "Keep on Trucking" T-shirt enough so that his stubby fingers could scratch the belly that pooched over his unbuttoned pants. With the other hand, he reached up to his craggy cheeks and layered chin, stroking the stubble that had grown since this morning's shave.

A piece of his thinning hair fell against his temple. He reached up and pushed it back into place, using the paste from the rest of his coif to keep everything neat.

The roar of the engines from the televised speedway race droned rhythmically from the old set. He lifted one hip off the recliner and passed gas that had gathered like a thunderstorm in his lower gut. The poodle stirred, tucked herself into a tighter ball, and placed her small paws over her muzzle.

He drained the glass—his second of the early evening. He swirled the small ice cubes, making a cheerful clinking noise. Placing the empty glass on the end table beside him, he stretched his arms high above his head and grunted.

How he loved Friday nights—the end of a workweek and the beginning of each weekly holiday.

Friday nights were like Christmas Eve. Saturdays were filled with presents and Sundays were his reward days.

Sundays provided him with a day of rest generally, although sometimes they were his day of travel to the farthest outreaches of his district as he worked his second job. He had earned a handsome sum of money over the last five years in his second job, but he didn't like the hours. He had to work extremely hard. He put in overtime and worked on the weekends.

A cranky operator was to thank for his idea to start his second business. Five years ago, that operator became intolerably belligerent toward him. All he was trying to do was conduct a follow-up inspection of a complaint filed against the guy's quarrying operation: The crushing spread was obviously in violation of the allowable emissions in the operator's permit. But when he told the operator he was going to issue a notice of violation, the guy became so enraged that he started shouting and cursing.

Offended, he threatened to issue a cease and desist order. He had told the operator he had an hour to comply with his recommendation, reduce the emissions from the crushing spread, or he would write the cease and desist—which just further enraged the operator.

Unfazed by the operator's verbal blowback, he calmly explained that he was leaving to find a uniformed officer to assist with his order. The operator instantly changed his tactics, pleading with Dick to forgive him and not to take any of his reactions and behaviors as a reflection on how seriously he considered the issue of air quality.

Ignoring the operator's pleas, he strode confidently toward his vehicle. The operator walked briskly past him and stood between him and his car and begged him to listen. He tried to reason with him and suggested he would do anything if he would simply forget the whole incident had happened.

Testing to see how far this man would be willing to go, Dick jokingly suggested that the man give him five hundred dollars. Then he might forget. The man pulled out his wallet, extracted eleven twenty-dollar bills, and handed them to Dick. He took off, saying he'd be right back with the balance.

Stunned, Dick watched the humbled man head toward his portable office trailer. While he waited, he stuffed the money into his pocket and looked around to make sure nobody had seen or heard what had just happened. And that was that.

The operator returned with the rest of the cash. Dick snatched it quickly from his hand and shoved it deep into his pocket. "If you ever tell anyone about this, I will deny it under oath. I'll tell the court you tried to bribe me. And believe me, they will never believe your word over mine, considering your background. Now, get this place into compliance before I come back. And have two hundred more for me next time."

It was the easiest five hundred bucks he'd ever made.

He couldn't believe his good fortune. What would have happened if he'd asked for a thousand? Or five thousand? *Who knows?* he wondered. Maybe the guy would have paid it. He knew without a doubt that the next time he visited that operator, he would be greeted with a friendly man bearing a gift of more cash.

He quickly discovered that many operators were willing to pay cash under the threat of being issued a notice of violation or under the threat of repeat and consistent visits from the EPA regulator. Regardless of their compliance with the permits, they eventually paid.

He had never before realized how much power he had been given as a federal enforcer of the cumbersome air quality regulations.

It took him no time to pull together a list of names from all the air quality permit holders in his region. Starting with the most obvious violators, he quickly learned the infallible system of feigning a complaint, threatening to report a violation, and demanding cash to ignore it.

After accumulating nearly two dozen steady clients throughout the state and accumulating nearly $25,000 from each of them in the first two years, Dick had amassed a small retirement pool.

But he wanted more.

He'd exhausted the easy targets: violators and typically less ethical operators.

He pulled permits by size, visiting the compliant, small operators who were just starting out in their businesses. He changed his tactics and repurposed his pitch to *protection* rather than hush money. He knew those operators had too much at risk in the tender, early years of operations and that they were generally not savvy enough to know that this was not the standard way of doing business with the regulators.

He quickly discovered that the more ethical the operator, the easier it was to convince them that they had to keep their mouths shut since the money they paid him on his first visit would appear to be a bribe of a federal official. Mortified by the prospect of being accused of bribery, the operators continued to pay the quarterly demands—no argument, no protest. They had no other choice.

Over the years, the collection of what Dick called his "insurance money" had accumulated to nearly $300,000. With his current client base of forty, he could visit an average of three clients each Saturday and visit each one of them four times a year.

Limited to forty hours a week by the federal government, he became creative in how he used those hours, putting in his full week with the EPA by Thursday afternoon, which allowed him to collect on Fridays and Saturdays.

He tried to avoid working on Sundays. That was his day of rest.

He crossed his legs and leaned back in his recliner as far as it could go. Lighting up another unfiltered cigarette, he took a long, slow drag and blew the smoke above his head. A thin-lipped smile spread across his face.

He was proud of himself. His tongue flicked across his teeth as he calculated how much he would collect by the time he retired from the EPA in four years. He had had the discipline and intelligence to know that he should continue living his modest lifestyle until he retired so as not to raise anyone's suspicions about his moonlighting activities. By spending more money than his EPA salary would support, he would not only draw unnecessary attention to himself but would also give credence to someone's allegations, should one of his clients decide to grow a spine and a conscience.

Instead, early on he'd decided to rat hole the money he made from the various clients and let it grow as interest was earned. He had already added nearly 25 percent to his earnings over the past five years.

At the rate he was collecting, and assuming he would be unable to pick up any new clients primarily because his time prohibited it, he figured he would have saved a total of nearly three quarters of a million dollars. He had already opened three bank accounts in separate banks throughout Denver.

In four years, along with his retirement from the EPA, he would be a millionaire. Then, he could live off the interest and spend nearly $50,000 a year on himself—maybe more—without ever touching the principal. That would afford him a more luxurious lifestyle than he'd ever enjoyed during his career. If he chose the right investment broker in Florida, he could double his principal within five or ten years.

He finished his cigarette and crushed the remains into the overflowing ashtray beside his chair. Pushing his calves against the recliner, he rose to his feet and padded toward the kitchen to make himself another drink. The fat dog sprang to her feet and waddled behind her master, hoping for a portion of whatever food item he was about to prepare. Happy with himself, Roth began to whistle. The poodle perked her ears at the shrill sound and cocked her grey head to the side expectantly.

Dick spoke to the little mongrel. "What do you think about Florida? I've always wanted to live in the Keys. Nice and warm down there."

The poodle stood perfectly still, not to dissuade her owner from tossing her a scrap if he were so inclined.

He stood at the open refrigerator and tossed the dog a scrap of fried chicken and then ate two pieces himself. Around a mouthful of partially chewed meat, he added, "Then girls will be begging me for a piece. Bitches always go for money, don't they, sweetie? I'll have money. Lots of it."

He grabbed a half-eaten summer sausage and a chunk of cheese from the cold cuts drawer and bumped the refrigerator door closed with his padded rump. Freeing up one hand by wedging the chunk of cheese between his lips, he grabbed his iced tea and tequila and made his way back to the recliner.

Then someone knocked on his door.

He froze. He hadn't been expecting anyone.

There was another knock.

He set down his drinks and snack, hurried to the door, and peeked through the peephole.

There were two police officers, a man in a crumpled white shirt and dress pants, and a heavyset, disheveled woman with thick glasses and frizzy brown hair.

With the woman motioning to knock for a third time, Dick swung the door open.

"Richard Roth? Dick Roth—inspector with the EPA?" one of the uniformed officers asked.

Dick nodded, puzzled.

The disheveled woman stepped forward, extending a badge toward him. "Special Agent Laurie Frumpley. Meet the district attorney." She motioned to the man in the crumpled white shirt.

As the officers flanked him, while the district attorney read him his rights, Dick Roth realized he was most unnerved by the chubby woman's expression.

Her confident sneer meant his holidays had just come to an end.

CHAPTER 39

"OH MY GOD," I gasped as I rose to my feet and started pacing.

I had been utterly shaken by his story. Streeter's undoing, his long, excruciatingly painful life, overwhelming personal grief, and trauma in the aftermath, underscored the true tragedy of Paula's murder. It was worse than Dillinger's letter.

A cold sweat had broken out on my forehead and chest. My hands and knees were trembling. I'd hoped that pacing would calm my nerves. I understood now why Streeter did it so often—like a caged tiger.

After nearly ten hours of purging, he'd long since left my side and retreated to the deck with his back to me. He was stooped from the weight of the nightmarish memories, and he seemed to have aged from those recollections right before my eyes.

No wonder his hair had turned white overnight.

I mumbled, "He killed her. To get back at you."

He drew a silent breath and lifted his gaze again to the distant woods. The sun had begun its early ascent over the mountains, and ghostly greys with threads of pinks were beginning to spread across the sky.

His words were broken and uneven. "I came home later than I told her I would. Maybe if I'd called or come home sooner . . . "

He buried his face in his large hands.

I was glad that he had turned his back to me now, so he couldn't see the genuine pity I felt for him at this moment. I walked up behind him and wrapped my arms around his waist. "If you had, you'd both be dead. Paula wouldn't have wanted that."

The shadows of the evergreen trees stretched across his deck.

He cleared his throat and wiped his face. He patted my arm. I'd laid my head between his shoulder blades.

He folded his arms across his chest. "I've never talked about this since the day it happened. Not to anyone. I spent so much time telling the story from a clinical perspective, a lawman's view, over and over in the days that followed her murder, that I swore I'd never talk about it again. And here I am, spilling my guts to you."

I felt his body tense.

"I didn't think it would be this hard," he continued. "I thought time would have lessened the pain somehow. But it hasn't."

I held my breath during the quiet moments that followed and waited for his free flow of thoughts and emotion.

"When I opened the door, the first thing I noticed was the smell. She'd been making dinner on the stove. My first thought was that Paula had made my favorite homemade vegetable soup. But the smell—it was off."

I squeezed him tighter.

"Then, I pushed the door open. I saw her lying there on the floor. It was just her torso. She was on her side with her knees tucked up against her waist and her arms splayed out in front of her. She looked so small, so . . . fake."

I felt the tremor ripple through his body and held him closer.

"I couldn't believe what was happening. I must have stood there staring for who knows how long. My mind couldn't accept what I was seeing. The horror was too great. I knew it was Paula. She was wearing the sweater I had given her the Christmas before. And the faded blue jeans she always wore. I knew it was her." His voice grew increasingly thin. "But there was a very small crimson pool on the carpet where her beautiful head should have been."

I shuddered. I didn't know if I could take much more of this. Yet, he had lived with it for decades. And I loved him. I told myself to buck up and stay glued to the saddle.

"I wanted to see her face, her hair, her beautiful winter wheat locks spilling across that floor, just as I had seen them spilled across her pillow so many nights when I'd watched her sleep. But her hair wasn't there. She wasn't there. It was her, but it wasn't her."

My arms squeezed tightly around Streeter's waist. I rubbed my cheek softly across his back.

His memories were disjointed. "There wasn't much blood, considering. I always thought there would be more in a . . . with a . . . there was hardly any."

He shuddered again. He couldn't say the word "decapitation" or "beheading"—words that flowed so easily from Coyote Cries's stories to Dillinger.

I stroked his chest with my hands.

"It was horrifying to witness. Even if I hadn't known her and loved her, I would've been forever haunted by the gruesome sight. The nightmares were always there, whether I was alseep or awake. I couldn't shake that image."

The quiet chirping of the birds pierced the silence. The forest was awakening.

The sun would soon be shining brightly, the cool air rapidly warming in the coming dawn. I felt his sweat-soaked back against my cheek and his shivers come and go like a tide.

"They say I called Sid Carter, the Denver SAC, my boss. But I don't remember that. I don't remember much. One minute, I was coming home, finding her like that. And the next minute? I was sitting in a pew at her funeral in a church I didn't recognize, being consoled by people I'd never met. I think Sid must've handled everything. Sid and Roger Landers. Roger flew to Denver from Rapid City and stayed with me until after the funeral."

I recognized the names from my research. Both had been his bosses: one in Rapid City, one in Denver. I adjusted my hold on him, pressed my hands flat against his chest to protect him from the cool breeze. The chirping grew clear, distinct, and cheerful.

"I don't remember much. They gave me sedatives. Lots, I suspect. One minute I was in Denver, the next, in Lead-Deadwood. I don't even know where I stayed. I can't even tell you what was said at Paula's funeral. Can you believe that?"

I answered, "I can. That had to have been the most traumatic event a human being could experience."

He stared at the sunrise, shaking his head in disgust. "Some husband—can't even remember the words spoken about my own wife at her funeral."

"You were beyond upset. It's understandable," I comforted him.

"I love you," he said absently and unexpectedly.

"I know," I responded evenly. "And I love you, too. To my very core. And for always."

"My hair turned all white the day after I found her."

I knew that. I had either read it in one of the articles or someone had told me . . . Father Shannon . . . he'd told me. He had officiated the Mass.

"It had been brown, dark brown, without a trace of grey all my life. Then, it was white. Overnight," He babbled. His thoughts rambled. "They say that happens sometimes during moments of severe stress or shock. I guess I'm one of those classic cases that proves it's true."

"You could have died, Streeter. From the shock," I said.

"Believe me, there were so many times that I'd wished I had," he replied honestly. "This all took its toll on Roger, too. He was terribly upset about June Chase being killed by the car bomb.

I didn't know who June was and hadn't see her name anywhere in the files I'd read. Maybe she was a relative of Roger Landers.

"Her murder happened on the same day that Paula was killed. She died when she started her car that morning. On her way to work."

"At Roger's home?"

He shook his head. "On the reservation. She was a witness in one of the cases he was working."

I'd have to look into that case and read the files. Then, something dawned on me. "Then Coyote Cries couldn't possibly have killed both women, could he? He couldn't be in two places at once. On the reservation in South Dakota and then in Denver."

He sighed. "He could've planted that bomb sometime during the night and driven back to Denver. He had plenty of time. They never found June's killer—just like they never found Paula's. They never found enough evidence."

"This guy is an expert."

Streeter scowled. "If he didn't kill June, he ordered someone to do it. Roger suffered a massive heart attack two weeks after June's death."

I gave him another loving squeeze. He rubbed his eyes and forehead with his right hand.

I waited quietly so as not to interrupt his thoughts before saying, "I'm confused. Why didn't Coyote Cries get a stiffer sentence? I'm surprised he wasn't given a life sentence without parole—or even death. For such a heinous and brutal crime of revenge against a federal agent, I would have thought they would have put him away forever. It makes no sense to me."

I'd read everything in the files and, although circumstantial, as a juror, I'd have ignored my duty to the law and nailed the bastard because he clearly murdered Paula. Maybe I'd been prejudiced with Dillinger's letter.

"He was never charged with Paula's murder, or June's.

"What about the advances in DNA? Maybe he could be tried now."

Streeter sighed. "We did fiber searches, dusted for fingerprints, and scraped under Paula's fingernails and teeth for any DNA we could get on her murderer."

"Nothing?" I asked. "Not even DNA?"

"Nothing. No prints; no witnesses. No weapon was ever found. Nothing was missing from our apartment. No apparent motive. For some time, they even investigated me as a potential suspect."

I let him go and leaned back, stunned by the revelation. Of course they'd suspect the husband—especially with no evidence. "How could they ever believe such a thing?"

He shrugged. "I can't blame them. I had no clue who would've done such a thing at first. The thought never crossed my mind that Coyote Cries was the culprit. I was in a fog for weeks, wondering who would do such a thing and why. I think Roger suspected it all along. But he was probably trying to spare me the torture."

He stretched and grabbed my hand. He led me to the couch. I slumped down into the soft cushions beside him. Just as I was about to ask how he was so sure it was Coyote Cries if there was no evidence, Streeter took the conversation in another direction.

"I didn't see . . . the rest of her at first," he whispered, averting his eyes.

"Maybe I did, but I avoided it. I saw her hair—behind the couch. I remember a lot of commotion going on around me. The police and the bureau, arguing over jurisdiction for the case. I stared at the men who were all milling around our apartment, while . . . my wife was in pieces."

I didn't dare move. Or breathe.

"I saw everyone. But I didn't really see them. It was kind of like a blur. I remember the flashes of cameras. Picture after picture. Of my wife, the floor, the wall. The apartment."

The wall? Of course: where he'd thrown her head. I wanted to scream. I closed my eyes tightly against the images that had begun to burn in my mind's eye.

He stopped breathing and stared at the floor—for a long, long time. "The guys never talked much about it with me. I guess I really didn't want to know."

His voice and thoughts trailed off.

I wanted to throw up, but I forced back the bile that rose in my throat. I didn't dare move.

Minutes later, he straightened his spine and stood up. "Anyway, they say the funeral was nice. The other guys did everything they could to find Paula's murderer. And I buried myself in my work after that. They wouldn't let me be involved in anything regarding Paula's case. Can't say that I blame them for that."

"That's how I met Tony Gates. He was the investigator at the time with the Denver PD."

"And now he's Chief," I said.

He nodded. "He was good. He never doubted me. And he was the one who connected the dots to Coyote Cries and went after him as ferociously as I did after that. I was far too devastated emotionally about the whole thing—to the point of hysteria."

He looked straight at me. "I wasn't right in the head for a while. You're justified in warning me not to let him have power over me, Liv. He has before. I can't let him now."

I nodded.

"I mostly worked on helping build the arguments and gather the evidence against Coyote Cries in the other murder case on the reservation. It was a drug overdose case. The one that earned him his conviction. Drugs would also land him behind bars—but not for long. Not long enough, considering it was a first offense. So we focused on the murder. It was tough without our witness, June. She was the only one who saw Coyote Cries near the vic at the time of his death. We had a motive. But we had no concrete evidence that he'd killed the man or that it was premeditated. It was a tough case to win."

"I didn't remember you saying that Coyote Cries was convicted of murder." I was thinking about everything I'd read compared to what he'd told me, so I could keep my reactions to his news genuine.

"He wasn't. Based on the jury's decision, we had to settle for the judge giving him the maximum penalty allowed for involuntary manslaughter, illegal possession, and drug trafficking convictions. Which was life with possibility of parole after twenty years."

"And for what he did to Paula? And June?" I asked.

"Nothing," he answered flatly. "He got nothing; not even charges pressed against him."

He'd been so open with me. So willing to let go.

I had a risky question that I feared might shut his progress down. But I had to ask. Especially after reading that damned letter.

"If there was no evidence found, how were you and Tony so sure that Coyote Cries was the one who killed Paula and June?"

His body stiffened.

And he grew quiet.

CHAPTER 40

LAST NIGHT, OR RATHER, early this morning, I ruined the mood.

After all this time, Streeter had finally uncorked his bottled demons throughout the night. And early this morning, I pushed too far.

What an idiot.

He immediately grabbed my hand and led me to bed, telling me he'd had enough and needed sleep. When I woke up around noon, he was already in the shower. He barely spoke to me all day as we took a long hike down the canyon, holding hands, thinking.

Tonight, I would make it up to him.

We sat on the deck, a blanket wrapped around both of us.

"Streeter, we need to talk about it."

"No, we don't."

"I'm sorry about my question this morning. About how you could be so sure it was Coyote Cries who killed Paula and June. I think you misunderstood my question. I wasn't doubting you. Believe me. I don't. I know for sure that Coyote Cries murdered your wife. You couldn't be more right about that. I just wanted to know how you and Tony knew it so long ago."

I stopped short of telling him about Dillinger's letter. I needed him to tell his story his way, without interrupting, if I could get him talking again.

"And it was probably a really stupid question. But you sounded so convinced. And I believe you. Please, don't think I doubt you. Not for one minute."

From his profile, I could see the jaw muscles working against his angry thoughts.

"Talk to me. Please."

He let out a breath that hung in the cold like a suspended balloon. "I suppose it was partially my fault. I approached it all wrong. I wasn't myself when it came to issues regarding Paula. Like I said, I'd pretty much lost it. So we all agreed that I'd have nothing to do with Paula's murder investigation. I blew up a few times at the guys handling the investigation for not finding anything. I said some pretty awful things about them."

"Understandable." What I was really thinking was how impressed I'd been at his composure. From what I'd read, I'd have gone ape-shit on everyone around me if I were him.

"Better for all of us that I focused my attentions elsewhere. So I immersed myself in another case, even though I had worked the drug overdose on the reservation, which involved Coyote Cries as a Top Ten fugitive."

I imagined he had to seriously compartmentalize his work from his life to accomplish what he had on that investigation.

"I attended the sentencing but not the trial. I couldn't bear that. I wasn't even called as a witness, thank God."

"Which meant you did a great job providing evidence to the prosecuting attorney," I offered.

He shrugged. "When the judge announced a life sentence, I almost blacked out with relief. Just as they were about to take Coyote Cries from the courtroom, he leaned over to me and whispered, 'I should have raped her before I killed her, but I don't like white meat—especially pregnant white mean. Did you enjoy your carrots?'"

I tried not to gasp aloud. This was exactly the way it was described in Dillinger's letter. Proof of its authenticity.

But it was brutal for anyone to hear. Let alone for Paula's husband.

I asked, "What did you say?"

"Nothing. I just froze. I knew he was trying to tell me he had murdered my wife and had gotten away with it. The autopsy report had indicated she was pregnant. Twelve weeks. I didn't know. She hadn't told me."

So he had known—through a cold, callused autopsy report.

A tear streamed down my cheek.

He'd lost his wife and a baby he never knew he had.

"I learned later that nobody knew Paula was pregnant—except her doctor who had seen her the day she was killed." He turned toward me and leveled a stare. "That's why I'm so convinced."

"There was no way for Coyote Cries to know she was pregnant unless she had told him before he killed her." I had as much conviction as he had—and the letter to prove Coyote Cries's admission to the murders.

"And Tony Gates pointed out to me later that the carrots didn't even show up in the police reports. Anywhere," Streeter said. "That's why he was so convinced. The only mention of the vegetable soup she'd been making was that a pot had nearly boiled dry by the time I came home. Tony surmised that she was bagging up the leftover carrots she'd used in the soup when Coyote Cries arrived. He'd used those details to help determine the time of death. She was killed only ten minutes or so before I came home."

I understood. "Only the killer would have known about the carrots."

The cold breeze through the trees of the early evening had quieted the birds outside. Fighting off the chill, he got up and pulled the glass door shut.

Rubbing his upper arms with his hands, he added, "I shouldn't have done it. After I got over the initial shock of his confession, I threw a punch at him. As the bailiff led him away, I lost complete control of myself in that courtroom. The guards had to pull me off him. I was yelling, 'He killed my wife. The bastard killed my wife. And my child.'"

"He provoked you," I said.

"I just kept shouting over and over. Everyone in the courtroom, including my boss, Sid Carter, thought I had finally gone off the deep end. Even the judge came back into the courtroom to see what the commotion was all about."

"You aren't crazy. He was taunting you. He's evil."

He wrapped his arms around his own waist. "Everyone assumed I'd had a nervous breakdown. They'd assumed with the stress of my wife's brutal murder, the subsequent months of trial against this Top Ten fugitive, and the option for parole after twenty years that I just couldn't handle it anymore. But I didn't even hear the part about parole. They thought I'd gone mad, out of my mind."

"Streeter, anyone in your situation would have reacted the same way."

He nodded. "When I tried to explain what Coyote Cries had said, no one believed me, except Tony. When I told them that Coyote Cries knew about my wife being pregnant, some said it was because I had screamed that he'd killed my unborn child. Others said his lawyer had probably obtained the autopsy report."

"And the carrots? How'd they dismiss that?"

"Some detectives suggested sour grapes on my part and desperation to place blame on someone for killing my wife. They argued that misplaced anger and blame were classic emotional stages of the grieving process."

"Don't you hate how everyone tells you what grief is all about?" I asked.

He offered me a crooked smile.

Streeter gazed down at his shoes. "A few who believed me suggested that I had ruined my chances of making the charges stick against Coyote Cries by my outburst and by divulging confidential information about the murder in a crowded courtroom."

"Did he provoke you on purpose to prejudice a jury?" I wondered.

"He's smart enough to have done that. But we were never taking the other murders to trial anyway. The practical situation was that we had no evidence, no witnesses, and no murder weapon. Nothing had ever materialized, which made the other murder cases against him even weaker than the overdose trial, the manslaughter case we'd just completed. All we had was my word against his about what he'd said to me."

"And any defending attorney would have a heyday with that," I said.

"Not to mention with my credibility when it came to this issue. I had punched him and screamed at him in front of dozens of witnesses."

"You must've been devastated." Rising to my feet, I approached Streeter and grabbed his hand. I led him to the window where the sun had completely set.

"I was. And I have no doubt in my mind that Coyote Cries killed June Chase to avoid prison and that he murdered my wife to get back at me."

I draped my arms around his neck and leaned against his shoulder.

"The worst part about the whole thing for me was the torture Paula must have gone through before she was killed."

I stiffened. No way could I ever share Dillinger's letter with him.

"Death is quick the way he killed her. But the autopsy report indicated that Paula had been sweating before she died—and worse, crying. The report said that her cheeks and neck were 'streaked with saline excrement.' With tears. I wonder what he'd done to frighten her so badly."

"As much as she loved you, it was probably the fear of knowing what you would go through when you found her," I said simply. "She loved you. And knowing how tortured you would be was probably terrifying for her. The same horror that's consuming you over me."

Streeter tilted his head curiously. "I guess I never thought about it like that. I'd always assumed he'd hurt her somehow. She had a broken bone in her wrist and an odd bruise on her shoulder and on her back. I just assumed she was crying because of that."

I shook my head. "There are worse pains than broken bones and bruises. You of all people should know that."

He stared at me for a long time. "Thank you for that."

I assumed he meant for giving him something else to think about other than the physical pain she must have been feeling.

"Obviously, I never forgave myself for letting Paula down that night . . . If I'd only come home ten minutes earlier."

"You'd both be dead. Like I said, no way Paula would've wanted that. You can't think like that. You can't blame yourself."

"Easy to say, hard to do. I can't help but blame myself. He was getting back at me. I was late coming home. Maybe he was laying low for me that night, and Paula came home first."

"And if you had, Paula would be going through the same torture you've been living with for the past twenty years."

"At least she'd be alive—with my child. Maybe if I'd come home earlier, I could've stopped the whole thing from happening. Maybe if I hadn't lost my cool in the courtroom, we could've convicted the bastard. Maybe—"

"Hush," I whispered holding my finger against his lips.

"But maybe I could have—"

"Stop. You can't keep torturing yourself with what could've been. That won't solve anything for you. And you can't possibly springboard into any kind of future by wallowing in what could've been. Don't give that thug so much power over you, Streeter."

"I loved her so much," he said, averting his eyes.

"I know you did. But she wouldn't want you to die of a broken heart. Roger had a massive heart attack from the guilt and remorse he harbored over June Chase. Both of you went through something more tragic and more horrific than any human being should ever have to endure. I can't imagine a greater burden."

He nodded. Glanced up at me.

I offered him a kind smile. "But you can't make that burden heavier with the guilt and remorse you continue to pile on yourself. You'll be crushed by the weight of it all. You can't end up like Roger. Suffering a massive heart attack."

"And now, he's so . . . jaded about everything."

"Paula wouldn't have wanted that for you. You have to live for what's now."

I leaned over and kissed him gently on the corner of his mouth.

"This lunatic is up for parole. If they let him out, I am seriously concerned about your life," Streeter said sternly.

I didn't want to argue that the parole board wouldn't let Coyote Cries go. They had. So I had to think quickly. "Why would he come after me? He punished you twenty years ago, Streeter. Wasn't that enough? Why would he want more? What could he possibly gain from that?"

He stared at me for a long moment. His blue eyes were flat with weariness. The lines of concern around his eyes had deepened. "I couldn't bear to lose you. I couldn't take that chance. I won't take that chance."

He released my hand and walked out on the porch through the sliding glass doors. I followed him outside.

"I saw the look in his eyes when I punched him. It isn't over. He will come for me—with vengeance."

I sidled up beside him. "Maybe so. But even if he's been harboring a vendetta for you, which is highly unlikely after all this time, you're prepared. Right?"

Streeter nodded reluctantly. Then his eyes filled with fury. "But I can't protect you—even when he's behind bars. He's already gotten to me by hurting you through Chavez."

"You don't know that."

"I do. And on Tuesday, I'll know for sure. He'll tell me. When I look him in his eyes, I will know if he has changed after all these years—at his parole hearing."

"Then stop worrying," I scolded. "I've remembered a quote from the book of Luke ever since I was young, because worry had a hold on me even back then. It was something like, 'No one who puts a hand to the plow and looks back is fit to prosper.' Something like that."

His expression changed. He stared at me as if a light bulb turned on inside his mind. I wondered why that quote mattered to him that much: I'd been grasping at straws for anything that might encourage him, strike a chord.

"Luke. A book in the Bible. Isn't there a book of Jeremiah?"

I nodded and added, "So the passage by Luke makes sense. It's hard to keep driving forward if you're always looking in a rearview mirror. And Streeter, that's what you're doing. Don't let fear of him sneaking up from behind stop you from moving forward. Understand?"

But I'd lost him. He'd excused himself abruptly to make a phone call. Something I said must've triggered his reaction. But I had no clue what it was.

When he returned, he was grinning, happy, a different man. He lifted me into his arms and kissed the top of my head. "I love you so much, Liv. You are my only weakness and my only strength."

I kissed him back. "You can't kick me out of here tonight, if that's what you're thinking. I ordered the full weekend kidnapping, not just the 24-hour bit."

And that was the last time we ever spoke about Coyote Cries again.

CHAPTER 41

STREETER HADN'T BEEN ABLE to sleep that night.

He lay beside Liv with his arm beneath her head and stared at her in the moonlight as she slept. Her silky auburn hair glistened against the crisp white pillowcase. Her gentle purr, barely audible, rose and fell like the distant sound of waves steadily washing ashore.

Her soft, white skin glowed. He couldn't resist the urge to stroke her arms gently as she slept. He lay there all night studying her and watching her sleep. He imagined what it would be like if they were married and if it would always be this peaceful for him.

As the darkness of night began to recede in the early hours of morning, he'd rehearsed at least two dozen versions of what he might say at Coyote Cries's hearing tomorrow. The hearing was scheduled for nine o'clock, which meant Streeter would have to leave his house by seven.

And he wanted so badly to go into work this morning to follow up on the lead Liv had inspired him with. He thought about the passage from Luke, about the rumored preacher who'd been terrorizing the residents of Pine Ridge, and about the book of Jeremiah.

He didn't want to awaken her. He didn't want his time with her to end. He'd enjoyed spending the past few nights with her, holding her, listening to her sleeping. He knew that he had to do anything he could to make sure she was safe and protected.

That meant keeping Coyote Cries behind bars.

He had to be persuasive, convincing, with just the right amount of emotion. He had to stay controlled and professional, regardless of the impact of seeing Coyote Cries after all these years. Just receiving the letter notifying him of the parole hearing had made him regurgitate.

What reaction would he have when he saw him in person?

He and Liv had a quick breakfast together before they both left for work. He knew Gates had officers watching his house all weekend and that Mully would tail Liv the instant she left his house this morning. He knew she'd be protected until he could return to her—after parole was denied.

"Monday morning," she said. "I used to love Mondays. Because I'd get to see you."

"And now?"

"I like weekends much better. Kidnap me anytime you'd like." Liv flung her arms around his neck and kissed his cheek. "He's not going to win. You have a second chance. Don't let him ruin it for us. Keep your hands on the plow and your eyes on the field ahead. Or for you, hands on the wheel and eyes on the road ahead. Not on your rearview mirror. And we stand a chance."

Joy consumed Streeter. He adored this woman.

She kissed him deeply, cupping his cheeks in her long slender hands. "Are you sure you don't want me to go with you tomorrow? Or on your dry run today? I can wait in the car."

"No, sweetheart," Streeter said calmly. "That's the last place I want you. I don't want him to know you exist. You understand that."

Liv nodded and made her way to the Jeep. As she crawled in behind the wheel, he opened the garage door for her.

She rolled down her window and said, "I'll see you at the office this afternoon."

Streeter nodded and waggled his fingers at her.

He watched her drive off over the hill. His smile faded along with the sound of her Jeep. Dread filled him, and he wanted to call after her. Bring her back. Shelter her.

A shiver skipped along his spine. A protective and weary instinct conjured up frightening images to flash through his overactive mind.

He shook it off.

No rearview mirrors.

Told himself that he was simply anxious about tomorrow morning's hearing and today's dry run.

He would be there both days to make sure there was no snag in the process.

He climbed into his car and peered around to see if he noticed any of Gates's men standing guard near the driveway. He saw nothing.

He drove through the streets of Conifer and weaved his way through traffic onto the highways heading into Denver. The roads leading into Denver in the mornings were so congested that he'd learned other routes and would probably beat Liv to work with his fancy back road maneuvers, if he were heading to the federal building. But not today.

When the highway forked, he waved out the window toward the northeast road, knowing Liv had just taken that route only minutes earlier. He took the southeast road as a trial run for the timing tomorrow.

He calculated that he'd arrive at Englewood at least a half hour before the hearing. Maybe even by 8:15, depending on traffic. He would have time to discuss the case with some of the parole board staff ahead of time and learn what kind of people he would be dealing with.

The traffic congestion of rush hour slowed his progress, but he arrived in Littleton at the administrative office next to the Englewood Federal Correctional Institution by 8:30.

Perfect.

He'd drive the same route tomorrow and be a half hour early to the scheduled hearing.

He adjusted his rearview mirror, so he could straighten his tie for a final time. He stepped out of the car and slid his suit coat over his short-sleeved shirt.

The morning sun beat down on him. He had another hot day ahead of him. The reflection off the car nearly blinded him as he marched through the parking lot.

At the security desk, he announced who he was and that he was confirming the time and place for tomorrow's parole hearing scheduled for Jeremiah Coyote Cries. After checking his credentials, the woman behind the desk made a phone call and pushed the button for the security release on the heavy metal door.

An obnoxious buzzing noise sounded. He entered.

The woman said, "Down this hall. Third door on the right. Mary will help you."

"Thanks," Streeter said with a nod.

Mary was an attractive woman at least ten years his senior with stylish grey hair piled high on top of her head. Her petite, feminine voice matched her five-foot, slender frame. "May I help you?"

"I'm here to check on everything for a hearing tomorrow—to testify at nine o'clock in front of the parole board. I'm Streeter Pierce from the Denver division."

"FBI?" Mary said, as her eyes widened. "I don't recall requesting your assistance on tomorrow's hearing. Manfred Z. Rana?"

Streeter frowned. "Sorry? Manfred who?"

She studied him. "Manfred Z. Rana. He's the one scheduled before the board tomorrow at nine."

His stomach turned sour.

"I think there's been some mistake." Streeter retrieved the letter from his pocket.

Mary quickly scanned the letter. "But this says the parole hearing was scheduled the week before last, Agent Pierce."

"Right." He produced the second letter from his pocket. "But then you sent me this follow-up letter saying the parole hearing had been rescheduled for tomorrow morning."

Mary scowled as she read the letter. "This isn't right."

Confused, Streeter asked, "What isn't right?"

Mary frowned and removed her cat-eye glasses allowing them to dangle from a shiny silver chain that encircled her neck. "Wait right here, Agent Pierce. Please? I want to check on something."

She retreated around a corner.

Puzzled, he began to whistle to calm his nerves. He checked his watch. It was 8:40 a.m. He was glad he'd come down a day early to iron out any wrinkles. There was plenty of time to untangle any confusion that might come up.

Mary emerged around the corner followed by a short, pudgy man in a pinstripe suit.

The man extended his hand. "I'm Norman Sheehan, the administrative coordinator for the parole board."

"You send the letters. I recognize your name," Streeter said.

"I coordinate all the notices, yes," Sheehan said. "But I think there's been some mistake, Agent Pierce. We did send you the notice of Jeremiah Coyote Cries's parole hearing for the week before last. But we didn't send out this second letter." Sheehan lifted the sheet of paper and waved it in the air. "See the signature? That's not mine."

Dazed, Streeter stared at the letters Sheehan had extended toward him. "What are you saying?"

"The hearing tomorrow at nine o'clock is for Manfred Z. Rana; not Jeremiah Coyote Cries. His hearing was two Thursdays ago."

Stunned, Streeter said nothing. He'd tumbled headlong into a nightmare. Again.

"I told the same thing to someone from your office last Thursday since you were out of town."

His head spun. His vision narrowed in a kaleidoscope of greys. He reached for the desk, steadying himself before he passed out.

"Who?" he managed to ask.

"Special Agent Liv Bergen."

He sat down hard on the floor and put his head between his knees. He drew in deep breaths to ward off unconsciousness.

He heard Mary and Sheehan call to him. They were concerned, and their voices seemed muffled and distant.

"Water, please," he managed.

When the paper cup of water was shoved under his nose, he took it and dipped his fingers in it. He wiped the water over his face and drank the balance. He rose to his feet. His vision had returned but was still blurred.

He leaned against the counter. "Where is he?"

"Coyote Cries?" Sheehan asked nervously.

Mary and Sheehan exchanged a concerned glance.

Streeter growled, "Where. Is. He?"

"We're not exactly sure," Sheehan stammered. "He didn't show up at his scheduled time for his return to the correctional facility after work the weekend before last. We're still trying to locate—"

"*YOU LET THE BASTARD GO?*" Rage blinded him. He grabbed the man by the collar.

Sheehan batted at his hands, which made him snap out of his fury.

The pudgy man cleared his throat and straightened his shirt. "The parole board released him. He was on work release. He had several people testify on his behalf to his good character—including some of the prison guards. No one was there to testify against him."

"Because I was told the hearing had been rescheduled," Streeter said through clenched teeth.

"That's not our letter." The anger behind Sheehan's words was as passionate as Streeter's.

Streeter pounded his fist on the counter. "Damn it!"

Sheehan and Mary silently studied the federal agent. Sheehan finally offered, "Would you like us to see if the warden has time to talk with you?"

Streeter pushed himself away from the counter and quickly regained his composure. Rubbing his fingers through his hair, he asked quietly, "When was the last time he was seen? And where? Exactly."

"He was dropped off at his work assignment at two o'clock the Saturday before last," Sheehan answered sheepishly. "He didn't report to work. And he hasn't been seen since."

"Work? Where?"

"At the Colorado Cardboard Corporation. Three miles northeast of here."

"Liv," Streeter gasped.

He snatched the phone from Mary's desk and punched in numbers. Staring intently at Norman Sheehan he ordered, "Call Denver Chief of Police Tony Gates. Tell him to put an APB out on Jeremiah Coyote Cries. Immediately. Tell him he's armed and dangerous."

Liv's cell phone went straight to message. He dialed her again and then Mully. Neither answered. Panic rose in his throat.

He dialed the office. "Bessie? This is Streeter. Has Liv been in this morning?" She told him Liv hadn't. "Transfer me to Kelleher. Hurry."

Streeter covered the mouthpiece of the phone and instructed Mary, "Tell Sheehan to inform Gates that Liv Bergen is missing. Have him put an APB out on her and her Jeep."

Mary nodded.

"Kelleher, its Streeter. Jeremiah Coyote Cries was released a week ago last Thursday on parole. He skipped work release the Saturday before last. The US Marshals are probably looking for him, but I don't know that for a fact. No one has seen him since two o'clock that day. Liv's missing. Help her."

Kelleher rattled off several possibilities. Streeter's head was swimming. "I don't know, but let me think about it. I'll call you from my mobile. I've got to find her."

Streeter ran from the administrative offices and jumped into his car. His tires screeched as he tore out of the parking lot. He slammed his fist against the wheel and sped through traffic, hoping a police car would stop him. He needed an escort. No luck.

As he expertly darted between lanes and cars, his mind raced. The image of Liv as she left his home earlier that morning flashed into his memory.

He sped through traffic. It wasn't as bad as it had been an hour ago. People had already arrived to work for the day.

He ran the timeline through his mind: the beatings, the murders, Webber, Alcott, Long Soldiers, Blue Owl, Norma, Jeff—not by CCG; by Coyote Cries himself, the preacher from Denver. The Two Bears had been right.

How could he have been so stupid?

What would Coyote Cries do next?

The cell lying on the passenger's seat vibrated with several short screeches. He snatched it. "Pierce."

"Tell me where to look," Gates snapped.

"Were your people at my place?"

"All weekend. Followed you out."

"Anyone follow her?"

Silence by Gates.

"Have you sent someone to her apartment?"

"Done."

"How far are any of your people from Conifer?"

"The closest is about fifteen minutes out."

"Get someone back there to check my house," Streeter ordered. "He'll kill her if he hears any sirens, Tony. So keep them dark. Everyone on a short leash—got it?"

"Already done," Gates said.

"Get Kelleher on a three-way with us," Streeter commanded.

"I'm working on it. Why the hell did they let this guy out anyway?"

Streeter realized Gates had been catapulted back in time, just as he'd been—to the same stress and fear caused by the devil, Coyote Cries.

Only this time, they knew who the man intended to target.

Liv Bergen had also become a dear friend of Gates since her nephew Noah was abducted. And he would fear for her safety as much as Streeter did.

The moment was very real for both men.

Streeter didn't have time to answer Gates.

Phil Kelleher cut in on the call. "Streeter? You there?"

"Gates has Liv's apartment and my cabin in Conifer covered. Get some of our guys out there with them."

There was a pause and then Kelleher said, "Got it."

Gates interrupted, "Got a line on her Jeep. It was found on the shoulder of the eastbound lane of Interstate 70 about five miles west of Interstate 25. The rear bumper was creased, but the Jeep appeared to be operable."

Streeter's stomach twisted. "He got her before she ever made it to work."

He remembered the instinct he had felt to call her back to him, to hold her, to never let her out of his sight.

"Keep your cool," Gates warned Streeter. "There's more. We found a man at the scene. Beat up, but currently clinging to life at Lutheran Medical."

"Who?" Kelleher asked. "What do we know about him?"

"Don't know yet. His Harley Davidson was discovered next to the Jeep," Gates said.

Bile rose in Streeter's throat. "Mully."

Kelleher asked, "Who?"

"Carl Muldando. A friend. Head of the Lucifer's Lot motorcycle gang.

He probably tried to help her. I'd asked him to keep an eye on her when he could." Streeter held his breath. "Is he going to make it?"

"Touch and go," Gates said.

Kelleher said, "Streeter, think. You know this guy better than anybody. If she's still alive, what would Coyote Cries want with Liv?"

"The book of Jeremiah," he answered in a low voice. "He warned them. The people ignored his warnings."

Gates and Kelleher grew silent and waited.

Streeter added, "He's carrying out his own prophecy. He's annihilating everyone who's wronged him. He kidnapped Liv to torture me."

"Again?" Gates gasped.

Kelleher asked, "Think. Where would he be taking her?"

Streeter paused. Then said, "She's still alive. He wants me to find him, and he . . ."

After a long moment, Gates asked, "What is it, Streeter?"

Kelleher said, "Streeter?"

Streeter answered quietly. "He's playing the game a second time. He wants me to get there early this time."

"Where?" Kelleher barked. "What are you talking about, Streeter?"

The silence that followed was broken by Gates. "Listen to me. Whatever you're thinking, you'd better share it with us. This guy is dangerous. He'll kill you. He'll kill Liv. Tell me what you're thinking. *Where are you going?*"

"This is between him and me. He wants me to come alone," Streeter answered absently, terminating the call by powering down his phone.

He made an illegal U-turn through the grassy median on the highway. And headed in the other direction.

CHAPTER 42

"**WHERE ARE YOU** taking me?" I asked evenly.

Coyote Cries ignored me.

He hadn't said anything since I first saw him on the roadside except for the guttural words he spoke as he jabbed the barrel of his pistol into my ribs, "Get in."

I worked the ropes that bound my hands behind my back. I strained against the seat belt, which Coyote Cries had pulled tightly across my chest and lap.

I could feel that the ropes had not loosened any. I had tried to ball my fists and align my knuckles to allow the greatest space between my wrists as he bound them—just like I'd learned at Quantico—to give me room to wiggle once I relaxed my muscles. But it hadn't worked.

I wondered if I'd made a tactical error. Maybe I should have head-butted Coyote Cries while he was tying my hands. I'd thought about it but decided against it after a quick assessment of his size and apparent strength.

I'd underestimated him. I'd thought he was old. But his arms were huge. He clearly spent a lot of his free time in the gym.

And then I completely fell apart after I saw what he'd done to Mully.

Coyote Cries had rammed my Jeep from behind. I had wrongly assumed that it'd been an accident. I pulled over on the shoulder to exchange insurance information and stepped out from behind the wheel and made my way along the Interstate to the man's car parked behind me.

I saw him standing by his front bumper assessing the damage. He'd had his back to me, and I didn't see his long braids tucked in his T-shirt until it was too late. He was wearing a Rockies baseball cap pulled low over his eyes.

The only thing I'd determined was that the man who had rammed my Jeep was a very large person.

I'd approached him and stood beside him, looking down at his front bumper.

Before looking over at him, I'd asked, "How bad is it?"

Before I knew it, he'd spun to face me, worked the barrel of the pistol against my ribs, and grunted, "Hands behind your back."

I panicked at first and then quickly thought of what I should do while he bound my wrists with one hand. He yanked the twine tight and tied a knot, using his teeth to anchor it.

He pushed me toward the passenger side of his car, and I saw his long grey braids swing free from his T-shirt.

Before getting into the car, our eyes met.

Instantly, I knew who he was: the lifeless eyes, black and cold; the sharp copper features; late forties, maybe early fifties; certainly Native American.

He looked exactly as Streeter had described him to me, only decades older and much more menacing. For a brief moment, I thought Coyote Cries had noticed the recognition that must have flashed in my eyes. His eyes narrowed, and I thought I saw a slight grin on his thin, tight lips.

It was then I'd thought to head-butt him. But I didn't.

Instead, I scowled. "I'm not getting in until you tell me what this is all about."

I thought I detected amusement on his face. I hoped I'd successfully convinced him that I didn't know who he was.

Coyote Cries jabbed the barrel into my gut. Hard. "Get in."

"Ouch. Hey, calm down, buddy. I'm getting in."

Before completing my thought, I'd jabbed Coyote Cries in the gut with my elbow and slammed my forehead into his nose. When he flinched momentarily, I took a step back and flung my foot high to the sky, cuffing the side of his head with my side kick, nearly toppling without my hands to balance my quick movement.

I'd underestimated his speed and agility. He snatched my foot and twisted it hard and drove me into the ground—head and shoulders first as if he were driving pylons.

I winced in pain from the blow to my skull and the sharp tearing ache I felt in my once-healing head.

Then I saw stars and nearly passed out. I'm not quite sure what happened next.

One thing was sure: He wanted me to know how strong he was. Once again, he effortlessly lifted me with one hand.

I thought he was going to pile drive me into the ground again and finish me off.

Instead, he hoisted me to my feet and shoved me into the car and disappeared.

My head throbbed so badly, I thought it would explode. I was dizzy and confused. I felt like throwing up.

Then I heard something.

A shout. A scuffle. A grunt. A punch.

A loud thud that I knew was a kick to someone's ribs.

I cleared my head and steadied myself enough to find the side mirror of his car. I tried to see what was happening and who'd been fighting.

I saw Coyote Cries standing over whoever had tried to save me, and I watched as Coyote Cries pummeled the man on the ground.

I recognized the leather vest. The colors. It wasn't Streeter.

"Get out! Run Princess!" I heard him yell.

Prince Calaf to the Princess of Turandot.

Mully.

I tried to do as he said. My mind was muddy. I tried to fumble with the door handle, to get out. But I collapsed just outside the open door. I couldn't move.

I heard more beating.

But it wasn't on me.

Then I heard nothing.

I felt someone lift me and stuff me into the car.

My mind cleared and raced to what I could do next. If Coyote Cries had meant to kill me, he'd have left me there with Mully on the roadside, dead.

So he must not have wanted to kill me—at least, not right away.

I decided the best chance I had of getting out of this was to continue to make Coyote Cries believe I had no idea who he was. My head and shoulders throbbed in a syncopated gait with stabs of pain in my forehead. My only hope was that someone had noticed the two men struggling on the roadside and that someone had found Mully.

And called 911 for help.

My abandoned Jeep along the road would have drawn more attention if I'd thought to bring my SIG or other work-related items that could be found to identify me as a federal agent—or if Coyote Cries hadn't taken my personal Smith & Wesson revolver from the front seat before he left.

I'd tried everything I could to stay conscious. I engaged him in conversation as we drove.

He said nothing.

I'd asked several times where he was taking me. My words tumbled out like clumsy blocks.

I got no response.

We drove past the Bronco stadium in downtown Denver.

At one point, the only words that seemed to find coherency were in questions I asked, "Who are you? What do you want with me?"

He raised an eyebrow and stared straight ahead as he drove south on I-25.

I knew I was being taken captive to somehow torture Streeter. I had that much sense left in my muddled mind. But I couldn't figure out his angle. I needed to find out what he was up to if I had a prayer to live.

I thought I'd try a different approach.

"Do you need money or something? Because if you're kidnapping me for a ransom, you've got me mistaken for someone else. I'm not rich. My family isn't rich. I've got nothing except that Jeep we left behind."

He weaved his way expertly and slowly through the crowded lanes. At one point, just before the Yale exit, the traffic was at a standstill.

I accidentally spoke my thoughts aloud. "I mouthed 'Help me!' to the guy next to us. But he just blew me a kiss."

Coyote Cries grinned slightly.

I was scared. Terrified, really. But I didn't want to appear to be.

I wiped away the blood that dribbled into my left eye from the busted stitches on my forehead.

"Tell me the truth. Are you a movie actor or something? You look so familiar. Weren't you in *Dances with Wolves* or something?" My words slurred. I knew I sounded drunk. "You are an Indian, aren't you?"

For the first time since he'd pushed me into the car, he glanced over at me and scowled.

I shrugged and continued to work on the ropes tied securely around my wrists. "What'd I say? Did I offend you or something?"

I studied his facial tics, movements, and responses. "Should I have called you a Native American instead of an Indian? Or a Navajo or something?"

"Lakota," he grunted.

"You're Sioux?" I asked. I knew Lakotans. I grew up in South Dakota. I understood most of the tribes in our area. And I guessed what his response would be based on what I'd learned about him.

"That's a white man's term."

"Sioux? I didn't know that. Lakotan, then. Not Lakota Sioux."

Coyote Cries shook his head in disgust.

"What'd I say this time?" My heart raced. He was slowing down, preparing to turn off the Interstate at the Yale exit.

My anxiety mounted. I glanced at the clock. A quarter to nine. Streeter would probably have arrived at the correctional facility by now. Maybe he'd already discovered that Jeremiah Coyote Cries had long since been released from prison and had escaped.

Maybe he was looking for me.

Streeter would know by now all the details of Coyote Cries's escape— that he'd been sent a fraudulent letter about the delayed parole hearing, that the board had granted parole, and he'd be piecing together his connection to the trail of murder victims he'd left behind.

He'd be terrified for me.

Even more so, if he knew Coyote Cries was sitting right next to me with a pistol lying across his lap.

I closed my eyes and rested my head against the seat. I wondered what Streeter planned at this moment. I hoped he wouldn't step into any trap that had been laid for him.

With me as bait.

CHAPTER 43

I PRAYED STREETER would not do something foolish just to spare me.

I offered a quick prayer for strength and wisdom. And for Streeter's safety. When I opened my eyes, I could see Coyote Cries watching me.

"You scared?" he asked evenly.

"Yes," I answered simply. "Isn't that what you want?"

He stared out the window and drove through the narrow streets of the neighborhoods.

I watched and wondered where he was taking me. My heart pounded when we approached the street where I lived.

He knew where I live.

My heartbeat thrummed against my eardrums.

I was frightened.

What else did he know about me? How long had he been watching me?

Chavez, I remembered—of course he knew where I lived. He'd hired the guy who had followed me to my apartment.

A sigh of relief slipped quietly past my lips when he drove beyond my street and continued down the main arterial.

Coyote Cries pulled the car into the parking lot of an apartment complex five blocks east of my place. I wondered why he'd chosen this place.

I cursed myself for not being able to shake the fuzziness from my frontal lobe. I needed to think.

My concern began to grow when I realized we'd arrived at his destination. I didn't understand what it meant, but I knew he was where he wanted to be.

He pulled into a parking spot near one of the buildings and turned off the car.

With the pistol clutched comfortably in his left hand, he turned to me. "Listen to me. I will let you go unharmed if you do exactly as I say."

I knew he was lying.

He reached in the back seat and strapped the double shoulder holster around his back and chest. Into the ten-inch holster on his right side, he slipped an equally long Bowie knife with a five-inch handle.

In the smaller holster on his left side, he carefully placed the loaded pistol. The hint of a menacing grin played around the corner of his thin lips when he shoved the second pistol, my Smith & Wesson, into the front of his pants.

Reaching again into the back seat, Coyote Cries pulled on a long, thin jacket to conceal the holster. I watched him dress.

He pulled his purple cap low over his forehead and tucked his braids into his shirt. "I'm getting out now. I'm going to come around to your side and release you from your seat belt. You will not try to break free from me. You will not call out for help. You will not try to run away. You will go quietly with me, and you will not be hurt. Understand?"

"Where are you taking me?" I asked weakly.

I was genuinely afraid. The Bowie knife forcing the singular image into my muddled mind of Paula's tiny body.

He didn't answer. He got out of the car and walked around to my side. He stood by the door and looked around the parking lot.

I wondered if he was taking me into his apartment to use me as bait somehow for Streeter. I knew that being spotted by someone on our way into the building in broad daylight might be my best chance for help. I was hoping someone would see that my hands were bound behind my back.

Coyote Cries opened the door to the back seat and then to the front seat. He reached around me and released my seat belt. Grabbing me by my right arm, he pulled me out of the car and slipped a second oversized jacket over my shoulders.

So much for someone seeing my bound hands, I thought. Maybe someone will notice two people walking awkwardly through the apartment complex and wonder why we were both wearing jackets in eighty-degree weather.

I could only hope.

Coyote Cries draped his left arm over my shoulders and slid his right hand inside his jacket. As we began to walk toward the nearest building, I stiffened when I felt the barrel of the gun through his jacket poking against my right arm.

I painfully limped along obediently by his side. He wouldn't hesitate to shoot me if I defied him. I knew that much.

We walked up the stairwell of the old apartment building and stopped on the fourth floor. I smelled the wafting stench of rotting garbage, stale cigarettes, and moldiness. It seemed like an appropriate place for a cockroach like Jeremiah Coyote Cries to live.

He stopped in front of one of the apartments and removed his gun from its holster. Just when I thought I'd figured him out, Coyote Cries surprised me by knocking on the door.

When the chain was released and the doorknob began to turn, he grabbed me and jammed the barrel of his gun against my right temple.

The older woman in a bathrobe who opened the door was as startled as I had been. The second of hesitation before she tried to slam the door on her unwelcome visitors was all Coyote Cries needed to kick the door wide open with his foot.

The elderly woman tumbled backward with her robe spilling open to reveal a ratty nightgown beneath. Three curlers flew from her mousy grey hair, and the package of cigarettes she'd been carrying spilled onto the ground. The remaining sticks scattered all over the stained carpet around her.

I broke free from his grasp just long enough to collapse by the woman's side. "Are you okay?"

Coyote Cries closed the door and secured the chains.

The woman cried, "Who are you people?"

"Shut up, old woman. Who else is here?"

"What?" the elderly woman asked in confusion.

I ignored the sharp stabbing pain in my head, struggled to stand since my wrists were still bound, and clumsily helped the woman to her feet by letting her hug my neck as I lifted us both to our feet.

Coyote Cries leaned toward the old lady, clutched the robe up under her chin, and lifted her feet from the ground. "Who else is here in this apartment with you?"

The elderly woman let out a screech. Coyote Cries leveled the gun against her forehead. "Shut up. Just answer my question. Or I'll blow your head off."

I heard a trickling noise beneath the sobbing woman's robe and saw a pool on the floor beneath her. "Nobody. Nobody's here. I live alone."

Coyote Cries put her down and pushed her away from him.

The woman stumbled backward. I steadied her by offering her my shoulder to grab.

I spun around to face Coyote Cries. "Leave her alone. Can't you see she's frightened?"

"I kind of figured that. She just pissed all over the floor," he answered brutally.

The elderly woman sobbed. "What do you want? I don't have much, but you can have it. Anything. If you'll just leave."

He flashed me a menacing grin. "I have no intention of leaving. I just need to use your apartment for little while. I'm expecting company."

I suddenly realized where we were.

Coyote Cries had returned to the apartment where Streeter and Paula had lived.

Twenty years ago.

CHAPTER 44

COYOTE CRIES HAD BROUGHT me here knowing that Streeter would eventually come.

The elderly woman was simply a victim of living in the wrong place at the wrong time. I was overwhelmed with pity for her as she stood sobbing beside me.

Coyote Cries leveled his gun once again on her. "I said shut up."

The old woman continued to sob. And she'd begun to quake, uncontrollably.

I wanted to hold her and keep her from trembling. But my hands were still bound behind me.

Sensing Coyote Cries was losing patience, I tried consoling the old woman by talking gently to her. "It'll be all right. Just do exactly as he says. And everything will be all right. Try not to cry. Everything will be okay."

But I knew everything would not be okay.

Coyote Cries had grown increasingly more irritated by the woman's sobbing.

Within a few short minutes, he grabbed the woman's arm and dragged her down the hall toward the back bedroom. The woman's cries became louder, more hysterical.

I couldn't just sit there. I had to do something to stop him. I ran after him. Pleading, "Please, don't. She doesn't know any better. She's just frightened. Let me try to talk with her, please. I can get her to quiet down. Just give me a chance."

There were no chances for the woman.

Coyote Cries pushed her onto the bed, covered her face with a pillow, and fired one quick round.

The pillow muffled the sound.

I'd lunged at Coyote Cries and rammed my shoulder against the small of his back. But I'd been too late.

The elderly woman stopped struggling and stopped sobbing.

She was completely still, the smoldering pillow covering her face.

Coyote Cries barely flinched from the blow I had delivered, and I glanced off him like a penny skipping across a sidewalk.

I had tried to save the woman's life, but all I'd managed to do was enrage him further.

He swung his hand that still gripped the loaded pistol—my bureau-issued pistol—against my face.

My world went instantly black.

CHAPTER 45

I AWOKE WITH my face pressed against the smelly, stained carpet in the woman's living room.

I could hear the excited crowd blaring their cheers for the winning contestant on the daytime game show.

I could see the familiar cowboy boots inches from my face by the couch.

I could feel the pounding against the inside of my skull and believed at any moment my head would explode. The burning stinging in my cheek from where he'd hit me, coupled with the injury to my forehead, caused so much confusion and pain that I wanted someone to just put me out of my misery.

I wondered if the hot, dripping sensation across my cheek was sweat or blood.

I lay still on the carpet, wondering how long I'd been here. Then I saw the cigarettes and curlers on the floor nearby, which made me remember the woman. That poor dear.

Coyote Cries had obviously dragged me out of the bedroom and placed me here at his feet. He was sitting on the couch, watching a game show on television, waiting for Streeter to arrive.

What can I do to help? How can I warn Streeter? I needed a plan. I had to think. But I was so confused. The throbbing in my head was deafening.

Before I could even decide whether to sit up or not, there was a knock on the door.

I glanced up and saw that it'd been unlocked and unchained.

I heard Coyote Cries scramble to his feet and felt his knee jab hard against my back. I let out a loud grunt. I felt him grab a fistful of my hair and yank my head back so swiftly, I thought my swollen cheek might burst.

The blade of his Bowie knife slid expertly under my chin against my skin. I whimpered.

Coyote Cries whispered, "Shut up, Forty-Seven, or I'll finish you now."

I had no clue why he called me forty-seven. I couldn't think straight. But I thought I'd remembered him saying "forty-six" right after he shot the old woman.

Then it hit me. It was the number of people he'd killed. I was as good as dead.

I felt the cold, sharp blade against my throat, and I knew he wouldn't hesitate to use it.

I no longer had to imagine how Paula felt twenty years earlier. I knew. I was absolutely terrified. And I knew I was going to die.

My only hope was that Streeter wouldn't die along with me.

I'd been trained in many different ways to deal with people like Jeremiah Coyote Cries, yet I felt completely helpless and paralyzed in this moment.

Poor Paula. She'd had no training. She must have been utterly horrified.

I silently prayed that the knock on the door hadn't belonged to Streeter Pierce. I hoped it was a concerned neighbor who'd heard the muffled shot, or an unsuspecting delivery boy stumbling innocently onto the situation.

Ashamed at my wish, I didn't change my mind. I truly hoped an innocent party was at the door. Just not Streeter, who would be forced to witness my last breath.

I couldn't bear to think of how that would finish him.

He wouldn't think to come here, would he? Surely he would search his own house first. And mine, next. That knock couldn't possibly belong to him.

But when I saw the knob slowly turn, I knew it was him. Streeter had indeed come here to save me.

My heart sank, and for the first time since Coyote Cries had abducted me, I wanted to cry.

He'd gripped the clump of hair more tightly in his left fist and had pressed the blade closer to my throat with his right hand. I felt his left knee grinding into my spine.

I tried, but wasn't able, to call out a warning to Streeter.

The door flew open. Streeter crouched and leveled his pistol at Coyote Cries. His face contorted into a tortured grimace when he glanced down at my bloodied face.

As he made his way into the living room, inching nearer to me, his animalistic growl was nearly unrecognizable. "Drop it or I'll blow your brains out."

Coyote Cries shoved the knife closer against my throat. I felt the blade bite my skin. I winced, and my blood began to flow.

"Put the knife down."

Coyote Cries's response was calm. "Now, really. You are in no position to make demands of me. On the contrary. You drop it, or I'll cut your girl-friend's throat. Just like I did to your wife."

Streeter's steady hand began to waver.

"Drop it, Pierce. I mean it." He dug the sharp knife even deeper into my skin. I couldn't see the crimson trickle spilling onto the shiny blade. But I could smell it: two distinct metallic odors—blood and wet metal.

Streeter's hands trembled.

His face twisted at the sight of my blood.

He dropped the Smith & Wesson and held out his empty hands. He fell to his knees on the floor.

He pleaded with Coyote Cries. "Let her go. She didn't do anything to you. It's me you want. Let her go. Please."

Tears streamed down his cheeks.

CHAPTER 46

THE PAIN IN MY throat was nothing compared to the ache in my heart for the horror Streeter was reliving.

"You sound like your girlfriend, now," Coyote Cries said with a knowing grin. "She practically used the same words when she was pleading with me to spare the bat's life who lived here. It didn't work though. You're a betting man. Your chances with me?"

"What do you want?" Streeter demanded.

"Do you want to know what your wife said just before I slit her throat?"

Streeter swallowed hard and stared at Coyote Cries. His eyes were wild with confusion and pain.

I couldn't see Coyote Cries's face at this angle. But I imagined that he stared back with those dead eyes of his. "She told me that more violence wouldn't help matters. She was wrong. More violence is exactly what I need in my life. It makes me feel . . . productive."

I knew that Streeter was holding Coyote Cries's stare but could see me in his peripheral vision. I'd noticed numerous quiet and quick shadowy movements in the hallway under the door. I darted my eyes in their direction to warn Streeter.

And hoped he understood. I knew he needed to keep Coyote Cries talking. He had.

"Why did she tell you she was pregnant?"

Coyote Cries answered, "She was whiny, a wimpy bitch. Not at all like this one. This one has some spunk."

I noticed Streeter grimace.

"Your wife was pleading with me to spare her child. She said she hadn't even told you about it yet. Was that true?"

Streeter paused and nodded.

"I'll bet that's been eating you up all this time—knowing I knew she was pregnant before you did."

I strained to clear my mind, to determine if I'd truly seen movement outside the window of the apartment. I had. I saw the faintest movement of shadows. I recognized Chief Tony Gates dangling from one of the rappelling ropes, frantically directing his people to move into position.

No matter what happened to me, I found solace in the thought that at least they'd nail this bastard.

Streeter responded calmly and slowly. "That did bother me. But not as much as how you goaded me into making a fool out of myself on the day of your sentencing. You were clever. I bet you laughed many times about that while you were behind bars."

"That was clever, I must admit. And you never were able to pin her death on me," he said.

"A bit of a problem controlling your rage just like the prophet Jeremiah. Am I right? I paid a visit to your mother after you'd stopped by the other day."

I felt Coyote Cries stiffen at the comment. I wasn't sure what Streeter had in mind, but surely he understood that he was being antagonistic. And he hadn't told me about visiting Coyote Cries's mother, so I assumed he was bluffing.

Coyote Cries growled, "You ruined everything for me. I had a nice business. I had a good life. Then, you pop into my world with your Dudley Do-Right attitude and destroy everything. I got myself busted by a stupid rookie cop."

"I'm an agent, not a cop," Streeter corrected.

I noticed more shadows of movement under the crack of the apartment door. Gates's men were getting into position to break down the door.

I felt something dig deeper into my throat, and I closed my eyes. I asked God to have mercy on me, to make death come swiftly.

In a split second, my world erupted. I heard a crash, a shattering of glass, the splintering of wood, thundering footsteps, and voices hollering in front of us and behind us.

"Freeze!"

"Don't move!"

Coyote Cries tensed.

Realization flickered in Streeter's eyes.

I felt the knife cut deeper, and I felt a weight fall away from me.

I watched as Coyote Cries rolled off toward Streeter.

The movement confused me until I realized he was launching himself toward Streeter's discarded gun.

I tried to warn Streeter, but I heard nothing except a gurgle coming from my throat.

I felt a warm gush from the gaping wound and instinctively moved to stave the flow, realizing my hands were still bound behind my back. I told myself to forget about the blood and awkwardly scrabbled after the pistol that was lying right behind Coyote Cries. I slipped on my own spilt blood, and my chest hit hard on the dirty carpet.

Streeter dove for the gun in the same instant, and both men wrestled for the piece.

Clearly bigger and stronger, Coyote Cries twisted Streeter's wrist to force him to drop the gun.

Streeter's strength dwindled.

He was outmaneuvered by Coyote Cries, who quickly grappled with him and slung Streeter onto his back and then splayed his large body across him.

I scrambled on top of them both and used my teeth to gouge out one of Coyote Cries's eyes. He let out a screech.

An army of men instantly appeared from the hallway and through the shattered windows. Guns were leveled on the two men wrestling on the floor. I'd rolled onto my side to allow the men a clear shot of Coyote Cries.

Streeter managed enough strength to wiggle free from the Indian's powerful grip.

A single, muffled shot was fired.

Everyone froze. Guns were leveled on the pair.

I could see the two men freeze, staring at one another. Neither was moving. Both were in a death grip.

Then, Coyote Cries's arms dropped. Streeter shoved the man, and he tumbled to the floor with a thud.

Streeter pushed himself away from the lifeless body of Jeremiah Coyote Cries.

The Lakotan lay supine on the floor, blood pooling beneath him, with the blossom of red spreading quickly across his chest.

I'd half expected the floor to open up and swallow him like in every horror movie I'd ever watched. Jeremiah, the Devil's breakfast.

In the commotion that followed, I felt my energy drain.

I could do nothing but stare at the man's lifeless, hateful eyes and his angry mouth mocking me, even in death.

I collapsed onto the floor.

One of the officers grabbed a towel and pressed it to my throat. I felt a tug on my wrists as someone cut the binds. My arms flopped to my sides, too thick and numb to use. My eyelids grew heavy. But when I managed to lift them, all I could do was search for Streeter. I couldn't find him.

People were running, moving, scrambling.

My world blinked in and out of focus.

I was in a white room with white walls. No windows.

I saw my brother, Ole. Then my dad. They were smiling, telling me they were safe. Then all my sisters and my younger brother Jens joined them. And my beautiful mother. She was standing beside Mully hugging his waist, like he was one of us kids.

My mind struggled to understand what was happening. I was further confused when my grandpa stepped forward. Wearing white. He'd died when I was six. I was so confused. There was lots of light. Jack Linwood joined my family. Wearing a white robe. Like a frigging angel. Holding his hand out for me. I wanted to reach for it.

But I didn't.

I blinked.

I opened my eyes again, and I was back on the dirty carpet of the old woman's apartment lying on my back. Streeter knelt beside me on the floor.

It hurt to talk. My throat gurgled, and my words sounded garbled. But I managed to say, "You did it. Finally. The monster. Slain."

I wanted to cough but couldn't.

Streeter glanced over at the dead man, who was lying on his back staring at the ceiling. He shook his head. "He's nothing to me. You're everything. The monster was my fear of losing you."

He scooted closer on his knees, wrapped his arms around my body, and pulled himself close against me. His hug was tender and loving.

Neither of us had noticed that Tony Gates had joined us on the floor. Maybe Streeter had seen him come in, but I ended up in the white room again with all the light. And my family. At once, weird and wonderful. And pain free. I wanted to stay there.

But I heard Tony say, "The lab confirmed Coyote Cries's DNA on the work clothes found up at Alcott's mountain mansion, along with some of his other belongings. Plenty of proof that he killed Dan Alcott and Victor Webber."

I'm not sure what all he said, but I caught that much.

Streeter stared down at me and studied my face and neck. He dragged his finger lightly around my split cheekbone to avoid the swelling bruise and gash from the pistol-whipping I'd been given by Coyote Cries with my own gun.

"You need a doctor—soon," Streeter said to me.

Then he lay down beside me, his breathing heavy.

Tony snapped his fingers, and EMTs appeared out of nowhere.

I heard one of them say, "He's been shot. She's been cut."

They descended on both Streeter and me. I realized then that it was Streeter they'd been referring to when they said he'd been shot. Not Coyote Cries. The EMTs helped both of us with our injuries.

I drifted in and out of the white room—out of pain, in terrible agony, then back again.

I glanced over at Streeter, whose stare never left me. I warned, "Hands on plow. Move forward now."

I kept repeating the mantra over and over, hoping he understood.

Gates frowned at me. "She's in shock. Get her help. Hurry."

I heard commotion, but I couldn't make out their words. Every time I slipped back into the other room, the white room, with all my family and friends, my head felt better and the searing pain along my throat disappeared.

Then the pain was back when I felt Streeter grab my hand, when I heard him say, "Stay with me. I love you. Always."

I tried to speak but couldn't. I wanted to tell him to look forward. Not behind.

My energy drained. I'd lost far too much blood. I couldn't resist going back into the white room. And staying there forever.

The last thing I remembered was Streeter pleading with me. "Stay, Liv. The nightmare's over."

Maybe for me.

But not for him.

READING GROUP GUIDE

1. At one point in the book, Liv says to Streeter, "There are worse pains than broken bones and bruises. You of all people should know that." Discuss what this means in the context of the plot and the major characters in the book.

2. Streeter and Liv have openly declared and expressed their feelings for each other. Discuss how you felt when their relationship seemed to finally be on the path forward. Discuss how you imagine their future together.

3. Discuss what part of *Jeremiah's Revenge* took you most by surprise, either positively or negatively, and why?

4. Discuss Coyote Cries's childhood and what impression it made on you in the context of this story. Discuss the use of the Bible references in the book and why they were especially effective in highlighting his character.

5. What was your general feeling when the book ended?
   What point did the author make about revenge?

6. Discuss how you felt when you read how Streeter's wife had
   died. How did this change your thoughts about him and
   Coyote Cries?

7. Why do you think the author chose to have Liv physically
   resemble Streeter's wife, and why did Streeter never tell Liv
   about the resemblance?

8. Discuss the following passage in light of Liv's character and
   what you think it means when she says, "worry had a hold
   on me." What significance does the quote from Luke have
   in the bigger context of the story?

   "Then stop worrying," I scolded. "I've remembered a quote
   from the book of Luke ever since I was young, because
   worry had a hold on me even back then. It was something like, 'No one who puts a hand to the plow and
   looks back is fit to prosper.' Something like that."

9. Discuss which scene or scenes will be your most lasting
   memory of *Jeremiah's Revenge* and why. Discuss which
   scenes you think the author meant to be the most memorable and why, in terms of this book and the Liv Bergen
   Mystery Thriller Series as a whole.

AUTHOR Q&A

Q: Would you describe when and how the Liv Bergen and Streeter Pierce characters first came to you and who, if anyone, they are modeled after?

A: I love these two people. I have no idea who they would be most like today or how they came to be the wonderful people they are, other than they spoke to me through the pages during the seven journeys that are the Liv Bergen Mystery Thriller Series.

When I started writing, I had a particular fascination with the FBI because I admired and revered two very beautiful friends who were both FBI agents—Sue Hillard and Mick Sherer. I remember being struck by Sue's picture in a magazine. She was suspended in a harness picking through the debris of Pan Am Flight 103 from Lockerbie trying to retrieve evidence of the terrorist bombing and the remains of loved ones for the 270 families who were affected. I had worked on the 747 at Boeing and knew what a chore it must have been to search that massive area inch by inch to retrieve what she could. Her courage and dedication to her work were incredibly impactful to me.

And Mick was always there for me as a protector and friend until his death in 2012. I miss him. He even attended a book signing with me once, during a time when he was afflicted with dementia, and signed books as Streeter. I'm willing to buy one of those treasured books from a reader, if any of you lucky recipients are willing to part with your book.

Sue and Mick were my original inspirations for Liv and Streeter, although both were much more fascinating than the characters they inspired in these pages.

Q: In *Jeremiah's Revenge,* did you decide to edit anything *out* after you had written the initial manuscript, and if so, why?

A: As a matter of fact, I did rewrite several scenes in *Jeremiah's Revenge* because of some wonderful and necessary coaching from the lovely Danielle Dosch, my FBI beta reader, and two Lakotans who read the manuscript for me. Life on and off the reservations can be so harsh for some families. Ask any teacher, any priest, any grandmother, any FBI agent, or any tribal police officer. I don't think the world is ready to admit or acknowledge what a tragic destiny we sentenced our native people to for generations. We rounded them up like cattle in 1830 to live on reservations and then paid for our sins by doling out stipends. Monetary handouts, rather than meaningful hand ups, have not worked. They were doing fine until we Europeans came along. And most people don't know what tragically happened in 1830 under President Andrew Jackson when the Removal Act was passed by Democrats and fought voraciously by Whigs. I was coached that deleting the party reference might be the wise choice, which I did for the former, leaving in the Whigs. My intention was not to alienate one current party or another. This isn't about the parties. It's about a nation. The Indian Nation.

My intention was to show the goodness in those hard-working Native people living on and off the reservation who are dedicated to their traditions and culture. I wanted to show the temptations offered by a few evil people who live among them, who are trying to oppress them, shame them, and keep them from their greater purpose. But in my attempt to show how difficult the situation can be, the character of the long-time FBI agent working on the reservation appeared callous and hopeless about whether life there would ever change, and I feared the readers would believe he might be borderline bigoted or prejudiced. So I changed him. But my opinion on how hard life must continue to be for those dedicated teachers and priests, steadfast tribal officers and FBI agents, and welcoming grandmothers to provide hope for so many people remains firm. God bless them for all they do for so many.

Q: What were the most difficult and most pleasant scenes to write in *Jeremiah's Revenge* and why?

A: Streeter's ultimate cleansing, if you will, about what happened to his beloved wife who was murdered, had been overdue for six books. His hair turning white overnight should have been a clue to readers that he suffered a terrible shock. And allowing the readers in on that secret along with Liv as Streeter shared the details, it was extremely difficult for me to write, yet necessary.

I loved not writing anything about the blissful five days that Streeter and Liv spent together. That time should have most definitely been off-page and left to the readers' imaginations. Those two needed some well-deserved space and quiet time, don't you think?

Q: Can you describe your familiarity with life on the reservation and inside a prison that allowed you to so vividly describe both of these settings?

A: I have lived most of my life in South Dakota, which has nine reservations and tribal lands—more than any other state. I have had the good fortune to learn about Lakotan culture and the reservation throughout my entire life from school friends, competitors in sports, coworkers, and mentors. Most of my time spent on the reservation was with friends, including an FBI agent who took me on ride-alongs with him. My friends and I made several stops at Big Bat's while passing through Pine Ridge.

In recent years, visiting the schools on the reservations as a guest author has been one of my favorite pastimes. The kids are awesome!

I also served on the board for the largest museum in the world dedicated to the North American Indians at the Crazy Horse Memorial nestled in the Black Hills of South Dakota. If you haven't seen the massive monument carved in the granite mountain by the Ziolkowski Family, you must.

As to prison life, hasn't everyone had a chance to visit an incarcerated relative or two? I haven't yet experienced prison life as one of the population, but I have had the experience of being locked in a jail cell once (Don't let that mind of yours get all slippery on me: I was on a tour of the prison.), which was enough to make me keep my nose clean.

Q: How do you manage to get inside the head of individuals like Coyote Cries to be able to conceive of the actions they take?

A: Storyline inspirations, for me, come from that tiny grain of irritating sand that forces me to work it into a pearl. For this book, *Jeremiah's Revenge*, the inspirational and excruciatingly irritating grain was a man I've studied for years—his writings, news articles, blogs, and books. The more I've read about him, the more I realized that evil does exist. He was convicted for the execution deaths of two innocent FBI agents—Agents Coler and Williams—on the Pine Ridge Reservation in 1975.

His name is not worth mentioning. But Agents Jack Coler and Ron Williams are worth remembering and thanking. God bless those agents and the men and women just like them who put their lives on the line every day at work to make us all safe and secure.

Q: What emotions propel or compel you to write in general?

A: I write because I can't stop. It's a passion, an addiction. I'm still hoping someone creates a Writer's Anonymous organization to help people like me who suffer from this affliction.

Q: Besides writing, what are your passions?

A: I love work, being productive, getting things done, thinking differently, and creating a vision for future generations. Problem-solving is a passion. Results are a passion. And helping other people become productive, creative, results-oriented, self-reliant human beings is a huge passion for me. One of my favorite quotes by an unknown source is "Who we are is God's gift to us. What we become is our gift to God." My biggest passion is to encourage everyone I know to discover what they can become. Be you!

Q: Is there one person in your life who has been your hero or heroine or who has inspired you more than anyone else? Can you tell us why?

A: I am fortunate to be surrounded by so many extraordinary people that it's hard for me to narrow down my list of top heroes and heroines who have inspired me to just one. From childhood to adulthood, let me at least list my favorites.

I'd start with my parents, who are eighty-eight and ninety-two at the time of this manuscript's submission. Both continue to work every day of their lives, never choosing to give in to the pains of aging or to give up in the face of adversity. They have always provided a place to call home that is full of love and sustenance. They are exceptional human beings.[*]

My six sisters and two brothers were my tribe growing up in the woods, and my best friends as adults. Their stories are incredible, their achievements great, and their families, awesome.

I had a handful of wonderful teachers who inspired me to do things I didn't know I could do—like write fiction.

My children have taught me more about life and love than I ever believed possible. They are my joy and happiness and my reason for getting as close as I can to God in this life. I live to see my sons in heaven for eternity. And now they've given me grandchildren, a whole new generation of life's elixir.

And I have come to realize I was born to be my husband's wife. God had a plan for us, for me to be with him. He will always be my hero.

---

[*]   Sandra's father died in April of 2018 after she wrote this answer.

ABOUT THE AUTHOR

AUTHOR OF THE HEART-POUNDING Liv Bergen Mystery Thriller Series, Sandra Brannan writes about the mining world she's lived in her entire life and about the FBI she's grown to love through her best friend. One reviewer has described the series as "Gritty. Liv Bergen is the love child of Jack Reacher and Kinsey Milhone."

Native to South Dakota, Brannan incorporates not only suspense and twists into her plotlines but also the color and richness unique to her home state—often so vividly that the setting becomes a character all on its own.

Her mysteries have received numerous recognitions, including being named a *Denver Post* Bestseller and earning places on the American Booksellers Association Indie Notable and Next List. They have also found places on *Suspense Magazine*'s Best Suspense List, Amazon's Top 50 E-booksellers List, and honors as a USA Book News Best Book and Best Suspense Finalist.

In order of publication, here is the complete list of Liv Bergen Mystery Thriller Series titles:

2010 » *In the Belly of Jonah*

2011 » *Lot's Return to Sodom*

2012 » *Widow's Might*

2013 » *Noah's Rainy Day*

2014 » *Solomon's Whisper*

2016 » *Jacob's Descent*

2018 » *Jeremiah's Revenge*

To request an appearance by the author—particularly in classrooms, for library events, and at book clubs—email Sandra at

Sandra@SandraBrannan.com.

Sandra appears in person when possible and via Skype, FaceTime, or telephone if schedules make in-person travel impossible.

CPSIA information can be obtained
at www.ICGtesting.com
Printed in the USA
LVHW04s1735260718
585040LV00003B/403/P

9 781632 991737

8